This Book Belongs To

This Book Belongs to

THE VICAR OF BUTTERMERE

Printed in the United States of America

Ironmantle Books

THE VICAR OF BUTTERMERE

By

STEVEN KAY

Ironmantle Books
Publishers Since 2012
An imprint of DonnaInk Publications, L.L.C.
601 McReynolds Street, Carthage, NC 28327

Ironmantle Books

Library of Congress Cataloging-in-Publication.

Kay, Steven, author.
　Title: "The Vicar of Buttermere" / Mr. Steven Kay.
　　546 p. cm.
　　　Subjects:　FIC027000 FICTION / Romance / General; FIC031010 FICTION / Thrillers / Crime; FIC027300 FICTION / Romance / LGBT / General; FIC027390 FICTION / Romance / LGBT / Bisexual; FIC027190 FICTION / Romance / LGBT / Gay; FIC027210 FICTION / Romance / LGBT / Lesbian; FIC015000 FICTION / Horror.

Identifiers: ISBN – 13 - 978-1-947704-83-1 | 978-1-947704-59-6
Printed in the United States of America
First Edition: 12 11 10 9 8 7 6 5 4 3 2 1; 2021. All Rights Reserved.

For more information contact:
DonnaInk Publications, L.L.C.
601 McReynolds St., Carthage, NC 28327
www.donnaink.com

About the Book

THE VICAR OF BUTTERMERE

While most people were mentally ill, the state had been run by people too. Living in a natural environment, surrounded by beautiful landscapes and among fauna and flora, would have helped to heal the people. The masses though, were too scared to live without modern technology and the shopping centres. For all too many mortals, during the last days of the cyber age, family life was broken, and a man's best friend was Facebook.

Beth, while living at The Howe due to the stress of the tsunami, went into labor earlier than was expected. She escaped from ending up in the red river as a corpse with her sister, Sophie, and the hedonist, Roger. Together they went to a safe house well above the reaches of the tidal wave and this was thanks to the kindness of a nurse, Jennifer.

In part one of this trilogy: Roger was a despicably evil man. In the second part he used Beth and Sophie, possibly inadvertently, since he sincerely wanted a child, but didn't want the responsibility either. Worried about the fertility of either girls; he got both pregnant immediately and simultaneously to him one night. Apart from that, he was in his own special way good to both women and with a great remorse for his wicked past deeds towards the fairer sex. In theory he was a feminist and was well known in the liberal circles as a lawyer who for the right price achieved everything for his female clients. Sadly, when it came to his own relationships, he enjoyed step by step revealing to his women about his evil past life and using it as a means to trap his belles into feeling sorry for him and later making them too scared to leave him after he damaged them psychologically. In the first part he was confused about his sexuality, but a master in his profession. In part two no longer totally lost as to who he was, and with a new identity he moved on with his life and was then leading a quiet and semi-retired life. At the end of *Wordsworth's Baby,* he became a father for the fourth time and was expecting his sixth child from his seventh pregnancy and would be the third child of his whom he would actually see.

On the day Beth gave birth, his beloved Lake District due to a man-made tsunami was plunged back to the days of Wordsworth. At a stroke: the cyber age ended. A new dawn began, and people in order to survive would learn to live with each other again. For Roger, survival of the fittest meant earning as much money as possible to survive at the mercy of nature. Now, his money is worthless, the population has been almost wiped out, yet Roger wants to impregnate as many women as possible, without any emotional ties. Since in his schizophrenic mind he is Genghis Khan and Beth's posterity, he cannot decide what his place with her is. He believes, like his rivals, that Beth is simply the most adorable being on the planet.

As for his women, they too, like him find out that their ideas about life after the floods are different to the ones they had in mind, and like him, Beth and Sophie are still learning things they never knew about themselves. After getting over the shock of corpses floating down the rivers, life goes on. The women are still in love with him since although he is the evillest man they have ever encountered, he makes them realise that they are far from being angels themselves. On top of that, the few other men left are far from ideal too.

Other Books By

STEVEN KAY

For the Love of My Children

In Wordsworth's Shadow

Pebbles: Love Across the Morecambe Bay

The Satanic Court

Wordsworth's Baby

You and Me

Table of Contents

THE VICAR OF BUTTERMERE

The Vicar of Buttermere

PROLOGUE

Wearing his no-nonsense clothes, the vicar has an interesting presence. The formal attire helps radiate from him his penchant for a great semblance of an orderly dress code. Christianity, with its rules, appears to keep his very active mind in balance. For him, having the power of God in his services as he orders the couple to obey and respect the vows bestowed onto them along with the grace of the Lord and via, he, the vicar himself, gives him his narcissistic satisfaction. Everything is working with synchronicity apart from his eyes which appear somewhat sad and confused. Nevertheless, as a well-respected pillar of society, the couple, being married by him couldn't ask for a better village elder than that of the Mayor of Buttermere, who also happens to be the vicar of the church where a eulogy of the famous fell walker Alfred Wainwright took place a few decades earlier. The couple after becoming husband and wife kiss. Looking no less than Romeo and Juliet; it is strikingly obvious for those present that; the blissful couple are well connected in mind, body, and soul.

He had no woman, there were none available anyway. He had married the couples out of his newfound love of God, his two loves of all people, to his rivals. As such death was on its way to him. To merely commit suicide was no longer a viable option for him. After taking a deep breath his mind was made up. He believed that either of the women would stab or beat him to death. With thoughts of their hatred playing on his mind he felt that he might as well go out with a bang and do something to both girls that would affect them for the rest of their lives.

Thanks to his high standing and the food imports which arrived via coach from the south after arrival from Dover, he was able to provide his guests with dishes fit for royalty. In turn the five-course dinner was a blessing for each and every one of his visitors. This was merely the eye of the storm of his own making.

Introduction

BACK TO BASICS

Before we continue with our story about dramatic romance, and family life, this chapter has been written as a preamble in order to place a perspective around the main characters. Given they were plunged back centuries; this introductory chapter will help the reader understand the mammoth tasks that lay ahead for Roger and his women. It also serves as a reminder that as much as Beth was happily getting on with her new humble existence; that she was still a product of the consumer age.

Given that the population had less in the way of distractions from the cyber age, the human race became more passionate. It also became more pious, and more family orientated. This conundrum was one which Beth would battle with herself more and more. In order to seduce her and at his evil mercy, Roger became increasingly sanctimonious as well as unhinged. Equally, his powerful rhetoric would consume Beth as if he were her savior.

Unlike in the days of old, the survivors had no idea as to what was immediately happening around them. There was no longer any televise-ion, radio and of course that meant no Internet too. Cars were obsolete and trains too. For the survivors in came once again the horse and cart and travel on foot. The printing press would return, but mechanically, and that would mean visits to museums in order to have the machines that would help bring back newspapers, since without electricity, many of the goods people relied on were then obsolete. Given that there was no mention of events relevant to them on the day of the tsunami since they had no modern technology, several years after the first part of this book was written, this piece was added in 2029 on the tenth anniversary of the tidal wave and when civilization was getting back on its feet. Below is an account of what we think as the survivors is important for the reader to consider before finding out more about Roger, Beth, Sophie, and David.

It was then the eleventh of April 2019. Until yesterday, the population of Cumbria had been serving in the interests of the elite who wanted people to work themselves to death so that they could go rocking all over the world with their riches. Simply put, the more goods produced; the more the elite would have for themselves. At the same time, they wanted plenty of space for themselves and their sacred families. The useless eaters, the vast majority of the population, were being made redundant due to robots. Suicide rates were rising among single people who were depressed to be working, running a house, and having no time for pleasure, let alone love in their lives. More and more people were sexually confused and less fertile as they were being encouraged to butcher and mess around with their sexual organs. Too many women at best were waiting forever to find the perfect man who all too often never materialized; at worst they would make love to their pet dog. So many single men at best were waiting forever to find a woman who loved them and at worst were having fun with other boys who looked like girls. In turn the birth-rate was falling rapidly. As for the living, so depressed with being in the chaos of the modern age, they cheered themselves up in the material world, which was destroying health, children, and marriages. Spending hours driving to shopping malls for superfluous products meant that husbands and wives had no time for each other as they worked more and more hours.

As the people were becoming more paranoid, many bought several freezers in case they would need to stock up if a war broke out. For all this food, plenty of toilet rolls would also make sense and many a loft looked like the shelves in the local chemists. Often, they would stock take on their own domestic supplies, and were dismayed that most of it needed to be thrown out.

Many couples slept in the same bed, but not at the same time. As one was sleeping, his or her other half might have been watching porn at best or if the other half was babysitting, the hedonistic half might have been taking part in an orgy just a few doors away at the house of a single person. Hopefully as far the Illuminati were concerned, families would break up as couples turned from heterosexual to homosexual ones and produce less and less children. As for men such as Roger, they had made a huge amount of money destroying families in court while getting more than their fair share of women in the family way. On top of that, most teenagers no longer wanted to have a family since they believed that having children was a crime for the environment and that the family court would destroy their children's lives as well as those of their own anyway.

Unsurprisingly, Cumbria was the county, with her beautiful valleys, where the masses escaped to away from the modern society which was driving them nuts. In turn these city dwellers from all over the world brought with them an urban feel to the honey pot in the centers of the Lake District as exclusive shops sprung up all over the national park. While most Lakelanders bemoaned the good old days and believed that they had the same problems as the rest of the world, life in the rest of England was much more chaotic during the final days of the computer age. While one was not perceived to be somewhat out of the ordinary if he or she walked to work over and down a fell in the lakes, where people appreciated more the sublime beauty of nature, the Internet age and pornography was biting out the love of many a couple in these beautiful valleys too. Still, at least the traffic jams and the miserable commuters on public transport had not become a major part and parcel of Cumbrian life.

Sadly though, the ideals of Lebensraum posed no solutions for the lucky ones, who wanted more space for themselves, in many ways too much wealth and not enough appreciation of what they had, meant that too many high earners were destroying themselves with, decadence, debauchery and deception. While living in the lap of luxury and far away from reality, the real elite made sure that they brought up their own children in a traditional family environment. They banned their offspring from the overuse of computers, had no TV and lived lives similar to those of the middle classes just after the second world war when people were humble and lived for their loved ones. Simply put, they did not want their own families destroyed from the consumer society which was how they made their own personal fortunes from the sales of their products which they did not even like themselves. They knew themselves that images on mobile phones were replacing human relationships and making love between men and women was becoming obsolete. One lady even planned to invent furry robots with feelings so that people could carry out their desires on a machine instead. The same scientist had four children, was happily married, and lived far away from the masses. Of course, some women already had sybians if they were bored and rich. Just a few more years and men would have been able to make love to a fury android instead of with some wild animal. Even so, most of the elite themselves were wiped out through their own greedy actions when the tsunami came, and the sea levels rose higher than expected and caught them out by surprise. Their plans to wipe out ninety-five percent of the population went wrong as more than ninety-nine percent including and many of the elite themselves; turned into floating corpses which Roger had been dreaming about.

Electricity was gone. All modern appliances were sat looking pretty and nothing more. How would one cope without internet porn and without laptops? At least those who survived no longer had to work themselves to death due to their consumerist addictions and disorder in their lives. Then again, it would not be so tranquil. Without running water in taps and modern medicine, diseases would be back. All of the surface water had been running through the corpses and the rising sea level had further contaminated the waters.

How would one cope having to cook one's own food with wood instead of poisoning oneself with a packet of crisps and a can of coke for dinner or a McDonalds if they went behind with the rent? Now, with so much time on one's hands, cooking for those who survived would be back in vogue. If only the masses had realized how lucky they were when they had it all. Had the men and women been united instead of tacitly agreeing with the depopulation agenda, the words of Macmillan with, "You have never had it so good," would have depicted the modern age which had been wiped out in 2019. As disgusting as it was, because of the tsunami, there was plenty of meat. The problem was not so much as cannibalism as for the fact that without modern day appliances the corpses would turn rancid before one's hunger after eating so much protein would return.

The elite prior to the genocide were planning on bringing in Martial Law. This would have been a first in the UK. Instead, and thanks to wipe-out being greater than expected, the elite did not have the resources and manpower to control the masses with police and soldiers as well as pharmacists who were needed to keep the masses docile via drugs. The elite were concerned about a revolution; but most of them had disappeared along with the higher-than-expected amount of commoners.

On a more positive note, people would enjoy the simple delights of nature. Those lucky enough not be alone would appreciate their loved ones more than their previous addictions for soap operas, as more and people would return to the thinking of Wordsworth and how beautiful the world was and especially in the Lake District where this story is set.

Instead of going to the shops, those who survived would grow their own crops and in turn enjoy more than ever the fruits of nature which they themselves had nurtured, as opposed to simply collecting nutrient poor produce off the shelves from a shop. People became more physically active by day while at night all was calm and without the disturbances from electronic gadgets.

In reality not all of the survivors were living in the utopia that the NWO had been mapping out. Thanks to the Tsunami which went wrong, and obliterated more of humanity than had been expected, common utilities were all too often beyond repair and the manpower shortage was worse than expected. Many of those at the top of the Illuminati tree were at best mentally ill, and at worst as evil as the worst dictators who had ever roamed the earth. While Roger had saved two sisters from the genocide directly, he had pretty much destroyed them psychologically. Equally, his mind was far from being that of a simple loving man, but of one twisted and confused megalomaniac and typical of his former masters who believed that they ruled the earth in every way and served benignly in the interests of humanity.

Cumbria, the county with the highest mountains in England was expected to have many survivors in comparison to counties such as Kent, Essex, and Sussex which were low lying. Still, the largest settlements, Carlisle as well as Barrow-In-Furness were hardly above sea level. Workington and Whitehaven had lovely views of the Isle of Man and had a fishy smell in the air. Now the views and the smells had changed somewhat thanks to the terrestrial victims, meaning that in all the aforementioned Cumbrian towns, there was not a sole survivor at the time as a direct result of the flood.

The planned tsunami at seventy metres would have led to many people surviving in the national park, but at more than one hundred metres, things were worse than expected. Of settlements with any significance within the national park, only those around the Ullswater Valley were flood free. Those around Windermere, Coniston, Derwentwater and the other lakes were locations where more than a handful of people lived, had been swamped. In turn it would be anybody's guess as to how many people out of the forty-one thousand Lake District inhabitants survived. Many of the people who lived high up worked down in the valleys when and where the tsunami swallowed up the innocent masses including most of the elite. As such a survival rate of five percent seemed quite reasonable for the park when out of the thousand inhabitants of the Ullswater Valley, lying well above the tidal wave limit; the old were probably at home, the small children at the local school. As such more than fifty percent survived in the villages of Pooley Bridge, Patterdale and Glenridding. As for those who were working away that day from these villages, it was indeed anyone's guess.

Many were working at levels much lower than those of their homes in Carlisle and Windermere. Penrith at least was flood free. The three largest settlements, Windermere and Bowness, Keswick and Ambleside came off much worse and were well below the tsunami limit, their combined population was fifteen thousand. As for those at work, some were in villages such as Grasmere, Hawkshead and Coniston but these villages were well below a hundred metres too. Others were in Lancaster, more or less on the Morecambe Bay, and close to sea level itself. These mentioned places would obviously be ghost towns. As for wild campers high above the valleys, in summer there were many, but it was only April. Many of the survivors from outside of Cumbria, due to the chaos, claimed to be inhabitants from other valleys in order to be given priority housing, and no checks could be made since all of the data had been stored and since lost on computers.

Globally, while the NWO planned to send population levels to around those in 1,400 and around three hundred and fifty million, at less than eighty million, the amount was less than when Christ was born.

EPIGRAPH

VICTOR HUGO

"To love or have loved, that is enough. Ask nothing further. There is no other pearl to be found in the dark folds of life."

THE VICAR OF BUTTERMERE

Chapter 1

UNITED IN SIN

One day after giving birth, Beth was settling down nicely with her baby and enjoying the spring sunshine in the delightful grounds at her new home; high above Ambleside and nearly halfway up Loughrigg Fell. It was hard to believe that the day before terrible events had taken place down in the valley, when everything looked exactly the same at Fell End before and after the tidal wave. Everything was so peaceful and beautiful with the spring flowers, the warm sunshine, and the breath-taking views around her. As miserable as she was, at least she was proud of her physical fitness. All the swimming the walking and of course plenty of passion she had had recently meant that she would very quickly get back into shape from her labor that had taken place the day before. In fact, she looked incredible and as beautiful as ever, and deep down she knew this too.

Roger was overwhelmed about the amount of work that would now be needed to be done at Fell End. He wanted to seduce Jennifer and believed that he needed to show her how good a gardener he was. In turn and with a rake, he got rid of the moss. He also noticed that there were plenty saplings of bushes for berries in the shed. Delightedly he planted bilberry, raspberry as well as blackcurrant bushes. On top of that, the moles had been around and there was plenty of fertile soil and he didn't need to worry about water for the loamy soil. Close to their new home ran a small uncontaminated mountain beck. Roger was also indebted to the former owners who had obviously been preparing themselves for the wipe out. They had been spearheading a campaign to help encourage people to use less water at the local library. As for their own water an astonishing one hundred bottles of water had been stored inside their cellar. While this amount doesn't so incredible; when one looks at the size of the bottles it does. Each cylinder contained twenty litres. They had not just their local stream but two thousand litres of drinking water to help them during the early days of the planned crisis. While making sure that other people were using water sparingly, they had made sure that they would have more than enough for themselves for a few days at least. A big smile went over him as he was so thankful that they had died in more ways than one.

In many ways Roger had changed. Previously he enjoyed jet setting all over the world, but now life for him was all about his home, his garden and the nature around him. Other Lakeland valleys were now another world as far as he was concerned. Now was the time to simply get to know, his own watch in more detail.

With the women on a long maternity leave, hopefully with several more pregnancies at least, he would have to take care of the manual labor himself. This was something he had never done before, now it was survival, although in recent months he had been taking up gardening as a hobby and a means to prepare himself for the aftermath of the holocaust. Feeling exhausted from just a morning's weeding, one pretty and seductive thing took his mind off his toils in the garden. As far as Roger was concerned and with visions in his mind, she was very soon going to be impregnated again by him and she was lucky to be with him, since he was the great survivor and without him, she would be dead. Even so, as much as Roger saw only the beautiful things connected with her, Beth was intermittently planning on taking her life. Her mind was going through with plenty of confusion and turmoil. Most of it had been caused by Roger, but David hadn't helped matters either. In many ways David had broken her heart more than of Roger. Simply put, Roger was often known simply as; 'The Beast.' Her expectations of him were lower than those she had for David who was meant to be her Christian savour, while Roger was her satanic aphrodisiac, who had equally taken advantage of her because of her sweet nature.

At least the weather was good, and she hoped that Erik would save her from the Beast before she would do something that she would later regret. Unlike David, Erik, the man she met on holiday three months earlier, he accepted her child with Roger. Sadly, he was in Poland when the disaster struck and if he really loved her, he would have by then followed her from their romantic holiday in the sun, on the Canaries, to the Lake District a few months earlier. In some ways he was useless for her. Given he was so morose from living without a woman, the fact that he had done nothing at all to be reunited with her meant that love wasn't so important for him after all. At least she was relieved to be away from The Howe, where she lived during her pregnancy until just yesterday, which was the day of the birth and genocide, and now too littered with the corpses of humans and other life forms due to the tsunami. While she knew, in recent months, that the genocide was on its way, the day before seemed as though it were one year earlier and more.

As far as he was concerned, Beth was just as potent for him as ever, and as he walked up to her while she was sat on the grass and breastfeed-ing in the mid-morning spring sunshine, he couldn't take his passionate eyes off her. Just looking at her was enough to make him drool and long for her. She though, simply felt repulsed by him and wanted him to leave her alone, but his presence was unnerving her. At least Erik had promised to visit her, but knowing about his jealousy, she decided not to remind him about the man who was coming over from her homeland especially for her. "I don't how you can smile after what happened yesterday. I am so depressed about it." She said thinking about the tsunami as she was still numb from giving birth on the same day as the holocaust. As much as she felt born to be a mother, it was something she never expected until she was at least twenty-five and after her university education.

"As a father, all I care about is my children. If you were the last woman left on the planet, I would be looking after you more than you could ever imagine."

"Enough people have died; I don't wish for this to happen."

If you were a true romantic, then all that would matter would be us." His words were beautiful, but his actions were one of a different paths and even if there were millions of other women around, she would still be his one and only if he was sincere. She continued breastfeeding and this was something for her to block out his unwanted presence with.

They were both parents, and as much as she was just a baby making machine for him, William would be their connection. He simply stood there smiling at his son. Although it was in the direction of her breasts, her woman's intuition told her that he was looking fondly at their child. "Thank you for naming our first child after the great poet."

"My pleasure." She said politely.

"I am so proud of you." He said as Beth was also still recovering emotionally from his sounds of lovemaking with her sister that took place a few hours after she gave birth and could hear in her bedroom just the night before. She didn't reply. "When you wear the jewellery next time along with your seductive hourglass figure, every thought of mine will be running through my fertile mind as the impending passion will be one of a night to remember." He said as he was leering at her breasts and trying to provoke some passionate response from her.

"Roger, I have just given birth, and all I can say is that I am so grateful to you, and proud of you that you weren't making love to Jennifer while I was in labor." She said ironically.

"I would never want to hurt you. You look so tender and fragile and make me want to be the man who deserves your part time love." He said, and then kissed her on her lips and walked off and was disappointed that she hadn't accepted his friendly gesture towards her with alacrity.

His words part time love made her angry, but what else could she do if she didn't want to feel hurt by him? There were three women and just one man. He wasn't able to deal with her emotions when his mind was full of three women, whom he wanted to put in the family way again and again and again. Equally, he wanted to behave as a real gentleman to all three of them, so that, Fell End would be simply one great love factory in every sense of the word. Then he wouldn't need to heap on so much praise on the women whom he hoped would be fighting with each other and over him. In his eyes he was the most important being on the planet, and little Rogers had to take care of the planet for the survival of mankind.

Beth simply felt like nothing. If only she was ugly and with a caring monogamous man. Being so stunningly feminine and beautiful was doing her no favours whatsoever. All she wanted was love. Roger was a dangerous forbidden fruit for her; he spoke so excitingly to her. At times, his love for her sent her on highs which made her feel as though she was in heaven, before making her feel as though she was merely just literally a hole for him. Sadly, because she needed a man so much, she was at his emotionally destructive mercy whenever he wanted to bring her back down to earth with his less than romantic talk of death, infidelity, and sexual confusion while his image of that of a debonair was a bewitching enticement for her. Even so, and despite her passionate mind, the idea of making love ever again was as attractive as bathing in a cowshed full of excrement.

Sophie was relieved that Roger had survived the beating she meted out onto him, which could have been fatal, and was busy with the cooking. It seemed to her that due to the floods, he was the only man who had survived. All she could hope for; was that he would not jilt her after she would give birth now that a third and beautiful woman, who had literary connections with Wordsworth, appeared on the scene. Less sensitive emotionally than her sister; she found it in some ways easier to get on with her life, but in return, deep and meaningful love came less than she would have liked. At least the night before he was with her, and she was enjoying herself more than her sister whose body was exhausted. Other times she was jealous, her sister had her birth behind her, but then again, since her baby wasn't yet there, she knew that although tired from her own pregnancy more tiring days were ahead of her. In short, she knew she had to make the most of things before she too, any day now, was a full-time mother.

As for Jennifer, given Roger had been cheating with both sisters and that she had lost her David in the floods, she needed some cheering up and believed that she could easily become a partner of his. Briefly, on the day of the disaster she had shed few tears for the people she knew who had died in the disaster. Now she had even more pressing problems to deal with. For all of the three women, Roger was a rough diamond, and there were no other men left. She went up to him nervously just after her breakfast time which was later than the others. He was sat in the garden thinking about his future plans and admiring the spring flowers and licking his lips with glee as he thought about life without anyone telling him what he could do or more to the point should do with his life. "You have done terrific work this morning. You make me feel so lazy." She said to him.

"I am happy to be doing something useful." He said.

"I am very lonely without David." She said as she was still shaken by the events the day before, which seemed to have ended her stable life unexpectedly.

"I am not at all surprised. It is a pity you fell pregnant to him so recently. I would have been quite happy to have got you in the family way. At least I am still alive." He said gentlemanly with a benign smile in front of her dreamy looking face.

"There are not many men left." She said wondering if a man would ever touch her body again. He seemed so faithful to his two women. If only she hadn't let the cat out of the bag the day before. Her being pregnant meant Roger was out of her reach.

"I plan to get both girls pregnant again well before you give birth."

"My God! Well, I must admit they are real beauties." She said as his speech was exciting her, and her heart almost skipped a beat. Sadly, he wasn't interested in her, even though he was along with his women staying at her house.

"I like the idea of keeping the pregnant flow alive." He said as she felt mesmerized by the love, he had for his two women. "Of course, I find you very beautiful too." He said as he was looking straight at her ample cleavage.

With his words of tentative affection for her, she looked at him in a dreamy and hypnotised trance, as her body felt galvanised by his words. How could she survive without the touch of a man? How much she longed to be caressed. David was dead. She had to survive, and he had just flattered her and seemed to be a gentleman too and was thankful that having her own house might just help her get to some romance in her life and to join his exclusive harem that was hopefully less tantalising than before.

After feeling mesmerized from his earlier words and still looking at him for more than a few moments and waiting for him to do more than just look at her lecherously she was about to walk off. "I have a bad back from working so hard here and I need the soft touch from a beautiful nurse." He said as she was then excited by his words. Together they walked inside the house when the other women were in their own world and went upstairs. There were four large bedrooms: one for each person. Of course, Roger hoped he wouldn't have to sleep in his own four walls alone. Once inside the house, they went to his room. "I guess you have a little backache too. Sit down and I can give you a massage." He said to her as she accepted his offer exultingly. In turn his hands which had the combination of David's gentle touch and his own manipulative and erotic feel meant Jennifer was being turned on by this rogue and on the day after Beth gave birth, which she attended as a midwife. That was also the day when she found out that she was pregnant. For some reason, his confidence made her feel relaxed. While David was sweet, nice, and good, this man seemed to have the chemistry that other men she knew were lacking. Suddenly, and to his great delight she started massaging him too.

Roger made love to Jennifer on the same bed where he planned to once again; place the three women living at Fell End along with some other young maidens in the family way, during the coming months.

After making love he looked at her. "Normally I should have made love to Sophie. Any day now she will be giving birth and I really love her maternal body." He said as Jennifer then thought about her own growing boobs and a curvier figure to excite him further with. Later with a bit of luck, she too would carry his child. If she wanted to a part of something exciting, that being the rebuilding of mankind, then Roger was her guy. "You only made love to her last night." She said: she knew everything. The night before she had been gently masturbating herself outside Roger's bedroom, and heard lovemaking taking place to a woman who like herself was pregnant, but at the opposite end of the gestation epoch as she could then without David only imagine what it was like to be sexually fulfilled with a voluptuous, maternal, body like that of Sophie's and of Beth's just one day earlier. Since the tsunami along with her sudden pregnancy hormones, events had sent her subconsciously somewhat crazy and hornier too. Like Roger, without society's norms she was at risk off going off the rails. She was used to the Internet and had been cyber cheating on David. She didn't want to physically cheat on him, but now without her eyes being excited from the images of other men she needed Roger. What was more, David was dead anyway, so what was so wrong in making love anyway?

She was now getting used to other forms of entertainment. She was jealous of both girls and felt that in not being impregnated by Roger, that she was the odd one out. "To be honest, my dream is to produce at least a dozen children, with Beth still a teenager there is plenty of time, and I plan to live until I am one hundred and twenty." He said proudly, as she was simply going weak at the knees and just wanted him to quickly seduce her. For her very own survival she needed him. The day was still young, and they had a nap together. He knew from the sounds downstairs that the girls had been in and out of the kitchen. With the weather being fair, he thought and hoped that his women might not be coming into his room as he thought about Emma from Silverdale and the time the sisters saw him making love to her.

After a quick sleep, he looked at her. "Would you like to visit my old house and see my collection of paintings, after a quick swim in the tarn?" He asked her with a cheeky smile.

"I would really like that." She said. She knew her place, she wasn't so young in his eyes and fertile as the sisters, but she was at least still on the right side of being thirty. She believed that things had changed dramatically around her; and that in order for her to survive both physically and mentally, she had to adapt to the New Order of things. She also recognized that; Roger unlike David, wasn't a submissive type.

As they left the house, the girls seemed to be unaware of the passion between them and didn't even register their departure. The walk was so peaceful, and they had the whole world for themselves and were walking with cheeky smiles on both of their faces and hand in hand. Nobody would have guessed that they had just survived from a holocaust worse than any other. As they arrived at Tarn Foot, Roger looked at her. "Normally in summer, this place is full of campers. Normally a Tsunami wouldn't reach this level, and up to around three hundred campers could have survived, but as we can see some people weren't so lucky as us." He said as if the only people who mattered; were each other. He looked at her, hypnotically with his shiny eyes, and together they French kissed. Jennifer smiled, she was luckier than the waitress who had perished and felt that keeping on the right side of him was more than just beneficial for her.

After a few moments of kissing, she looked at him. "We will be lucky if three hundred people have survived the whole of the park let alone the Ambleside area." She said. This was to Roger's relief, since he wanted to be sure that enough people had perished.

"Shall we look at the campsite?" He said as she nodded her head. Together they walked to the site. They found a small tent. Roger opened it up and found no one inside it. "I wonder what happened to the camper."

"You never know, we might bump into him or her." Jennifer said trying to sound interesting to him. By then she saw him as her very own savior. She already knew something about the depopulation agenda and remained silent so as not to annoy him about her knowledge. Rumours had been going around at university that a whistle-blower who was about to release something big on YouTube had been silenced, and his body had been found in a river after an apparent suicide.

What was strange was that she was the junior partner in this relationship of convenience. The simple fact was that; Roger was a very manipulative man. Common sense should have prevailed. She had given him the safe haven of her newly acquired manor. She would have survived without him. Instead, and without her, he would have been sharing his home with two angry women who would have been wondering where to begin with regards to cleaning The Howe which had the stench from the red river that contained the debris of rotten flesh. Not all women were quite so adventurous as Jennifer, who despite being a nurse, she didn't always worry about hygiene standards. Of course, Sophie and Beth were adventurous ladies too, but he was by then bored of both of them.

Walking down towards Loughrigg Tarn, her mind was once again on other things. She thought about how just the day before the world seemed so different in every way, until the moment she met Roger. If only she hadn't taken things for granted, but now was not the time to worry about the past and together they got inside the waters and had a quick swim in the bracing waters. She kept her mouth closed since she was paranoid of swallowing skulls and limbs, which were not so far away. As a nurse, deep down with death all around, she did worry after all about hygiene too. Accidentally she swallowed some water, spat it out and was a little frightened that she might end up ill from a virus in the infested and bloody waters.

There were a few corpses close to the shore of the lake and together and after their swim, they moved them away so that the waters wouldn't be later contaminated. Roger by accident came inside his pants. He seemed to be producing more sperm than ever. It seemed that the recent events had given him a new zest for life. Everything seemed to be going his way, and as soon as possible he would turn the area around the tarn of Loughrigg into a baby making factory of his very own and exclusive making.

After the swim, they dried off in the sunshine together. It was funny. The day before her mind was on dead bodies and today all she could see everywhere outside was the spring flowers. As they arrived at his home, they walked inside and could smell the damp from the flooding the day before. His walls looked as though they had been painted in slime too from the vegetation tide marks. Once inside his bedroom he looked at her. "Why don't we spend the night together alone?" He was the only man around. She needed him more than ever and was going weak at her knees with him. In this house she was away from his other women. As she got on the bed, which was still more than a little damp she wanted to laugh. She hoped that his passion would take her mind off the wet mattress. Feeling so tired after their passion, she simply wouldn't care about the souvenirs of death which were staring at her on his walls with the faint smatterings of slime and the odd dash of red.

They were a little hungry; at least they had eaten well at her new home. He did have chocolate bars and nuts lying around upstairs and some bottles of water too. The rest of his food in the kitchen due to the flooding was no longer fit for consumption. At least they wouldn't starve. After having so much fun together and talking non-stop and very soon it soon got dark. With several candles which had been placed safely above the water level along with matches, together they studied the three paintings of Beth together as he held her in his arms. "My God, these are so beautiful. I can see a lot of Beth in them. It is no wonder that two women fell pregnant to you with the amount of love that you give." She said.

"My favorite is this one." He said proudly as they were close to the painting of Beth nursing two babies with her toddler watching on fondly and heavily pregnant.

"David wanted me to end up like this, I guess. It wasn't my desire, but now things are different. I don't have a career anymore and have so much time on my hands. On top of that, I have never found a man who I fell in love with. Why are you with two women anyway?"

After what seemed like eternity but was just a few seconds, Roger's answers were at the ready. "These things happen, I can't say I am pleased, but one evening Beth sneaked into my room and completely unawares I made love to her in the dark while Sophie was taking a bath."

"What a terrible thing to do to one's sister." She said looking shocked as Roger was feigning a decent code of morality.

"I know. I didn't know what to do when I found out a few hours later as I woke up after making love passionately. In vain I decided to make the most out of things, but once you have been deceived it kind of takes over you. Both girls wanted to fall pregnant to me, and I was a fool."

"Women often play cruel games against men. For me as such an honorable man as you are, you are beyond reproach." She said. Roger knew she was trying to move his affections solely to hers as he thought about the deception she had towards David. If she was a loyal partner, so soon after his death, she wouldn't be making love with someone else. "I bet you met many famous people."

"I did but I think that they are all dead and buried." He said as they giggled from his words at each other. He didn't wish to discuss his sordid past with the elite to her.

"I think we have met a match in each other. I met the randy prince who couldn't settle down with one woman." Roger merely listened. "He was a friend of Joe Goldberg's but what the media didn't wish to report was they were having sex with each other." She said as he was in awe.

"I know, because the male media big knobs were having sex with both men and to divert attention and due to their jealousies, they only mentioned the teenage girls because that was nothing to do with LGBT of which the media are big players." He said as they then embraced into a passionate kiss together.

After a long and deeply sensual kiss and then holding each other's hands romantically he began; "One doesn't really know a woman until she carries his child and shows him that she is still the girl he first met." He said planting the seeds of a second pregnancy inside her as she started to blush like a beetroot in her face.

"Would you start a life here with me?" She said as she felt as she was being along with her womb swept off her feet by him.

"I live for the moment, and I want to impregnate you now, but I will have to wait for eight months at least. Still first come; first served." He said as she was in shock with his passionate and cruel audacity. She sensed that he was ready to impregnate Beth before spring was over and would willingly have a threesome with her or then with Sophie, but being a newcomer in his harem, she was merely testing the waters.

"OK you old dirty bastard! Here we are, united in sin, just fuck me senseless!" She said as her dreamy romantic thoughts about him turned to simply those of a naked lust instead. Willingly, he did as he was told. Neither wanted something tender. Neither wanted to kiss and to cuddle, all that they both desired was their own orgasm and didn't really care about the other.

On the other hand, if only he had the sweetness of David as well as the potency of the Don Juan he was. Then she would have wanted him to treat her like a lady all night long with the caressing and tantric love that as a teenage girl she dreamt of before her first man disappointed and used her.

Thanks to seeing death and destruction around her, and knowing that she herself was with child, she certainly believed in the survival of the fittest, and didn't care if she could trust what he had been saying to her earlier that evening. What he had said chimed with her desperation as she was worried about dangerous wild men walking around of lesser intellect. She also felt safer with him, than being at the mercy in a world without order. In her native Cumbria, David was a respectable gentleman.

She believed with hindsight that when she was down at Cambridge where she met many well-heeled cads, that they were training her for Roger the sophisticated philanderer. On top of that, she was no better a person herself. If she were the only woman around and several suitors were lurking, she would gladly offer her body to them in turn for them to look after her home, which required so much manpower. She dreamt of having one man to collect fuel, another to farm the land and another to satisfy her erotic desires and another to make babies with. Of course, these role positions she would mete out on the men, would not be fixed either. In turn though, and feeling all woman, she would clean and cook. Once the gas cylinders would run out, life would return back to the stone-age and she would need a strong man, or more to the point men more than ever. As such, by then she was convinced that her thoughts about him were about love and nothing less. He was the only man around after all; and she needed him more than ever.

A few hours later the damp bed was a little uncomfortable for her and feeling so alone and unloved she shook him gently. He woke up. "Could you ever love just one woman?"

"That was my plan. As I told you my love, I was taken advantage of by both sisters. This really messed me up so badly. Imagine the pain and torment I went through with when I realized that they had both premeditated all of this?" He said with his shiny and deceptive eyes.

"It must have been terrible." She smiled at him gently as her eyes lit up radiantly as she reassuringly placed her right hand onto his upper left leg, and he was ready for her again.

"At least I am still standing." He said as he smiled back at her.

"You are such a strong man to have stood by both of them."

"What about you?" He said changing the topic and too scared to accept too much flattery when he only wanted to play around.

"I have waited all of my life to be in love with just one man. Sadly, none of the men I met were real men for me or were simply bad guys." Roger was licking his lips with glee, even David, the man he himself would gladly be his bitch or sweetheart for, and carry his babies if he could, wasn't good enough even for Jennifer who for him wasn't nearly so beautiful as the Pollack girls. He sensed that exciting times lay ahead for him. She knew being the great deceiver she was that she had simply met her match in him and more. She respected him.

After another round of lovemaking, Jennifer found a side of him unpleasant to say the least. She was angry that she was able to be attracted to a man who was going to use her, but equally she wondered if she could offer him more than the sisters together. Given the chance, she would happily gloat at the girl's expense. As much as her intuition told her she was going to be disappointed with this rogue if she really believed that he would make an honest woman out of her, feeling so sensual all she wanted was for him to fuck her senseless again.

The night started off beautifully as he wanted to pound her again and again. Being away from the other women in his life was a blessing for both of them, as they could romantically concentrate on just each other. Even so, he thought about Beth and wished that he was alone with her. She wasn't pregnant and all he could think about were the paintings of her and how much he wanted her to be as slim as the painting with her standing on the island just after she lost her virginity and to be ready to be pregnant once more. In turn she would then be a step nearer to the painting of her after being impregnated by him three times where she epitomised the female goddess in all of her fertile glory and with an even bigger belly and wider hips than the last time. In turn the excitement of imaging her being slender as well as big; proved to him that he needed a few women at a time. Simply put for this man whose desires included making love to a pregnant woman and impregnating a woman simultaneously, meant that monogamy simply wouldn't work for him. On top that although the disaster happened less than two days earlier, it seemed like a lifetime since he was last at The Howe. In turn memories of Beth, the first time he saw her, with her T Shirt showing the contours of her breasts, her shorts which didn't cover the whole of her soft and beautiful skin were always on the back of his mind as he was lying next to Jennifer. After his pounding of her several times, a dark cloud went over him as he desperately wanted to make love to his other girls.

Unlike at Fell End there was no dry toilet. As such and with no running water, they made use of a potty, wet wipes, and common sense for hygiene. As for the smells, they quickly got over them.

She woke up and was truly ashamed of herself. She had lost everyone she knew thanks to the tsunami and seen death everywhere with the corpses. As much as Roger was a villain, at least the way he treated women, wasn't this man merely carrying out the dreams of many other men she knew who had perished? Divorce, broken families, cheating domestic violence and mothers having children to a few partners proved to her that Roger wasn't so bad. Many men left their girlfriends when they fell pregnant; at least Roger was looking after both of his women. All she could hope for, was at worst he would take her into his harem and excite her. Not too infrequently.

After breakfast Roger inspected his former garden. One thing that surprised him was that the floods hadn't damaged all of his future crops. The cherry tree still had her blossom. The vegetable plot still had her plants to some degree intact. The greenhouse looked safe and sound and had plenty of future crops inside, he just had to re pot and sort out the compost which needed replenishing. He was then suddenly only too well aware that he would have to work hard physically so that his growing family could be sufficiently fed. Luckily, he was well prepared and went to the garden shed for his compost. In short, there would be a decent harvest at The Howe. He carried the heavy compost, and, with her hands she re-potted the greens. They were working very well together and not once did she think about the dead bodies until he had a plan for a corpse or two.

After working somewhat on his land, a flash of inspiration went across his mind. "You see the compost heap over there?"

"I do." She said.

"Why don't we add a few dead bodies onto it?"

"That isn't much of a compost heap."

"I know, but after we have cleaned up the mess, there will be plenty of vegetation and with the flesh we will have something like one of nature's own Lancashire Hot Pots!" He said half serious and half in jest.

"How will you cook it!" She smiled at him.

"Don't be silly, it is going to be used as a fertiliser!" She then looked at him.

"Never!" She said sarcastically. In turn they both burst out laughing as they looked down together on the garden corpses.

After making a start on the compost heap, they started giggling at one another. Together hand in hand they left The Howe and followed the path which was normally full of boots moving in both directions. "Shall we see what happened to the mystery camper?" She asked him.

"Yes, it was a rather nice-looking tent and sleeping bag and we have plenty of storage space." Both of them were taking a chance. A male camper would be good news for her. Either sex would be good news for him, as his mind was no longer thinking about the dozens of different genders which he was used to, the choice between homosexual and heterosexual ones seemed to be enough to satiate him with.

As they reached the campsite, they looked at each like brothers in arms. Both were sad that the camping gear was no longer there. The excitement had gone, the mystery had been solved and wasn't nearly so exciting as they had been hoping for. Then it was time to move on.

In the distance she spotted a being, she had to extricate herself from him and moved her hands away from Roger. If only this person could save her from this dirty old man, who was two decades older than herself as she put him on in being forty-eight years of age, as opposed to her twenty-eight. She had to move onto the next desirable person available. In the meantime, Roger was her steppingstone. After a few moments, the man was looming into their vision vividly. "Roger, I think it is my David." She said. Roger was aghast, he was happy having three women at his command, now the only other survivor apart from his women was a man, and David of all people.

Her heart started beating wildly as she was hiding her guilt. She approached him as he was waiting in front of her, she burst into tears. "David!" She said, as Roger was listening attentively. "I wanted to die without you! Fortunately, two women, who needed my help, have offered to look after me while I am bereaving you! Oh David! If only you knew how much I wanted to die with you in the floods since without you I would have died here alone. How much happier I am now in seeing you alive!" She said to him with her florid words which she knew chimed in so well with his own paper-thin piety.

"I think I ought to leave you two love birds alone for some time." He said in a way he hoped might arouse both suspicion in David and fear in Jennifer. David's mind was awash with plenty of suspicions and riddles. Why was she with him and who were these women?

Roger walked off towards The Howe while the other two simply stood next to each other. Jennifer started to cry, she wanted him to speak. "Don't cry darling, as least we have both survived." He said, as he wished that it was Beth who was standing next to him.

"I would have died had I lost you!" She replied. If he found out later that she had slept with Roger, it wouldn't be so bad as then for this woman who lived for the moment. Then at least she was showing him her great devotion to him. He then kissed her passionately as they started to French kiss. "We must be strong David; we are parents to be!" She said as she believed that his devotion to her had been sealed.

"This is the best news since we have just been reunited. Maybe things are not so bad after all." He said as his inner strength was enticing her desires towards him and away from Roger. Maybe, perhaps, maybe she would love David. He seemed delighted that he was a father to be, and he had touched her heart to some degree at least.

After a few moments of euphoria, David was scared. He wondered if it was Beth who was one of these women. Was Beth going to spill the beans to Jennifer? Had she already done so? Was this why Jennifer was sleeping with Roger? He wanted to be sick. Luckily, he used his head and decided not to find out the truth, since if Jennifer knew how much he loved Beth, he himself would be closer to the devil, in her eyes, than to the good Christian boy he wished others to believe that he was, which he wasn't. Like Roger, his image was more important than the acts he carried out. Simply put, he was still madly in love with Beth. For him, Roger's plaything was in the eyes of the church, forbidden fruit. In turn, with his mind back on the present, Jennifer, took the lead and guided him towards Fell End. "I hope you will like our new safe haven." She said. He was then thankful that as it seemed to him, Roger was living at The Howe. Who were then these women Fell End? He wondered, and was she trying to distract her from connection with Roger?

"Sadly, our place; got flooded. My workplace was submerged. Luckily, I was in the grounds of Dove Cottage and as soon as I saw the rising waters, I simply ran uphill in the direction of Alcock Tarn. I didn't look back; I was too scared to see people drowning." He said with a voice full of emotion.

"I am so proud of you," she said without thinking about the others who died, whom he might have been able to have saved.

"The waters were rising so fast that I didn't believe that I would survive, but it was well worth the chance." He said dramatically.

She suspected that some of his colleagues had drowned, but she didn't know any of them and wasn't at all concerned. True, she was a nurse by profession, but she believed that her life was not only about looking after others. In fact, as she had realized from her hedonistic night with Roger and knew from her own past life that; only one thing mattered, herself.

As they arrived at Fell End, David smiled, this house was better than his flat and he didn't shed a tear for the masses that had drowned, and he simply couldn't believe his luck. His new modern manor was a palace for him. All David cared about was his own fortunes. His partner was carrying his child in turn his life was complete and with more children together his three prayers would be answered. His first was a woman. His second was a family. His third was a detached house with a garden. All three were now coming beautifully into fruition for him.

He was in great trepidation and curiosity; the first of the sisters to greet his terrified eyes was Sophie. In turn he realized that these two women, were simply Roger's women. At least Sophie had prepared him for the inevitable, that of him meeting up with the women he loved like no other. She saw him before he saw her, and she felt as though she had been slammed into some psychological hell. So wild with emotion she ran inside her house, crept into her room where her baby was sleeping, put on a pair of trainers and wanted to jump out of her window and escape by running up the hill. Instead, she erratically placed the running shoes onto her feet after taking off her boots, and with her heart beating as though she was running for the marathon, she held her breath, left the room and walked downstairs. As soon as she opened the outside door, she simply ran out of the grounds of Fell End. At least she had the sense not to run too after, although she was very fit, her body needed time to recover from her labor.

Roger had only made love to Jennifer for one night. Even so, it was nice that he had got his sweet revenge on David who had made love to Beth. Should he tell David? He wasn't so sure. For Roger, his main concern was his genetic code, and the fact that he had merely had a night of passion with her, was nothing more than an innocent act for him.

Hopefully one day, he would carry out his dreams of posterity on Jennifer as well as with the sisters too. On top of that, the idea of raping a Christian man was more exciting than making love to another homosexual. In fact, David had so many pure and good qualities that he wanted to devour for just him only. David was the quintessential English gentleman, white Anglo Saxon who had something of the Blue Blood in him as far as Roger was concerned.

With Jennifer around, David acted as though he didn't know Beth and was sat tightly next to Jennifer with his eyes discreetly on his recent; and former love of his life's sibling, who for him looked more beautiful than ever. As for Sophie, she seemed to be completely absorbed in her own melancholic world. For her, people were evil. Nobody seemed to be shedding tears for the deceased. She was in no way an innocent either, but at least her lack of tears was due to her being still in shock and too weak to accept that she was still alive. What a horrible world it seemed to her. Still, her younger sister had just given birth, she had to remain strong, she was going to be giving birth herself too; very soon. Knowing how vulnerable and emotional Beth was, Sophie was pining over her and was scared of what the sight of David might have done to her psyche. She had seen her running out and was terrified that she might have in turn harmed her recovering post-natal womb.

Roger concocted a delightful meal especially under the primitive circumstances which they were going to have to get accustomed to. Beth had returned at the right moment just as everyone had just sat down at the dinner table and had other things on their mind. "Hello." She said uncomfortably. The others returned a smile without making any fuss and merely replied in one word to her greeting. David though, was more than just awestruck with her innocent like beauty. Sophie was frozen, and hoped that with David on the scene, Jennifer wouldn't throw them out of her house. At least her sister must have only run out of the house and slowed down to walking pace, since she looked as though she was glowing from her outing. While eating, his diners seemed happy and were devotedly serving their bellies. All was eerily calm until, David, unable to cope with events he started puking all over the table profusely. Jennifer smiled nervously; he ran out of the dining-room while his partner carried on eating. "Do you think David is OK?" Beth asked.

"Of course, he is, but at times he is a bit of a drama queen." Jennifer said. "If you are worried, you can check on him." She said as she was trying to work out what kind of girl Beth was. She then walked out with her heart beating rapidly, yet relieved that she had the blessing to see that he, her one and only true love, was alright. The fact he was going to be a father was a double-edged sword for her. On the one hand she more in the way of respect for him, while on the other, she was also in pain that his paternity had nothing to do with her child.

Beth then found him sat on Jennifer's bed upstairs. "Why does Jennifer address him as Roger?"

"That's his real name. He is a Frenchman, an impostor. If you don't mind, I don't wish to speak about him, I am more concerned about you."

"I am sorry. When the floods came, and while I was running uphill, I heard screaming, it was from a colleague of mine who was working with an electric saw outside, and lost control as the waters arrived at his feet. In a panic he dropped the saw which was battery operated and then it slipped and sawed off his left foot." He said as he saw once again the images of blood pouring out of his popular colleague.

"Why didn't you go and help him?" She asked him.

"Of course, I wanted to help him, but I saw no point in drowning along with him."

"Is that why you threw up?" She asked him with care.

"Yes and no, I am still suffering psychologically. Back to the incident, I don't know how this happened but as I was running uphill, a dog ran past me carrying a blood-stained leg and was being chased by hungry crows and it was that of one of my colleagues. I have never seen something so disgusting in my entire life. He was screaming in agony until the river of blood silenced him. Please don't tell the others. I don't think they care."

"I care." She said wanting him to know that she was of a moralistic sort as she smiled at him gently and wanting him to kiss her as her body suddenly felt no longer disgusted from a man making love to her even though it was too soon after giving birth. While, in his mind all she had to do was to kiss him and he would be hers.

"I know you do, he said meekly." He said as he was confused as to where his loyalties lay.

"Was there any other reason as to why you felt sick?"

"Yes, there is, I love you, but I can't understand how you allow yourself to be humiliated by that man."

"Your words don't flatter me in any way. To think that you love me more than the mother carrying your child, yet all you can do is to berate me, obliquely. I am little more than a child and all you can do is blame me for all of the misery around us!"

"No, no, Beth, as if I would blame you for dear for the Tsunami."

"I have lost more than just my dignity as a woman. I have lost my family, my roots. I am Polish, I will never see my country or my origins again, as far as I am concerned it has all been wiped out of my memory. Don't you see that a part of me doesn't even care about this! I know I shouldn't as a Christian be speaking like this, but all I want now is you." She said as she started crying and to his great horror as his piety was taking over his mind as in turn, she looked less alluring for him.

"I am going to be a good and honest father." He said coldly as his words brought tears to her eyes as well as a shock which went running through her body. Without his love her mind went on to other things as she was once again feeling traumatised because of death, especially that of the waitress. This was the young lady Roger impregnated just two weeks before he met the sisters. After running out of the house a few hours earlier, she went to visit the scene of her former neighbour's death, where she asked God to bless her body and soul, as well as that of her baby and her boyfriend who thought he was the child's daddy.

That night all was peaceful at the beautiful home where her deceased employers lived until the tsunami and Jennifer felt safe. No longer upset about the demise of all the people she knew, she was delighted to be living in such a lovely home. David was making mad passionate love to her, so in turn she trusted him. Jennifer was making mad passionate love to him, so in turn he trusted her. That night with shivers running down her spine she eventually fell asleep. She knew that David was a good man for her and that she was lucky to have him. All she could hope was that she would never cheat on him again and that he would never find out about her meaningless affair with Roger. Suddenly an attack of sadness went over her. She was feeling very sad about the people who had died after all. There were some she loved dearly. Her Facebook and Twitter friends whom she had never actually met, but for her were just as real as Roger and David combined.

As for him, even on this night with her, Jennifer, David was thinking about Beth. In their hedonistic flesh they were in more than one way together and making love to each other but out of habit. In order to get excited; Jennifer thought about Roger: as he thought about Beth. In their hearts and in their minds, they were devoted to other people. As such they were simply living a life of latent infidelity at best that would have made The Beast himself proud of both of them.

As for Roger and Sophie there was no trust. She might kill him, and he was cheating on her. She hadn't once cheated on him, but Roger could never feel fully satisfied with her. Even so, the poor good girl, Beth, was sandwiched between the two walls of the sounds of love making taking place between the two most important men in her life with women other than that of herself. In short, she wanted to die. She wanted to leave her beautiful son with Sophie and to jump off the nearest suitable crag to her demise. It was bad enough listening to Roger and Sophie making love the night before, now she felt more alone than ever. David and Jennifer would remind her about the beautiful romance which she herself was missing. Even so, both sisters were pretty disgusted with Jennifer as well as with Roger and had pretty much an idea as to what they had got up to the night before.

The next day after a difficult night with her restless baby and knowing that her beloved David was with someone else, Beth was sat in the sun breastfeeding minding her own business and trying to build up her life for the sake of her son. As a woman full of love who wanted to look on the bright side of things, she was enjoying the ambience of nature around her. The sounds of the birds singing seemed louder than usual, and they were since in a jiffy, tourism died. While she recognized their singing in the early morning as being normal, it was the middle of the afternoon and almost as if they were celebrating. Beth loved the flora and fauna but was never in a million years going to relish in the genocide. Suddenly, she was disturbed by his voice. "Does Jennifer know anything about us?" He said as she looked around in horror.

"My God, David what do you take me for?"

"I am sorry. I know this. I do though have a right to know if Jennifer slept with Roger?"

"My God, how can you ask me such a question? You have betrayed me. Roger has let me down. How do you think I felt when I was alone last night and heard four people making love, who have all let me down, when I feel so alone? I am not a snitch David. It works both ways as far as you and Roger are concerned. Jennifer is your woman, and if she loves you, she will speak with you about things which are of no concern of mine!" She said as her words made him more suspicious than before that he was being cuckolded by a lesser woman than the one whose beautiful eyes he was looking into.

"But Beth, how can I confront her about Roger when I cheated on her with you?" He said in desperation as his desire for her was rising.

"Oh David, leave me alone. Can't you see how much you are killing me with your manipulation and trying to put the blame on me regarding your infidelities?"

"What do you mean?"

"I did not force myself onto you."

"But you lied to me about being with his child."

"If you were a real man, things would now be very different." She said as she thought about how they could have been happy together and was offended by his far from loving speech directed at her.

"Beth, you will always be at the mercy of Roger. That was the reason why you chose the name of William for your son." He said as he was feeling somewhat offended by her too, and his passion was being replaced by his boredom of her lack of unconditional enthusiasm for him.

"Perhaps, if you hadn't stopped going to church you might be fuller of love instead of the hatred you have for me."

"Now is not the time to speak about religion when many of the survivors are less humble than of those who perished. I often wonder why I myself survived."

"Oh my God! David, how can such evil thoughts spew out of your mouth?"

Tears then went down her face as she believed that she had chosen the wrong name, while he believed that her child would basically be a mini-

Roger. Her pride had been wounded, but she didn't wish to harm Jennifer and to spill the beans. She simply didn't wish to fall down to the level of a gossip merchant. Her own happiness was more important for her than gloating over the misery of others, while at the same time David had just deeply injured her emotionally and she wondered if he had obliquely implied that she too should have drowned in the Red River.

She was after all a victim of Roger's, a good girl at heart. Couldn't he accept that she would be so loyal and true to him? Feeling guilty himself, he walked meekly away from her as she wondered if she was going to lose her mind. She loved David, but in her mind, there was something about him that made her feel uneasy about him and was more than just his jealousy towards Roger. Once again, she would try to fall asleep after her baby had quietened down and before the opposite sides of her wall would keep her awake with the unwelcome stereophonic love productions. That was the way of her routine and nothing more, so it seemed to her.

A meeting was held underneath the beech tree the following day. "As we are well aware, it is important in one's life to have some order in one's life." Roger began upbeat. "It is now Saturday the thirteenth of April 2019. In turn I think we should follow to some extent with our daily routines. Our week will as normally begin on a Monday and I will ask us to meet here and to discuss let's say around ten. We will discuss what happened the previous week and our plans for the current one. I will be keeping an eye on the future harvest at The Howe. David will be doing this here at Fell End. We will make sure that there is enough food for all of us. Today we will have a short meeting and I will be planning our first official meeting after the weekend. David, I have a question for you?"

"What is it, sir?" He said smiling kindly.

"As our head of Christianity, I would like you to make sure that the Sabbath will be of one that satisfies all followers of Jesus here. Do you agree?" He said as David smiled and nodded his head as Beth's heart was touched. "You can also concentrate on cultural affairs. My bosses were meant to have contacted me about the next steps. Unfortunately, many of my superiors perished too because more people were within flood range than had been forecast for this region. I think I even recognized one of them when we were swimming to safety, but I had Beth to think about instead." He said proudly as the object of his words of chivalry, Beth, felt a warm glow running through her heart since someone at least cared about her. "Finally, I wish us to end on a high note and to thank the women for carrying our babies!" He said as Jennifer couldn't take her eyes off him.

Later that evening Jennifer and David were together. "Beth is so beautiful." Jennifer said.

"I am a one woman, man." David had been waiting for this. So, frightened of his secret he knew what to say. In turn his love was too scared to ask more questions. Lost for words she merely started to French kiss him even though she was suffering from nausea. With thoughts of Roger at the back of her passionate mind, feeling guilty, she had to keep David sweet. She wanted to praise Roger too, but it was David who was being put to the test of fidelity rather than that of herself, she believed. Even so, if she needed to berate David, she had to be whiter than white herself.

That night Jennifer couldn't sleep. At least David didn't know about Roger, but then a dark thought came across her paranoid self. David might be a one-woman man, but given Roger was cheating on Beth and Sophie, what if while she herself was away on holiday David was with Beth? Given she had cheated on him when she went on holiday to the Canaries just before she fell pregnant to David, why shouldn't he have been cheated on her too while she was away? In one sense she thought she had a woman's intuition that David had slept with Beth, but she needed him, and she had slept behind his back with Roger, which in wild days was in her mind a normal thing to do. On top of that it was better not to find out the truth. In one sense the idea of him sleeping behind her back excited her. In another sense, it maddened her.

The next day David found Beth breastfeeding outside in the sunshine and the rhododendrons almost coming into bloom. "I am sorry for asking you about Jennifer and Roger.

"I understand."

"The problem is, Beth, I love you." He said nervously as a bolt of energy went through her body only this time instead of shedding tears from his words, she was ready to make love to him.

"But you are a good Christian boy, and your lady is pregnant." She said almost gasping for her breath. Her heartbeat started to run out of control as for a brief moment she wished that Jennifer had drowned. A moment or two later, she was feeling sick with guilt, and to make matters worse, the way he was looking at her with his smile seemed as though he understood her pain and her wild emotions. If only he would force a kiss on her. They had already made love so many times together, why was he being so meek, as his presence was making her go so weak?

"If she is cheating on me, I will have good reason to leave her for you." He said to her somewhat lost, as his cold words dampened her passion for him both suddenly and with profusion.

"David, as I have told you many times before, I need a real man who loves me and not someone who is confused and doesn't know what he wants." She then walked off with her baby and wanted to kill herself there and then. She wanted him more than ever. She wanted him to want her for reasons of love and not out of malice and to be bold and brave too. Deep down, she wasn't sure if she really wanted him, since she felt that he really wasn't strong enough for her.

Later that morning David held a Christian service. Sadly, for him nobody came. Neither his apparently beloved Jennifer nor his moralist spiritual other half, Beth, attended. Beth merely saw a hypocrite in both herself and in him. At least one thing the survivors had in common was that they didn't miss the demise of modern technology in any way and were concentrating more on the real world instead.

Roger believed that since more than ninety percent of the population had been wiped out and probably much closer to a hundred percent and was something that even he in his wildest dreams never expected; that peace would return and that the agenda to destroy families further via the media, the law and social services would cease. Of course, without modern technology there was no more politically correct brainwashing with feminist as well as Gay Muslim icons appearing on British TV and explaining why they are so happy to have broken free from their families. If there were still too many people, then, the elite would have to resort to other forms of warfare against families instead.

As for events closer to home, David and Jennifer would often go to and fro between Fell End and David's flat. She was relieved that all of her heirlooms and things of value had already gone with her from her parents' home in Windermere, to Ambleside. David wanted to visit his childhood home in Kendal but given his love had made no mention intention of visiting hers which was much closer, he decided against it.

Chapter 2

THE DOG FEAST

Roger had plenty of other things to do apart from dealing with women and babies. The Howe was his workplace. Given he swam daily, it made sense that the area around the tarn was his domain and covered if he included his new home a good square mile. Luckily for him, the tenant farmers John and Maria had survived and were acting caretakers for all the dwellings around the water's edge. He hadn't found any maidens yet, but he needed people to help him watch and to maintain the houses close to The Howe. In turn John and Maria were very busy. What Roger didn't know was although they did their job properly, they avoided him like the plague. Maria, like John, despised him.

Now that he seemed to be keeping on top of things, he went out in order to visit Ambleside. He knew that the place would cheer him up since the disappointment of David's return. Death was never far away from his thoughts. In turn and in need of settling some scores, he walked down into Skelwith Bridge. Thanks to the two most important people in his life, he had a pretty good idea as to where Anthony lived. With ease he found the location. The front door of the house was still left unlocked.

He went inside with great anticipation. Sure enough, the bodies of the Fleming family were there. Maybe there was some bastard Wordsworth blood too. The name heralded from Flanders, maybe in order to keep things quiet Anthony had been given the position in being of the sage responsible about the life of William. After thinking that he might be distantly related to Anthony, he then looked at the four dead bodies lying on the floor complete with terrified looking faces. It was then that he burst into tears and could take no more as he thought about his unholy urges of which he had no control over. He felt that their honor was going to be taken away and put the blame on the fact that his baby making factory was looking like some pipe dream. If only he were happy, then he would then leave everyone in peace.

As much as he wanted to have some necrophilia, he was somewhat put off by the blue bottles devouring the bodies. Equally, as much as he wanted to seek revenge on the dead man's honor, he was desperate. As much as he wanted to smash the bodies up when they would be of no more use for him his mind went onto David. If Anthony weren't David's boss, he would have had no qualms for his fetish. The conundrum was a simple one: he worshipped and admired David but he had no respect for plebeian Anthony. The inconvenient truth was that; Anthony was David's boss and in turn, he was closer to that of a Wordsworthian gent than Roger wanted to admit to himself.

With his vivid imagination, he walked over to the twins and masturbated with images of them screaming as their parents were drowning as he wondered what it would be like if he could have had sex with them. They were dead anyway; it wouldn't have done them any harm. He then walked over to the bodies of the parents. It was time for his second orgasm, first though he needed a rest. His mind then went back to the tsunami. Anthony's wife was too young and beautiful for his nemesis. If only he had ran down into the valley and taken Rebecca against her will and saved her. So distraught over the loss of her babies, he could have replaced her peasant offspring with that of whose origins would be of his noble Illuminati blood. As she would have been wailing over the demise of her twins, he, the great impregnator would have been her savior. On top of that, Roger believed that he looked better than her husband. As these thoughts left his mind, he had reached his second orgasm during his visit to the house of death. He then went upstairs and miraculously he found some photographs of the family, including a portrait of Rebecca. Without the frightened look on her face before she drowned, she looked more desirable than she was downstairs in the flesh. He then lamented that he had never met her before this special day and felt as though he was being buried alive.

After getting over the horror that he had been unable to save her, he then continued walking in the valley. He was sure that there were other dead families. He was sure that many of the fathers in some of these homes were younger and more attractive than Anthony. Instead, and feeling too tired to make every dead body rise from the death during his moment of passion with his unwilling corpses, he continued on for Ambleside.

In the eyes of an ordinary observer, he looked as though he was some official. He was dressed the part and had been taking notes with his pen and paper. Just like many a common being, what was taking place in his mind was somewhat different to what another viewer might have perceived in being the truth.

Some of the dead bodies were of really fine specimens. They could have been placed in museums as examples of what men and women looked like before mass vaccinations, oestrogens in the water, and modern life had turned so many into androgynous looking beings. He then burst out into tears with his infinitely excruciatingly painful grief.

His mind went onto cyborgs. A shiver went through his spine. Without the national grid human experiments would cease. It was then for the first time in his life, he wondered if he would have been quite happy replacing his brain with artificial intelligence if it would help him live forever. Luckily for him, his mind went back to his transgender tendencies. That was until he burst out crying. Without modern technology, what was the point in having his balls cut off when no womb could be inserted inside of him? It was then that he found it appropriate to gloat over the deaths of the smug Luddites he had seen who were wearing their country clothes and were littering the Vale of Ambleside with their frightened faces when all of the sudden their untimely deaths came. At least, with his gloating over the fate of the plebs, he had at least found a reason to be cheerful.

He came back satisfied after what had been for him an exciting walk. He had seen flies on bodies, rotting flesh and he wanted to share the delights with both Beth and Sophie. Ambleside wasn't far away, but it being a town and low down in the valley meant there was plenty of death around to show his subordinates and to remind them how lucky they were. Only Roger could face seeing the corpses which excited him between his legs and in turn he orgasmed with glee. He then thought of a plan to entice the others at Fell End to share with him his own personal delights, at their very own emotional expense. As for the family in Skelwith Bridge, he had to keep mum on this.

In the dining room as they were eating their evening meal, he looked at everyone. "I don't know what to do or say. There is a stench of rotting flesh down in the dale, and this is turning into a health hazard. We can't move literally hundreds and hundreds of bodies. Equally, disease will spread if we do nothing. Beth you will probably stay at home." He said to her in front of the others.

"No, Roger we are all in this together."

"Thank you, Beth. We are all working very well as a team together." He said as the others smiled wryly at him. "If anyone else decides to drop out I understand, but if Beth who has just given birth is brave enough to move forward in life for the benefit of humanity, then I am sure that; the rest of us can too." He said as David's stomach was turning. He knew what Roger was up to, and calmed down inside when he realized that his, Roger's, own heart was for Jennifer and not Beth. If Roger wanted Jennifer, why not? In turn he would end up with Beth, his one and only true love. All he asked was for Jennifer to commit the act of adultery before him, so that he would then have an excuse for running into the arms of his Juliet.

Sensing that the others had had enough he changed the topic. "One thing we need to think about is that everything has its place. As such we will keep the cups in the same places as they were before for the previous owners. Everything has its place. There is no point in moving things around, just to create more confusion." He said and with that, David smiled, he too didn't want the women to be fussing around about as to where the items of crockery should be placed.

"I think we have other things to worry about. What about all the people who died, and we didn't even say goodbye to them?" Sophie said.

"I almost went out to visit the Skelwith Bridge Inn the evening before the floods. Had I known I would most certainly have bid my farewells to everyone." He said as he alluded with his smile that he was in fact delighted over their demise.

"What use would that have been? Would you have told everyone to camp out high above, or taken them into our home?" Beth asked.

"I am sure he would have locked some maidens up for their own safety." Sophie said trying to embarrass the father of her child.

"Now girls, we are all upset, the thing is he didn't know what was going to happen. It is so easy with hindsight to mark someone who did nothing in being evil. Somehow, we all have to unite, get along together and survive somehow." David said. With that Jennifer as she reassuringly placed her hands-on David's lap and smiled at Roger.

"One thing we haven't yet discussed is that I have some medical background, and that if anyone falls ill, I am here on hand." Jennifer said.

"I would also like to point out is that; women are generally excited at getting rid of the rubbish and throwing things out, but I think that it is a man's job when it comes to clear the area around The Howe of any remaining corpses." Said Roger as David looked as though he wanted to throw up.

That evening all was eerily quiet at Fell End. Beth was still sandwiched between the two couples in her bedroom, but the silence didn't make her feel any better. Like the others, apart from Roger, she was feeling sick thinking about the people who had perished, whom she was going to meet the very next day. Jennifer was by then getting over the men she had been flirting with on Tinder who had since died in the floods and hoped that things would work out well for her, and that she wouldn't find David too suffocating, who seemed to be fretting too much over the dead bodies for her liking.

In the other room next to hers there were different priorities. "I don't know if I want to visit Ambleside tomorrow." Sophie said.

"If you stay behind, you can practise breastfeeding."

"On second thoughts I had better go. I don't want you impregnating my sister again so soon after she has given birth."

"In that case you had better keep a close watch on us in our love making den!" He said lasciviously.

"If that is what it takes to prevent another disaster I will."

"The idea of you being into voyeurism turns me on so much that I would love a repeat performance of last summer, especially if it entails a threesome." He said as she was being increasingly disgusted by him but was being turned on by him whom she saw as some stud.

After battling for a few moments in her thoughts with her body wanting to make love before she would be recovering from labor and her contempt of him, she stared into his eyes. "I never thought that men as disgusting as you existed."

"Men were tamed dear. They have become too weak to confess their desires to sow their oats and to enjoy making babies thanks to the depopulation agenda. Those dark days are over. Now, we can flood these valleys with our genes, happily!"

"Roger, you are so disgusting, getting excitement about making babies at the same time as you are enjoying a genocide."

"Call me two faced, I don't care. At least I am more honest than most other living mortals."

"Or former mortals." She replied.

"Exactly my dear," He said grinning at her. As much as she hated him, he was right, deep down she was happy about there being a less overpopulated planet but had the decency not to relish in the necessary death and destruction like he did. On top of that she was disgusted with herself. He had turned her on to the point of no return. She felt as if she was walking on Striding Edge looking down on the corpses in the valley and the only way to stay upright and not perish, was to walk in the heavens and to make love to The Beast.

Knowing that she would be giving birth any day from then she enjoyed making love to him, but as he was getting close to his climax she was scared. What if she gave birth the next day and she fell back immediately in the family way just as in some of the stories she had read? That was clearly the last thing she wanted. Instead, as she was close to coming herself, all she could think about was her own special and precious blissful orgasm. After they had both been satiated by the other, she looked at him. "You will never be able to treat me properly like Jan did, will you?" He looked at her as though he was a little lost boy, and didn't know how to respond to her, while deep inside he was gloating over the fact that her first love was dead.

As for Roger, Sophie's doubts about him, made him feel unloved. It was then that he decided that the walk into Ambleside hadn't cheered him. As much as he was delighted that so many people had had their lungs filled up with water, he was sad about a particular plan. In short, how was he going to have a baby making factory with ten maidens at The Howe, when the only talent left in the valley appeared to be somewhat lifeless? As exciting as necrophilia was, bones alone without artificial intelligence wouldn't be able to fall pregnant. It was then that a veil of sadness went over him. Sex robots had only just before the tsunamis started to take over sybians and with a bit of luck; he believed that it was a matter of just years before these robots would have reproduced with a human partner. The Ullswater valley wasn't far away, but he had no intention in straying too far away from his home territory and was scared of other surviving

Illuminati moving in on his lawn in an area that was sought after because, lying high up, it had survived most of the adverse effects of the tsunami.

While waiting for Sophie as she was preparing herself for bed, he thought about what he wanted to say to David. He wanted to tell him that he dressed like a plebeian, and that a man of God should dress in clothes that would make him the man that he believed himself to be but wasn't. Ironically, Roger knew that his rival was a better person than himself and wanted to berate him about the inadequacies that he himself had. Still, as long as Jennifer was standing by her man, his thoughts about humiliating David were for then in his dreams only.

That evening Jennifer managed to get David to make love to her. Afterwards, all she could think was that with virile Roger, making love would have been so much easier and more fulfilling too.

Another day arrived, the days were long and making the most of natural light had a calming effect on the residents. Roger made breakfast for the five of them. There were still plenty of supplies of long-life milk left. He wondered if he could milk Beth, once supplies had run out. In short, she could be his cow in more ways than one he thought as he smiled to himself. It being a Monday Roger gave his first official meeting in the garden. "Five days have passed since those dreadful events. We are still here and enjoying the sunshine and have so much to look forward to. We will have a bumper harvest, to fill our bellies up for the winter with. In the meantime, we are all enjoying the summertime and becoming parents." Being more sensitive than usual Beth was unhappy that he seemed to have forgotten that she was already a mother and was in turn filed with fear as she wondered if he meant becoming parents again as in her case since, she knew exactly what he wanted to do with her. "Some of you might have noticed that the sky seems brighter. This is pretty obvious as to why. Not far from here is the M6 and closer to home plenty of A roads. Now that man made pollutants are now history, we will be able to enjoy this beautiful corner of England in a way that will make Words-worth proud. I am sure that the great man is looking down on us from the heavens above. Life is too short for sorrow, be positive!" He then took a deep breath. "Now; for more serious matters since we also meet here for our trip down into Ambleside."

It was then that the atmosphere became somewhat heavier. It was also the moment when he felt more comfortable. His pious like rhetoric would hopefully have anaesthetised any negative thoughts that might come their way about him when he would be enjoying himself at the others' expense, down in the dale later.

The sombre group consisting of the adults from Fell End set off together. The walk was more peaceful than ever without the tourists and it was lovely to think that they could do whatever they wanted without the prying eyes of others as far as Jennifer and Roger were concerned. Even so, the destruction was at the back of the thoughts of the others as they were still grieving over their loved ones and for humanity at large.

As they met their first corpse shivers ran through their spines, since they were well above the tidal mark they wondered if on this side of the fell the waters had risen even higher. Jennifer walked up towards the deceased person. He had unkempt hair and was wearing rags. "Don't go near him, he might be contaminated." Pleaded David who feared a virus might kill off all of the remaining survivors. She then walked back to the others.

"He wasn't caught up in the tsunami, it looks to me like a suicide. Judging by his appearance I think he was a drug addict, who couldn't get hold of his next fix." She said.

"Why was he here? I mean he must have been some homeless person on the streets of Ambleside, how did he survive when the town was flooded?" Asked David, a question Beth would have asked too.

"For Christ's sake David, how the fuck would I know, how would anyone else know, let's just get on with our own lives." Jennifer said as Beth secretly agreed with her.

As they all dropped down into Rothay Park, the smell was appalling. More to the point, it was simply a stench of rotting flesh. They went without Beth's baby. Since there were no laws, they didn't see a need in giving their babies a twenty-four hours watch. Beth's lonely mind was elsewhere, the penny dropped. This was the place where Beth said hello to David before she met Roger one day later. Now though, was simply not the time to dwell and to mention this with Jennifer being around. Even so, she wanted to cry when she thought about how shy he had been. On top of that, he didn't seem so coy with Jennifer, together they looked so happy; maybe he never really loved her after all. So, saddened with everything, she felt pain in her organs. She had to be strong. She had to block out all of her vulnerable feelings of love. In turn she enjoyed the beauty all around her and the sunshine on her face and was thankful that she was still alive.

Roger looked like a leader as he was thinking about what he wanted to say to the others. As for the others they looked so sombre and grim faced. Beth at least had her mind on other happier things. "What a waste! There's enough food to feed our growing families for generations!" Roger said, who brought dreamy Beth back into the miserable present. "Why don't we bring Dexter and Timmy along with us next time?" Roger said as he was enjoying himself at the others' expense. Jennifer found his comments somewhat hilarious but as she looked around, she sensed that David was trying not to listen, while the other girls looked bitterly angry. Jennifer couldn't understand why, he was only joking after all.

As they continued walking with the sights and smells of death everywhere the morbid silence was broken. "Oh my God! I can't bear to look at this!" Beth said as she was looking at a devouring taking place.

"Darling, I told you not to come with us." Said Roger the master of deception as one or two faces smirked furtively in his direction.

"It is literally Dog eat Dog!" Said Jennifer, whose words chimed in with his perverted mind. In turn Beth hated her and found her as sick as The Beast and couldn't believe that she was a fully trained nurse.

"Those dogs being eaten obviously perished along with their owners. They must have gone really crazy. I mean they knew that they had to escape onto higher ground." David said thoughtfully as he was thinking about his own lucky escape from the jaws of death.

"Maybe they bit the dog owners out of frustration." Said Roger reasonably as like the others he saw bite marks on the corpse's legs. Roger then walked off smiling nastily and found a well-dressed dead man lying next to a dead dog on a lead. The man had been bitten. The faithful friend had a terrified look on its face. As far as he was concerned money wasn't everything. As wealthy as the corpse was, he wasn't a part of the establishment, hence why he wasn't invited to the Travellers Rest. He then thought about the Illuminati members who perished high up on the way to Dunmail and was enjoying the moment in more ways than he could ever imagine. Like the others, he was well aware of the crows lurking around like vultures. There certainly seemed to be more of these hungry birds than ever before. As for Beth, although she loved animals, there was something about these birds that she found creepy.

He then walked back to the others who were in a trance and watching a vulgar depravity of the Dog-eat-Dog feast. "The dogs don't seem to like human flesh. I think David is right. I wonder how these dogs survived." He said relishing in the conversation. By then, even Jennifer was looking very sad. Sophie simply tried to block out the others. Both Roger and Jennifer disgusted her, or Beth and David made her feel suicidal. As such, too scared to go back home on her own she simply hung around waiting for the others.

Beth threw up. She simply couldn't cope with his vile rhetoric any longer, equally how could she reproach him after he advised her to stay at home? Thinking about life without labor saving devices, he wanted to tell her that she had to be more careful at home. Vomit wasn't very pleasant after all. Hygienic standards were now more difficult to maintain. Still, at least he had the decency not to say a word to Beth, who like her sister was responsible for the cleaning of the house. Jennifer though, had some empathy for the sisters and did more than her fair share and David helped out too. On top of that he sensed that the poor girl who had just given birth was at breaking point with everything. In turn he wondered if he should show a more caring side of his nature towards her.

Before he could bring out a more sensitive side to his nature; there was one more thing he had to show the others. "I am sorry about the disturbing events down here in the valley. The thing is; when I came here on my own something disturbed me, and I need you to give me a second opinion." He said as the others looked as though they were trembling with fear. What could be so bad that it disturbed him of all people? Together and with fear, dread and anticipation they followed him.

Roger wasn't at all disturbed of the sight of the man, who was nailed to a cross. The Illuminati had merely found an unlucky man and were using him for their propaganda purposes. The victim was also at a prominent location, where more survivors would quickly read the message. In the dead man's hands was a sheet of paper protected inside a plastic cover.

It is with great regret that this man is standing here on show in such a humiliating way. The sad fact is capital punishment in the national interest had to be reinforced on this criminal. His crime was simple; he simply took over a house without asking for any permission from the authorities. For your SAFETY, precautionary measures have to take place.

As disturbing as this sight of the dead man is, we have to maintain a semblance of law and order in these uncertain times. We hope that we will not have to carry out any more of these punishments and that you understand that the stealing of a house which is owned by the state is an act of treason.

Roger was hiding a secret from the others, and now was not the time to reveal his treachery against them. Instead as the great pretender he was, he had to act. He slumped himself to the floor as the others were still in shock. He then burst out crying. "I can't take any more of this madness!" He said. In turn it was Beth, the softest, gentlest and kindest being who had the strength, power and persuasion to get him back onto his feet.

Roger was delighted; everything was going to plan.

During the walk back the atmosphere was once again subdued. Roger was deep in thought. He decided in turn not to provoke the others any further. Instead, he concentrated on admiring the natural beauty of the area as he was thinking about ruling the whole place in more ways than one. As for the others, while they left sombre to say the least, on the way back they had more than a look of despair. As for Beth she was worried about William, how could she have left him alone for one hour?

Back at Fell End, Beth was relieved to be back with her son. Later on, Roger decided in order to celebrate that they would eat plenty of meat which he had carefully salt-cured from a cow which had drowned close to The Howe and was waiting for the right moment for the special feast. He sensed that the copious amount of flesh after the visit down in the dale would make their stomachs somewhat queasy.

A meeting was held by Roger after the dinner of the special beef the next day. "I was thinking that instead of allowing all the flesh to turn rotten, why don't we carry the corpses to the top of Scafell so that they will stay fresh longer?" He said trying to make the others' stomachs turn.

"It is too far." Sophie said.

"What about to the cave?" Roger asked.

"Even that is too far." David said.

"Dead people don't weigh as much as living ones." Said Jennifer as Roger winked at her and they were both being turned on by each other.

Beth then collapsed onto the floor; she couldn't take any more of his wicked and disgusting words. "Beth dear: we have to stay strong." Said Roger who was then more concerned about her feelings.

"What for? I wish that I had died instead." She said.

"No, Beth, I wish that more people had survived." David said.

"Here here! Jennifer said who suddenly had some respect for David and was worried that he was secretly in love with Beth while equally she had some sympathy for the young damsel in distress. Roger was looking on blankly, and she didn't to lose his favour either. As for Roger he was then feeling depressed while Sophie simply felt that she was having some bad dream and found everything so surreal.

That night Roger was delighted when while making love with Sophie, he heard the moans and cries from the others while they were thinking about the horror in their dreams of the rotten flesh all around them down in the beautiful and lush vale of the former pretty market town from his morbid tour the day before. For him making love and knowing that the others could hear him enjoying himself while they were scared about death, in their sleep, was bliss.

Beth's life had changed more then she thought it would without electricity. The home had batteries, but it had been decided that lights would only be used during the autumn and winter as a means of conserving energy when it would be most needed. As such she found herself making more use of natural light and going to her bed earlier. On top of that, she had more time for herself, and more time to think and that was something that scared her. The last thing she wanted to have on her mind was the corpses which would drown her own desire to continue with living.

The dwellers of Fell End were all stood underneath the beech tree again. "Once again the start of the week has arrived." Roger said in front of his housemates. "I do not want to make this meeting too formal. I do however wish to say that the air seems cleaner than ever. I am certain that the bees will return and that in many ways the mental health of all of us will improve as mother earth is healing herself. Rhubarb is now being harvested, things are going to plan and to be honest there is nothing more to add, and we should move on and not dwell about things too much." The final part of his speech had been deliberate since he wanted the others to be reminded about their recent trip into the valley.

While Sophie believed in the power of nature and her healing powers, she believed that Roger was too damaged to benefit from nature's return to a more virginal environment. "I do have something very important to discuss and that is water. This is the key to our survival. While the taps will be turned back on again once the system is ready, we must think about our back up supplies. We have plenty of bottled water to help us get though the aftermath of the tsunami, but my main concern is the local stream. We are the only local inhabitants and people are allowed to walk wearing boots and contaminate our supplies if they wish. As such David and I will build a dry-stone wall as some kind of tunnel leading from the front gate of our house to the stream. This will split the bridleway into two. It is merely a safety precaution. I know almost nobody apart from us uses this path, but it is better to be safe than sorry. We also have two other main gates; one is very convenient for walking to Langdale, the other for Ambleside." For the others, he seemed to be as leader acting responsibly. For Sophie, he was still flawed beyond help.

Day by day, all she could do was to analyze and to think about the year that had passed. The first season, the spring, she was still an innocent schoolgirl. In the summer, too much excitement had destroyed her integrity. In the autumn love was snatched away from her in the jaws of victory. As for the dark winter just gone what a nightmare, what a hell. Roger along with his deception and confusion was a living snake for her. Spring had returned again and If only she hadn't volunteered to bring back her sister home and could have died innocently along with her parents instead. David was in pensive mood too, but unlike his soulmate, Beth rather than Jennifer, he was trying to look on the bright side of things and was thrilled about the prospect in him becoming a father.

Two weeks had passed since the tidal wave. A new dawn had broken, and Beth was delighted to have slept the whole night through without being woken up to the sounds of crying. Instead, she discreetly opened the curtain window that would send a beam onto her bed and if lucky, she could read a chapter from the book she was reading. Then it was time for breastfeeding and with the weather being so warm and sunny, she decided to have breakfast alone, and before the others would walk into the kitchen as couples or as reminders that she was alone and used. It was still early when she had finished tidying up from her mess and getting herself and William ready. She then sat below the beech tree and was surprised by how much she needed the leaves to protect her not only from the mid spring burning rays but also that of the air which wasn't so fresh as she had expected. With a bit of luck, she would be able to visit the tarn while leaving her baby with Sophie.

A few hours later, Beth was nursing her baby outside and instead of comforting Sophie who was in labor indoors with Jennifer and David.

Roger walked up to her breezily as she felt shivers running through her spine as he was walking towards her. "I will be making love to you before Sophie. Aren't you the lucky one my belle!" He said to her as she could hear her sister moaning in agony and in turn, she shook her head. "I can't wait for you to wear the jewellery again." He said as he was looking aroused to her great horror as memories of morning sickness came back to her. All she could do was take a deep breath and he would leave her alone with her breastfeeding. As such she placed her child on her nipples and in turn Roger was drooling at her openly and in turn, she thought about how proud she was of the fact that she had very quickly got herself back into shape and wanted to show him whom the boss was.

"I would much prefer it if you left us both alone." Instead, she had spoken meekly as she felt increasingly overpowered by his presence.

"I came here to tell you that your fleshy lips and your loving mouth is mesmerising me like never before." He said to her. As much as she was enjoying his beautiful words, she was terrified of them too.

"I am not planning on falling pregnant again so soon."

"Your hourglass figure has returned!" He said grinning at her as he imagined her with a bigger belly than last time.

"No, Roger, I am nothing more than just a hole for you!" She said in a panic as she was feeling repulsed by him.

"If that is the case, why do I enjoy running my fingers all over your body and kissing you all over? Why do I lie on top of you touching every inch of the front of our bodies? In recent months as I had to be gentler with you, I was unable to lie all over you while making love, but I did my best to stimulate as much as you as possible and you know this too." He said as his words were hypnotising her as much as she wanted him to be out of her life.

"I just told you that, I am not falling pregnant again soon." She said as her fears were turning him further on.

He then thought and worried in case she would flee his home he softened further somewhat. "Beth, I wouldn't advise you to fall pregnant again before July, no matter how alluring your body is to me. Until then,

I plan to be very careful with you. We can make love, but as for the jewellery this might have to wait a bit." He said as Beth was both relieved and scared.

After he reluctantly left her in peace, all she could think about was how she needed the touch of a man all over her body. There was more to life than being a mother earth figure. There was very little in the way of entertainment other than sex, equally she didn't wish to have another child with him. Reading books were safer, but they all too often ignited her flames of passion.

Sophie gave birth to a girl in the afternoon, on that very same day she went into labor on the morning of the twenty-fourth of April. She chose the name Jane, in memory of Jan. The name had been chosen in order to provoke Roger. Instead, it had a pleasant effect on him. He was delighted that the name Jane, would remind her of the thirty-eight deaths at surprise view. On the day Beth gave birth, he slept with her sister, at the time she felt so alone. Now that Sophie had given birth, there was no chance for making love to her for some time. As such, Beth was delighted when this evening he chose to spend the night with her. Since giving birth, with her painful breasts, her sleepless nights, and lonely nights with the unwelcome sounds from the next room due to David and Jennifer, her life was grey.

With him back with her for the first time in two weeks, all she wanted was for her baby to sleep so that Roger would feel relaxed with her. As soon as William started to cry, he held him in his arms. Beth, who was literally exhausted, fell asleep. After calming down, he then placed William onto her breasts, and he started to drink and very soon after she woke up. He then placed William into his cot. As he started to kiss her all over, her life seemed as though it was iridescent once more. And as he went inside of her and making sure that as much of their bodies were touching each other as possible, she felt as though those rainbow colors in her mind, were beaming at her bolder than ever.

By then everyone seemed to be adjusting very well without electricity. Of course, it being spring and the days getting longer, it couldn't have been a better time to adjust to being plunged back into the dark ages. On top of that they would very soon have plenty of salad in season. Rhubarb was around, next would come the lettuces and then the berries and later on the cabbages. Just like last year, only this time they were being cultivated at home as opposed to being brought back from the shops. Hopefully by the autumn they would all be strong enough to survive the long nights with the battery-operated LED torches and be fit enough for the cold Lake District winter.

The land on which they lived had two houses. The small one was the size of the average detached family home; the large one was the size of a manor. By rights, the latter was Jenny's and David's. Instead, and wanting their own privacy, they decided to choose the smaller one, so that the house could be exclusively for themselves. This was a sign of commitment, a sign that that their world was each other. David of course, unlike his partner, didn't wish to listen to Roger's noisy orgasms any longer. In the meantime, a delighted Roger kept walking to and fro The Howe and Fell End, the site of his new and large home and was carting things of value. Items included: the jewellery which he needed for the girls so that they could excite him as well the paintings, photographs and books which had a similar effect on him too. He also had some gold nuggets which he could use for barter, but decided to hold onto them, and if he were to fall onto less fortuitous times, he could flee Fell End and return to The Howe in safety. They might even save his life. If someone wanted to murder him, he would simply offer them his riches. Hopefully and unlike Colonel Gadhafi, he wouldn't be having his eyes gorged out.

One month since had passed since the tsunami and it was an important landmark for the survivors. The farms in the valleys were out of order due to the pollutants on the surface water, and any produce was considered unfit for consumption. Luckily, the survivors like most people had plenty of fat reserves. On top of that, homes were generally fully stocked up with tins as well as plenty of toilet paper for their waste. Many people thanks to the consumer economy had become hoarders. Closer to home, and him being a part of the elite, every second day, milk was delivered on his doorstep from Patterdale, less than twelve miles away. The Ullswater Valley, being much higher than the tidal limit, very quickly resumed her dairy duties. A week earlier just when the others were missing fresh milk, for the first time in years, Fell End became a part of the milk round again. Milk was planned to be produced again locally, but until the middle of summer at the earliest, survivors would have to wait, unlike the dwellers of Fell End, most people were not VIPs. Roger wanted to visit one of the dairy farms, where hopefully he could rekindle the acts of his grandfather, Sebastian, and rape a milk maid or two. Sadly, David was around, and although an atheist, somehow David put the fear of God into this Satanist. He believed that not only would David disapprove, but that another misfortune might move in on his patch like the weeds in his garden which seemed to be growing faster than he and David were able to deal with.

It was also the day when one month had passed since Beth gave birth, and she was already making love to Roger on a very regular basis, while he was still waiting for Sophie to open up her legs to him. One thing she didn't enjoy when they were in bed together, was that as each night was getting shorter, the images of the paintings of her were shining more and more in her eyes just when she didn't wish to see them. Although not content, the dwellers seemed to be getting on with their lives stoically. So, obsessed with a second round of impregnation, Roger had been inspecting the women for tentative signs of menstruation. Even so, he wasn't so worried; he knew that mothers could fall pregnant before their periods returned. Of course, bringing life into the world was a hobby of his. He also relished in the death which was a part of his depraved world and now it was time for regeneration. As much as he enjoyed the stench of death in the valley, he was sad that with so few survivors he would never again be able to experience such a massive genocide again. At least it would forever be in his memories and make his lovemaking all the more enticing, especially since his desires were of an ever-changing mood. If he could, he would try out many of his perversions, but felt that then wasn't the time to push the others too much and that he was for the moment at least, fairly satisfied with his life anyway. As he had done with Beth, his perversions would be revealed to the others by stealth. All he had to do was to analyze how he had succeeded with men and women previously. Exciting times lay ahead for him. Jennifer was an ally of his. Sophie had some previous desires of perversion when she wanted to whip him to death. In a democracy, with three against two, he could have his wicked way with both Beth and David together.

There was one big black cloud hanging over him. He wanted to impregnate Sophie before Beth but was scared of what she might do to him. A part of him was still shaken from the fact that she had almost murdered him. He found Beth so fragile and wanted to have this soft and gentle submissive being once more at the mercy of him after she had fully recovered from the birth which he believed was then. He would deal with Beth, after he had impregnated her sister, so that she would wait nervously for the inevitable with him. Equally, he was worried about her. He knew from her desperation over the fact that he couldn't commit himself fully to her, that she was maybe open to another unexpected male who might come into her life. Equally he was in fear of her exceptional beauty reigniting his transgender tendencies, when he would once again wish that he had a body like hers. He also sensed quite rightly if he got her in the family way too soon, she might take her own life. On the other hand, he was scared that David might want her instead. If only David could leave Roger alone in peace. That way he could impregnate the girls at his own choosing.

On even more sinister matters, due to the girls and especially Beth's Jewish ancestral roots, Roger often thought about World War Two. Thanks to the girls he wished that he had been born a few decades earlier, lived relatively luxuriously as a corrupt Nazi boss, shot many people dead and used women such as Beth as sex slaves. For him, that would be the ultimate in him having a beautiful gentle soul at his evil mercy. In fact, in his mind, due to the passion and pain, that this would be love of a highest kind.

In the quiet and beautiful setting of the lakes he was still as psychopathic as ever. He planned to build a coffin, dig his own grave and ask Beth to shoot him mercilessly before she would bury him out of his misery if he survived her bullets. Knowing how emotional Beth was, he had to think. Knowing how submissive she was, he just had to plan his words carefully. The excitement and thrill of seeing his Jewish sex kitten play the role of his Nazi boss as he played the role of a gay Jewish man excited him. In part he was ashamed of his homosexuality. He also felt inferior to Beth; but the fact she came from a race that had been victims of a holocaust made him wish to combine what he perceived both of his and her weaknesses. He would use both the race card and sexuality issues as a means in making himself immortal. Equally he would use these two issues as a means in bringing out the compassionate and caring side of Beth, as well as her own fears about her own mortality. This for him was an exciting mix of both good and evil.

Another conundrum for him was how would he be able to get such a heterosexual being as Beth to play the role of a man before his own demise? Yes, he had lots of plans for her. To make her pregnant again and again, while at the same time he believed that Sophie rather than Beth would kill him. In his mind, it was easier to manipulate the younger sibling without suffering the wrath and fury that the older one was capable of meting out onto him again. While on the one hand that soothed him, on the other hand it confused him. He also wondered how someone who had been provoked so nastily by him, never showed him any hatred or malice. What could he do to make her realise that she wasn't so sweet and gentle as she wanted to believe? He then smiled; at least he had taken her purity away from her and was proud of the fact that she ruined her reputation further when she went to bed hopping. One day, he hoped that her sister, Sophie, would follow in her footsteps of promiscuity. Their shame: was his pride and joy.

While Beth was both scared and excited of their lovemaking, Sophie was scared of being alone. As soon as possible, she would make love to him and didn't care if she would fall pregnant to him very quickly. She knew of course from the sounds next door what the other two in the triangle were up to. In some ways she was closer to Roger than her sibling was, since she didn't see things so much in black and white as Beth did. On top of that, her agnostic outlook on life was becoming more atheist and the evil around her made her think of morality as a means of putting people down, since David and Beth, the two romantic lovers, were apart from each other. For her events had been exceptionally cruel to her dreamy sister. She was sure that too much in the way of morality issues; had ruined it for David and Beth.

As for the meetings, they were very brief and becoming superfluous. On top of that, he knew that he had opened the eyes of the others to the benefits of the wipe out. They all had plenty of space for themselves. Despite this, no one wanted to leave Fell End. In one sense they felt that they were experiencing safety in numbers. They were only five plus two babies. The fair-sized detached family house of David and Jennifer's seemed bigger than ever now that modern technology was obsolete. As for the larger house on the site, it was large enough for plenty more babies which Roger living there with two fecund and very young beauties knew only too well.

One thing that excited Roger was the fact that despite of depopulation he seemed to have more control over more people's lives than ever before. Thanks to him, survivors couldn't take over empty buildings. There were too many dwellings left lying empty, but that was not the issue. For Roger it was all about control. He had to be in charge of all those at Fell End. This was why he had advised his bosses before the tsunami to bring in new laws. In turn, the girls were trapped: they couldn't run off with David and find some new abode. The scene of the man nailed to the cross had a devastating effect on the others. They then knew that they well and truly trapped. They simply couldn't leave Roger and find a new place to live without his consent. He was their savior apparently.

While many things hadn't gone to plan, it was his large degree of control over the others that kept him just away from the point of suicide. With his misery in not being able to become a transgender woman or a cyborg, he could still, when feeling unloved, ruin the lives of those around him.

Chapter 3

THE TREES FOR HIS CHILDREN

Often, Roger felt as though his head was spinning around. He had hoped that the tsunami would have cleared his mind and set him on the road into him having a peace of mind. Instead, he felt as though he was on the verge of losing his own control. While he was fully behind the depopulation agenda as a means of cleansing the masses from their insanities due to modern life, he was only too well aware that unstable people existed since the beginning of mankind, and feared he was more like Coleridge than Wordsworth. Even so, he had hope that given he had had more than his own share of strange experiences while living with his mother, that now he would be healed in the serene setting of the Lake District. Without the hordes and the long spell of fair weather the place was simply one of heaven on earth for him. Peace would enter his mind. Hope was his bread.

Firstly, he had other matters to deal with. One of his pastimes, which bordered on morbidity as far as he was concerned, was to analyze the three main women in his life. His main concerns were sex, children and love. On these issues alone, his number one was Beth, his number two

Sophie and his number three Jennifer. He often thought about David too ad this made things more complicated for him. If he were a woman, he, David would have all the benefits of the three princesses put together. In his own mind as a woman David would be like Beth with brains. As a man though, David was a rival and, in his eyes, had already stolen Jennifer off him. If the woman were himself, he was convinced that being pregnant himself his rapid bodily changes would keep any thoughts of boredom at bay. Roger was pretty much certain that he was at least a third generation would be transgender. He knew about his parents, and had heard plenty of rumours about his grandfather, Sebastian, too. One other problem was that in his moments of despair, death was the only way to clean up the mess that these women had meted on him. If only they knew the psychological torture that he was going through with because of them. Perhaps then, they would treat him kindlier.

Jennifer was for him great in bed, she was new. In the end he would tire of her, because she wasn't so beautiful as either of the two other girls. Equally she was less at his mercy, she had a faithful partner and although she had slept with him, he knew sadly all too well her alibi was that she thought David was dead. Luckily for him David was back so that was one less problem to worry about. Sophie was faithful she could bear him more children and if he opened his heart to her, which he couldn't, she would love him until death do us part. On top of that, he knew deep down that she was the best partner for him. She was beautiful, but not to the extent that she would bring out the confusion and insecurity in him which made his gender fluidity much more acute. Beth seemed to have the benefits of Sophie and Jennifer combined. He loved her like no other, surely, she was the one for him. Sadly, with his dormant confusion, this seemed too dangerous for him to contemplate.

One institution he admired then was the Church. If he could wake up as a woman, then he would be an avid church goer. Instead of following the laws of man, he would be supporting his man who was following God and looking after their children. He admired the strict rules regarding, gender, family, and morality, but so long as he was a man, he would remain an atheist. David believed in Jesus, couldn't he with the grace of the Lord perform a miracle? Lourdes was a place of healing, why couldn't he have been a transgender believer before the floods?

All he could do was to wait for time to heal his demented thoughts of his gloating over the demise of the masses and hope that he would end up in being more akin with the great poet. It was then and only then, could he accept his own body.

Now, he was spending less time with her as she was busy with their baby. Although he no longer felt like a woman next to her, there were times that he wished he was peacefully inside her womb and that David would be his father. Or should one say her father? The reason being, Roger quite fancied the idea of being born again as a girl, especially one being brought up with stable parents, such as David and Beth. They would be the parents he never had. If only they could save him from what he believed to be some evil spell from both his mother and of his father as well as his paternal grandfather for that matter. Deep down he believed that he was a good person who had been misread by people.

He really wanted to discuss his issues with Beth, but now that the tidal wave was behind, he worried constantly that he had less power over her and that she would run off. Equally, he didn't want to frighten the living daylights out of her. On top of that, if Erik returned, he would be on his own with Sophie. Sophie met the important criterium and he couldn't understand why, for him she would be nothing more than a piece of furniture. Despairingly, he didn't have the same feelings for her as he had for Beth. At times he wished that she had killed him. At times he felt like having a nervous breakdown so that the women would nurse and take good care of him. If he were some kind of lady boy, he was sure that they would love him more than ever as thoughts about his own mother and his father were on his highly tortured mind.

Other times he wanted to be their uber alpha male. If only he knew what he wanted. On top of that, David wasn't confused sexually. As such he felt somewhat distant from this man who in many ways he admired. It was a strange experience for him to be living in such a close proximity to this man. In Roger's eyes, Christianity discriminated against his homosexuality, while at the same time he would gladly swap places with David immediately to be a man who knew who he was sexually, and to be a pillar of the religion he followed. At times Roger was opposed to the satanic order which although comforted Roger at times made him bitter. It offered no solutions for those who as they got older would rely more on moral values connected with the young looking after the elderly. Despairingly there were times when; he wished that he could wipe out with all of his hatred any form of surviving life and smash the beauty of the Lake District to smithereens as if he was an atomic bomb as big as the great creator himself. It would be a moment of bliss and although he wouldn't be able to enjoy the aftermath it would be for him a much better way of going out with a bang than just merely falling off a cliff and killing only thirty-eight people as Jan had done.

He then went into philosophical mode. Even though the world was no longer overpopulated, his former hatred for mankind had subsided to just a very small degree. On top of that, he wasn't even much of an animal lover and their disappearing habitats hadn't been much of his concern. He had to believe in something, but what! He asked himself. He was relieved that he was surviving without modern technology. He knew that had been addicted to it. He was also well aware; that during the summertime the living was easier, and that winter would be more arduous.

Other times he thought about the fertile plantation of the garden at High Close. Still struggling with his confusion, his depression, and his anxiety he believed that the arboretum contained the trees for his children to cherish in. As such he went round to the estate which was owned then by a LGBT Feminist. He was marching up and down thinking about his forthcoming duel with her. In the end, with so many complications on his mind he decided not to meet up with this lady. In short, his biggest problem was that he didn't love Sophie and Beth enough to live on his own with them at the High Close estate. If he did, he would simply have got rid of the owner of the former youth hostel and National Trust property somehow and very easily. In turn, he often started crying on his own and felt as though he couldn't quite pull himself together.

Feeling as though his head was going to explode, he decided to take a break from working in the orchard at The Howe and went for a swim in the tarn. As he arrived the sun had stopped shining due to the heavy thunder clouds that had been stewing. Feeling nervous since he hadn't embarked on his daily swim due to so much necessary work on the land he didn't care if his swim would be the last thing that he would do. At least fearing for his life as the Langdale Pikes were being lit up made him stop worrying about his gender confusion as he simply wished that he could go back in time and to have made an honest woman out of either Sophie or Beth. As the lightning was moving closer and around Elterwater, more than ever; he regretted what he had done to the girls, especially to Beth. With her no longer being a maiden, a part of him no longer loved Beth. No matter how much she had got back into her wonderful lithe shape: her body would never be quite so nubile for him as it was the first time, he saw her naked. By this time, he decided to get out of the water, but the waves were starting to slow him down. Too afraid of getting drenched in by the then downpour, he decided to continue in the lukewarm waters, as the sounds of thunder were increasingly deafening, and the sky was blinding.

Later after he had warmed himself up, came inside his pants over the idea of him dying in the tarn, and, feeling smug, he went back to The Howe. Feeling safe and secure, as he was descending down to his abode, he felt once again invincible and that the word perversion was part of a religious concept against people like himself who did no harm to others and simply wanted to have fun. By the time he arrived home, the sun was shining, and the girls were hanging out the washing outside.

In many ways the communal living at Fell End had its advantages. Beth benefited the most from this. Her baby could be looked after by any of the five adults who were resident. She had recently taken up swimming again just three weeks after the birth when the waters were warming up nicely in the warm sunshine and was now swimming daily and managing at least a full round swimming of the tarn daily. On top of that, she was living with an important Illuminati member and four police officers had been installed in Ambleside for Roger. Their job was to simply make sure that none of the shops which were now owned by him; were looted or damaged. In turn as one of his women, she could acquire whatever goods in stock she wanted. One thing she couldn't find was the birth control pill; then again, that was against her religious beliefs anyway. Beth had recently called into Gaynor sports for some running trainers. She brought back five pairs, along with plenty of socks. In turn with her swimming and now running she had very quickly getting back into shape.

Although she wasn't living in the lap of luxury she was used to during her pregnancy, she was certainly living very comfortably indeed. With the shops full of everything she had plenty of clothes for the rest of her life. Of course, she missed perishable foods such as ice cream, but chocolate was still on the shelves and would be in stock several more months at least.

Roger had already been thinking about his future plans for her while secretly admiring her when walking the dogs past the tarn while she was in the water. One day he took a pair of binoculars. He was lying in the grass and watching her getting undressed when he came inside his pants as he was thinking about the day, she gave birth which coincided with the death of the masses. For him, it was a great shame that he couldn't control his confused sexual deviances for her. When he met her less than one year earlier, she was still a child in so many ways. Now she was a real woman, not only was she more beautiful than ever, but a real lady in every sense of the word. He was then about to start tearing out his hair as to why; given he loved her like no other that; he still had zoophile, necrophile, homosexual and paedophile tendencies which could once again send him back on the brink of an emotionally charged suicide?

So, distressed with everything, he started itching his bottom and licking off the faecal matter with his hands. Shivers went down his spine as it tasted better than even, he expected. In turn his body started to sweat and the second time he was collecting the dirty and smelly matter with his hands he started to excrete and pulled his hand away immediately. After calming down he then licked his sweaty left hand and was soothed somewhat by the salty taste. He then noticed that his fingernails were still brown and wanted to lick them clean. After a few pensive moments: he cleansed them with his tongue until they were looking pristine.

Some people bite their fingernails. Some people pick their bogies. While others scratch their bottoms and taste the fruits from their bowels.

Normality was anathema for him. With his deviances he felt unloved, a victim who had been bullied by a pretentious society into following rules that made no sense to him. So long as people were happy, they should be free to do whatever they wanted so long as they had plenty of money according to him. At least he was one of the lucky ones, unlike the deviants of the lower classes, whom he despised. Being a lawyer, he was at the crux of the breakdown of the old order. Being a lawyer, he had the satanic law on his side since money protected those against those who were penniless. He made his money in an unscrupulous manner and he was also a judge. Previously and in his courtroom building, wearing his black robes, his paedophilia, necrophilia, zoophilic and homosexual deviances he fitted in nicely with all too many of his judicial rivals in law.

It was only in his megalomaniac mind that they were a threat to him, in short almost all of the other judicial members feared him and were terrified of him being able to read their minds as much as their profession was based solely on making money. Even so, for these unscrupulous souls, Roger had gone more than a step too far. Equally they were scared that the mad monk of their profession would sink the whole ship rather than be a loser if tried for justice in a truly moralistic court. In short, the laws were meant to be based on Christian ones, and his colleagues knew that this cunning fox was quite capable of being Jesus himself if he could get his own back on those who had crossed him or help shift the blame onto those he could use as his fall guys. With him, anything was possible. All his former colleagues saw him as their evil and unwanted God. He was in turn, their very own satanic master. They were too scared to kill him and equally they believed that as a leader, he kept some kind of order and control for everyone else. In short, lurking in his shadows were snakes even more sinister than himself and like himself, puppets of the real Illuminati. Oh, how he missed those days. Now it seemed to his glee that most members of the judiciary had died too.

Sophie had given birth after Beth and was much less physically active. She would take it or leave it regarding the swimming. When someone wanted to go with her to the tarn, and if she had the time, she would take up the opportunity to do something which although she felt too tired to participate in, thoroughly enjoyed whenever she did it. A couple of times the two sisters went with their babies in slings together and managed to swim while they would be taking it in turns looking after the babies. Sophie never left her baby with the others when she left the house. She was far from happy with her life too, nothing excited her. At least she wasn't suicidal. Knowing how fragile her sister was; she felt that she had to remain strong and help Beth with the nursing and never complain about Beth's daily routine of sport.

The sisters were sat together breastfeeding on the lawn at Fell End underneath the beech tree whose foliage had opened up magnificently and just in time with the fierce rays of the sun which heralded the return of hot and sultry days. As each day went by, Beth was finding the living easier. Being a single mother had never been her intention, which in some ways she was. Still, she was feeling stronger as she was enjoying herself in being pregnant no more and with the recent weather there was no place like her home. "Remember what daddy used to say to us?" Beth said.

"Of course, I do, it certainly resonates with now doesn't it?"

"He was such a man." Said Beth smiling.

"Go on say those words!" Sophie said enthusiastically.

"The strongest men and women will survive. The rest will be childless or bring their children up into a broken society. The strong men and women still love each other. Even if the rest are crazy, they remain a beacon of hope for mankind." Said Beth.

After their words of wisdom, the two siblings started to think about things closer to home. That wasn't such a fortunate setting, since they themselves had been too hedonistic for their own good. Feeling humbled, they started to feel the discomforts in their bodies. "My breasts are so sore." Said Beth.

"Mine too, but this is the usual course of nature." Sophie said, as both wished that they were each sharing their maternal weaknesses with a caring, loving and faithful man who would be protecting them exclusively.

"Are you sure, you really don't mind breastfeeding both babies when I go swimming?" Said Beth suddenly relieved and thinking about her keeping her body in shape which meant that; her zest for life returned.

"No, of course not. I have two breasts." Sophie said with a welcoming smile.

"If you want me to look after your baby I will." Said Beth.

"Thank you so much, Beth. Not just yet, I am too lazy to go swimming."

"Maybe, we can go to the lake at Waterhead with our babies together."

"Yes, as soon as I am ready for this, we will."

It was a sweet conversation between two siblings. Little did they know that Roger was sat behind them and quietly masturbating himself as he was thinking about them both being pregnant to him again. Trying to be more respectable and like his hero, Wordsworth, he did all that he could in blocking out his other deviant thoughts: those connected with children, men, and animals. Accidentally, he groaned louder than he planned and quietly walked away. Beth turned around, she saw no one and concluded that she was paranoid and was worried about her own mental health. As sick as Roger was, with David on site, he wouldn't go to such low levels of depravity. She hoped: She prayed. After several more minutes, she noticed him in the kitchen and his hands were all floury. Instead of thinking about his kindness for making some traditional home cooking, she looked at him behind his back somewhat deprecatingly and wondered why he was leaving all the hard manual labor to David. As nice as it was him cooking, she would have preferred to have done this herself and to be happy in the knowledge that he was with his hard graft, digging for victory for a bumper harvest with David. After visiting the bathroom, she then went back outside but felt a little uneasy as she worried that another nasty surprise might be on its way.

As she arrived back: Sophie smiled at her. "I read about survival. Why is that despite the fact we lost everything, yet we are alive and healthy, in some ways we don't have the positive survival instinct?" Asked Beth poignantly.

"It is a question I have asked myself many times too. Close your eyes." Beth did as she was told "Imagine if when you came over, I was expecting a child with Jan. Together we took you to the campsite and you met David. I gave birth around Christmas and you did in April just gone to David's child. How would you feel?" Beth was mesmerized by her speech and deep in thought. "I have thought about this so many times." Said Sophie.

"It is so soothing; with such positivity we would be happy. We would be getting on with our lives beautifully. If only!" Beth said.

"Yes, if only! This is how it could have been. On the one hand we are lucky, we are still alive. We could have been dead and buried; instead, we are living with someone who is cross between a beast and the Grim Reaper. It is no wonder that; six weeks post holocaust we are no less depressed than the times leading up to it." Sophie said thoughtfully.

"It is all very well what you are saying, but a man who didn't know about the tsunami, would not have saved us."

"I know what you are saying."

"Why don't we get out of here for the day? Wouldn't it be nice to spend some hours away from the dark prince and his energy which is like that of some blackhole?"

The following day, the girls were sat at the banks of the tarn, with their babies. Beth was sleepily thinking about Roger spying on the sisters and masturbating over them both, when she saw Jennifer and David walking hand in hand towards the waters but luckily at the other side of the tarn. A few moments later Sophie noticed her unease and sadness. "Beth you look as though you haven't slept for days, what is the matter with you?" She was worried that the death of the waitress and the baby was still on her mind, something which she herself didn't wish to discuss, since Roger could very easily have chosen the waitress instead of them.

Her words had quickly triggered off another concern of hers and Beth then took a deep breath and began. "Sometimes I don't care if he were to drown me. I try to lose myself in these very waters but there are times when I feel as though the pain, he is giving me is pushing me down towards the tarn's bed. I try with all of my might to deaden my feelings so that I can swim like some machine. I had so many dreams; to have a family with a man who loves me. Oh sister! Don't you see how beautiful it is here, yet at the same time the bad luck I am having denotes to me that I am in the wrong place, yet still alive. Sometimes I am breathless and want to give up, but I am scared of dying. All I can do is breathe and hope that I will die peacefully in my sleep. Sometimes I forget about everything and can have a beautiful dream. I can wake up happily listening to the sounds of the birds singing, but as I think about him, his cruelty, my dream for the day has ended. I then start my miserable day again. This is my life! I simply can't go on like this. All because I want a one woman, man. I mean; someone to care about me and to be the head of the household with his patriarchal love." She said with tears in her eyes.

"My God, Beth! So where does this place me in all of this? How selfish of you! There are just two men and you want me to be alone!" Sophie said as she stood up leaving the babies with Beth and started walking away in disgust.

"All this horror began at Surprise View! Until then my life was one of innocence." Cried Beth as Sophie continued as though she hadn't heard a thing, but her sibling's words struck her like lightning. She too often thought about ending her own life.

Sophie after analysing everything she came back quickly to the tarn and later on after both hers and Beth's swims, they had lunch, breastfed and placed their babies into the water.

Back at Fell End, Beth was shaken by her sister's reaction and simply cried buckets that evening. Her sister was cruel. If only she had someone who would listen to her. As much as a sympathetic ear wouldn't be able to help her, at least it would keep her sane in the knowledge that she herself had done nothing wrong. Poor Beth, she was feeling so sad that she woke up much earlier than normal. The second night was worse. As for the third night, her baby was up all night and she felt that she was being punished for her sadness. At least she had recently taken up with running.

As boring as her life might have been for her former city peers; for Beth, apart from her disturbing love life, it was one of bliss. She also enjoyed looking after her baby and wondered what she would do alone without having something to care for.

A few days later, it being late May, they all appreciated the long days. This time last year the days were the same length. Now though things were different. Without electricity they honored more than ever the power of natural light and opening and closing their curtains was simply like a light switch for them. At least the water supplies were back, as they had been almost immediately, but that was by way of carrying buckets to and fro the local streams. Now the domestic taps were back on. The next full moon was to coincide with almost midsummer's night on the seventeenth of June. In one of his thoughtful moods as he thought about the previous year, he believed that the second round of impregnations would be less exciting, but better than nothing. They had to take place then too, because of his advancing age which he feared to be threatening his fertility and his dream of a mid-winter impregnation several months later. He also believed that; day by day, he was losing his potency.

In great desperation Beth stormed into his room while he was writing a letter to Emma one late morning. This wasn't like her to come in on him like this. "Let's go for a swim." She said as she was holding their child in a sling. He was the father of her child and they were a unit after all. He smiled at her, and without any fuss he put down his writing pad and got ready for her, even though his mind was elsewhere.

They walked together like a normal family would. He walked the dogs too as was normal. It was just before they arrived at the area around Tarn Foot, that she stopped him in his tracks. "Why did you go for my sister first to get me?"

"As she is my Leah, you are my Rachel." He said trying to turn her on with his romantic rhetoric which he hoped along with its pious hues would impress her.

"But you are an atheist, how can you speak to me like this?" She said somewhat annoyed.

"God works in mysterious ways!" She looked at him in shock. There he was, the Satanist, who seemed to be in agreement with her. Was God putting her to the test? Without Roger, would she ever experience a man again? She wanted love. At best, the passion she was getting from him would remain plentiful. At worst, the passion would put her in the family way again with him. It was a strange kind of love she had with him and all she really got was sexual fulfilment of a kind of sorts with him since there were times when she heard ringing in her head his words of confusion such as: If only I were you! When he wished that he was carrying her child. Since his mind was demented, they were unable to enjoy fulfilling speech together.

Even so his answer helped move her away from matters regarding religion to things closest to his heart. With some connection regarding divinity, she hoped that she would be able to trust him. She then thought about how his previous romantic and daily speech towards her had deteriorated since the birth and was nothing more than hedonistic. In turn she had little in the way of hope for him.

She then thought about her father. What would he be thinking about Roger? She then blaming him for her father's death wanted to shine what she saw as the love and light from her daddy with his words unto Roger. "The strongest men and women will survive. The rest will be childless or bring their children up into a broken society. The strong men and women still love each other. Even if the rest are crazy, they remain a beacon of hope for mankind." Beth said. Roger completely taken aback didn't know how to respond. In some ways he viewed her words as a darkly veiled attack on himself. If she could so callously accuse him of being like the others, like the rest of the population and weak, then maybe it was better for him to show her who he really was.

After walking a little further on he looked at her as he was feeling very insecure from her words. "Why am I only attracted to lesbian Jewish women?" He said to her pleading with his hands moving around emotionally as they were stood in front of the woods on an incline. Although he looked crazy, he looked somewhat sweet too. His crazy thoughts about love for her gave him an interesting look on his face. At least the beagles were not afraid of his madness.

"I'm not gay, but I am Jewish." She said to him in great desperation as she too started looking somewhat confused. Somehow, he would love her. She just had to impress him as much as she could.

"I know, I know, I know." He replied. "Helene Berger was a lesbian Jewish colleague of mine, but I shot her in self-defence. Jodie is a lesbian but not Jewish and I fathered her child. She then moved to live with another lesbian who was black. My son went on to have gender reassignment surgery it all went so badly wrong, so her female partner stabbed him to death. You are Jewish but not a lesbian! I don't seem to get things the way I planned."

"Who was Helene?"

"Her husband was a pedophile and his skull was found in my garden and she blamed me: so, I acted in self-defence and shot her with her gun. Jodie was as I mentioned impregnated by me. It is all one big mess I know." He said hoping that she could help him with his issues.

"Is this the story you told me on the night you took away my innocence and made out that you were a widower and an impotent man?"

"Yes." He said as he smiled with a big leering grin at her as her response was arousing him.

"Oh Roger! Please forget about all this madness, I will save you." She was scared of him but trusted that he would never do any harm to her physically and she didn't want to be some spinster like figure either. In short, it didn't matter how much he lied to her, words were simply nothing more than movements of air as far as she was concerned. What was the point in taking him too seriously when if she analyzed him she would end up further in despair or worse? She was also scared that if she feared him, he would sense this and become violent towards her.

The rest of the outing was pleasant, and they spent a lot of time swimming and touching each other in the pleasantly warm sunshine. What more could she ask for in her life? One thing she didn't want was to be touched by him for a while because of his insane thoughts.

It had been a strange trip for Beth with Roger. She was relieved that she was a Christian and was pinching herself for going down to his lowest moral denominator by expressing her Jewishness. He had already impregnated her before he knew that her great grandparents had converted in order to escape Hitler. In short, she was a proud Christian woman, and totally ashamed of herself in trying to gain his affections by expressing roots which had never really meant anything to her. On top of that, she was worried about losing her mind over his views on sexuality. What could she do? Would she be able to imagine herself as a lesbian in order to turn him on? In turn as soon as Roger went behind a tree for a wee, she ran off for a run up Loughrigg Fell before going back to Fell End along with the beagles running after her.

That same evening after dinner he walked into her room. He was feeling sad because he was worried that her heart was moving away from him. "What are you doing dressed like this?" He asked her dumbfounded as she was wearing his courtroom robes which had been sent over before the floods and were much too big on her.

"I'm a gay Jewish man! Please bring out the woman inside of me!" She said loud and proud as she was hoping that he would take off the clothes of his she was wearing and make love to the feminine, Christian woman she was inside.

"Beth you are sick, you are mental. How can you do this to me?" He said to her horror. "You really are in need of medical help. If it were the pre tsunami days I would have had you placed onto the psychiatric ward for making fun out of LGBT, Jews and different races. This is a criminal offence! This is a hate crime!" He looked at her as she stared into his glacial eyes. He had shot a Jewess and a sixth sense went over her. She had to take a chance to restore her dignity.

"Your hero is Adolph Hitler!" She said as she was still looking into his confused eyes as she was half serious and half joking. His arms then went up in the air flailing wildly as he started groaning like a werewolf. He then lost control and fell on the floor as Beth didn't know what to do. In fact, she was somewhat terrified of him as she could imagine him as some four-legged friend. Sophie then stormed in wondering what all the commotion was about.

"Stop provoking him!" She said screaming at Beth.

Sophie knew that her sister was right since she had more or less heard the twisted conversation as she had been listening outside the bedroom door. Roger was indeed some kind of freak of nature, but what else could they do now? They simply had to make the most of their circumstances. It was also her turn to be with him for the night. Scared of him losing control and destroying their lives even further; she placed her hands on his shoulder and Beth left her own bedroom while her sleeping baby was in his cot.

The door closed. "She is so provocative." He said dolefully and feeling sorry for himself.

"I know." She said as she reassuringly placed her hands on his shoulders.

"I wanted to confide in Beth something, but can I in you instead?"

"OK, what is it?" She said somewhat apprehensively.

"You know I used to be attracted to children?"

"I do, why was that?" She didn't know but knew how to help him open to her.

"Sometimes I preferred women without the curves and thought of them as little boys. I know the simple solution would have been to have found a woman who was androgynous and looked like Annie Lennox, and legal too." He said as though he was a law-abiding citizen.

"I think you simply see human beings as simply being meat for you to do whatever you want to with."

He froze she had hit the nail on the head, now it was time for him to change track. "What she doesn't understand is that I am black transgender woman." Sophie was then in shock, but on the outside, she seemed somewhat composed perfectly. "I'm not a black transgender woman when I am with you."

"I see."

"I feel safer with you."

"Then why do you spend more time with her than with me?"

"Close your eyes." She did as she was told. "Imagine that you are a black lesbian. Would you go for men or women?"

"Women I guess." She said confused about his words.

"Exactly." He said as she felt provoked but couldn't quite put her finger on exactly as to why.

"Why do you feel like a woman when you are with my sister?"

"It is her perfection. She thinks that she is a good Christian girl." He said, too scared to tell her that he found Beth more attractive.

"Look Roger, you are the only man apart from David left."

"I am sorry, but for me, you are just my blow-up doll, my safe haven." He said as he was unable to conceal his despair over Beth.

For a brief moment she wanted to kill him, how could he make out that she wasn't all woman for him? All she could think about was how she was his lover and mother of one of his many children but instead of feeling angry, she simply smiled at him. "If another two men arrived, I would run away from your insanity!" By then she wondered how Beth was able to deal with him.

"I am sick and tired of being nothing more than a radical feminist's dildo!" He bawled at her.

"You have such a high and almighty opinion of yourself don't you dearest." She said smirking at him.

"You are nothing like your sister! You are the cause of all my problems!"

"Then go to her! And I will find a man in time."

"You don't appreciate how lucky you are with me. I am a very strong man," he said almost bellowing at her. He wasn't going to allow her to try to kill him again. In turn she became frightened. "I can make any man gay if I want to, you included." He said almost tearfully. By then she was angry, what right did he have to have the monopoly of sexual conquests, how could he imply that she was a man? "No other men are coming, so I can be open and honest about myself." He said.

"I'm sure there are women who would treat me better than you." She said.

"Go on, go and fuck with Jennifer." He said both jealous and excited by the thought of the two women together. As she left the room, she believed that she had done so on a baby like and pathetic beast character. She then went to her room and was relieved to see that Beth had been watching over her baby.

That night he started screaming like a girl and was trying to pull off his penis in his sleep. Sophie then ran into his room. She saw that he was sleeping, and she knew that he was suffering from some horrific nightmare. Somehow, she had to save him. She then shook him.

"I have to pull my penis off!" He cried.

"No, no, please don't do this!" She pleaded.

"OK, I will postpone this act but not indefinitely. I simply can't go on like this!" He cried pathetically. She stayed with him with his head on her lap and once he fell asleep, an extremely fatigued lady left his room.

The next evening while on her own and actually pleased about this; Sophie was thinking about Roger. He was mentally ill, but she was by then getting used to his insanity and was beginning to accept it and to wonder if it was nothing to be concerned about. One thing she couldn't fathom; was why before the tsunami he was less crazy. Luckily for her, he was in Beth's bedroom. In fact, he hadn't left her sister's bed since the evening Sophie walked out on him. The days were long, and searching for answers, she crept into the lugubrious setting of his room and looked through his letters. It was there that she found an unfinished letter of his.

My dearest Emma,

Should I write? I do not know. Are you alive? Again, I do not know the answer to this either. I posted you three letters, and am still waiting for your reply, which won't come soon enough for this man who is pining constantly over you. When I said that ever since I caught the sisters cheating on me that my feelings of love turned to dust, I meant it. I know that they are the mothers of my children; I also know that being a father is important to me. Oh, if only you knew what you mean to me! With you I think about love and nothing else. I have visions of the pain that the sisters cause me, and in turn I am incapable of treating them with respect. They are both using me: using me because I have saved their lives due to my connections. They are simply two scheming women. They have no respect for each other either. Each time that I try to escape from the love tryst of their own making, I fail. I tried to commit myself to one of them, not once or twice but several times. Each time I sink further into the abyss. They ruin my plans. In turn I become so utterly confused. To be with you and focused on just one being is better than this hell that is sending me to despair and destruction.

After reading Sophie decided to place the letter in exactly the same spot where she had found it. Given she had nowhere else to go; all she could do was place the words of his letter into her thoughts and not to dwell on them too much.

The following night and while he was in bed with Beth, he was feeling happy. In turn he had what was for him a most beautiful dream. Wrapped inside his miserable sorrows of self-loathing, he had a vision. In it his penis had grown to the length of three feet (100cm) and was five inches thick (15cm). In turn Beth sliced it off with a carving knife and the residents at Fell End feasted on it including himself. His head then fell off, his limbs fell apart and with his energy flowing all over the place he had set of violent lightning which seemed to be engulfing everything around him towards a black hole which was growing and growing as everything around his former self was disappearing. He woke up after everything had disappeared and all that was left was simply a black space. He had never in his life seen something so beautiful. As far as he was concerned, life was meaningless, what was the point in being put on death row at the point of birth? If only he could share his dream with Beth. Instead, and feeling amorous due to what seemed to her his positive energy in the air, she aroused him, and they made love together as though heaven and earth were moving.

Now that they were living close to nature, Roger expected both girls to start menstruating on the night, of the new moon, that being June the third. Beth had already menstruated sometime in the middle of May, but he had been too scared to mention this, in case she would be wary of him and ruin his exciting plans for her. He was sure that both girls would menstruate together like they had done last year, and with them both being fertile simultaneously, this would make a double impregnation easy for him.

On warm afternoons he was lying in wait and admiring the young mothers of his own making. Still schizophrenic, he no longer saw his illness as being a problem. In fact, it made his orgasms more exciting than ever. For him being aroused by death and impregnation simultaneously proved to him that he really was someone special. Being aroused by corpses alone or by sex alone was like a sandwich without all of the trimmings. Having an orgasm with thoughts of floating corpses and his women falling pregnant was what made his life simply worth living. In turn he believed himself in being the great savior of the human race. He had helped to put the masses out of their misery while he was bequeathing to earth a gift; and one of simply life, that being his own posterity. For him it was time for sadness, sorrow and regret as he was thinking that he could have started with his impregnation program when he was still a teenager. He could have travelled from country to country, but it was better late than never as far as he was concerned.

As a 33-degree Freemason, his offspring could have been leaders throughout the world and puppets like himself of the New World Order. At least he wasn't Joe Goldberg, the man who had the same ideas as himself and was dead and buried and according to the media, which controlled the masses, had died childless. Now of course there was no media as he knew. Newspapers were starting to come back slowly into circulation but only in the big cities such as London which had perhaps as many as twenty thousand inhabitants and one daily newspaper. Manchester, Leeds, and Bristol had five thousand a piece and a weekly rag. Liverpool and Newcastle were for some reason deserted. Eventually the Manchester Guardian would be posted into homes as far north as South Lakes.

Back with him after his stint with Beth, Sophie was still reeling from his comment about her being nothing more than his blow-up doll. In the bed with him she looked at him as she saw what she perceived to be an ageing mortal. "Beth is right, you really are a Satanist!"

"This is the same as discrimination against the Jews!" He said. Sophie decided to remain calm. For some reason Beth was listening in on their conversation outside his bedroom door and something was festering inside of her. She was scared that one day she might end up in killing him.

As for Roger, Beth had nowhere else to go. She was alone. Even so, if she shared with her then, before she fell pregnant again, his sinister dream, he might sacrifice his chance in becoming a father once again.

It was on the fifth of June when Roger was feeling overwhelmed. His plans for the middle of June seemed to be moving away from him. One day earlier Beth had had her nineteenth birthday, but there had been no mention of this. As much as she was calmly getting back on with her life and making the most of it, how could she celebrate her birthday when just one year earlier, she had had such a lovely party with her family and friends who ended up dead just several months later? As for him, day by day, he was scared, he was worried. Was he going to end up even more insane than he was already? So long as Beth seemed to be getting on with her life, he felt as though he was losing his controlling power over her.

One thing that took his mind of his personal life was when he could use his power at work. In turn, he walked to David who was busily building the trail towards the stream which was being covered with a wall on both sides. "The girls are so proud of the way you are looking after them." He said, before promptly walking off. He knew his manner would keep David on his toes. For Roger, people not getting too close to him personally, was what made him feel more in the way of being in control of his life.

Sometime around the tenth of June he recognized from the blood on her bed, that Beth was or had been menstruating. She later cleaned her sheets, but with Roger inspecting daily, he had already noticed her shame. Her shame was his pride and his joy. Without a washing machine and having to clean the bedsheets by hand, Beth was learning more and more how much easier her life was before. The day she gave birth coincided with the tsunami. What a terrible coincidence that was, she thought as she was reading a book on the lawn, it was sadly for her a recurring memory. If only her life could get better. At that moment as she was feeling guilty in being a survivor, he came up to her as she was sat in the garden with William on her lap as she was minding her own business. His presence had provoked the fury that was inside festering inside of her that she had against him. "Don't you find it sick, that I am reminded about terrible events whenever I look at our son?" She said to him with an icy tone which wasn't in any way at all of her normal persuasion.

"In short I don't. Life and death excite me. You are beautiful and I want to offer you all of the world's riches. All the shops in Ambleside are owned by me, and what is mine: is yours. Equally, isn't it exciting to think that when you are bringing life into the world that other people are dying so that there is more space for us?" He said as he walked off. She then followed him. "No, I don't Roger!" She said as he turned around and stood in his tracks listening to her.

"Come on love; stop trying to dismiss the facts."

"What is the point in us populating the world when some madman is only going to destroy our own posterity one day?"

"You know as well as I do that the earth was overpopulated and that now we can live in peace, procreate and not worry about the rest. Millions of people were starving to death. Millions were dying in Bangladesh due to flooding. The world is much more peaceful now. My only regret is that you cannot produce as many children as I. There is no woman so beautiful as you. If we are strong; we will survive, isn't that what your daddy said?" He said as he was hoping for some reaction from her as she was in shock over the way he had abused her daddy's words.

"If you loved me, you would not be speaking about death and destruction at the same time. You would not be thinking about other women too. Instead, you would expect us both to be role models for our child." She said as she looked into his eyes. He was full of defiance and wondering when was she going to either admit to him that she was with him because he was her shield? Why hadn't she slapped him across his face when he spoke about her deceased father? How could anyone remain so composed in the face of evil and keep her beautiful mind intact? She then ran off immediately in tears back to William as his hateful words depressed her.

"Please don't leave me alone! I am scared that if I am unhappy, I will turn into a black hole and swallow everything in my path which will be more than just the earth!" He said as a veil of sadness went across his mind and he knew that she hadn't heard him and felt that it was better that way. He calmed down and believed that he had had a very lucky escape. He didn't want her to see his vulnerability, since a part of him was genuinely depressed about the wipe out. In his eyes she had given him the go ahead to punish her; but instead, he wanted to do something that would have given them both pleasure. There was nothing that made him happier than when they were both enjoying something together. If only he could keep his transgender thoughts at bay and love her the way that she wanted him to.

He was Satan for sure. Equally she was far from in being the good girl she wished to be in simply so many ways which for her were too numerous to mention. If only she had tried harder with David the first time, she set her eyes on him. He was shy, but sometimes especially in the modern world it was the women who were expected to take the lead. Many men were too frightened to approach women due to false allegations of rape and harassment. Equally, when a woman wanted a man, he was expected to seduce her. If only she had tried harder with him. All she could think about was how she had made such one big mess of her own life.

While Roger was busy with her sister as well as herself for his procreation, she was relieved that no one else other than the two sisters was involved. On top of that, she knew that a man like him would, given the chance, take over the whole of mankind with his deranged genetic code and was thankful for small mercies.

At least she was menstruating. As such she didn't need to fear him. She then decided to walk to him in the garden as he was gazing into space. She wanted to tease him somehow. As such she was stood upright as he was admiring her chest. "It is strange. I am still menstruating. If we make love the blood will excite you, but my infertility will depress you. What a pity we don't make love when I am bleeding." For once Roger was lost for words. For some reason he believed that making love when she was having a period, would reduce his chances in making her pregnant later on. In shock, he simply walked away from her. After a few moments he composed himself, thought about how he got the date of her menstrual cycle wrong, and vowed to get his own back on the only woman he really loved Beth.

Beth then walked away from him and was pleased to see David alone. "How are things Beth?"

"He said that life and death excite him!" She said as tears ran down her face.

"That is so disgusting. I need to have a word with him about this." He then walked off as he saw Roger. For once David was acting like a real man in her eyes.

"Roger!" He said as he approached him. "How can you say that life and death excite you?"

"David, as lovely as the girls are, their English isn't perfect. What I had said originally had obviously got lost in translation. I have been explaining to her that what saddens me most is the squalor, deprivation, and hunger that the people in overcrowded countries such as Bangladesh were suffering. How can anyone equate my own nervousness about bringing a child into the world with the beauty I see in procreation with that of the destruction due to the genocide?" He said looking as though he was a caring man who would never say something horrible.

"Excited and nervous are synonyms." David said diplomatically. Roger smiled like a gentleman. Now in David's eyes he was still a bad person, but not quite so evil as Beth wanted him to believe.

He then walked up to her, "Beth my love," he said as he returned to her where she had been waiting for him as she went weak at her knees. "Nervous and excite are synonyms." He then walked off. She was both insulted he was trying to make out she misread Roger and insulted he didn't believe her. Equally she found his use of the word, 'love,' as being highly and poignantly insulting towards her when he merely saw her as some silly little drama queen.

In a fit of fury, which she managed to control inside of herself, she ran into her room put a pair of running shoes on and went off up the fell. She didn't care if she had an accident, although inside she was a little scared since she had never before ran up a small mountain like this before. As she got to the top of Loughrigg she was so proud of herself. She was glad to be still alive. As she ran back down the fell, with all her adrenaline pumping inside of her, this fit young and sure-footed girl felt stronger than all of the others combined down at Fell End.

One afternoon and due to his boredom in the garden he was in deep thought. What if he sent a letter to Beth asking her to carry out some macabre acts on him? The problem was that, if he was still alive, he didn't have enough faith that she would kill him. On top of that, he didn't have a gun. Even so, he believed that time would solve his problem. For him, Beth was the closest thing to perfection. If he could drive her to the point of no return so that she would kill him, he would be able to prove that no matter what, there was a dark side in the saintliest of beings. As he thought about her purity: his own self-loathing was killing him as he wished more than ever that he was her, and not himself.

Meanwhile at another end of the garden, the sisters were together. "When will the stretch marks disappear?" Sophie asked.

"Just give it time." Beth said a little uncomfortably.

"Have yours gone yet?" Beth then showed her sister her belly and her thighs, they were sisters after all. "Lucky you and poor me. Just make sure that Erik moisturises you next time. You don't have any stretch marks. It is as if you haven't been pregnant let alone given birth. I wish I had your skin, Beth."

She felt so guilty: she knew the reason why. Roger had told her that the pregnancy creams were for her exclusively, since she was his beautiful lover as opposed to his dowdy common law wife. He wanted her to look as sexy for him as ever, while he wanted Sophie to be more of mumsy type being. On top of that, without a pool of young maiden survivors he painfully treasured her more than ever.

Back in her own world: and as far as Beth was concerned Roger wasn't giving their baby as much attention as she would have liked. He often seemed to be showing William off with Sophie to her fury, but as a nuclear family, he didn't seem to care for their mutual child as much as she would have wished. Maybe it was because the child was still so small, but she doubted that in several months' time that he would be teaching the child French and reading bedtime stories.

Chapter 4

A MAN FOR ALL SEASONS

Often, he would sit in a trance and plot his next steps. Looking out of his window he simply believed that time was running out for him. Other people his age had already died due to their unhealthy lifestyles, and while he was a living testament that looking after one's health paid dividends, he had to act. He was in fact frustrated with Beth. Since giving birth, she had already had her second menstruation and he believed that she was wasting too many of her precious and fertile eggs. Tired of pulling out of her when they were together alone, before he reached an orgasm, he had to think again. At least Sophie hadn't yet menstruated, and wasted her gifts from nature, and this for him was yet another sign that he should leave her alone but for several weeks at the most only. By then, any acts taking place between this fecund and beautiful Adonis as he saw himself and his lucky woman were meant to be. As such, it being too soon for Sophie, his main focus was on Beth. Equally, he wasn't sure that the others would approve in him making this nineteen-year-old mother pregnant again so soon. At least the women had been tamed by events and he didn't feel threatened by them, although he still had the odd twitch in different parts of his body from Sophie's savage attack on him a few months earlier.

He then sat on his chair and as far as Roger was concerned, David was a wimp. He knew how much Beth loved him; he knew how much of a user Jennifer was and couldn't understand why under the circumstances David wasn't having some pleasure with Beth behind Jennifer's and his own back. In turn he felt that David was weaker than himself in every way of the word and would one day pay the price for not standing up against him. One thing Roger didn't at all respect was feeble men and wanted to destroy them psychologically. At the same time, he wanted to kill robust men such as Erik.

He knew that he was being watched by everyone. He wanted to remain the leader. As such he planned a beautiful three course meal and instructed David to follow his command under his watch. That simply meant he had to clean up after Roger's mess and do all the menial tasks. At times he felt some soft and effeminate energy from David when he gently scrubbed the potatoes. Even when holding a knife, David had for Roger the Midas touch. In turn he would sometimes sing love songs about women as a distraction from the fact that they were being directed at him. Calmly he remained resolute that even with Jennifer around, that one day he would bugger him up, physically and mentally. What was also amazing was that the previous owners had already prepared themselves for the genocide and as such they had a fully convertible oven. This meant that they could cook with electricity or with wood burning underneath. For Roger it filled him with delight that; his former rivals were dead and buried and he was, thanks to Jennifer, now living in their luxury home.

He was the only French person in the kitchen, in turn he felt like a Gallic Emperor as his humble followers enjoyed his meal with relish. On top of that, he sensed that he had to heap plenty of praise onto David if he wanted him in his trap. The energy of heat from the wood was different to that from electricity, and simply added an extra dimension of added exquisite flavour to the dishes. He then thought about how certain cannibals would have cooked using wood and wondered as he had a vision of human flesh with its skin peeling off in the heat, if they were capable of appreciating the blending of charcoal and bone, before moving onto his guests. He was their sun; they were his fruits. Like a shining star he was feeding them and one day as his love for them was entering his stomach, the food he had fattened them up with, would make them into one big feast for him. The big question was, when how and with whom?

After the meal he was ready for a change of scenery. "I am glad you all enjoyed dinner. I am proud to announce that the dry-stone walled tunnel path to the stream has been completed." He knew that the wall was superfluous, but he had to show the others that he was in charge of things taking place at Fell End. "Beth and I will retire for the night." He said regal like, before the others were to comment about the unveiling. While David was disgusted, secretly he wished that he could alternate between Jennifer and Beth and could blame his lack of decency on the grounds it was Roger who had created this mess between him and his women. In short, the pain and torture due to his conflicts between his heart and his head were making life at times unbearably difficult for him.

As for Jennifer, she saw nothing at all wrong with the effect he had on her. She believed that she was a lucky one in having one faithful man, and that she herself deserved love from the only other man available. The one she wished she could experience behind David's back, again. If David weren't a man of piety, she would be able to express herself more. Simply put, David was for her a true Christian. How could she discuss the fact that she wanted a threesome with either one of the sisters, or with Roger, to David? Beth scared her somewhat. She seemed so pure as snow. In short, having sex with a predictable man was better than not getting it, and she didn't wish to lose respect in front of the others about her bi curiosity from her Cambridge days, which was resurfacing since David wasn't giving her enough satisfaction in the bed. He was passionate, but too predictable and not adventurous enough for her. Unlike most men she knew previously, he wasn't into dressing up as a woman or BDSM. On top of that, she was finding the sisters as being more and more beautiful every day as these stunning mothers were reminding her of her changing role from being a single girl to that of a mother earth figure herself too.

In one of his contemplative moods, while Beth was sleeping, he started to realise that his impregnation plan had to be postponed. Without electricity, he saw no sense in a midsummer conception. He wanted to wake up during the night and admire her pregnant body in the twilight. A March birth would mean that during the last trimester, the most enjoyable part for him, due to the then short days he wouldn't be able to see her curvy body as much as he would like. On top of that he believed that during warmer days she would be hornier too. In short, he had to wait so that the birth would take place at the end of the summer. This would coincide with the harvests too. In winter seeds were sown, in spring they were flowering, summer they were developing and autumn they were crops in a harvest, it all made sense to him. In short, he had to think about each and every month very carefully indeed.

As far as her conception for him was concerned June was out. July and August would create a similar problem. September would have her in full glow at the zenith of her pregnancy in midsummer, but he believed that that was too early too. October, as soon as she started to really show he wouldn't be able to enjoy the natural light shining on her curves. November was still a little too early. December he would have her in the second trimester during the spring and the third trimester during the summer. January, at the end it would already be autumn and maybe she would be a little too cold during the night. December it was he had to get her pregnant then. This was the perfect month for a conception as far as he was concerned. During the first trimester she would be suffering from nausea, so he wasn't so worried about her being too cold to make love then. At least he had some old-fashioned hot water bottles and was sure she would prefer to use these during her first flush of pregnancy before they could cause any harm to her baby bump. With the longer days and warmer nights during her second and third trimester, it would be the best time for him to enjoy her pregnant body.

After a lovely start to the day with Beth, Roger decided to spend extra time with her. He planned a long romance with her before she would be with child again. While she was delighted that he wanted to be with her there were issues that needed to be resolved. It was in the garden when after lunch that she needed to get things off her chest. "Roger, we need to talk?" She said earnestly.

"Why don't we do that in front of the tarn." Ever the optimist, Beth smiled at him. She wasn't asking for much, she had been through with so much hell, and that lesser women would already be dead.

Together they waked hand in hand to Loughrigg with William in his sling. She looked at him as they arrived at Tarn Foot. "One year ago, I was an innocent virgin, now I am all messed up."

"Then we can support each other." He said as her confusion was soothing him while the sunshine beating down on his face made him look more attractive for her than ever.

"I am messed up because of you." She said as her words were turning him on. "Did you really mean it when you said you wished I were David, and you were me?" She said in fear of him.

"I did. But there is nothing we can do about it now; we no longer have the resources to change our sex. If I could, I would have myself as our child's mother and you as the father. Then again, I should be happy, since if we stay as we are, we can have more babies." He said as her confusion wasn't quite so enjoyable for him as he had hoped.

"And how do you feel about this? I mean being unable to change sex." She asked him in all seriousness.

"I can live with this. We have other things to worry about now; our very own survival."

"I just wish you knew who you were. I know I am a woman through and through. It is difficult for me to love someone who doesn't know what sex he is."

"I think it is because my love for you is so strong that it is some sort of punishment. There is nothing I want more than to be happy. Please help me. I am so sad that my life is so. I am in such despair!" He said to her as though he was with great difficulty controlling the tears inside of him.

"Roger don't you think that another man would be happy with me? What more should I do for you?"

"Of course, a man should be happy with you, you do everything for me and much more . . . I am happy with you. No other woman is as special to me as you are." He said. She was then repulsed inside thinking that he might have sent her on a road to transgenderism and in turn she would have fallen pregnant while on some gender hormone transition treatment. Thank God the world had gone back to the pre-industrial revolution she thought as she was hyper ventilating and disgusted with the way she had allowed him to take over mind.

As soon as she calmed down, he looked at her somewhat sternly. "Do you discuss my confusion with Sophie?" He asked her worried in case together the sisters were discussing his weaknesses. He didn't want them talking about him behind his back, when he expected them to idolise him.

"No, I don't. She has enough problems to worry than going on some downward transgender spiral with you." Her words as icy as icy as they were, reassured him.

"Thanks. I don't mention this to her, because she isn't so sympathetic as you. On top of that I am sure she would have nothing more to do with me if she knew. The strange thing is I find you somewhat surer of your sexuality, yet you seem more tolerant. I guess Sophie is afraid of her deep self in being revealed."

"Roger you scare me. Even I sometimes question who I am because of you!" She said alarmed at him.

"Don't worry, Lyla was about to have a sex change for me, I guess even David would become a woman if I asked him too!" He said in awe of her, as her speech was arousing him. "You hate his Christian values, don't you?" She said as her fear and fury of him was multiplying.

"Yes, his, David's, hypocrisy. People like him have had millions of gays murdered throughout the world."

"What a load of utter and complete nonsense! So, if homosexuality and transgenderism is so fantastic, why are you so messed up?" She said as she was staring into his eyes.

"I know, I know, I know!" He cried as he looked at her hoping that she could cure him.

With that Beth hated herself. What he said resonated somewhat with her. David was outwardly her Christian gentleman, but she wondered if Roger could actually trigger something off with this weak individual. In fact, she wasn't convinced that he really was all man because of the way he acted when he was confused over their relationship and didn't know if he could stand by her or not. Most importantly of all, he wasn't with her. Her distaste for some aspects of his flawed character was because she loved and missed him like crazy and he wasn't hers. Somehow, she had to get him out of her ever thoughtful and analytical mind. On top of that, she abhorred herself too, for being in this contemptuous mess.

Beth was confused, and after calming down after the conversation; if it were so simple for her to change sex and to be an honest man for her beloved wife, Roger, she would. Anything was better than being in the mess that she was in with him. Now though, there was nothing either of them could do about it. She had to bring up her children in a stable family home. At least the wonderful views of land and water were able to prevent her from losing her own mind. "There are some things about you I find incredible. Your hair is still black without a grey hair. Your skin is so smooth. You could be twenty years younger."

"So, you can make the most out of the situation."

"I know I sound clinical, I guess in some ways I am. Even so, I really think we can live happily together, but that would mean you being a one woman, man. If Erik were to be with Sophie and not I, would you do everything to treat me right?"

"Yes, I am with you a real man, and I want to get you pregnant again, and again and again."

"But I don't want this." She said as she was regaining her inner strength, "I want to know that I am more than just a baby machine for you. I would prefer it that we got to know each other a bit more. That we learn more about each other as friends rather than just producing nonstop."

Her response scared him as he worried that his dormant demons might wake up. "You know that I have led a very complicated life thanks to my mother and my father. Dearest, you are going from hourglass figure to mother earth figure and back are the things that simply keep my transgender desires at bay."

"Look Roger! If we have had a sex change, we wouldn't be having children. As for the sex changes, I have thought about my life as a man and yours as a woman, but to be honest I don't see how it would work. I mean I am small petite woman and even if I developed biceps like those of a body builder you would still be towering in height above me." She said as the repulsive conversation had its tentacles of fear wrapped around her, as she wanted the best for her children and was too scared to be alone. "I admit that I have never thought of that. Yes, you are right this would be a problem. I want you to fall pregnant in winter, so that in summer I can admire in the long daylight your luscious pregnant body." He said as she wasn't fully listening to him. By then Erik would be back in her life, she hoped.

In turn Roger felt bad about himself. He accepted that he had gone too far in messing with Beth psychologically and that he wanted her to trust him. She was only nineteen, and he could wait several months before impregnating her, and that his mental issues through her love and compassion would be solved. By then, he hoped that she would simply fall pregnant to him at her own demand and most importantly, willingly. If not, he would have to do this by force somehow.

Beth was saddened that he was unable to control his perversions, his desire to impregnate her again and again without any commitment as well as his desire to be a woman, which brought out a feeling of hatred towards him, made no sense to her. She was also frustrated and wondered if she should control him instead. How she had no idea. Maybe she could threaten him with Erik. If she loved Erik, Roger would be so scared to lose her that he would see that he had to treat her right. Beth didn't believe that he would arrive from Poland, but his possible legacy during his absence in bringing Roger closer to her was something worth thinking about.

Roger and Beth took it in turns to swim in the tarn. Both took it in turns to look after William. With no one around making love was no problem. Although she didn't that day wish to be touched by him, his massages rather than his weird mind had got the better of her judgement. "Are you happy with Sophie?" She asked after the second time they made love and close to the tarn and hoping that he would be faithful to her.

"Kind of. It is our fate as you know."

"You know that Erik is now setting off and heading here for me. Will you be OK with this?" She said hoping that he would give her his exclusive attention.

"I must be." He smiled wryly, to her expected disappointment. His emotions were confusing her as she couldn't work out if he was being hurt by her, didn't care, wanted to hurt her instead, or was simply trying not to overwhelm her too much. They continued taking it in turns with the swimming and during the middle part of their visit they had a packed lunch which had been prepared by him as she was looking after their baby in their home earlier that day. As much as the sandwich was delicious, with the uncertainty surrounding them, she couldn't enjoy it.

Suddenly he started to panic. He pretended that he simply needed a wee behind a tree. If Erik came within the next month or so; he would had missed his chance in getting her pregnant for a second time. He then thought about how she told him the other day that she was menstruating. Surely this was longer than usual. He had forgotten all about the full moon and had missed the boat. She had been taking him for a ride, if only he had trusted his own judgement. Suddenly he calmed down and realized that it was the sixteenth of June. Once again, his life had a purpose for him.

A few hours later and together as the sun was lowering in the sky, they walked back and ate a meal that Jennifer had prepared in the garden. The meal had been made with love. What a turnaround of events. Several months earlier when she was with Roger, she came home to a meal served with hatred from her older sibling. Now it seemed that it wasn't just herself who was being tamed by events. She knew previously that, David's belle wasn't the most domesticated of women, but without modern life, what could one do other than look after domestic duties when life had gone back two centuries? David came along and a sing song about the beauty of the world was sung by everyone. Secretly, Jennifer who was obsessed with her figure: had taken up belly dancing when she knew that she was expecting. Since then, she had been teaching both Beth and Sophie how to dance in oriental fashion and was wearing jewellery from her wild days, which she had luckily taken over to David's flat before the tsunami. The girls then had their erotic bodily parts covered, as the men were awestruck. This lasted for thirty minutes. Sophie was not so delighted. While she had no problem with David watching her, it was Roger's manner that haunted her. In her mind he looked as if he owned the women. Even worse was that Roger was seriously thinking about how he could discard of the other males as the belly dancing was reminding him about Genghis Khan.

The couples needed privacy. After the belly dancing, Sophie was cleaning up the mess from her cooking with her baby close to her. Jennifer and David were having a passionate and early night together and both were thinking of some other being than the person whose belly and chest was touching them.

It had been a beautiful evening for Beth with Roger. He had been sketching her breastfeeding as they were sat together on the lawn outside in the warm setting sunshine. Later in his room as she was breastfeeding and putting their baby to bed, he was coloring in his erotic portraits of her. She was wearing the jewellery too, and he had the gold drawn into his portraits of her. As she put their baby to bed, and had taken off the jewellery, he started to kiss her body from head to toe. His smells were homely. Now without all the mod cons he was less obsessed with his grooming and personal hygiene. She wanted him badly, but instead he gave her a massage until she could take no more.

Without taking off their underwear he pressed himself firmly against her as he was on top of her, just like the first time. For a brief moment her mind wandered back to when she had for the time in her life felt so bonded with a man, what a feeling that was! She could feel his passion and his gyrations of lust and felt honored that he was caring about her needs as she deeply regretted in saying that he was simply just a hole for her. He could feel her excitement and felt that she was one step closer in being knocked up by him. Thoughts of the night she became a maiden no more, her conception, and her maiden pregnancy, were exciting him. This time he had things better planned out. Sophie could wait a few more months and then a few months later it would be Jennifer's turn with him. Her mind was still on that first night, and she was disappointed that as soon as she experienced lovemaking, that was just as thrilling as now, she fell pregnant. Things were different now, he had promised her, and very quickly she climaxed. With their bodies locked closely together from their heads down to their toes, she felt safe with him, and Roger wanted to excite her further. After a second orgasm she wanted to sleep. His mind went back to her wearing the jewellery and Roger couldn't take his mind off the previous time she was wearing the gold and was heavily pregnant and while their baby was quiet, he got on top of her for a third time without taking their underwear off. On top of that he was worried about Erik arriving in on the scene.

Now she found it difficult landing into the land of nod and was a little afraid of the fact that she had worn the jewellery but as she remembered his desire to make her pregnant when he could combine her glowing pregnant body with the long days of spring and summer she calmed down, especially since they hadn't fully taken off their clothes. He excited her mentally, and Roger sensed that she needed an orgasm. He wasn't sure if she was sleeping or not, and Beth was dreaming while she was still half awake. She couldn't fully sleep she needed to experience the truest, simplest and most exciting carnal pleasure naturally. After a few minutes rest, he took off her underwear as well as that of his own and got inside of her for the first time that evening and by then she was feeling relaxed as she enjoyed the sensations.

Normally she would tell him to pull out when she was about to climax and expected him to wait for her hands to help him reach his orgasm. This time she was so serene. She was calm because she was also too tired and so she would deal with Roger later. After a while, Roger's kissing of her breasts was starting to help drift her away gently from her light sleep and any remaining fears of hers. She was being turned on by him more than ever. No longer pregnant she could feel his hips pressing against hers and this was something she had missed with her large belly. He had promised her several more love making months without her being with child, and she had never before felt so sexy and relaxed. She had thought about going on the pill, but thanks to his promise to her, fortunately that wasn't necessary for her and thanks to the new agenda, birth control was off the cards again.

As they orgasmed together as she was lying on her back and as Roger felt a warm glow running through his heart, she couldn't believe that this loving and tender immortal was at times vituperative. So tired she then fell happily into sleep. Roger looked at the paintings on his walls in the twilight and was delighted as he could make out her silhouette in the dark and enjoy the fact that as she was lying on her back that his sperm had filled her up, which he already knew anyway.

The next morning, she woke up. She smiled at the paintings of herself above his bed. Without TV this was the nearest thing to Facebook for her. "Did you enjoy our lovemaking last night?" He asked her as he was admiring her body. Her skin was still delicate and soft, and he had a good supply of cream which he was still rubbing on her body in order to keep her youthful appearance.

"It was all so dreamlike: I was half awake and half asleep."

"Was it beautiful?"

"Indeed, it really was."

"Why don't we do the same thing again?" He said as she looked on lovingly at him.

"Why are you looking at me like this?" She asked a little coyly as he was leering at her and thinking about her body expanding more than ever the coming nine months.

"You have an amazing combination of your old hourglass figure and bigger boobs from breastfeeding!" His words were turning her on and he kissed her breasts. Some men didn't like the idea of women lactating and, in her mind, he was at that moment at least, a real man for her. At the right moment for her, he kissed them again and fed off some of her milk. He then got inside of her and was feeling hornier than ever. It being June the seventeenth with his mind over matter, he was producing sperm like that of a flowing fountain. As for her, she was thinking at the back of her mind about her baby alarm and had a flash of herself in the family way again but with the excitement of a lifetime; she dismissed this from her thoughts. His phallus, her drug, was her elixir.

Without all the modern cons of the electrical age, making love was more exciting than ever, as people were no longer living in the virtual world. As soon as she reached her blissful moment, she would simply tell him to pull out. She wanted him to be careful, but equally she was over excited and had no control. Roger was delighted and enjoying every second inside of her. This time he was making sure that he knew when she would reach her orgasm.

As soon as she got there, he climaxed with her too as he quickly glanced at the paintings of her before looking back at her body in the flesh and felt as though he was in paradise. She had never felt so horny in her life and wanted him again and again. For some reason with him keeping himself in such good shape she didn't feel as though she was making love to a much older man. Also, with her being a mother herself, she felt a generation older in her wisdom than one year earlier. Feeling in heaven she then followed his eyes which had returned away from her and saw that they were on the paintings. It was at that moment when her mood suddenly changed, and then she burst out crying. "You bastard! You were supposed to wait for me and pull out!"

"You said you wanted it just like last night!" He said to her calmly as his eyes were lovingly once again looking at her body.

"I don't remember it being this way."

"Maybe you were asleep." He said as a matter of fact.

"I might be pregnant again." She said trembling.

"I hope so darling. I hope so. I want to know what it is like to be making love to you while you are pregnant and still breastfeeding." He said as his eyes on her body were then looking lecherously at her.

"But what about Erik. I don't want to be pregnant when he is here." She said in great desperation. All it took was for him to tell her that, he wanted her forever and then she would feel safe with him.

"He will arrive dear, don't worry. If you are with child when he arrives, he will understand that he arrived too late for you. You can't just sit around waiting when we can have so much pleasure together. You know precisely what your hourglass figure has ignited inside of me." His devastatingly hedonistic response was too much for her to bear. Silently she prayed to the Lord Jesus for both herself and Erik to be reunited as soon as possible.

He didn't believe that this dull Polish guy would return. He sensed that Beth was using Erik as some emotional bait for him. Had Beth not distressed him with the unpleasant news of the Polish boys return into her life, getting her in the family wouldn't have been a matter of great urgency for him. All he could do was to pretend that he accepted her with Erik and in turn she wouldn't be able to get the better of him with her manipulation. As far as he was concerned: he simply had to remain calm. He wasn't sure when exactly he had got her pregnant the first time, it might have been on their first night together or on the island all he knew was the child was his. Back with his mind on the present, he simply had to fill her up again and within twenty-four hours.

He looked at her, she looked so vulnerable and was turning him further on, as he wanted her to fall pregnant, give birth and have her hourglass figure back temporarily as a part of a cycle again and again and again. Opening the bedside table, he took out the creams. "Your skin is so beautiful; you have no stretch marks." He said kindly as she was then terrified. She certainly didn't want to have unsightly stretch marks like those of her sister; equally she didn't want to be with child again so soon after the last accident. Shaken and numb, she allowed him to moisturise her skin. She was silent. "Even before you fall pregnant, it is good to know that before your skin is being stretched that it is soft and supple and won't look unsightly." He said.

"Thank God, I am not pregnant then!" She cried with relief.

"You are not yet pregnant." He said as he saw some of his juices coming out of her and simply kissed her womb and re inserted some of his white liquid inside of her. She then started to relax. She had to trust him. He then gave her a massage. She felt so vulnerable. At least he had told her convincingly that she wasn't with his child again.

Beth was scared, she was enjoying his touch. He then got inside of her again; making babies was giving him an incredible appetite for sex. She was fully turned on by him. "Don't worry; you will be going through with the implantation stage in a few days' time thanks to my love swimming around inside you. A sperm or two is fertilising one of your eggs, and then you will be with child. When I came inside you, it wasn't that you fell pregnant immediately, the sperm embarks on a journey for a day or two." He said with great satisfaction. "I feel so alive and so happy. What a beautiful world this is, we are so lucky together, don't worry. You won't fall pregnant from my love juices this time." He said as they were both being so turned on by his words of passion.

Suddenly, as he was thrusting against her body tightly as she could feel him from her head down to her toes, she suddenly had visions of herself looking enormous and trapped inside a cage with Roger wearing a black leather cat suit and wanting to try out some perversion on her. After making love she was frozen. Instead of enjoying the sperm filling her up, she felt as though she had been injected with poison. He then walked off eerily and looked inside his cupboard and took out his tape measure as her mind went back to the present, which seemed no better than being behind bars. With him, she was imprisoned in so many ways. "I want to measure your breast, waist and hip size." Visions came back to him as he hoped that she was now as slim as she was when she was still a maiden. He then saw the terror in her eyes. He then quickly measured her chest, 'thirty-six inches. Your breasts are fuller. Waist twenty-four inches you got back into shape very quickly. Obviously, all that belly dancing, hips, thirty-four inches. Must be all that swimming, walking, breastfeeding, and making love." He said leering at her.

"I was less before I fell pregnant."

"You are a mummy now." He smiled at her as she noticed that his phallus was growing.

"Making love is dangerous."

"I know it is also the reason why I am measuring you now." He said to her horror. "Darling, as you grow, my love for you will multiply as much as the changes which are going to be bigger than the last time when you carried only one child. As you know from reading novels, in the past women had babies throughout the whole of their child rearing age. No matter how many children you are having, I will always want to make you pregnant again and again and again." He said as he was enjoying his power over her which was turning not just him on further but a terrified Beth too.

In his life everything was turning out so well for him. Beth was the best, the purest the truest. If only he was able to impregnate another beauty whose body hadn't experienced stretch marks and was ready in his mind to bear a child to him. Then and only then, could he make Beth realise that even she was indispensable for him. She had to be kept on her toes. His mind then went onto his hopes that she was with child again.

After a night and early morning of passion she was then feeling exhausted started thinking while he was still sleeping from their last session. For Beth, there was no pleasure. She had wanted to end her life and to pass on the responsibility of her motherhood over to Sophie. It was thanks to the warm and sunny spring days that she had put her suicide on hold. Now though, thoughts of taking her life before she would be with child once more were coming back inside her mind to haunt her.

As she was waking up, she then started lashing out at him with her arms and punching him. She didn't know what had got inside of her and simultaneously in the background she heard the sounds of a cat screaming who was probably being impregnated there and then. Having empathy for the feline she gained some extra strength as she was then throwing harder punches at his face. Roger wasn't worried. She had no control over herself. Her upper arms were locked, her lower arm was weak. She was a slightly built girl, and her hands were flat. Her punches were nothing more than tender caresses for him. All she had done was turn him on once more as the excitement that she must have got fertilized from one of his orgasms was making him hornier than ever.

What was going on she thought as she heard another cat screaming and being terrorised by a phallus as both she and Roger were in the throes of an orgasm a few minutes later. Well for Roger it was heaven, but for her as she heard the terrible shriek from the cat she was reminded of her own plight. After making love to her she looked at him demonically as he was enjoying his power over her. "What's wrong dear?" He asked her.

"I have nothing against homosexuals, but a man who uses women when he is in love with men at the same time is a woman abuser!"

"Beth, you are nothing but a homophobe!"

"No, Roger, don't you care about the feelings of women?"

"Yes, indeed I do. I am inside very effeminate."

"Roger, this is not what I meant."

"I don't know exactly what you want out of me."

"Do you want men or women?"

"I want both."

His honest answer wasn't enough. As much as it repulsed her, she had to get to the bottom of this no matter how hurt she would feel. "Just be honest with me." She pleaded in vain since she didn't trust him.

"OK. I am attracted to men and repulsed by them. As such I am partly homophobic and partly straight. As for women I am attracted and repulsed by them, as such I am partly heterosexual and misogynistic."

"You can't love a woman when you are thinking about men."

"That is one of the most narrow-minded things I have ever heard!"

"But Roger what you do isn't right!"

"Nobody wins in this world by doing the right thing. The world is about simply making money. Now we are experiencing a lull in the monetary world, but it will return. Once we get back on our feet, people will look for pleasure. Drink, drugs, perversion whatever, I just call it all fun. Forget the fairy tales that don't exist. God works in mysterious ways; look at Romeo and Juliet they simply perished!" For once she believed him but with that Beth ran out of the room nakedly and to her shame David and Jennifer saw her as they were walking to their room.

David saw that she was distressed but was too scared to say anything to her. He was worried about Jennifer finding out that he had more than just a soft spot for Beth. Roger was a much bigger man than himself, he simply wouldn't dare annoy him. Trembling in fear in case she asked for his help, he acted as though there was nothing untoward with Beth's behavior.

He needn't have had any worries; Beth's beautiful body was helping to resurface his partner's bicuriosity. As for her being jealous, he had nothing to worry about.

Feeling depressed and nervous about Beth who had hurt his feelings; he then placed his hand up his bottom and it was hot from the sweat and remains from his last excrement. He then scratched himself gently and collected as much as he could as the sweat and faecal matter was soothing him; before placing his hand below his nose and breathing his natural man-made delights in. Roger then decided that the next time he went to the toilet he would collect his excrement and burn it. After calming down he decided against this on the grounds that it could backfire against him. As such he felt that he wasn't quite the free man he wished himself to be. At least the others wouldn't be aware as to what he had been up to, so long as he washed his hands in the local beck, since he was too scared in being caught out in the house regarding his new fetish. Once again, he would lick the whole of his hands until the brown smelly marks had disappeared. Until then, he thought that smokers were hypocrites. If they could see the inside of their lungs, they would see themselves as being just as dirty as this lover of excrement.

Later that day as she was sat in the garden enjoying the warm sunshine and fearful of her future, she saw Roger lurking around and knew he was thinking about Sophie. Beth left her baby on the grass and ran off wearing just her shoes. Given there was no one around, thanks to depopulation, being naked was no longer a crime. She needed a swim around the tarn. She enjoyed the swimming there so much. After the birth she felt what she believed to be was the healing power in the waters and her reason to continue with living. Now though things were different, as all she could think about was that the tarn was simply Roger's den as her memories about the emotional traumas at The Howe were on her mind once again. Rogers's cheating and the unfortunate consequences of his entrapment of her which had all taken place there. In turn the place was looking like a very sinister and creepy place for her.

As she was swimming, she felt as though the water had been infested with his spermatozoa. She felt as though she was going insane. Of course, she knew deep down it was his sperm rather than the fertile waters that would impregnate her, but her thoughtful mind was overactive. If a lily pad tickled her, she felt as though Roger's tentacles were floating around and when one of them brushed up against her groin she felt as though she couldn't breathe and that her face was covered in some suffocating mask. As she got out, she cried without any words. If only the waters could wash away the sperm of his that was fertilising her egg. She then thought, it was probably too late for that. As a good Catholic girl, if her egg was already fertilized, she shouldn't be thinking like this. She was prolife and had to accept, "what is done; is done."

Although Roger was meant to be taking it in turns with the girls, he decided to spend a second consecutive night with Beth. He had caused her so much pain and torture but now emotionally weakened from her latest fears of a pregnancy she needed him more than ever, as far as he was concerned. As the great manipulator, any vitriolic thoughts of his had to be kept under the surface. As successful as he was in sowing his oats, this was no time for complacency. Beth was as sweet and kind as he was vituperative. She wasn't Jodie or his mother who longed for a child of Satan. Instead, she was a loving child of nature and he had to check that his work was done for a second time with her. Equally his gender fluidity was also the reason why she didn't want to be with him. That evening as they were in bed together and under the candlelight, he noticed a white egg white vaginal discharge pass through her. "I think I hit the jackpot!" He said as Beth froze submissively. "Tonight, my darling, you are at your most fertile. I hope that your womb is looking after my sperm which has filled you up the past few times, we had sex and thanks to my everlasting love and devotion to you." She didn't want another child with him. Equally she hated the lonely nights. Had she believed played her cards differently, she would then have either Roger to herself or be with David full-time.

She then started crying. He didn't want to lose her, it was the seventeenth of June, and he couldn't be too complacent regarding her conception. "I am sorry my love. I have never experienced something so powerful as our passion. I have to be honest with you, your alluring silhouette in the dark turns the night into that of a pleasant summer's day. Please come with me to the window and let's hold our hands together, and may I kiss your sweet and tender lips underneath the moonlight." Together they got out of bed and quietly he opened the curtains. Sure, enough the full moon was out with her full glory and being low and close to the horizon she was a moody big fiery ball of red. She was overcome with the romantic setting as they held their hands together and kissed each other's lips under the moon of love. After some French kissing, he gently kissed her bottom before kissing her navel. It was so sweet, and he had ignited her fires. The lovemaking that evening and night was stupendous but was equally breaking her very fragile nerves. As for

Roger, he was certain that another maternal cycle of hers had been conceived.

After breakfast the next day, there was plenty of work to be done on the garden. Grass was a problem. No electric lawnmowers. A few sheep might come in useful but would bring in disease onto their patch. As such Roger decided to weigh things up over the next few days. He knew that the mothers relied so much on the grass; equally, long grass could spread illness. With thoughts of more babies being born, hygiene standards had to be maintained. Yes, he had his filthy fetishes, and this fuelled his at time neurotic hygienic tendencies. Like the tides going in and out at the Bay, which carried the corpses into the sea and nourished the sea life too, he too was a man of both the vulgar and the wholesome.

During the next two weeks Beth had a constant fight with herself. She wanted to avoid Roger, she certainly wanted him to be more careful. Equally, what was the point? If already pregnant she might as well enjoy the feeling of his love juices flowing inside and out of her and enjoy the swimming in the lukewarm waters of the tarn. As far as she was concerned, those who followed every law of God had never lived. They were perfect because they had never experienced love. For them being able to deprecate others was so easy. All it took would be for them to look at their own imperfections be humbled and to experience the joys of romance. Without love, whether it be romantic, tender or passionate was like that of starving oneself to death. Beth was determined to enjoy her life.

Roger too, was enjoying the hot weather, and wanted to walk in the footsteps of Beth's maiden pregnancy, where he could bring back to life her first flush of pregnancy in his mind as well as literally. As such, they visited Grasmere Island together while Sophie was nursing both of his babies and David was doing some hard work. The swim to the island was heavenly. "Isn't it so nice that we have the whole lake to ourselves." He said. Beth didn't respond. She shed a tear for the beautiful family she saw who were sitting on a rowing boat during the previous summertime. The man was a good decade younger at least than Roger, the women more than a good decade older than Beth. They looked so perfect, she looked so radiant and was with child, and their small son was having fun blissfully waving at Beth who was swimming at the time. Now they were more than likely corpses. How evil; how cruel, how could anyone has wished their beautiful family away?

As they got out of the water together, she had tears in her eyes. "What's wrong love, everything is so beautiful." He said.

"I was thinking about the perfect family I saw here last summer; they were doing no harm to anyone and your wish to exterminate them along with many other beautiful families has been granted."

"There is nothing we can do about this now is there? Just wait here while I go in search of some berries."

"I would rather eat the thorns surrounding any of your fruits than give you any credit in being the loving man which you wish yourself to be known as." As he went away, she simply burst out into tears. Suddenly a fear went over her. What if another tsunami came? Something had to take her mind away from such deathly and terrifying thoughts.

He came back with the berries and was looking at her relatively innocently for him. "Remember how much I was getting turned on when you were scared of being pregnant to me, and how much I was so excited and wanted to fuck you over and over again, as you enjoyed it. You were confused, would I make you pregnant from so much sex or was it too late and better to just sit back and to enjoy it? What a Deja vu situation this is, since then you were already having my baby!" Beth then ran off as she felt that she was in exactly the same situation. He then, placed the berries down carefully which were luckily inside a tub and then he ran after her. In no time at all he was massaging her all over. She was enjoying it so much as well as hating it so much. What was the point in hoping for her next period when he would only make her pregnant one month later anyway? In turn she closed her eyes and made the most of the excitement he was giving to her body despite her mental aversion towards him. He was hot and sweaty, but his extremely youthful appearance made her succumb to his lust which she enjoyed as she felt that there were worse things than to be carrying those Peter Pan genes of his inside of her womb.

A while later, she was then sat frozen and numb as her mind went back to the time she was there with Sophie as they were both fighting over him. He had been away for a long time and just as she was about to leave, he arrived. "I can't think of anything more beautiful than for you to place dozens of raspberries all over my body." He then lied down. She then placed the berries from the tub all over him. He was sensitive enough to feel each and every berry. One by one she ate them all.

"I want to lie down, and you can do to me what I have just done to you." She said as she wanted him to think that she was in control of him while she was both scared of the effeminate side of him coming out again. He then placed the berries all over her. As he ate them one by one, he made sure that he placed his phallus closer and closer to her as she felt the temperatures rising inside of her.

He then got inside of her. After a few moments they were both excited. "Darling what do you find most romantic. What's done is done! Or I am going to get you pregnant again and again and again!" He asked her. It was too late, his speech although repulsive for her didn't dampen her desire for her own orgasm and she sensed that he knew this too as together they came, and his words brought out her tears as she felt that she was simply at his evil and lasciviously passionate and fecund mercy. After making love together, they dozed off together in the sunshine on this English version of a desert island.

They swam back together, but Beth felt that he was humiliating her. At least they had gone back home together. Even so, she felt so alone in knowing in her heart what he was going to be doing with her sister behind closed doors later that evening. She felt as though her simple heart was breaking.

They were walking back together hand in hand; it could have been so beautiful. They could have been enjoying a perfect day of romance together, but his mind was distracted. If the National Grid was still up and running, he was sure that experiments on human bodies could have been taking place and that there would be cyborgs lurking around. One thing about the Cabal; was that they had been honest regarding their intentions. They had revealed all their plans in their Satanic Hollywood movies and cartoons, even so, not everything had gone to plan. "How can you say what is good and what is bad?" He asked her as he imagined that her head had been wired up had the floods arrived a little later.

"We need rules so that they we are kept onto the straight and narrow." She said to him.

"No Beth, we don't know what is right or wrong."

"I have never heard such rubbish in my life." She said.

"To be honest you are full of hatred!" He said.

"Me!" She replied.

"Yes you. Your hatred of homosexuals makes you the same as a Mullah!"

"That's rich coming from you, who believes in the depopulation agenda! It is you who is full of hatred, not I!"

"The depopulation agenda has nothing to do with your hatred of LGBT." He said trembling inside.

"OK, then call me a homophobe I don't care." She said to his surprise.

"It is what you are." He was then relieved he had won the argument.

"At least I wasn't behind a plot to wipe out the vast majority of the human race, ninety-nine percent in fact!"

"It was in humanity's best interests!"

"I have nothing more to say to you Roger; you hate ninety-nine percent of the population while the same cannot be said of me. On top of that, you have ruined what could have been a perfect day." Beth then walked off. She needn't have worried. She had won the argument leaving him badly shaken.

There he was the fully experienced lawyer, who had never lost an argument until then. Back in his native France he had fined mothers who had similar views as she had. Now things were different, he was addicted to her. On top of that he respected her more than anyone else he had ever met in his whole life. If only he could be worthy of her and be cured of his confusion and once and for all make an honest woman out of her. On top of that, a shiver went down his spine as he sensed that she could destroy him literally if he pushed her too far.

She then walked ahead of him in disgust. He soon caught her up. "I love animals, but I am never in a million years going to make love to a dog, a sheep or whatever?" She said waspishly as Roger was feeling very uneasy. "Does this make me as zoophobic as I am homophobic in your eyes?" She said as Roger turned white in his face. Once again, he was lost for words as Beth had outsmarted him and wasn't sure if he wanted her to lose her temper with him or not.

Back at Fell End and in front of the others, which often and on this occasion included the indigenous Westmorland couple at the table, all members present were behaving with grace. After dinner that evening, Beth was thanks to her running and swimming able to control her feelings of hatred. Feeling nervous, she wanted to run up and down Loughrigg Fell twice over. Instead with the sun getting lower in the sky she decided that once was enough and was proud of the fact that she could run up and down the mountain as safely as she walked up and down it the first time on her maiden visit in the area.

The next day a meeting was held on the lawn. By then they were held as and when was necessary, rather than weekly on a Monday. Beth was for once feeling happy as she was breastfeeding on the soft grass and waiting for the others. Now she valued nature more than ever. Roger, David, Beth, Jennifer and Sophie along with Jane in her arms arrived. "For hygienic reasons we have to get rid of the lawn." Began Roger and surely things couldn't get any worse than they were, she hoped as she feared that with him, they could. She also believed he was seeking revenge on her because he had lost an argument or two with her.

"No Roger, I don't want this." She said as he seemed to be once again taking away any pleasure away from her life.

"Neither do I, but as I said we don't want diseases here."

"What about if we get a sheep?" Said Beth.

"Yes!" Said David to Beth's rescue. Roger was thinking that if David could put up with a smelly sheep then so could he.

"Let's think about this over the coming days." He said.

Given that she was hopefully soon to find out that she was with child and that he had been neglecting his mutual born baby with her, Roger felt that he had to give Beth a beautiful day, no matter how boring it might be for him. Fortuitously, for her, she wasn't on her own crying about David or Erik, and they were together in the bed as he was thinking this. He made love to her before placing their baby on her left breast as he himself started drinking from her right breast. "The milk is for our child, not for you!" She said a little coyly.

A warm glow went inside of him. "Normally you have no problem with this, what is going on with your hormones?" He said as a fear went over her. "Darling, a bit of stimulation is no bad thing." She then froze, did he mean she had to prepare herself to feed two babies? She didn't dare ask, she wasn't pregnant, and it was romantic of him to make love and then place their baby on her body so that she didn't need to get out of bed. On top of that, wasn't it nice to think that her milk was delicious enough for him?

They woke up after a refreshing sleep together at 6 o' clock and before the others. They had breakfast together which he made and then went out along with the packed lunch he prepared as he was carrying their baby in a sling. For Beth he was a gentleman with the Midas touch. It was exactly how she wanted things to be: the parents with their child together and him helping her. On top of that, the beagles looked so sweet together too.

At the tarn they were both sat enjoying the views, the weather and family life. Beth decided to make the most of this beautiful day. As she looked around there was just the two of them and their baby. Roger was the attentive husband and father. With no one around she wanted to breed and breed. Having so much space for herself, with her family, she felt that she was the luckiest girl on earth and had every right to enjoy her life. Now was not the time to dwell on the misfortune of others and to simply feel blessed that her luck was that of one in a million. "Do you mind if I go for a swim?" She asked him.

"Why should I, when we first met, it was your swimmer's body that shone in my face and made me want to make days like today come true." He said as she was lost for words. She looked at him and kissed him passionately, before going off on her own to the tarn. As for the beagles, they never ran off and were as good as gold, as usual.

After lunch and some playing together with their son; Roger went for a swim. She admired watching him swim around the lake clockwise and then anti-clockwise for his second round. She was missing him. As he got out of the lake, she was proud that he was looking after his body and delighted that he read her so well and made love to her. She then fell asleep. As she woke up, she saw him lying next to their child. It was so sweet, if only she had a camera she thought. Never mind, seeing this in real life meant so much more to her than in just a two-dimensional picture.

What a beautiful day it had been, she thought just before her mind was about to retire for the night and after a lovely dinner, he had made for everyone, which the others ate after they had finished their dinner in privacy. She was so relaxed. He had carried their child to and from the tarn, while she was responsible for Timmy and Dexter. He fed them three meals and apart from his one-hour swim, when she followed him with her eyes, he had spent the whole day with just her. Roger fell asleep too. After his nap, he felt that: given she would find out very soon that she was pregnant, he knew that in showing her what he was capable of as a doting family man who looked after their family pets too; that this meant that her body at least wouldn't reject his child. He also decided not to make love to her more than once on the outing, so that she would see a gentler side to him. Even so, in the middle of the night she badly wanted him, and neither of them thought about pregnancies since all he could do was wait and see while she often heard ringing in her ears around this time was, what's done is done!

Not everything was as blissful as Roger would have liked. He felt sure that forces were trying to usurp his authority. One such example was at the dinner table the following day. "Given that the water supply is back, I don't think we need the private trail to the stream anymore." Said Sophie. Roger was angry. While he agreed so privately, he had to show who the boss was and his position in his eyes was being testing thanks to the issue of the lawn too. Instead, he merely looked into her eyes like a mafia boss and in turn the others remained silent.

Roger gave Beth another day of his full attention, but at the end of this second blissful day for both Beth and William, he felt somewhat bored. In turn, he started spending more time with Sophie the following days.

It was two days before she was due for her period. Beth was feeling very low, in fact she was feeling angry too as her emotions were becoming more pronounced. What was Roger doing to her? She wanted the grass so badly, of which she was sitting on; it reminded her of the old English novels. Now it seemed Roger wanted the worst of the old ways of life, the difficult lives, and the worst of the modern ways of life, the confusion. She felt as though she was losing her mind. On top of that, she wished that she had seduced David when he wasn't sure if he could trust Jennifer. She knew what Roger was doing behind his back with Jennifer, why hadn't she confessed this to David? All she could think about was whether she was with child again or not. She wanted to end her life. Maybe it didn't matter if she was pregnant or not. Her life was meaningless. Even so, she was wondering if she was going insane, and hoped that either way, once she knew whether she was expecting or not, she would kill herself. At least Roger, Sophie, Jennifer, and David were around. She could leave her baby under the watchful eyes of the others and swim as usual in either the tarn or the lake at Ambleside. Staying fit and in good shape, meant so much to her. If only David, Erik or Jan was able to pay her compliments about how beautiful she looked. Simply put, any male apart from The Beast would do for her.

She decided to leave her baby longer than usual. This was a test. Sophie would breastfeed her baby, she had already done this, but now she would have to do this more often and for longer. As such she spent the whole day at Loughrigg Tarn swam around the lake three times and had plenty of rests in between. As she arrived back home, sure enough, Sophie was breastfeeding both babies. In turn she felt useless and surplus to requirements. Nobody would miss her demise, not even her own child. In short, if she took her own life, Sophie would look after William. William would see Sophie as his own mother. Her death would lead to a more traditional family as the father of both of the siblings' babies, with herself out of the way; the honor of her family would be restored. Then, Roger and Sophie would look like a normal traditional family and could bring up her William as their own.

Beth was going out of her mind, she felt as though she could hardly breathe, she had to speak to him, but he was there with her rival, Jennifer. If she wasn't pregnant, she wanted him to make sure she would be, before The Beast got his wicked way again with her. He was of course no other than David with whom her lust and broody desires were running around. "David." She said as Jennifer walked off. "What would you do if I were in bed on my own got out of bed and kissed you as I caught you going to the bathroom while Jennifer was asleep?" She said as she was imagining the kind of language Roger would use to seduce her and using it in a less vulgar way.

"Beth, I haven't thought about this." He said as looked shocked by her temerity. Inside he was feeling on top of the world as he believed that anytime he wanted her, she was always available for him.

"Don't say I haven't warned you." She said cheekily to him. While deep down her heart was breaking.

He looked at her in awe. The passion between them inside was palpable, all it took was one small thing and there would be no more stopping them both. She was feeling weak, he went up to her and held her in his arms and was opening his mouth which was turning like jelly, as he was feeling guilty too. She sensed that he was about to kiss she then bent her head forwards towards him. Finally, her dreams were coming true as her heart started racing wildly. Life was beautiful again, finally.

There was simply no turning back. All he wanted to do was to rip off her clothes there and then. David and Beth were meant to be. Nothing was going to stop them now. Her heart was still beating wildly. She felt so happy and like the contented child she was not so very long ago. Oh, how much joy was inside of her! As for him he didn't care who saw them. Four hands were gently caressing each other on their faces and were ready to move downwards. "David! David!" Jennifer said as she came back outside calling him inside as Beth went red in the face. Reluctantly she moved herself away from David. All it took was for him to grab hold of any part of her body; to show her that he didn't care about the other woman, and Beth would be in heaven.

That evening as Beth was alone in her room and angry with herself in being scared of Jennifer, who had already slept behind both her back and David's with the Beast. She then heard what sounded like an envelope being posted underneath her bedroom door. In turn she lit up a candle. This was a matter of urgency for her.

My dearest Beth,

I am writing this in the candlelight and find myself being able to express myself much better now that we are living more like in the days of Wordsworth. I love you more than you will ever know. I regret that I hadn't forced you back into my arms when you escaped from me because of Jennifer. I simply didn't care what the others would have thought when our two hearts were beating as one. If only I had acted more proactively somewhat: when you gallantly warned me of Jennifer's arrival. I would have pounded you in front of the others since all of my senses where being focused on you and nothing else.

Her breath was taken away; she looked around in her room and had visions of running away with him. A warm glow went throughout the whole of her body. She then reread the beautiful paragraph, since she wanted to make sure that her eyes were in no way deceiving her, before reading on.

You think that you know me so well, but in reality, you don't. I am not so nice and sweet as you think I am. I am in fact a very weak and pathetic soul. I am living a big lie with Jennifer. She deserves better than this. I want to leave her right away. As soon as our child is delivered safely, I want to leave her and run off with you. I know I sound such a hypocrite, since I left you, when you yourself were with child. The problem dear is, she is carrying my own flesh and blood, and as the father of her child, I want to make sure that my son or daughter will enter this beautiful world safely.

How could she reproach him for being a responsible father to be? In short, she couldn't; but this last paragraph had dampened out all the amorous feelings she had as she felt so shaken and numb that their reunion wasn't imminent. As for the word, "safely", perhaps he meant, respectably, but didn't want to offend her.

Secretly I have been admiring your beautiful body. Oh, how I long so much for us to be reunited! I admire the way you go swimming daily. Your body is so heavenly. Six months waiting when we can be six decades together is a small price to pay for the dignity of my unborn child. As I am sure you will appreciate, I have no intention in having two women at the same time in the family way. Equally I cannot wait another twenty-six weeks before being able to kiss your heavenly body all over.

We have many things to plan, and I look forward to our secret swims together, as I will be at your call.

Love David.

Of course, she wanted to meet him at the tarn or the lake, but his words for her were in fact a thinly veiled message; that if she were pregnant with Roger a second time, that he would no longer want her. He seemed to be thinking too much about Jennifer as he wrote the letter too. Full of the importance of his own genetic code, he was in some ways no better a man than The Beast for her and knew nothing about unconditional love. After a few seconds of being disappointed with him she then thought about herself and wished that she was as pure as he believed she was when he first spoke to her. Until he found out she was carrying Roger's child: he was besotted with her. Trembling with fear she saw herself on some downward spiral. She wondered if she should simply run away and hide alone: where she could drown her broken heart in her tears of sorrow. As far as she was concerned, if David had made two women pregnant simultaneously, this would be a million times more appropriate than when The Beast had done such a thing. One man made her happy in both her heart and soul, while the other only excited her in the bed.

She then thought about when David said that six months is not long to wait. Oh, how she felt so differently, when living another day seemed one day too many for her. All she could hope was that since it was the end of the month; that the next one, July, would bring in happy days into her life. Feeling all of a sudden hungry; she ran downstairs, took out some homemade bread before wondering if it had gone off since it smelled somewhat queer, and feeling so tired she went back upstairs to bed.

The following day was the start of seventh month and the day she was due for her period, she breastfed William, had breakfast and left him with Sophie. She was also surprised that the bread which had gone off had been finished off by both Jennifer and Sophie, who were eating it as she first arrived at the dining room table. How could they have eaten such smelly and old dough? She wondered. She wanted to find out for herself without making any fuss whether she was with child or not. She then walked out to the lower ridge on the way to Tarn Foot with the view of Windermere. The sun was shining on her face she was deep in thought. She thought about Roger's pregnancy test and she was in no mood in giving him the same pleasure this time around. It was then that she fully understood the inevitable. Apart from feeling so sleepy, she felt nauseous, certain smells repulsed her and she felt so emotional.

She then ran back distressed to Fell End and to Roger as he was admiring the orchard whose apple and pear trees were doing nicely. "You got me knocked up again!" She said in tears.

"Don't worry; you look beautiful no matter what circumstance you are in. You will always look even more beautiful than in the painting."

"Is Sophie pregnant?" She said trying to dismiss his flattery.

"No, she isn't."

"Why is she not pregnant?"

"I saw getting you pregnant as a greater urgency with Erik coming. The first time we made love I got you pregnant. The first time we made love since you gave birth, I saw how quickly your body was getting ready for another precious baby of ours. My dreams came true again during these long hot days with the moon blessing our heavenly souls as we were enjoying our bodies together in perfect harmony without you asking me to ruin our bliss. As for Sophie, it is you who turns me on more!"

"So, you got me pregnant in case Erik is coming?" She said as she was trying to dismiss his beautiful, yet annoying words of wisdom to her.

"Yes, I did." He said smiling and looking very proud of himself.

"As for the bliss, you mean in getting me pregnant?"

"Yes dear."

She didn't know how to respond. He was in her eyes a terrible man, but he was much too strong for her mentally. He was her psychological abuser and somehow, she hoped that as the submissive one that eventually he would take pity on her. She could see from his eyes that in making her pregnant that he felt as though he was in paradise. He had taken advantage of her yet again and she wasn't going to allow him to penetrate her ever again. Maybe he would love her the way she wanted if she gave him a chance. He had such powerful feelings of lust for her and surely, he needed her as much as she needed him. "Please Roger, let me live with you as your wife!"

"That wouldn't be fair on Sophie would it?"

"Then I might have to kill myself, in fact the tenderest thing you could do to me right now is to put me out of my misery!" She said hoping that he would save her. Instead, Roger then ran off to Sophie as Beth was getting on his nerves. His behavior shook her to the core as she then decided against seducing David. She had lost all confidence within herself. Maybe all she could do was to look after her physical health and not worry about her depression and to have no more amorous feelings of love.

As far as Roger was concerned, Beth was a moaner who was always feeling sorry for herself. The only feelings that mattered were those of his own. Women were meant to be more compassionate and sensitive than men. These were some of the reasons why he was a feminist. If he wanted to discuss things on his mind there was Beth. She had listened about his confusion for hours on end before she gave birth, now she seemed preoccupied with her son and he didn't feel relaxed in telling her about his feelings so much as before. Simply put, he was trying to deal with his mental issues himself and couldn't deal with her own personal problems too. He also believed that instead of acting like some poor baby, that Beth had to understand as his mother had told him, "we come into this world alone and we leave this world alone."

On top of that, no woman could help him either. Since he didn't know what he really wanted; he couldn't really love a woman. Often, before he met Beth, he thought that his biggest problem in finding a woman lay in his personal interests. In France, it wasn't so easy to find a woman who loved the Lake District, like he did: a woman who loved cycling, swimming and walking as well as fine cuisine. While Lyla and Hannah were of this persuasion, at the time he wasn't ready for their love. Maybe he was with Linda, but that was a short-term romance. As for Beth, she loved all the things he did; she had given up her roots for him and left her beloved family behind back in Warsaw for a new life with him. If only he could control his perversions, which he knew Beth didn't fancy. If only she would follow him since one of them had to submit to the sexual desires of the other. Once again, he wondered what had gone wrong, and was convinced that from the former days of consumerism that the human race was beyond repair. In his world all people were fucked up and those who said otherwise were simply nothing more than lying bastards.

A few minutes later and feeling dazed and confused, Beth went into a corner of the garden and was crying buckets of tears. Once again, he put her one step nearer into being a dowdy mother earth figure. With David, Jan or Erik and bearing children in faithful wedlock, she would have felt like some beautiful and sexy wife, instead she felt like a fallen woman. Suddenly she felt a soothing but firm arm over her shoulder. As she looked up and saw him, she jumped in fright. "Beth, when you fell pregnant the first time, I was deliriously happy, and I want us to repeat the magic that we had the first time around." He said feeling very guilty about his current treatment towards her.

"And you are so much in ecstasy because you had got two stupid teenage girls pregnant!"

"No dear, I came here to tell you beautiful things. I came here to tell you that I never expected that getting you pregnant a second time would mean so much to me. Your hair is beautiful. Your eyes are so lovely. You haven't lost the innocence in your face or the allure of your lips. It is moments like these that I wish that time would stand forever still. I love you so much!" He then placed his hands onto her waist. She wanted to look at Facebook or to swim in the tarn anything was better than this mess and being right by his unwelcome side.

There was no technology, she was too tired to exercise non-stop. With nothing else to do with her life she could only submit to the beast. He then took off her top. She wasn't wearing a bra and immediately he started suckling her breasts. She was enjoying it, he was enjoying it too, but he wasn't being aroused as much as he wanted to be. His distraction was that he imagined that they were in bed together. In fact, that wasn't the only distraction. As she was enjoying feeding him with her milk, he was vividly seeing in the serene beauty of his imagination that he was a baby girl. Knowing that she judged him by his potency, he was concerned with his image. He then; imagined that she was a pregnant transgender man, so that he would be able to satisfy her. Suddenly he was ready to go. She too was more than ready to go.

After making love she looked at him. "If you could, how many women would you have living with you at Fell End?"

"I would turn David into a woman if I could. Then I could be a man of all seasons. You would be my: autumn fruits, Sophie my winter warmth, David my spring flowers and Jennifer my summer breeze."

"So, you mean you want a woman for all of the four seasons?"

"Maybe, what I mean is that every three months one of you would be impregnated by me and one of you would rest for three months, like that of a fallow field. This would all be a part of a sustainable and loving cycle.

That was what I meant in me being a man of all seasons." His answer had neutralised any feelings of repulsion she had for him, as she respected him once again as a real alpha male. He had homed in his honesty inside that of her mind. Basically, she was too tired to think about him being of a moral persuasion and didn't care since she could always end her life at any given moment. His mind went back to Rebecca. When he said David, he had been thinking of her, but was too scared to make Beth more jealous than ever. By then, she had got used to his gender confusion and so David's name was the safer option. Then was not the time to discuss his gender dysphoria or his other desire in becoming a mask wearing cyborg. At times he hated himself so much, he would feel safer if people couldn't determine the expression on his face, and it was times like these when he wished he had a collection of sex dolls.

Deep down, she saw him as a twisted and bitter megalomaniac. She knew of no human being worse than him. She also sensed that he wasn't so interested in being a father since apart from the day when they went to the tarn together and he appeared to be the doting father of her son, he hardly bothered with William. Equally, she took her family views seriously. She also felt that with her mind elsewhere on David; that she herself wasn't so pure as the impression she wanted to give to the others at Fell End. No matter what, she would always put herself down instead of standing up for herself and in turn this belle was always ready to forgive The Beast.

Could things get better for Roger? He didn't think that they could. The fact that no one came round looking for his babies made him smile. He was sure that the men he was meant to contact so that they could buy his babies off him; had died. He was trying his best in being a straight male and felt that; Beth's news was heralding great tidings for him. He hadn't seen Richard since the Tsunami, and in turn he started gloating about the deaths of those who could have made his life one of sadness. He had to somehow appreciate his children from both mothers and somehow learn to be a good father. He then almost burst out laughing as he thought about the contacts, he was meant to hand over his babies to. One was a transgender woman and a former Liberal Member of the European Parliament. The other was a former BBC Presenter who wanted to bring up children with his husband. It was with these deaths on his mind that he believed that his conversion to being a traditional gentleman had saved him. At least he hadn't worried the mothers of his children about the fact that Illuminati wanted them to produce many babies and to hand them over to the VIP men.

As for his baby from one of the cottages at Tarn Foot who had died during the tsunami it was living proof for him that he had to make as many babies as possible in order to guarantee him leaving a pronounced mark on the planet with his posterity. He was also relieved that the girls hadn't spoken about the waitress too. He didn't want to be reminded with the fact that there were times when he wished he could swap Sophie just so that he could have a night with the deceased waitress whom he would never see alive again.

During the next few days, she felt dazed and confused. How her life could have been so different. Shivers went through her spine daily as she thought about how on the first week of July the previous year, Jan would die, and she would meet Alan as he was then known. Then she was a virgin, and now she was with child for the second time. How could he have knocked her up again just two months after she gave birth?

As for Rebecca, like a historian reading about the Great Plague of London, he wanted to ask David about the corpse he had orgasmed over but was too scared in doing so.

Chapter 5

TORN BETWEEN TWO HELLS

She had recently taken up with running, but with so many things on her mind she gave it up. Walking down towards the tarn, just over a week since she found out she with child, Beth was thinking about how she was now as terrified of David as she had been of Roger around the same time last year. While she was scared of losing her virginity from Roger back then, this was nothing compared to the trauma of being a second time pregnant to him. Still madly in love with David, she was feeling emotionally weaker than ever. How much she loved him, but equally how scared she was of him breaking her broken fragile heart even further. David didn't fight back when she needed him most; his unwelcome silence spoke volumes to her. At least Erik would accept her the way she was, if and when he came back into her tempestuous life. In short, it was David, who was scaring her the most. While she could block him out of her mind, she knew all too well that subconsciously he had got right underneath her skin.

As she got inside the water; she felt calm. No one was around and all was peaceful so that she could ponder. As usual she enjoyed being in the water despite her morbid sadness. As she was heading towards the southern side, she saw a man running towards the tarn. She continued swimming around the waters as if he wasn't there. Even so, she couldn't help but notice that he was heading towards her. He was just seventy yards in front of her, on the banks of the tarn. She was in awe, who was this gent? Not many handsome looking men were around since the floods. Very quickly he stripped off and got into the water and swam. Her heartbeat was pounding. She refused to look at him and had nothing at all whatsoever to say to him as she was feeling both scared of her feelings of dignity and her desire for him. She decided to swim as if he wasn't there. This meant she could neither swim to him deliberately nor swim away from him on purpose.

All he could do was show her that he was a good swimmer as he couldn't take his eyes off her. For him it was such a crime that; as a father to be to someone else, here in such a beautiful place that in his eyes he felt as though he had been touched by the hands of God, since he was swimming next to such a beautiful woman. All he could do was think about the days he worked at the Wordsworth Trust and felt that his life back then was a dress rehearsal. Now he was living a life more akin than ever to that of The Lake District poets. Southey was a man of probity, where did that get him, apart from ending up with a woman who was insane? Wordsworth had a rock-solid marriage, but the grim reaper stole too many of his small children. What was the purpose of life if he wasn't happy? Only Beth could make his life one of joy.

Very soon he would tire, stop getting on her nerves and leave her alone in the water. While she no longer felt that her body was hers alone: nobody had the right to stop her from taking her own life. She had only wanted to swim one circumference around of the tarn, but she continued because he was simply getting on her nerves. He was still there after she had swum her second lap, and she was determined that she wouldn't leave the water before him. Strangely she had gone from being very sad to very angry. After her second lap he was still there: and she was tired. All she could do was to carry on. In total she had swum three laps around the small mountain lake and nearly two miles in the eerie silence. He had swum two and a half rounds of the tarn. He was simply happy to be with her and together they got out of the water.

With her suicidal thoughts put on her hold thanks to her long swim she was reeling with David. Nobody had the right to stop her from taking her own life. He looked at her. "I said hello, but you didn't reply."

"I cannot talk and swim at the same time." She said.

"We didn't have any problem talking and swimming together last year." He said to her with good grace.

"I am not in the mood for speaking." She said thinking about how his last sentence was complete nonsense since back then they were a loving item together while now she simply felt masked from his presence that was in turn making her breathing difficult.

They got out of the water and she made sure that her legs were tightly closed and that he wouldn't be able to see her sensitive parts. Shyly after she had dressed herself, she was sitting as if she was some frightened maiden. She had her shorts on and was scared that the naked skin around her legs was more than enough to ignite his carnal desires that he had for her when he first spoke to her. He then tried to touch her gently. "No David, don't touch me!" She cried hysterically.

"Beth what has got inside of you?" He said wanting her to start a new life with him.

"He got inside of me and now I'm fucking pregnant again!" She cried. All she wanted was for him to ignore her speech. To simply grab hold of her and show her how much her body meant to him.

Time stood still between them both. He was angry with himself; she had given him an opportunity recently to make love to her, but he was too scared of being unfaithful to his pregnant partner with a woman who had got herself into a mess for a second time as his presence had made a bigger and more complicated mess in her mind. "Oh my God! If only you had waited!" He said without thinking about the consequences of his painful words, when suddenly he remembered that he was also a father in waiting. She then had tears running down her face.

"If only this were your baby." She murmured.

"If only!" He whispered as his desire for her was flowing back once more since he knew of no woman as feminine as she and was getting over her shocking news.

"So, you don't want me now, do you?" She cried raising her voice.

"I do, I do, and this time it is going to be real." He said as his mind was in turmoil and getting over the shock that she wasn't pregnant to him, when things could have been very different.

"No, no, no, David I am suicidal. Last time you said it was going to be real you bought me a maternity dress, I had dreams of having children with you, but then you dumped me a week later. I almost died from a broken heart."

In turn he looked at her meekly. "We have to wait until Jennifer gives birth." He said dolefully.

"I have to wait forever for you! There will always be a reason for you to break my stupid heart that still loves you, David! Nothing you say will take my mind away from the fact that you are disappointed with my condition." He then tried to kiss her again. "Leave her and then we can be together!" She said before running off with him following her.

"Beth, just give me six months, like I said in the letter." Suddenly she started screaming at him. David had never seen her behave in such a tetchy manner. Jennifer would never carry out such a churlish act. In an instant, he was scared of her. He knew that he was pushing her to the limit, but he had to do the right thing for his child. Also, if she could act in such a feral manner, he was scared that behind closed doors the energy of her voice could be turned towards her hands and she could simply strike him in his sleep, and he would die. "Beth, please stop screaming at me as if you are some petulant child."

"You don't own me! To think that my love for you is sending me to the depths of despair that makes the instant deaths of the corpses recently look like some holiday as opposed to my tears of sorrow when all I can think about is what could have been with you!" She said full of tears, as her screams turned to more benevolent crying.

"Beth, what would you do if you were me?" He asked her desperately as he was looking shaken.

"David, Roger takes the lead on so many things concerning me, I wish you were strong enough to save me from him! You dumped me for being pregnant, and had you taken the bull by the horns, I would not be expecting a second time to The Beast and you would want me!" With that David was shaken and they walked off in silence over the lower slope of the fell.

He then looked at her; he couldn't control his confused feelings of love for her. "Beth, let us spend the night together at The Howe, please ask Roger to lend you the key."

"Why do you want me to do this?" She asked as she was breaking inside and desperate for his unconditional love.

"I want us to see how things go between us."

"Am I right in my understanding, you want to try me out and then decide whether or not you want me? No David, you must leave her first before you can take me and in turn, I will be yours." Inside he too was breaking. With them both carrying so much baggage, he was no longer sure if things could work out between them both and felt that his request was a reasonable one of his. Due to her embarrassing act when she was screaming at him; she was eating humble pie and gave in to his demand. Her mind went back to when she entered a competition at school to see who had the loudest voice, and she won! Back then it was funny, but now she was more than just a trifle ashamed because of her shrills.

They arrived at The Howe after collecting the key without any fuss, since Roger was happy that David was cheating behind Jennifer's back. In her former bedroom, Beth was looking forward to him satiating her. She took off her clothes while David was waiting downstairs. She looked at herself in the mirror, she was sure that this was how her body more or less looked the first time she saw him. That was the time when he should have made love to her and before The Beast had set his eyes on her and let alone entered her. She then got dressed into a dress Roger had had sent over from France, for her, along with a semi veil, that gave her more than just the look of a good country and well to do Christian girl from the eighteenth century. She had never worn this outfit for anyone before. It had arrived too late, and the day after she found out that she lost her virginity under less than sacred conditions. After the flood she left it at The Howe for good luck. Recently on a visit, she came with some washing powder and washed it along with the rest of her clothes there, in the beck, allowed them to dry before placing them back on the shelves. Downstairs she looked at David. "I am tired will you join me upstairs?" She said sweetly to him and waiting for him to tell her how beautiful she looked, as all she could hear was Roger ringing in her head as he was in awe of her lips.

"Of course, I will darling." Said David as he then followed her upstairs.

There was no doubt at all that they both badly wanted each other. Even so, he had hurt her, and she needed to know that she could trust him. "I love you so much, but I don't know if I can trust you.' She said as David looked at her dolefully. "Please speak to me, my love." Her request was a reasonable one, but he was scared of her. He had never seen such beauty in a woman before and felt as though she was out of reach. All she could hope was that her Christian clothes like those from the days of old; would melt the ice inside of him, before she would hate him forever.

"I am sorry Beth; I understand every word that you say. I don't know how I can answer you, but it is breaking my own heart as much as that of yours." He said to her enormous dismay.

"How can you behave so priggish?" She asked as he decided to remain silent. As much as he loved her, she was no longer the perfect girl he first saw in his mind when they first met at Grasmere. Her innocent looks and beauty were deceptively hiding the fact that she had been bringing into the world a bastard. Yes, she was a victim, but there were times when he couldn't cope with the fact that he was with Jennifer, loved Beth and the easiest way out was for him to think of her as some stupid slut. How could she at the age of eighteen have involved herself with him? How could she when she knew only too well how much he loved her, could she have ended up in trouble with the Beast again? "I am sorry David." She said when in fact she was begging for his love.

"That bastard, he is like some petulant child, that's how he gets away with murder! Everyone feel sorry for him, and I wish he had never been born!"

"How can you behave in such a sanctimonious manner?" He said.

"I am sorry."

"I am sorry too that I am lying next to such a cold fish who can only fall in love with someone who is perfect. You might as well make love to a corpse; at least those bodies have stopped with their sinning."

That night neither of The Howe's former Romeo and Juliet could sleep. She had gone there against her will. She didn't want to be touched by him. All she could see was Roger's slimy grin as he wanted to imply that David was weak and up to no good. Both were thinking about how the goalposts were being moved. He dumped her for being pregnant to Roger. He then got over her love child, wanted her and then found out that she was expecting again to his foe. Now he needed more time to get over this. Both were wondering what repercussions would follow. On top of that, he was a father in waiting with someone else.

As soon as the early dawn arrived, David who hadn't been getting any pleasure from Beth fled The Howe and went back to Fell End. A few hours later a heartbroken Beth was with Roger in the garden.

"Roger, please don't tell anyone that I am carrying your child, I mean Erik will be back, won't he? You said he would."

"I am not looking forward to his return. I will miss your body so much and have to think more and more about you while making love to Sophie."

"Roger, I need a man every night in my bed."

"I will make a deal with you."

"If we make love once a week during your pregnancy when and if he returns, I will keep mum on this."

"No, Roger this is not fair."

"Life is not fair; I love you so much Beth."

"You are a pervert Roger!" She said as she terrified of him.

"No Beth, I was a pervert. I was a part of the depopulation agenda. We encouraged women to have abortions and spoke about the dangers of falling pregnant. We also wanted girls to have their wombs ripped out. Those dark days are behind us. Nature has taken over and it is normal for a man to make his woman pregnant, to love and cherish her body as she gets back into shape and for her to fall pregnant again and again and again with him. Look at history, pregnant women were worshipped by men, many old statues were dedicated to women just like you. We have no freewill and I will make you pregnant again!" He said to her as shivers running through her spine.

"But Roger, if you had your eyes for me only, they to be sharing what we are producing together would have been so beautiful. All I wanted was a man to love and to protect me, not someone who would have shared my body, without my knowledge, all over the Internet. To have been alone with you, in every sense of the word, would have made our lovemaking one of heaven." He then grabbed a hold of her face with his hands. "I don't want this." She said. He then moved them to her belly, and she felt as though she had a fluttering. Of course, it was too soon for that, but his touch reminded her about her impending fate. Maybe once showing, Erik would have by then found someone else, how much longer could she wait for him anyway? He then started to kiss her face. She could smell the sweat and the smells from his previous conquest a few hours earlier. She knew that he had made love to Sophie; she recognized this nauseating aroma from the first time that she was pregnant. Now she felt as though she was drowning and couldn't breathe, as all she could imagine was that prophetic painting of her looking heavily in the family way for the third time was coming closer to reality. On top of that she was still in distress thanks to David. More than ever: she felt so used and unwanted. Equally she was still suffering from post-traumatic stress from the tidal wave, the death of her parents and not to mention her own personal situation. If she wanted to entice him, she had to remain positive, and hopefully he would make an honest woman out of her now that he was expecting a second child with her. And so, it was, although she was seriously thinking about her demise, although she wasn't in any way in the mood to make love, she did. For her children to be brought up in a traditional nuclear home, she would suffer the humiliation from his using of her, so long all as would end well.

On top it all, she expected David to be an honorable gentleman with her, but he had created a greater humiliation for herself even more than any she had encountered with The Beast. Love was more important for her than hate. She loved David, and one unwelcome word from him, wounded her as much as a thousand slaps across the face from the man who was simply a sick and deranged pervert for her. Roger would never slap her across her face, but she believed that she deserved this for being so stupid. What a humiliation for her it was that in the eyes of both men, she was a loving and seductive second best.

Back at home it was her turn for a lonely night, The Beast was with her sister, and she cried herself to sleep almost incessantly. All of her beauty was being wasted. There she was, like a rose but was surrounded by so many thorns. So, traumatised by what she saw as her stupidity she simply saw herself as being jinxed. Yes, she believed that modern life was degenerate, but equally she was sure that even two hundred years earlier a woman like herself would have made the same mistakes back then.

The following day, everything was going to plan. She left her baby sleeping. Sophie was around as usual nursing her own baby, and she had asked her sibling to keep an eye on her son. As she left the suffocating atmosphere of her home, she looked at the beauty around her. There couldn't be a more delightful place to end one's life she felt. She then looked up towards the crags and believed that she had planned everything smoothly. Life was so surreal. She was one in a million in every sense of the word. All she had to do was to imagine Warsaw. How many women there; were more beautiful, and living in a more pristine environment than she was? Of course, no one else, like all the other women, the beauties perished along with her parents. The thought that her luck was greater to when someone had won the national lottery made her so angry. How could she feel blessed for her good health, her healthy and beautiful child, her good life in the Lakes, when all that she wanted was love?

Planning her own death was more efficient for her than planning her own beautiful world. Being a good girl had failed her miserably. Had she cheated on Roger, she might now be carrying David's child and not Roger's. Instead, doing the right thing and trying to be bring up her child in a nuclear family had got her right into this mess. On top of that she wanted to stab herself for being so stupid. David loved her, he seemed willing to accept her with one of Roger's babies but believed that he would never in a million years accept her in the condition she was in then. He knew she was pregnant again, and he dumped her last time on finding out. She had had enough and had to get him out of her head. All he wanted was to play on her mind with his games. He would make love to her if she begged him to, and out of spite dump her for being with child to someone else. He was nothing but a cruel and heartless bastard for her. If only she could be in love with Erik, the only one of her lovers, who had never done anything bad to her, apart from not be there for her, just when she needed him most. Equally like Jan, another decent man, no other woman truly wanted him either. "Oh, Erik please save me! Come to me!" She screamed in her silent and vivid thoughts.

She wanted to tear out her hair out of spite and because of her beauty. Instead to calm herself down she started walking towards the tarn. David ran after her. As he arrived, she was delighted. After a few minutes of them walking together without either of them uttering a word, she was feeling depressed once more as her hormones, all too poignantly of a pregnant kind, were running wildly. As they reached the tarn's shore and were still walking, she then began. "Sometimes I don't care if you were to drown me. I try to lose myself in these very waters but there are times when I feel as though the pain you are giving me is pushing me down towards the tarn's bed. I try with all of my might to deaden my feelings so that I can swim like some machine. I had so many dreams; to have a family with a man who loves me. Oh David! Don't you see how beautiful it is here, yet at the same time the bad luck I am having denotes to me that I am in the wrong place yet still alive. Sometimes I am breathless and want to give up, but I am scared of dying. All I can do is breathe and hope that I will die peacefully in my sleep. Sometimes I forget about everything and can have a beautiful dream. I can wake up happily listening to the sounds of the birds singing, but as I think about you, your cruelty, my dream for the day has ended. I then start my miserable day again. This is my life! I simply can't go on like this. All because I want a one woman, man. I crave for someone to care about me and to be the head of the household with his patriarchal love."

David then looked at her, fell to the ground and Beth was worried about him. He cared about her after all. Her hopes had been raised. She needed to reassure him that they were made for each other. His pain was her gain. He loved her after all. Instead, he started crying like a girl or a child but not like that of a real man. His voice went high pitched. "I am sorry, I am sorry!" He said sounding as though he was pleading for her forgiveness. All he did was to make her feel more masculine than him and she walked off to the tarn in disgust. She swam around the tarn and imagined that he was a girl and was relieved not to be carrying his child. As she arrived back, he was still there, annoyingly for her. His eyes were red and his face so soft and gentle. He was nothing like the rustic hodge she desired from a man who was in her mind a true Lakeland man. On top of that she was disappointed that he hadn't joined her for a swim. He was even worse than Roger for her. As they walked back, he was one step behind her, as if he was the Grim Reaper, as she felt as though she could be just a heartbeat away from death.

Back at Fell End, another meeting was held. Finding a sheep was more difficult than they had envisaged. They wanted a clean and tame ewe. Suddenly a vision of himself sketching Beth breastfeeding a lamb came to his mind. "Beth, lambs are cute."

"Yes, they are."

"They are friendlier and easier to control. What if you breastfeed one? After a few weeks we will have all of our grass problems solved." Beth didn't know what to do. Although she no longer wanted to be the submissive slave who was aiding and abetting his perversion, she was scared of a having a garden without any grass. There would still be endless weeding to do. She wanted instead to be swallowed up and to be placed somewhere else and in the arms of a real man, if as far as she was concerned, he still existed.

"If I have to mow the lawn with my bear hands, I will, then instead for one of our residents to be placed in such shame!" Jennifer said.

"Eventually we will find a sheep." David added. Beth was shaken. Roger was crazy, but at least Jennifer had stood up for her and David had shown her once more that he was a wimp.

That evening, Roger's mind went back to his macabre thoughts. He then thought about how he planned to rape Beth if she would leave him after giving birth. This would be an act of kindness from him, since he had the best genetic code. All he wanted was to impregnate her again and again and that she would kill him so that his deathly wish would come true.

He thought a little more and too deeply than he wanted. He then came to the conclusion that, premeditating these events and given he was relying on an unwitting partner, things might not turn out the way as he intended. He then thought about how successful he was when he was spontaneous. He trusted Lucifer willing, that his dream would finally and once and for all come true for him.

Together Beth and Roger were in his bed. It was Sophie's turn to brood. She had woken up before him and was staring at the beautiful but poignantly prophetic paintings of what she believed more and more to be herself. Roger woke up. He held her hand went up to her in a spooning position and placed his left hand on her belly. Both of them dozed off to sleep together. "I wish it were just the two of us living here." He said as they both left the land of nod again. As for Beth she was certain that she was going to have a beautiful day with him.

"I want us to have a pleasant day, but first I just want you to honestly tell me that you really think that the tsunamis were the best way to have culled the masses?"

"What difference does it make? You are never going to understand this humanitarian agenda, are you?"

"Just try me." She said.

"When my mother was a child, which is a very long time ago, there was a plan to reduce the population. The idea was to free women from the shackles of childbirth. Instead, we saw an explosion of single mothers with loads of kids. That didn't work. We were doing this in the interests of the people. We then wanted to homosexualize the masses, but all we saw was a gay parenting explosion. True, we encouraged sex changes, but stupid governments were banning this. So then, we had one more card to play." He then paused. "Go on tell me."

"The race card: we brought in millions of immigrants who hated the west. All we wanted was for the race riots to kill of millions of people in the cities. Sadly, that didn't work." He said as Beth looked at him in shock. She then gulped. He then tried to kiss her, but she turned her head away and burst into tears.

"And the viruses." She said as he started shaking. "David and I saw a science fiction film about some top medical scientists who deliberately let out a deadly virus. They kept it quiet for a few months, and once the epidemic had taken root, they simply locked the people up under house arrest. They were forced to wear masks. Many died from suffocation caused by hypoxia. The suicide rate was fuelled. In many countries people were starving to death in their millions because they weren't allowed to work, and the crops failed. They were then vaccinated the survivors and basically all the masses were sterilised. Finally, that wasn't enough for the evil agenda. The masses had nanobots inside their bodies and the government spied on their minds. Like a switch on a remote control, along with the metals inside of their bodies, a powerful transmitter could simply cook them to death with its emissions if they thought the wrong thing." She said as he had thoughts about Stalin and Saddam Hussein.

"Never, never never mention this again! If anyone hears this, they will kill you on the spot!"

"But you said your fucking bosses are dead anyway."

"Yes, that's right, just as with my hero Hitler, things didn't go to plan!"

"How can you saw this when you know about my ancestry?"

"I am sorry. I just wish that I had never been born!" He then burst out crying, leaving Beth shaken and numb with everything. The last thing he wanted was for David to know how evil he was. As for Beth, yes, she hated him, but equally, she needed him to look after her. As a part of the elite, she was granted extra privileges. Unlike the masses she had survived, and unlike the ordinary survivors, she was still living in a life of opulence.

She then left the room, prayed, and begged the Virgin Mary for forgiveness. Just as she had finished in trying to atone herself, he appeared. "It had all been written in stone. Drowning is not a pleasant way to die, I know. Still, it is much better than in putting the masses on death row for twelve solid years from say 2018 until 2030 when they hoped to have gradually reduced the population to half a billion. Life on death row is never a happy experience. You know about beheadings, mass executions etc. If I were you, I would be thankful that you have got this far. Please don't rock the boat." He pleaded. As for Beth, what was the point in protesting anyway? All the people she wanted to save had died anyway. As for Roger, he felt that then was not the time to reveal his regret that cyborgs were unable to roam the earth. "The tsunamis were a quick and painless death for the masses."

He made breakfast when she was looking after William and brought the dish which he made with love into the bedroom: whole grain cereal with local berries and scrambled egg, tomatoes, onion, and bacon. He was taking the lead on making her happy and she was dreaming about a normal traditional family. "Darling, I would like us to go walking together with William and the beagles."

"I want the same as you." She said romantically as she was drinking the tea, he brewed for them both out of love.

After they got ready for their outing, Beth was enjoying walking through the English countryside which looked day by day more like that she imagined from the books she had read from a bygone era. The silence between them both was beautiful, but for her somewhat strange, since normally Roger would never shut up throughout certain periods of the day and would basically keep on repeating himself with his monologues which were all about his confusion, his abstract desires he had for them both as well as about his unfortunate background. Poor Beth, all she wanted was to be in heart, mind and soul with him. At least with him being quieter than usual she had some hope that he was a reformed man.

Together as they were sat at the water's edge and their baby was calm, Beth looked at him as he looked at her. She wanted to speak to him. Instead, he started to French kiss her. He was acting like a gentleman, but it was the wrong moment, she needed to talk to him.

Although she was enjoying the kissing, too many things were on her mind. "I don't feel nauseous with the kissing." She wanted to start of gently with him. She wasn't pregnant after all.

"I promise to look after you, and to make sure that you will feel less sick this time. Also, with you breastfeeding your mammary glands are already large enough. They will only grow more if you are expecting twins." He said, as it made no sense to her what he is saying but was equally unnerving for her, and she once again believed that she was expecting.

"You know I want us to live together."

"You know that I am often confused as to what I want."

"I do, and as a man you should know what you want."

"How can you say such a sexist thing?" He said provoked.

His response hit her like a bomb, but she had to remain calm if she wanted to win his love. "I am sorry Roger." She replied meekly.

"You should know better than this. You have read the novels from my collection. You know as well as I do; that in the days of old, it was the woman who simply wanted a man to take them."

"I spend too much time thinking. All I heard back in Poland was that women didn't know what they wanted, and that men did." She replied.

"As I said, this doesn't depend on what sex you are."

"I am sorry. I just want you to look after me."

"I have a love hate relationship with David." He said.

"What significance has this got for us?" she asked him.

"Everything, and had I not taken advantage of you, you would be with him. You know this Beth, but something brought us together. For some reason I believe that everything will work out well. I am still learning about myself. All I want is to be happy. I want to live, but if my past could be wiped out, and to be born again as yours and David's daughter that would be the perfect solution for me."

Beth was lost for words and finding his words sick beyond sick, she wasn't fully able to absorb the meaning of them. He knew that she wanted him to expand in more detail about this new revelation. "As my love rival, I hate him, but as my father and I his daughter I love him. I cannot imagine a more blissful scenario to be in and most importantly with you as my mother." He said to her as gently as his words were full of perversion and fantasy for her.

"Roger dear, this won't happen. Please make the most of everything. I need you to look after me and our children."

"I can't, I can't. I am not who you think I am! I am a sheep in a wolf's clothing!" Roger then started sobbing like a baby as she had her baby on her lap and was sat between his legs on the warm grass and felt him raining down on her with his grief. As for the beagles, who, were on this trip too, they started howling in grief and almost as if they were in tune with Roger.

Roger had ruined the outing for her.

After putting her genuine baby to bed, at Fell End, she fell asleep instantly. Her baby was neither Roger nor David though in many ways she felt as though she was their mother even though they were much older than her. In turn she was having crazy, wild, and scary dreams about Roger. She saw him slicing off her breasts and placing them onto his chest.

She saw herself slicing off his penis and sticking it between her legs. Suddenly she saw a sheep, which resembled David, dropping out of the sky in a sixty-nine position with Roger. The perversion was simply too much for her and she started screaming in her sleep.

As she woke up, she thought that she was dead. She thought that she was Roger, until suddenly with her mind playing tricks on her she thought she saw him making love to their son.

Her mind was clearly running out of control. The others were in a relationship. She was alone and pregnant and losing her mind. Fortunately, this was her last night. She had to kill herself before she would a die from a heart attack in a frightful nightmare at best or end up insane and to be cared for by someone even more disturbed than herself, Roger. She then calmed down. She would never be in the darkness again alone. She then realized that she wasn't alone, her child was with her in his cot and in turn she felt that she was a useless mother.

Miraculously for her, Roger came into her bed. Her suicidal thoughts were then put-on hold. He had heard her screams. She then felt calm lying next to a man. As she woke up, he was still there, all she could think about was the humble women who were living and married to wife beaters in the days of old. Men who put drink before their women. Like Roger, these men were traumatised. All they wanted was to come home to happy and submissive wives. Roger was in every way but one, better than all of these men. All he had to do was to stay with her. Maybe those poor examples of a man in the days of old knew what love was all about; since they were usually married until death do them part. After breakfast together they went with William in a sling to the tarn along with Roger's specially prepared lunch. Beth didn't say a thing. Roger sensed her black mood and had the sense to remain silent.

As they arrived; they both played with their son together. Beth even managed a smile. She then thought about her recent night at The Howe with David. They obviously had strong feelings for each other. The attraction was there, but equally the repulsion due to the consequences of the man lying next to her was also present. Suddenly she looked at him. "Sometimes I don't care if you were to drown me. I try to lose myself in these very waters but there are times when I feel as though the pain you are giving me is pushing me down towards the tarn's bed. I try with all of my might to deaden my feelings so that I can swim like some machine. I had so many dreams; to have a family with a man who loves me. Oh Roger! Don't you see how beautiful it is here, yet at the same time the bad luck I am having denotes to me that I am in the wrong place yet still alive. Sometimes I am breathless and want to give up, but I am scared of dying. All I can do is breathe and hope that I will die peacefully in my sleep. Sometimes I forget about everything and can have a beautiful dream. I can wake up happily listening to the sounds of the birds singing, but as I think about you, your cruelty, my dream for the day has ended. I then start my miserable day again. This is my life! I simply can't go on like this. All because I want a one woman, man someone to care about me and to be the head of the household with his patriarchal love." She said as she wanted to fall into his arms or better still for him to take her into his arms.

"If I didn't know you, I would say that you are autistic." His words struck her like that of an unwelcome cut. He then waited for her to respond. He had nothing more to say.

"What the hell does that mean?"

"You have read this over and over again in your mind and whatever you wanted to tell me has lost its resonance in the monotony of your nauseating words." He said to her.

In turn they had nothing more to say to each other. Then, she closed her eyes started sobbing, and saw herself sandwiched between Roger dressed as the devil and David draped as a woman, with her sister looking down imperviously at her from the sky above. From his response she wrongly believed that the three most important people in her lives, Sophie, Roger and David had been speaking behind her back about her. She had simply had enough. The rest of the day she functioned like a robot and was stunned from the fact that; The Beast didn't seem to care whether she was dead or alive.

In their bed she had to humiliate him somehow. She put her baby in bed. He then started to caress her. "Please don't! I don't want to be touched by you." His touch was welcome, but she felt no respect from him towards her.

"Why dear? Don't you enjoy our lovemaking?"

"Knowing that I am autistic in your eyes I have no desire for you."

"But I want you more than ever!"

"OK, in your eyes I am merely your slave. Fine, I will do my duties and be screwed by you. I feel emotionless but if you still need your sex just quickly get it over with." She said feeling sure that Roger would be upset from her sharp words. As he was taking off his clothes impatiently and breathing heavily from excitement, she was feeling sick inside. She had every right to say that she had changed her mind but was instead curious as she was learning more about this troubled man.

As soon as he was ready, Roger was delighted. No feelings, no emotions all he had to worry about was himself climaxing inside of her. Her hole was clean, like that of his hands after he washed them with soap and cupped them around his tool. With her being so young and tender she wasn't dry, and Roger was pleased that he wasn't with Hannah after all. Then just over forty, Hannah would be too dry for him if she didn't want him. After he had done what he wanted with his young and wet lady she was already fast asleep and oblivious to the world around her. With that he then wondered if that was a woman's place in the world: to simply be there at her husband's command and to be conquered by her master as she was his servant of love. If then that was what life was all about, why couldn't he be Beth herself and David be his man?

That day after, he made love to her in what was a normal way between two lovers, and after it, he prayed and prayed as he was holding her body that his spirit mind and soul could move into her body and that she could move into David's. He strongly believed that a lot of his anger and confusion was as a result of him being born as a man. His mind was made up; as soon as Beth woke up, he was going to dress up as a woman and she could be as manly as she wanted as he would be her submissive queen.

While sex change operations were no longer available on the NHS, Roger believed in mind over matter. If fish and amphibians could change sex, then so could he and his love.

Daylight came, his hands were no longer on her body; he then moved his arms around the body but was unable to reach out to her. In turn he started sobbing. She had walked out on him and left him alone in his bed and he felt so rejected and had suicidal thoughts. His life was no longer worth living. His hopes to become Beth's submissive belle were one of an elusive dream.

As far as Beth was concerned, she wasn't a snowflake. Her mind went back to stories she had been told from a visitor, a nurse, to the tarn about swimming baths along the Fylde Coast, whom she had first met along the sea front at Fleetwood. At one of the pools there was alarm. Some people thought that a terrorist bomb had hit the building as the lifeguards were seen in a panic. All that had happened was that a child had vomited in the water and for that reason; the pool was closed for the rest of the afternoon and evening. At another pool, the temperatures were around twenty-five degrees in the water and so this pool was closed for several days until temperatures were around thirty. The nurse pointed out that when before Beth was born, Derby baths had temperatures around nineteen degrees and people went there to swim only and not to stand around talking as though that they were sat in a cafe. The worst was when the nurse told her that her skin had been damaged due to too much chlorine in the water, but that she needed to swim to prevent her body from seizing up. She was horrified that her local pool was closed for a week due to the fact that level of chlorine in the water wasn't meeting health and safety requirements.

For Beth, family values had been replaced with hypochondria and wholesome people like herself, were simply the new underclass. Prior to the tsunami she had never thought about this; but now as she looked back and saw how people were acting around her when the living was easy, and how cruel the people around her were then, she had simply had enough of human beings. She had simply had enough of life in general. What life was it for anyone to be working in the pits all day, and to die from emphysema? What about those gallant and brave men who had died in vain; building the railway line that saved the lives of others from sinking in the sands around the Morecambe Bay? Both deeds ended in tears. Where was the National Grid, where was British Rail? They were just simply dead and buried, like everything else, thanks to the tsunami

As for Roger, he was content with his life. With Beth being at his mercy, he wanted to wear a dress, so that Beth would understand what it was like to be making love to a woman. Somehow, he had to bring out the masculine side out of her.

Chapter 6

A CORPSE REBIRTH

Beth simply felt that, whenever her mind was focused on Roger and then in turn on David, as though she was torn between two hells. If it weren't for her child relying on her milk, she wouldn't have taken her very last breakfast. Poor Beth, her head was spinning out of control. She didn't really want to kill herself; it was simply that she saw no other way in ending what she perceived to be a dark energy that was engulfing and hurting her so much psychologically. At times she wondered if Roger deep down hated her with a deadly poison that he wasn't even aware of. There were also times when, she wondered all too often if David was as weak as a snowflake. As positive as she was by nature, the emotional environment around her was bleak. Seeing no end to her misery, she had to take the bull by the horns, and die. At least she had no pregnancy symptoms; so, either she had miscarried or lost her baby. Either way it didn't matter, at least she wouldn't be murdering her unborn child.

As she left Fell End for the last time, she felt as though she was Jesus and carrying a heavy cross on her back. It was heart-breaking, she was now in so much physical pain from her fragile nerves and saw visions in her mind of Jesus walking to his death as she looked up to the sky above. "Oh Lord Jesus, please have pity on me, I am in so much physical pain!" Her plea was promptly answered like magic as the pains throughout her body were gone, but still her morbid depression remained. What a poignant end to her life. Bang in the middle of July, the weather was fair, and it being St. Swithin's day this heralded according to folklore, forty more days of fine summer's days. What a pity she wouldn't live to see those days.

Walking up towards the top of Loughrigg she knew that her final vision would be that of Loughrigg Terrace. What a beautiful end, with thoughts of Wordsworth on her mind as she would be walking as lonely as a cloud towards her ignominious demise. There she would jump to her death and maybe end up in Grasmere Lake. The first time she came here she felt on top of the world. Still devoid of a nasty streak in her soul, even as she had hit rock bottom psychologically, she wasn't going to involve others in her farewell. She wasn't Roger and there weren't many people left either to die with her anyway. Everything was simply too much for her. If she were here in winter and walking during a storm, seeing nobody around it would have soothed her. It was though, high summer and wherever she looked the place was verily of one of solace. She then wondered what kind of Christian she was. If she was a true follower of God, she would believe that she had everything and that she wouldn't be feeling mortally lonely as she was. As she continued heading up towards the summit, she spotted a dead man. He was lying among the ferns and close to a stream. It was an incongruous sight. While she had seen many dead bodies, this one was above the flood level. She then continued on her way. Feeling guilty she wanted to carry out one final act of kindness and decided to walk back to the corpse. Maybe she could give him a makeshift funeral for the two of them together, and without any fuss, since nobody cared about her anyway. The question was thus, how would she arrange their burial? Still undecided about how she would die, the corpse would have to wait for her. Together these lonely skeletons would end up as carcasses in a kind of deathly matrimony. Lying next to this man forever, would at least tie them to some unity. Whatever that meant she had no idea, but it was better than in being alone.

As she arrived back at the scene of the deceased, she noticed that his head was covered inside of his jacket. She then shed a tear as she was thinking about how he tried to keep himself warm before he must have frozen to death. Surely, he was an innocent unfortunate who died all alone, with no one around who cared or even knew that he existed. She then took his left hand, and it was still warm. He must have died just before she arrived. She then had another thought, perhaps he had died just after her first encounter with him and before she returned. In turn she was thinking about nothing other than that of her own selfishness in not saving him when instead she had been then feeling sorry for herself. He died because of her lack of concern, now was simply the time to put herself out of her shame and die. She shook her head in despair, she let him go. The only man she had seen on his own; in literally months and she let him end up like almost everyone else she knew.

Suddenly, she was almost frightened to death, as the corpse began to move. If he were to strangle her to death: she simply didn't care. Was she going insane? She had simply experienced too much for a teenager to cope with in just one year. "Beth!" He croaked eerily as she looked at him in horror, it was terrifying for her to see a dead skull calling out her very own name. What if she had been in the water and the corpse had spoken to her? She was sure that then she would have been put out of her misery there and then and drowned in her own blood and tears of sorrow. "It is me; it is Erik." He murmured as he was a corpse rebirth. She cried tears of relief. "I thought I was going to perish out here in these wilds!" He said. After he had come back to life and was a corpse no more. Beth sobbed buckets of tears. She had been so close to her own demise. After a few moments she looked at him. She tried to get words out of her mouth but couldn't. His jaw was locked, and she was shaken.

She then went up to him, and his putrid smells made her realise that she was still with child. "Let's go home, my love!" She managed to blurt out. Her stomach was feeling queasy as she wanted to vomit all over him, with nowhere else for her head to turn. Of course, he would have understood, the shock of him coming back to life, was enough to make anyone feel nauseous, but alas, she had to keep her secret intact. With her Erik back in her life, once again the world around springing back to life as if the sun was shining on a meadow and bringing the flowers out into bloom.

Together hand in hand, they walked to her home together. The last time she saw him, she had since made love to David as well as to Roger while he had been saving all of his love for her. "It is such a lovely and beautiful path." He said. She nodded her head. She was still getting over from the shock that she had been very close to taking her own life and now Erik was finally back in her life, she had the second pregnancy from Roger to live with. She then wanted to forget about everything and to bury her head inside his loving chest. Even so, she didn't want him to have another surprise upon his arrival at Fell End, and, explained to him that Alan was really called Roger and came from France rather than from England.

Back at Fell End, later that evening, Roger had prepared a big feast in order to celebrate the return of Erik back into the close-knit fold. Beth was delighted, Roger wanted her to be happy, he wasn't so cruel as her sister believed. In reality Roger wasn't at all pleased and didn't wish for Beth to know how much Erik's arrival had hurt him. He had been so looking forward to cross dressing with her until Erik had ruined his plans. He had even been considering blackmailing Jennifer into forcing David into a threesome along with her because of her own infidelity. Instead with the arrival of another Pole, a new problem arrived, and he decided to use all his of his energy positively and heterosexually in order to woo Beth back to him. With Erik in the house, Roger's energy would have to adapt somewhat. Erik was a real man, and not a weakling like David, and for the love of the women, whom he didn't wish to annoy, he was too scared to act too soon against him. Deep down she suspected that the feast was to celebrate her second pregnancy to him but decided to think positively so that nothing ominous would happen. David then hoped that with three men and three women that the house would become more Christian and that the days of cheating, which included his own adultery were then over. After two hours of eating and drinking slowly, a dehydrated and hungry man was replenished.

Feeling very maternal, she needed a man to support her babies. Feeling sentimental, her mind went back to when they were last together. Back then, it was another world as far as she was concerned, yet still only six months earlier. All she could hope was that her then dreamy nature could be reignited as day by day he would satiate her simple needs. Feeling desperate for her love Erik was sat happily holding her in his arms. Given that she had a child out of wedlock it made Erik feel that she should quickly have a child with him. He was already thirty-three and feeling broody. What was the point in allowing her to wait because she had already borne a child? If she loved him, she would bear him a child too. His close shave with death, made him desire a baby sooner rather than later. For the time being at least, he kept his thoughts to himself.

The silence was then broken. "The meal is lovely Roger." Said Jennifer. By then the sisters were tiring of her fawning towards Roger.

"Well, we have one big celebration here." He said as the others looked at Erik who smiled, while Roger quickly stared powerfully at a timid and nervous Beth.

"I am honored." Erik said to Roger's delight.

"It is a great pleasure. I know we lost so much due to the genocide, but I hope that you will feel and learn with joy that we are celebrating many things including our very own survival." He said as once again Roger quickly gazed at a very pale Beth. His words, "celebrating many things," were terrorising her. Roger and Beth certainly had something worth announcing and preferably put off indefinitely. The deliciously tasting food might as well have been just bread and water, since when in the presence of Roger, she couldn't appreciate a thing.

As for Beth, this disastrous evening dinner had to turn into a night to remember. She had to act in her mind that she was being impregnated by

Erik. This she knew she could. In her bed with Erik, she was imagining that she was willingly going to fall pregnant, they made love. Everything was now so beautiful for her. Erik didn't have much to say but the satisfaction on his face spoke volumes to her. All she could think was how her life had turned for the better since Erik came back into her life. How could she think of him as anything other than that of being the love of her life?

Morning came, her baby was still sleeping, and she made sure that Erik would make love again to her. When she would be five months pregnant, she could tell him that she was only four and a half months gone. In two weeks', time she would be able to confess that she was suffering from morning sickness, until then, she had to keep mum.

At the breakfast table Roger made a special breakfast for everyone. He decided that he didn't need Beth once a week, and for his generosity he expected her to pay him a small price. Erik was sat next to Beth, and he couldn't take his eyes off her slender body, as thoughts of making her pregnant were more than being implanted in his heart. "It is great to have you here Erik." Said Roger.

"Thank you." He said. Beth's heart started beating wildly, as though she was going to be sick. In fact, her nausea was getting the better of her. Roger was doing this on purpose. If she left the room Erik would ask her many questions. She had to remain mum on this.

Fortunately, Roger had nothing else to say. Beth then left for the bathroom and was scared of all eyes being on her. She wanted to throw up, but it was simply a nervous reaction and she had to calm down. Then she would go upstairs and wait for Erik. She then remembered that she had left her small handbag in the dining room. As she entered Roger was tidying up. "Beth, please help me with the dishes." He said to her. She then started to help him. "Is everything OK?" She asked him nervously trying to hide the fact that she herself wasn't and wanted him to feel as though he was the problem rather than herself. She was scared, was he was going to reveal her pregnancy to the others.

"Oh Beth! you are so much stronger than I. Please cast Erik onto Sophie and tame me so that I can be saved!"

"I want you to be saved, but I don't know if I can do this."

"This is easy for you to say. Unlike myself: you were brought up in a loving family." He said trying to play on her sympathies, but instead she didn't know how to react. If he wanted her it was his place to act like a man and to love and to cherish her. She then continued helping him with the dishes and tried to ignore his brushing of his body against her bottom and ran off as soon as she had helped tidy up the place with him. As for the rest of the day, Beth avoided him like the plague since she didn't wish to hear him step by step blackmailing her. Her duties were William, and once she had done what she had to do, her time was for Erik. So long as he was in her presence, The Beast would be keeping his thoughts to himself.

In the garden the next day Roger was feeling forlorn since Erik and Beth still seemed to be an item together. As Beth came up to him, he nearly jumped out of his skin. She was torn between living in fear of Roger spilling the beans about her second pregnancy and living with him when his transgender tendencies could resurface without any warning or at any given time. As for him being a bigamist, so long as it was heterosexually based that was the least of her worries. "What the fuck are you playing at telling him all the time how happy you are with his arrival?"

"You wanted me to act like a man. So, I am trying to make him feel very welcome."

"Well, it wasn't very romantic of you was it?" She said emotionally. Her answer for him was confusing. Why did she expect him to be romantic with her?

"Beth, I am scared of you leaving me." He said hoping she felt the same way too.

"Stop with your bloody feeble excuses." She said, trying to hide the fact that as much as she wanted to repel him verbally, her strong desire to bring up her children in a respectable way was making her desire him. He then grabbed hold of her arms as she was scared since he was normally so gentle with her, as every thought was running through her overactive and confused mind.

"Beth, if only you and not Sophie had beaten me up. I am scared of myself. I am not scared of you; I am scared of rejecting you because I cannot accept that I am good enough for you! Why can't I be a one woman, man! If only you had killed me!" He said as he then burst into tears and was wailing like his father: like a girl.

"Roger, this is crazy, I beg you to move back into The Howe with me, and we can live in peace alone together. For God's sake, I am carrying another child of yours." She pleaded.

"My problem is that; at best you don't love me for my gender fluidity, you love me as the man you want me to be. At worst, you want me so that our children will be brought up in a better environment than I myself had been." He said as she didn't understand what was wrong with her humble desires to have a man and children together.

"You know that I can have another man, he has traveled all the way from Poland for me. With love, we can solve our problems together."

Her words were too much for him to bear and frightened of his emotions getting out of control; he then composed himself. "You are right about everything you say, but sadly I must do everything to accept that I cannot have you, but please tell Erik that you are expecting my children; please!" She dismissed his plural of the word child and wasn't concerned about his grammatical error.

"No Roger, this is the lawyer inside of you. Your reputation means everything to you."

"Yes, of course it does, our children have every right to know who their father is. I never saw my own father." He said pleading.

"The words selfish and manipulative have a whole new set of meaning when they describe you."

"Stop talking about yourself. Don't you realise we are still alive thanks to me?" He said to her annoyed.

"And to Jennifer too."

"Yes, I agree and there is something else that deeply concerns me."

"You might as well tell me." She said a little fearfully.

"The oven at Fell End is convertible."

"I think we all know this by now."

"The oven at The Howe isn't." He replied

"I think you are looking too much into this." She said as she was waiting for him to reply to her.

Luckily, there was so much work to do in the garden. Yes, he had two useless eaters, David, and Erik, who were able to work for him, but deep down he knew that there was still a lot of work that needed to be done on the land and decided to turn all of his confused and demented energies of his to the vegetable plot at The Howe instead. As such he walked off leaving Beth to stew and to ponder about his disjointed designs on her as well as his threats. All that powerful energy of his could hopefully be used productively on something useful instead. Now was not the time to worry about her hormonal behavior, he had to get away from her since he didn't like the way in which she was negatively behaving towards him.

Sophie was in the garden nursing when Beth walked past her with her baby. "I need to talk to you." Said Sophie. "I didn't know when to tell you this; but Roger is eviller than you will ever know. He told me that he wanted to have a baby factory, and for us to produce a master race with him. He also wanted to impregnate ten other maidens again and again and that their children would be used as our servants . . . He said that we are special."

"Sophie, why the hell didn't you tell me about this earlier?"

"I was worried that you would think I was looking for trouble. I mean, if I told you to leave him alone, you would have thought of me as being a jealous sister. Now that you have Erik, I hope that everything between you both will work out. I hate him as you know, that's why I almost killed him, but what else can I do now? I really wished that he had died, but I can't face going through with the horror in trying to kill someone again, it was a one-off thing."

Shivers ran through both of the sisters' spines as the silence was haunting them. "Oh Sophie, if only had you told me this earlier, I wouldn't have allowed him to make love to me. Now I am pregnant." Said Beth as her revelation came out of the blue.

"Oh my God, Beth," she said as her jaw dropped.

"How could he have done this to you so soon after you just gave birth? Even if I warned you about him, what use would that be? He would probably have raped you anyway. He keeps going on about himself as being Genghis Khan."

"Maybe it is better you hadn't told me. The day I met Erik here, I planned to jump off a crag and die. So, are you planning to have more children with him?"

"No of course not, but I am resigned to my fate. I hate my life; if I could die in my sleep, I would be happy." Said Sophie.

"But what about your child?" Beth asked: who was no longer having morbid thoughts thanks to being with Erik.

"I don't care. It is Satan's baby anyway! Don't worry I am not going to take my own life." Said Sophie.

"Should we kill him?" Asked Beth.

"I don't know. I guess we survived the tsunami because of him. Would we survive with one less man to protect us from whatever? I don't know. At least we know the bastard, and he will in some way protect us."

That night Roger couldn't sleep. Beth was right. His reputation was important to him. She was right; he was a bastard to Beth. He had no control over himself. He couldn't bear to see Beth happy and to move on with her life without him. In turn and in order for him not to sink further into a depression and to be racked with guilt, his own needs took precident to those of hers. As much as he loathed himself, wherever he would look, he saw her allure everywhere he went but with Erik standing next to her too.

Once again Roger made a gourmet style breakfast. Beth was sat looking somewhat frozen. She had so many skeletons in her closet. She was pregnant. She had Jewish ancestry, not that that was something to hide. She had even been willing to become a man for Roger at one point. For Roger she only had one skeleton. While the others had thanked him for his culinary effort in recent days, Beth was showing him no gratitude. If she were a man, he would punch her in the face. He looked at her as he had a paranoid fear that she wanted to kill him. "Don't threaten me!" He said to her looking ready for a fight.

"What are you on about?"

"You know what I mean."

"I am sorry Roger I have no idea what you mean." She said as she dazed and confused by his bewildering insanity.

"Just think about what you said to me three weeks ago when you threatened me." In fact, she hadn't said anything; it was all in his dreams. She wanted to know as to what he was implying but was too afraid to ask.

A few moments later the others had arrived for breakfast and sat down. While the others were observing their cereal, he was delighted that he was able to look into her eyes and full of anger for a few seconds. Beth was terrified and remained silent. Luckily for her there was no fuss, and the others went outside together. Roger seized his chance, placed his hands on her mouth and took her upstairs to his room. The setting was the paintings. He then started to undress her as she was terrified of him raping her. Equally his passion was confusing her. Still, if he raped her, she would get the others to kill him. Instead, he was merely looking into her eyes. "Why am I sat here like this in front of the painting?" She Asked him.

"I am torn between my paternal duty and my kindness towards you, and I was hoping that I would find some answers here."

"Have you." She said in fear.

"No, dear I haven't." What was the best way to deal with his blackmail? Make love and he would only ask for more favours from her or snub him and suffer the consequences.

"Oh Roger, these paintings are so beautiful." Was the best answer she could give to him.

"Indeed, they are. You look so tender, so innocent and as beautiful as you were one year ago." He said as she saw his compliment as a double-edged sword.

"I am honored that you find me so alluring."

"Yes, but if I make love to you now, won't you think given the way I brought you here that I had forced myself onto you?" He asked her as either way he would win this weird and psychological power game.

Shaken and numb she then left his room and went outside for some fresh air and wondered what he was playing at. As she arrived back in the house, he was behaving kindly to the others, and insisted on David and Erik having a day of rest while he himself was dripping with exhaustion from his garden toils. He had certainly ploughed with his own hands and some simple garden tools much of the land.

Sure, enough at the dinner table that evening he decided in his demented mind that he really was her conqueror. All she could think about was the strange and creepy moments they spent together in his room. "Beth has just found out she is expecting again, and I hope you will look after her properly." He said looking directly into Erik's eyes.

"I don't think it can happen so quickly."

"What do you mean?" Said Roger.

"I only just arrived here." Said Erik as Jennifer was in heaven listening to her hero, Roger, speaking.

"I know, and the day before you arrived, she missed her period." With that a highly tortured Beth stormed out. Sophie was in shock; she too wasn't ready for baby number two herself and felt really bad for Beth with the less than dignified manner that he had reported his gloating. While Jennifer kept her head low. For her, Roger was more exciting than David. As for David, he hoped that his Christian values would somehow save Roger. Erik decided to simply look for Beth. He was scared that he would lose her and that she would go back to the love tryst.

He found her lying on her bed prostrate. "Why didn't you tell me that you and Roger are still an item?" He asked her. By then, Beth decided that being truthful wasn't always going to help her after all. Desperately fighting for his love, she started to cry so that she would have enough time in formulating an answer.

"Erik, he said that there are no other men. I spurned his advances, oh Erik if only you knew!" She then started to cry. How could she tell him the truth that she only wanted to have sex with him and not for him to make her pregnant?

"He raped you?"

"Yes."

"How?"

"What question is this?"

"I want to know, as your man I have every reason to know about your suffering."

She looked at him and smiled and bought a few seconds so that she could think about what she was going to tell him. "I was falling asleep, when suddenly he walked into my room and grabbed a hold of me. He then tied my hands and arms together. He didn't need to do that, I am a slightly built girl as you know," he nodded in agreement with her, "but he knew what he was doing was evil. He then raped me and once again he hit his jackpot and the day before you came, I found out I was pregnant. If I knew you were coming, I wasn't going to tell him." She said without thinking and regretted before the words left her mouth but was unable to retract from her forthcoming lexis.

"You wanted me to think it was mine?" He said in horror, while feeling very sorry for his damsel in distress whom he wanted to look after.

"Yes, I am just an innocent, I was taken advantage of, and I didn't want to lose you." She said as she started crying.

"Beth, Of course I am in grief that he took advantage out of you, because I myself am desperate to have my own child, with you!"

"If only I had kept my mouth shut!" She said as she was thinking about her unborn child and that she had lost Erik's love.

"I have cycled, swam and walked from Poland for you!" He said wanting her to be quiet and happy to be in his loving arms.

"My God, why didn't you take the train?"

"Are you serious? Poland is obliterated too. Nuclear explosions took place; the official government line before they too went dead was that;

the tsunamis created a chain reaction of events. I don't want to talk any more but the whole of Europe has been plunged well and truly back into the dark ages. As such I had to swim across the channel and felt sick in the sea of blood. It was full of corpses, and I was scared that sharks would have come around me. In England, speaking the language of Chaucer saved my life. Somewhere near the Cotswolds I was given a horse to drop off just north of Preston where the owner's sister lived. I was lucky; I couldn't face cycling and besides I had already rode from Nancy to Cherbourg with flat tyres on my bike. Oh, my dear belle, please don't ask me more, I am so traumatised by everything."

As she saw him in her mind on horseback gallantly as some knight heading across the continent due to his love for her; she wanted him so badly. He then got into bed with her with his arms around her and wanted to protect her. "One more thing, as I reached Bolton-le-Sands, I was already exhausted. I thought about taking a short cut to Grange-over-Sands via The Bay. Instead, all I could see was the corpses everywhere of mainly humans, their pets and farm animals and decided against that. I later found out at Windermere that going via Milnthorpe and Levens that I followed the best route which was in fact along the A6. As soon as I got into the Lythe Valley, I wondered if I had reached heaven but was in fear that I wouldn't get any closer to you. All I could do was to think about your beauty that helped me fall asleep. I did the same thing when I woke up the next day and that gave me a purpose for the rest of the day." She then slumped her head into his body. He had taken her breath away with his love and devotion for her.

After many minutes the beautiful silence she was enjoying as he was holding her in his loving arms was broken. 'I do though want to restore your honor and to kill him!' With that she was scared as she thought about all those passionate times, she had had with him, The Beast.

"No, no, I hate him as much as I love you Erik. But if you kill him then you are as evil as he is, and I will no longer love you." She said as she wished that Erik was with Sophie, since she believed that she wasn't good enough for him. Equally, this former innocent who had waited all of her life for just one man then believed that sex and love were intertwined, and in turn she loved not just Erik, but David and Roger too. After a few moments he looked at her

'You must know that things in the UK are bad?'

"How can I? I know nothing as to what is going on outside of the Lake District. All I know is that there is almost nobody here and that the tsunami reached one hundred metres above sea level."

"Beth, there were a few tsunamis, but it was much worse than you could have imagined. Very few people live above a hundred metres in England. All I can tell you is that; London is of course well below a hundred metres as are most of the other English cities. I could travel through places such as Oxford and meet just a sole survivor. The survivor wasn't at Oxford at the time the whole city was flooded. All I can imagine is that the person I saw was from the Illuminati. If you think there are very few survivors here, imagine what it is like in the lowlands of Southern England. I also forget to mention, that when I was in Lancaster, as a vagabond I was arrested and put inside the castle gaol for two months. The real reason was that Satanists had taken over the city and had made the wearing of masks compulsory, on the grounds that the corpses were spreading viruses."

His news sent shivers down her spine as she thought about Roger, the man she depended now so much on, who was relishing in the destruction of humanity. In order to ease her own guilt about her thoughts that the population had been too dense before, she needed to let some steam off with him. On top of that she was furious. He, Roger, had tried to convince her about the benefits of the recent holocaust. As if this wasn't bad enough, poignantly, she then thought about the times she had made love to The Beast after she gave birth while her beloved was in prison because of his love for her as she felt nothing more than some stupid scarlet woman. Once again, Roger had ruined her life. Once again time, like with David had been her enemy. If only she had waited.

Erik looked at her somewhat composed as she wanted to melt into his chest. "I am sorry Beth, but I don't think that we can be. I thank you for saving my life, but I think it is better if we are simply just friends." He said as she wanted to simply die there and then.

"I beg you to walk with me to the tarn, I am desperate to tell you something that I cannot let the others hear?" She said as he then nodded and felt flattered that she trusted him more than the others. As they arrived at the water's edge, she began and was ready for him to berate her for being autistic. "Sometimes I don't care if you were to drown me. I try to lose myself in these very waters but there are times when I feel as though the pain you are giving me is pushing me down towards the tarn's bed. I try with all of my might to deaden my feelings so that I can swim like some machine. I had so many dreams; to have a family with a man who loves me. Oh Erik! Don't you see how beautiful it is here, yet at the same time the bad luck I am having denotes to me that I am in the wrong place yet still alive. Sometimes I am breathless and want to give up, but I am scared of dying. All I can do is breathe and hope that I will die peacefully in my sleep. Sometimes I forget about everything and can have a beautiful dream. I can wake up happily listening to the sounds of the birds singing, but as I think about you, your cruelty, my dream for the day has ended. I then start my miserable day again. This is my life! I simply can't go on like this. All because I want a one-woman man: Someone to care about me and to be the head of the household with his patriarchal love."

He then looked at her mesmerized. "My God Beth, such wise, poignant and romantic words. Please don't think of me in being cruel! I am sorry I didn't come back to you earlier! I love you; I do, I really do!" He said. In turn he started to kiss her as she was still crying buckets of tears. She then had a headache but a short while later and desperate to hold onto him she was blissfully happy as they made love together. She then ran to the stream which was tumbling down from the fell and drank as much as she could for her headache until she needed a wee.

"I am sorry for being so hysterical. I am worse than when you saw me on holiday. My emotions spiral out of control nowadays. The more I think about you and what happened when the mother stopped you from seeing your baby the more, I hate Roger. It is a funny old world. I feel as though I have aged thirty years mentally in just over one year. I was a serious but typical teenager last year, but now, I feel as though I am ready to write my own memoires about the human race. The point I am trying to make Erik is this; for me the family unit is the most important thing in life. As a mother, I know how much I have failed. As a mother I see Roger as a bigger bastard than ever before; a man who doesn't realize how lucky he is. How he has treated me so cruelly, yet I never considered taking away his parental rights. Oh Erik! How much I have cried over you when I thought about how a man like you deserved to have made me with child. Oh, Erik how I have cried over you thinking about the pain you have gone through in not seeing your child when a woman like me would have done anything for a man, a father of her child, like you." Suddenly before she was about to fall into a morbid depression, he started to kiss her slim belly and once again they made love. She had got everything off from her chest, except of course her growing boobs and now was the time to enjoy herself with him.

After telling him Erik's news, while William was asleep in the pram the next day near them in the garden, about how virtually the whole population of England had been wiped out, Roger looked at her in shock. "My oh my Beth. This probably accounts for the fact that the shops only stock healthy food nowadays."

"Well of course they are, I mean with less people there is less demand for things like coca cola which have anyway gone out of business."

"No, my dear you don't understand. We were happy when the masses were poisoning themselves with junk food. This was the reason why life expectancy rates were falling as well as fertility rates too, as sperm counts were plummeting. Now, people are probably being encouraged eat and drink healthily." He said.

"This is so horrendous, Roger. How could you have got involved with such evil creeps? I used to think that leaders were meant to serve and to look after their people, now I realise that I have the wool pulled over my naïve eyes." She said to him with somewhat disgust.

"As for the wipe out, I thought only ninety-five percent of the population would be wiped out, a mere ninety nine percent at the most. Based on Erik's observations the wipe out was one survivor for every hundred thousand. This is not what I expected. I am so sorry. That would mean a mere seventy thousand survivors globally." He said shaken that there wouldn't be enough slaves for him. "I have had reports that London had twenty thousand people, who must have either been in hiding in the hills on the day of the genocide or simply came from afar looking for some help. Liverpool, the former second city at the time of Victoria, has still simply no one."

"You don't care about the ninety-nine percent, do you?"

"Not really. Look, I feel more stable now that there are less people. I feel recovered mentally. At times I feel sadness due to what happened. Even so, if what you have told me is accurate, then I am devastated. This has simply gone too far. There won't be enough manpower for us. This is why we don't have electricity running again; there simply isn't the demand for it. I was hoping after the tsunami that we would have gone together jet setting all over the world and seen the seven wonders of the earth. All I wanted was for us to be happy."

"Your answers don't wash with me." She said.

"OK my love, I will come clean with you. Had only ninety-five percent been wiped out and the elite survived, things would be worse than now. They would have locked everyone up inside their homes forced them into wearing masks and said that this is in the national interest. They would have inserted microchips into everyone's fingertips. They could have cloned people and inserted artificial intelligence inside and turned them into cyborgs. You don't understand much about these things, do you?" He said patronisingly to her, while at the same time he was relieved that he had been honest with her.

"I do know some things about the NWO, but I don't quite believe that they are as sick as you say they are." She said as she felt breathless thinking about people masked and suffocating. With that Beth ran off to a secluded spot on the estate. With her baby sleeping in the cot alone: she couldn't leave Fell End for a run.

Away from the others she burst into tears. "Oh God, oh Jesus, I know that I know nothing. I know that I am confused. All I know is that; as a woman I want to love my man and for him to love me and my or our children. I respect that I am no more important than of all the others who perished through wicked deeds. I pray for humanity, and I am at your mercy. Please allow me to live in some kind of ignorance, please silence Roger, his words kill me." After her prayer and feeling numb and shaken, she merely collapsed down on the glass and fell into a deep trance. Falling asleep was the next best thing to death for her.

One person who took advantage of Erik being on his own in the garden while Beth was away sleeping at the other end, was no other than Jennifer. In a coquettish manner, she paraded herself up and down the area where he was working. She was wearing light summer clothes, which certainly helped to protrude her growing bump. He had after all met Beth when she was heavily pregnant, and she was certain that he would notice how beautiful she looked too. As she saw Beth arising from her nap, she calmed down and walked off as if she were some eerie yet discreet ghost like silhouette.

Her life was only slightly better with Erik maybe there was only one solution, given David was in love with Jennifer. "Roger, I think that it is time you grew up. I am willing to give you another chance and to live with me." She said uninterested about his confused ideas as she walked up to him as he was drinking a mug of tea in the garden, in his own world.

"When I say that I feel better I mean this. City life was depressing me. Now that I am out here, I feel so much more that my heart is full of love." He said as he was scared of never making love to her again.

"Then we will leave here and live our own private and beautiful world and be one big happy family." She said as her idea frightened him.

"It is a lovely and most beautiful idea. My problem is my guilt. At best I will be born again as a child of yours, and to be a girl just like you." She looked at him in shock and horror. For Beth something told her that no matter what, he would never be satisfied with her and there would never be an escape from him. In turn she believed that in order to live freely from him; she needed to be living with him as his equal; as husband and wife. The last thing she wanted was for him to be out of her life and to be controlling her inside her womb and for her to give birth to him. It was in moments such as these that she believed that even in death, his tentacles would be engulfing her as they were in life. In her mind, there really was no way for her to leave him.

He then looked at her. "Dear, in normal conditions I would be nothing more than a paedophile for you." He said as he was thinking about himself at his worst.

"I was eighteen when we met. I chose to move into your home. I could easily have run away from you. I was attracted and repulsed by you. You are a very handsome and sophisticated man, but much older than I. I fell in love with you because of your kind heart, but equally you have a mind full of destruction and depravity. Now I am desperate because of what you have done to me. Please take me to be your wife!"

"Desperation is never a good thing. You might think I am the best man now. You know how much I love you, but I live from day to day. I never know if my transgender desires will resurface again, because of you. On top of that, you have hurt my feelings with the fact that your love is not of a highest kind towards me." Beth then walked off. Roger was going to pay for this somehow. She never wanted him to touch her body again. A violent thought went across her mind. After killing him, she would in turn kill herself.

Beth was distressed. She then absorbed herself in being a mum. Evening dinner was served outside. As usual she put her baby to bed. Then she went to bed and Erik wanted to make love to her. All she could do was to lie like a log. He then sensed she was sad; he had no intention of treating like a blow-up doll and placed his hands on her face. It was dripping wet, but his touch had helped her open up her heart. "I am devastated because I wanted to carry your child. I must kill myself!"

"I am far being the most handsome, exciting and intelligent man in the world, but you can depend on me." He said as she heard his words just when she needed them most

"No, Erik, you have much more common sense than I or anyone else here." She said, as a warm glow went through his heart.

"Beth dear, I am man with few words, but please listen to me when I speak." He said as she fully respected him and smiled at him lovingly. "I can understand your pain, your sorrows but don't give up. Our country went through a similar hell during the World War Two, but life went on. Life still goes on. I have risked my life searching for you. I could have died had I stayed in Poland. It is our love that brought me back from the brink of death when you found me. You saved my life! My darling! My joy! Let's enjoy the beauties of nature together! We are simply living in a garden of Eden!" He said since, as far as he was concerned, the Lake District was simply amazing, and that Beth was the princess of the place.

She was touched by his sentiment. She felt safe in his arms. She also wasn't in the mood for passion, and he seemed as though he wasn't a danger to her. Equally she felt bad; she felt guilty. As lovely as he was to her; as kind as he was to her, she didn't feel as though she could ever really love him.

"I am glad that we have no National Grid." He said. "Me and a group of vigilantes were planning to take down the pylons so that there would be no 5G and worse still humans having their insides ripped out and being inserted with wires and being turned into something akin to Frankenstein's monsters." He finished. As for Beth, he was right. He was also a leader in waiting, but given her devotion to him wasn't divine, she didn't answer. Instead, tears ran down her face as she felt that they both deserved someone. As for Erik, he sensed that a quiet life with Beth was her preferred path as opposed to having some foolhardy leader.

As for Roger, he was enjoying his time with Sophie. He sensed he was driving Beth mad, and after making love to her sister, he fell instantaneously into sleep with a big and satisfied smile on his face in knowing that another child of his was on the way. With his life being so miserable, he wondered if he should have metamorphosed himself into the baby inside of her womb. Instead, he believed that his job as the sacred maker had not yet ended.

A while later his jealousy was getting the better of him. Beth was with Erik. Roger seemed to be in greater despair more than ever. Luckily, he used this energy towards protecting everyone from ticks and took up the initiative on paper with reducing the lawn area. Grass was lovely for sitting on, but now they would have to get used to sitting on rocks instead and he had to decide how he was going to place the large stones aesthetically. On top of that, he was more than somewhat sad, that his baby factory wasn't quite the successful program that he had had originally in mind.

The next day, just as he was about to place the maiden rock onto the lawn, Beth ran out screaming. Very quickly he got the message and took the rock out of their garden. Even so she fell into his trap as she started shouting at him over the rock. "You selfish and evil bastard, go and fuck yourself and shove those rocks up your arse!" She had never spoken to him in such a manner before. He was delighted; this little lady of his was capable of acting like any other commoner and was more proof to him that nothing was ever black and white.

"Are you related to the paedophile George Berger? The Zoophilic Markus Levy? The necrophile Abraham Israel or Nora Hahn the LGBT radical?" He said as he taunted her calmly. By then she knew what he meant. She was tired of his allusions and had basically had enough of listening to Anti-Semitism throughout her life and keeping her origins silent. Shivers ran down her spine as she thought about the Jews who had died in the Warsaw Ghetto. She with blood rushing to her face slapped him across the face. Her punch was so hard that he bled. He wanted to smile at her. He had done nothing wrong in his eyes, all he had done was explain to her that many from the true tribe she came from; were mass murderers and no different to himself. Roger wasn't the only important dangerous NWO being left on the planet and Beth had to learn that divide and rule was what kept everyone on Roger's patch on the straight and narrow. He believed that she had learnt this in their love trio too. Now she would have to learn that new rules would be applied now that two other men were in his house.

He then had a moment of fear running through his mind as he sensed for the first that she had feelings of real hatred towards him. "You hate me!" She screamed at him. Her statement sent his thoughts into free-fall and left him immediately thankful of his acerbic mind.

"I hate you as much as much as you deep down don't really love that wimp, who is only a man because of his Christian beliefs, a closet Satanist who would gladly be fucked senseless by me; if you, Sophie and Jennifer left this house! Oh Beth, don't you see how much I love you. You drive me crazy, and I am scared of losing my own mind, because of your beauty, purity and goodness." He then burst out crying with his crocodile tears. "I love you just the way you are! I am the only man who is delighted that you are once again with child. I am the only one who cares about our baby." He wanted to attack Erik verbally in his absence but felt that she would have sensed his jealousy. Destroying one man's reputation, that of David's, even if he wasn't a current lover of hers, was better than nothing for him. He also knew that his pro-life sentiment would go down well with her catholic faith.

Although she hated everything he said, some things struck a chord with her. What if David really was a closet Satanist? What if David, the soft English gentleman would secretly be willingly fucked senseless by a highly sexed and masculine Roger? In turn, she wondered if she could still trust Erik. As for him being delighted that she was having his baby, she wanted him to show his actions rather than his words and to show her that; apart from herself: he, Roger, too cared about their mutual posterity.

With other men in the house Roger felt as though he was walking on eggshells. As such and in order not to rock the boat too much he cooked a fine three course mean. "I am still celebrating." He said as they were all sat down together at the dining room table. "As you know, the world became messed up. Women were no longer enjoyed being mothers; they preferred to work themselves to death and to remain single. Some hospitals had during childbirth injected women with some substance that made then become repulsed by their men. Some of these mothers became infertile and less feminine in many other ways too. Of course, in most cases this wasn't necessary since family life was in self-destruct mode anyway. Now look how things have changed! Jennifer, what a fine lady you are for David. You are still in your twenties and not waiting forever to be a mother. You have proven your salt. You fell pregnant before the tsunami and are like the other women here; a living testament to the fact that during the anti-family days that you were still a good traditional woman. Sophie, you are doing a great job. What can be more fulfilling than looking after life itself! Just think without the tsunami you would probably be taking some Mickey Mouse course at university and surrounded by baby murderers disguised as girls who just wanted to have some harmless fun.

Sophie, who had aborted Jan's child only to have ended up in as what she believed to be his harem was full of contempt for him as Beth was angry since she told him in confidence about her sister's abortion with his darkly veiled attack when he spoke of baby murderers. "As for Beth, you are the super girl in this room. I am sure that Erik is delighted with you. I am proud that as the youngest in this room, you are ahead of the others, and I hope that you will set a new benchmark for them!" He said. Without any doubt, there was tension in the air, and Beth felt once again a victim of his manipulative turn of words as well as wanting to faint. The sight of his smug self was making her nausea worse than ever. How could she have got herself into such a mess with him?

"So many people are infertile. Now that we have been depopulated, we should cherish every pregnancy so that we will be able to defend ourselves." Jennifer said as she was sensing the disdain from the others against him. His speech was that of a statesman for her. For her he was the great orator. On top of that he looked great in the flesh too.

As usual, Erik was working in the garden, the day after Roger's speech. If only she could try him out. He was after the all the only man to whom she hadn't yet made love with. The way he stood by Beth was a great testament of the rustic Hodge's great loyalty for some fallen teenager who didn't deserve him. Unable to hide her feelings, she was ready for the kill. "Hello," she said as a warm glow went through her.

"Hello, how are things?" He said politely without any warmth.

"How are things?" She asked him in a flirty manner.

"They are fine." He said.

"It is nice to be able to get to know each other."

Sensing that she had eyes for him, he had to put out any embers of passion she had for him. "I don't know how Roger gets away with everything." He said a little upset.

"Well, he is the leader." She said on Roger's defensive.

"Great!" He said as he wanted the end of the matter.

"The world outside is run by dangerous people. I studied at Cambridge. If you want to survive, just keep your head down."

"And if he wants to make love to me what should I do?" He asked unimpressed by her vision and trying to sound facetious.

"There are worse things than that. Be grateful that you are still alive and have somewhere to live thanks to him. If you don't upset him: he won't upset, you."

"Well, he has already upset me."

"How?" She wondered in total bewilderment.

"I met Beth in January, and he got her pregnant a second time just before I arrived here."

"Stop being so bitter and twisted. He is obviously a highly sought-after stud, as Beth and Sophie are only too well aware." She said somewhat menacingly into his eyes, as she was distraught that she was carrying a baby from the wrong man.

She then walked off and decided to take the beagles out on a walk. What right did he have to turn her down? He was after all nothing more than a stupid peasant from a former communist country.

This pregnancy was different to the last one. She seemed to be suffering much less from morning sickness, her breasts were sore from the breastfeeding and not so much from the gestation, but her belly was much more bloated. On top of that, she was more tired too. In spite of everything, she still wanted to remain active. After feeding her son she gently woke Erik up with her caressing of his face. In turn, this down to earth man from her homeland who had a little more sexual prowess than David made love to her.

"Darling, would you like to go swimming with me today?" She said to him after their mutual passion.

"Yes, but what about your baby." He asked as she was touched by his care for her child.

"Yes, you are right. I often leave him with Sophie. The day we met I did the same. I should also tell you something I need to share with you. You saved my life. The day we met I left William with Sophie. I planned to jump off Loughrigg Fell but I found you instead." She said as she wanted to emphasise that she could still kill herself if he left her. She was feeling confused and needy and wondered if she loved him after all.

"I understand. Life is very cruel at times. I would love to go swimming with you darling." He said as he held her hands tightly. She was satisfied, his love was soothing her. Although she was being honest, she also had developed some of the manipulative tendencies of Roger's and would use them if and whenever she needed to.

Together after breakfast they walked together hand in hand to Loughrigg Tarn. Together they got into the water and swam. He was kind to her as well being a gentleman. Her mind went back to when she was there before she lost her virginity. Those times were so free and easy. If only she was here with David. If only Roger behaved as a human being. Erik lacked sparkle for her. Still, he followed her wherever she went, admired, and helped her look after her child and was never far away from her since his work was at Fell End and The Howe. Hopefully one day she would learn to love him, she thought.

It had been quite an enjoyable day. Erik had proven to her that she could depend on him. Walking back, she was happy to hold his hand. Some semblances of stability was back in her life once more. Back at Fell End, as she was admiring the beautiful garden, she almost jumped out of her skin as she noticed Roger standing behind her. "I am ready to move back to The Howe for you. Beth, I can't live without you!" He said pleading and was scared of his heart giving up. His psychological abuse was tormenting him. She wasn't going to miscarry because of him, and he had to protect her. As far as she was concerned, he was a dandy of a narcissist and wasn't a man for her. With a rush of adrenaline pumping inside of her; she was ready for him. She took a deep breath and was hopefully that her words would be more than just some whimpering.

"And I am ready to drive you insane. I no longer want you!" Now that she had tamed him, she no longer wanted him it seemed to him. In fact, like him, she could no longer be happy with just one partner. He had confused her. Now all men were just as bad. She then thought about how Jan would have been good enough to have spent the rest of her life with, before her innocence had been taken away. For that, Sophie was culpable to some extent for her mess. She had longed for years to have a fairy-tale romance. How could she ever have been the same again? David's strange, effeminate behavior towards her was as a result of her moral imperfections. Erik, had he been her first he too like Jan, would have made her happy. She would have been happy with him following her around. Instead, men like David and Roger who had messed around with her, made Erik look somewhat rather dull for her.

"You are love on legs. Oh, how I much respect and admire thee! A simple country girl at heart, you will probably be the last woman on the planet who knows about love and how to look after her man!"

"Oh Roger: why don't you write fiction? You are such a wonderful storyteller and could make the reader believe any of your lies!"

In turn, Roger stormed off and decided that he would do a good deed. He climbed up Loughrigg Fell full of hope that his actions would win him some favours with the others. He had been walking there the other day and a friendly sheep came up to him and he fed the animal with some grass. As he reached the top, he couldn't believe his luck when he found the ewe again. The sheep was cleaner than the others he had met, and it was his second meeting with her and for the first time he made love to her just below the summit. With a view of Grasmere and loving memories of Beth and Sophie on the island he was climaxing along with the ewe and imagined that he could have some goatee child with her. Feeling distraught that he couldn't impregnate her, he then imagined cooking for dinner and clothing himself with her wool as a means of wearing her with pride.

Pride meant a lot to him. Had the tsunami not taken place, he would have been following events about the planned first ever Trans Pride in London for September of that year. There had even been talk about Paedo Pride, but the public weren't quite ready for that. One thing that the Pride movement was looking into was Zoo Pride. He then smiled, he didn't need to shout and scream about his love of animals. He could do this behind closed doors, and still make love to the highest priests and priestesses of morality, such as Beth and David. All he had to do was to give the image in being a country gent, be patient, and step by step he would get what he wanted out of both David and perhaps Erik too before his deathly dream with Beth would come true.

A few days later a tense and nervous Beth went up to Roger in the garden, while Erik and David were busy weeding at the vegetable plot in the warm sunshine. "I think that it was really nasty of you to have got me pregnant when you knew my heart was for Erik."

"You have known for a month that you are pregnant, today is the start of a new month, are you going to continue with this misery for another month?" He asked her.

"I had no time to rest, I gave birth in April and two months later I fell pregnant again."

"Look love, I wanted to wait several months, so that I could have enjoyed your heavily pregnant body with my eyes during the long warm days of summer, but with you being less than certain about our future I had to act. Beth dear, I am happy that you have found Erik, but what I did to you, I did as a favour to you."

"What favour can this be?" she said as she was feeling sick from his deluded words and was thankful that she wasn't wholly dependent on him for love and romance.

"It is simple, Erik is not very bright. We need to produce the crème de la crème!"

"I am not a baby making machine." She said to him in disgust.

"I am not saying that." He said as once again the lawyer was inside of his speech, while inside he was shaking that she knew him so well.

"But your unromantic words speak volumes to me." She said as she was feeling more used by him than ever before.

"Look, Beth, instead of thinking about yourself, think about our babies."

"I don't want them!" She said as his words had struck her violently. He was right, but he was of course the cause of this terrible mess.

"Beth dear, just remember I am looking after you. I am sure you remember Richard; he is hopefully dead. He didn't like you or Sophie, and I kept him well away from you. He wanted me to sell your babies to some gay couples. It seems he died in the tsunami." He said as his words were hypnotising her somehow as she was disgusted more than ever with Richard. Equally she was disgusted with herself. Richard was dead because the tsunami wiped out almost everyone and she felt sick in knowing that a part of her relished in his demise even though it meant in order for him to be wiped out, ninety-nine percent as opposed to ninety-five percent of the population had disappeared too.

With society gone, she was increasingly at his mercy. Given Richard had been so evil, she needed The Beast to protect her from marauding men. "How is your morning sickness?"

"Much better than last time."

"Don't you see, by having a positive relationship with me, you are being better looked after. If it weren't for your diminishing waist, you wouldn't know you were with child again." She looked at her waist. It was growing quickly, and she was sad that she was losing her hourglass figure too soon. Worse still was that his words were scaring the living daylights out of her. "Beth, you are the most beautiful girl in the world, the most beautiful mother in the world. Our babies are the most beautiful children in the world. I love you so much." As much as he was a bastard, his words made her feel good with herself. She was beautiful and wanted to make love, but not with him.

She was just about to walk off when he started to run his fingers through her hair. "Just fuck me!" She said as she was excited but deep down, she wanted him dead. At the same time, the touch of his fingers running through her hair, were hypnotising her.

"No, I will make love to you." He said. She then calmed down, deep down she hated the idea of making love in a hateful manner and allowed her body to be turned on by his body that was for her physically irresistible. A shiver went through her spine as she was appalled with herself. With so much horror surrounding her, she was able to make love in less romantic conditions, was she starting to become aroused with the idea of something akin to hate-sex?

After love making, she shed tears for the fact that he was taking advantage out of her. On top of that, she was tired of his ever-changing moods. "What's wrong darling. You know that I love you more than ever."

"You said that I am autistic."

"What I meant was that you are living in the wrong era. If the world was like in the novel; *Pebbles, Love across the Morecambe Bay*, you would be happy. If you want to survive; things have changed. People have different desires depending on the mood that they feel." He said gently to her.

"I can't! I can't! I need love! Not with someone whose feelings for me go from one wanting to fill me up one moment to wanting me to be carried downstream the next. That's why I have to take Erik."

"Can I ask you one question?" He said changing the subject since he found every word; she said an ordeal for him to listen to.

"OK." She said nervously.

"If no man found you attractive and loads of women were offering you their loving touch, exclusively. How would you choose your perfect belle?" He said grinning at her.

Hysterically she ran outside, calmed down. As she saw him standing in the distance she went as bright red as a beetroot. It was then that she wanted to faint. Had he sensed what was going on? She felt as though her whole insides were being monitored for any anomaly between what she said and what her body was craving for. Looking at her was no other than Erik. She then went up and kissed him while Roger jealously caught a glimpse of the embrace. It was no wonder that Beth needed the open spaces around her when she is living inside a suffocating hell of Roger's presence. Sadly, like everyone else at Fell End, she had nowhere else to go.

Not everything in his life was peaceful. One particular cup was being placed in the shelf above the kettle on the wrong side. Luckily for Roger he found the culprit red-handed. "Beth why is that everyone else seems to know where this cup is placed. Have you never wondered as to why it is placed onto the left-hand side of the shelf and as to why you place it on the right-hand side?" He said as this poor trembling young lady, who was trying to quietly eat her breakfast, and had simply not thought that she had done something wrong with the cup. Instead, she suspected that he was punishing her because she was with Erik and for the fact that his confusion was tearing them apart.

"I am sorry Roger." She said and walked off without creating a scene as Roger was lost for words.

Feeling sad with everything, she decided to go out on her own with the beagles and take them down into the vale and back. At least they would never annoy her and showed her love, unconditionally.

A while later Roger was observing David working in the garden. "David, please use the shovel with both hands." David sighed and started to use both his hands. Roger continued watching him. "David please, please! Work a little bit faster. By the time you have finished digging, the grass will have grown all over those worm holes you have dug." Once again David sighed and tried to please him. Erik had been observing everything. He too was working in the garden. David collapsed onto the floor through sheer exhaustion. Erik then marched up to Roger with his rake.

"You had better then get off your arse before the grass grows over it. Here is your fucking rake. Not for your arse, but for the soil! David go and relax wherever you want; while that lazy bastard does some fucking work for a change." He said before walking off leaving Roger as he had literally said; to do some hard work for a change.

A few minutes later and while he was still reeling over the verbal attacks against him; Beth arrived back with the beagles and was surprised to be seeing him working hard and gardening. "Oh, you people, think you are clever!" He said to her.

"What is that supposed to me?" She said glaring at him as she was sure that he was giving some veiled attack on her.

"You think that Christianity has saved you! Then you are stupid! It is I who saved you and everyone else here!" He bawled at her.

"Jesus saved us!" Said Beth.

"Jesus did not save you! You were in his eyes as you have already told me carrying Satan's child! It is I who saved you, Beth! It is I, it is I." He said as he felt as though he was losing his mind. He then thought very quickly, he had to mess with her piety and walked back immediately towards her. "Jesus is saving you, because he loves me too and I am his master as he is my servant and that's why are still alive!"

"Why would anyone in their right minds want to save a carrier of Satan?" Beth cried, as shivers went through her spine as she thought about the evil from his words and didn't care if she had to be sacrificed in order to purify the evil surrounding the situation.

"Because your loving Jesus; loves Satan too, we will all survive." Incensed he continued with his bawling with his vitriolic thoughts as she walked off. Beth was then deep in thought and prayed for forgiveness as she looked up at the sky to the east and away from the sun.

Chapter 7

SO IN LOVE WITH EWE

Beth was feeling much worse psychologically than the first time around when she was in the family way. Her body seemed to be filling up much quicker too. Beth was concerned. No longer concentrating about dates, as much as she knew that it was the middle of August, and as much as she must have known that she fell pregnant in mid-June as opposed to mid-July the previous year, she was horrified as she compared this pregnancy with her body exactly one year earlier. As she was standing in the garden and gazing into space carrying her child in a sling in front of her belly, her heartbeat rose as she saw the being who was on her mind. She needed to talk to him, but he was observing the garden with Erik. She was getting cold, she wanted to go inside, but she needed to catch Roger when he was on his own. A few moments later, Erik was busily trimming the hedges with a scythe and she gently walked up to Roger so that Erik wouldn't notice. "Roger." She whispered. "I need to ask you something."

"My dear, you can ask me anything you like, I am always here for you." He said so lovely, making her despise him further.

"Is there any reason as to why I am feeling much less maternal and filling out much quicker than last time?"

"Beth, that's a very good question and I wish I knew the answers." He said hoping to spend some special time with her.

"I really need to know." She said almost in a sweat in case Erik would suddenly appear as she went red in her face.

"Let me do some research, from my French books about pregnancies and meet me say here at the same spot tomorrow around two in the afternoon and I will tell you what I have found out. Please make sure that you get a good night's sleep in first." She merely nodded her head as he smiled at her.

That evening she went with Erik and her baby to watch the sun go down from Louhrigg Fell. While she was there, Roger was once again with his, one and only ewe. He spied Beth before she noticed him and was relieved that he had made love to the animal the evening before. Even so, he couldn't resist and took his four-legged friend down a few metres where they were out of sight and out of mind. The feeling of the female sheep licking his hand with her bristly tongue was simply one of heaven for him as once again his ewe had aroused him. Without any inhibitions, he took off his clothes and he made love again to his furry friend. Once again, she was delighted as he went inside her, and once again he felt as though he was in heaven. His heart started glowing and he was sure that the ewe felt the same way as himself. As she bleated Roger had forgotten about Beth and Erik and in turn he started groaning excitedly and in tandem with her.

Beth started trembling; she felt as those she was blushing with shame and that she knew what The Beast was up to. Inside she was praying that Erik wouldn't comment about The Beast, which wasn't the sheep, but the very own father of her children. She then wondered if she was going insane. Roger wouldn't actually make love to a beast. "Did you hear that strange noise?" Asked Erik.

"I didn't hear a thing." She said lying through her teeth and too scared to imagine that Roger was carrying out with such a disgusting act of bestiality.

Roger in turn took the sheep back down with him to his home. Although a little in love with his ewe, he came inside his pants as he thought about cooking her alive on a fire with him staring at her as she would look on helplessly at him. He knew that the sheep was very fond of him and he wanted to speak with someone about his confusion. It was times like these that he missed the good old days, when psychiatrists were everywhere. In some ways he needed more help than ever before but wasn't sure how much he could fully trust Beth, who was the nearest person to being his own personal psychologist.

The day ended nicely. Back at Fell End in the twilight, Beth spied the sheep and felt somewhat sick; equally she was right about the lawn. Grass was so much nicer than rocks. The sheep was grazing. Roger was sat in the garden. The sheep walked up to Roger as though they were both lovers and started bleating and licking him all over. Luckily, Roger wasn't doing anything with the ewe. Even so, shivers went down her spine as she thought about his idea for her to breastfeed a lamb. On top of that, she felt sick; she felt in her heart that the father of her children was a zoophilic beast. She had heard a groan a few hours earlier resembling that of his own as well as that of the bleating from the sheep. Beth was absolutely sure that more than just three women were fighting over him in their own ways and that the fourth female in his harem was nothing less than a four-legged sheep. It was times like these when she questioned herself. What normal woman could collude with such depravity?

As for Roger he had tried an ewe and decided that making love to humans of both sexes was just as pleasurable. He was pleased that he had tried and believed that you had try things out before one could say whether or not it was that suited someone. Nobody had seen him on the fell when an hour earlier when he was making love in such a beastly manner. In turn he felt that he was a kind man to have done such a selfless deed for the others. It was thanks to him that the lawnmower was on site.

So long as he had a hole for his penis, he was happy, and his pet served a good purpose for his lawn as well as for one of his fetishes too.

The next day they met up as agreed, as Roger knew his son was taking his afternoon nap. He also felt that she was probably carrying twins. "It is nice that the weather is warm again." He said. She merely nodded her head since she wasn't interested in his small talk. "I will need to carry out a simple test on you. Follow me." He said. As such she followed him to the garden shed. Once there, he took out a tape measure and a diary. "You are only eleven weeks pregnant, during the last pregnancy you were around your breasts thirty-two inches your belly twenty-five inches and your hips thirty-four inches at the same time. Please take off your clothes." He then measured her breasts. "That's an extra three." He said smiling and then wrote the figure down. He then measured her belly. "That's an extra five inches." He said with a broader smile then wrote it down. Then he measured her hips. "That's an extra four." He said grinning like a Cheshire cat and then wrote the figure down on paper since his laptop, without electricity, had no more of a use for him.

Her mind went into overdrive. "What does this all of this mean?" She said in terror. The last time she was pregnant, she looked great and well proportioned. Now she believed that she was dowdy.

"It could mean that because it is your second pregnancy this is normal, however, you got pretty much back into shape quickly. Look Beth, given you are breastfeeding your breasts shouldn't be growing much during the pregnancy, you have plenty of milk in there. I am wondering what else this could mean." He said as he was busily and excitedly fondling her breasts as she was feeling like some cow with large udders.

Feeling as though she couldn't take any more of his suspense she blurted out- "I need to know if I am ill or something." She said as she pushed his hands away from her bosom.

"There is no danger of that." He then started leering at her making her feel uncomfortable. "How does it feel when Erik kisses your breasts?" He said with his eyes fixated on her passionately.

"I don't let him, because they are so soft and tender." She said with her head bowed low as she was feeling overpowered by his masculinity.

"Let me see what's wrong with them." To her utter horror he then started kissing them with his mouth and made sure that he got some of her milk as he was suckling. For a brief moment she wondered if she should grab hold of his face and embrace as her mind was in such turmoil. Instead, she then felt extremely nauseous and wanted to run away from him. On top of that she could smell his latest conquest, in his hair, which made her feel even sicker than that of the pheromones of her own sister.

He then looked into her eyes. "You weren't like this, so nervous the same time during your first pregnancy when we were at Fleetwood and eleven weeks gone. There's nothing wrong with your luscious breasts, you are a real woman, Beth!" He said as he sensed her great unease. "What has got inside you all of a sudden? I need to see you again this evening."

"No Roger, you just want to fuck me!"

"Yes, I fucking well do!" He said without thinking.

"I refuse to see you this evening." She said loudly.

"Very well, I might as well let the cat out of the bag," he said as he came inside his pants thinking about the build up towards her becoming the submissive girl before she met David. Back at Fleetwood she was still free and easy, pregnant but not yet showing and he enjoyed taming her. Of course, she was a good girl when he met her, but he wanted her to treat him with love, respect and devotion as he would brag about his foibles to her. Back then, she wasn't aware of the depopulation agenda, while he was enjoying his strategic planning in being able to use his then covert fears of himself ending up as a skull flowing around the estuary. Instead, he had managed to pretend he was in fact feeling sorry for her since she was suffering from morning sickness. Back to the present, later on, he would once again have exclusively rights to her mind, body, and spirit as she would be his sex slave along with her sister. All he had to do was to find someone else for Erik. After climaxing over the recent death and destruction during these moments, he really wanted to fuck, rather than make love to her. He wanted it vulgar with her, since he was becoming a little bored and angry with her. Bored because she was so nice and angry and that she was Erik's girl. And Erik simply had to perish as far as he was concerned.

All he could think about was how much he wanted to get inside of her. "Your body is changing much quicker than last time. This is good news and means that you are expecting twins. I am so happy." He said as she looked at him terrified.

"You horrible man!" She said desperately.

"There is no woman I know as ladylike as you. Even now you keep your dignity and speak to me in a polite very dignified fashion and make me feel more than ever, a useless immortal as I see in you a giant of a goddess like being. I will never be so wise as you." He said as he somehow had to get inside of her.

"I am nothing more than just a teenager."

"In your romantic novels from the days of old, many a woman would have changed their shoes with yours. I also want to apologise about the vulgar language I used in front of you. I am deeply sorry." He said as she then ran off in shock as though he had just raped her. The news that she was expecting twins, made her feel as though he had just impregnated her once more. As much as she had been so close to allowing him to conquer her, so long as he had the smell of ewe in his hair, she would never allow him to get his pleasures with her. At least he had given off a glowing presence of lust and desire for her, which made her no longer feel that she was simply fat and ugly. However, a moment or two later she felt fat and ugly again as she thought about the ewe, who Roger loved, and was fat and ugly too. Suddenly she wanted to scream and end up on the psychiatric ward which probably no longer existed, where she could simply cut herself off from the real, depressing, and insane world.

Without Erik in her life, she would well and truly have been ready to hang herself. He then ran up to her. He noticed the terror in her eyes.

"Beth, I simply want to tell you one thing." He said as he wanted this beautiful, hot, sultry and sexy being so much.

"Go on then!"

"When I impregnate you, I do it with the utmost of love." He wanted her there and then. She wanted him too, even with the smell of ewe. If, however, she betrayed Erik: she would lose him. As for Roger he only wanted to use her as a hole for his penis, fuck her, and nothing more. If only Erik were less exhausted from his labor. Given that he was too tired to make love to her body; she still found The Beast exciting. Dazed and confused and thinking that she was dreaming about everything, she submitted to him, not for his love but to simply live a life of peace.

The sisters were still close together, they were both going through hell and preferred to spend as little time with Jennifer as possible, the woman who seemed to have it all. The babies were being taken care of by Roger and Erik who were sat on the lawn in the shade. "What have you learned since the tsunami?" Asked Beth.

"For me the tsunami began even before we met Roger." Sophie said as there was then an austere silence.

"Please let me know more." Beth asked who was delighted that Sophie was showing her rare tentative philosophical hues.

Sophie then looked at Beth nervously. "I need some time to breathe. I feel as though I'm suffocating in the insanity of our circumstances." Said Sophie.

"Why don't we go for a swim in the tarn?"

"I would like that."

"At least we can take our mind off things."

"Actually, I don't like the cold water. I am no longer used to swimming in cold water." Sophie said as she feared that her body might get a nasty shock in the tarn as memories of her father brought sadness to both of them. Their loving and sporty father who trained them both to swim in all weathers and in all conditions too.

"Look Sophie! I'm depressed too, if it weren't for Erik, I would most probably be dead already. I don't enjoy anything in my life, apart from taking care of my baby. I swim in order to survive. If I didn't swim, I would probably have no energy to look after William."

"Be happy you have got Erik."

"No, I can't be, I'm imbalanced, I no longer know who I am. I am no longer the person I was just one year ago, and I hope I am not going to go insane! Roger's torture has changed me into this ludicrous woman I have become. I spent all my life dreaming about a good man. Erik is so sweet, but I have no feelings for him. I am nothing like our dear mother. I have bad feelings about The Beast, yet at times I want him to rape me! I feel that I deserve to be punished for my own stupidity. Other times his passion excites me." Said Beth.

"I am also unhappy. I am anything but a normal girl and have been destroyed by our misfortune. I too enjoy fucking; I just wish it were an act of love too." Said Sophie.

"As for our mother, she was so in love with our father."

"Let's go and swim." Said Sophie. "Anything is better than this morbid conversation."

The two girls walked together to the tarn. They then had a swim around the tarn and were talking and enjoying themselves. Twice they swam around the water body and Sophie had forgotten her feeling that the water was too cold and was enjoying the landscapes ever changing moods.

As they got out, they felt so relaxed in the late summer heat. They were sat next to a small rock with a splendid view of the tarn and the fells behind them. 'I wish I hadn't done the dirty on Jan.' Said Sophie bringing back their moving reality. 'It all started when I told him to take a shower twice a day. He disagreed and so he told me that his health would suffer, and that he would have a skin rash if he washed all his natural chemicals away. I told him he was a dirty pig, and he called me stupid. I was so angry from his remark that from that moment on I was convinced that we had to finish. It was also around the time when I fell pregnant to him. I mean fancy me wanting to end our relationship because he called me stupid!' Tears then ran down her face, as Beth took her by the shoulders. 'Now I know that he was right after all. My skin is much healthier since I started washing less often than before. I bet that had I stood by him that; I would have been saved up on the Honister Pass when the floods came. Roger is my punishment." Sophie said as tears of remorse were running down her face.

"I just hope that there is a reason for this." Said Beth.

"Maybe we should be thankful that we met The Beast, he saved our lives." Said Sophie.

"And destroyed them too. There are times when I think nihilism is the only way to survive." Said Beth.

"Don't say that, you are so good, so true, and inspire me."

"Thank you for that. It is so hard for me to think that we lost everything back home. I miss my roots. But I must stay strong for our innocent children." Said Beth.

"Who would have thought that our conversation so soon in our lives would have been about babies all the time? As miserable as our lives are, we are much stronger than before, more grown up. I'm going to make sure I swim much more often." Said Sophie as Beth smiled wryly at her.

With the weather being so warm and sunny they went for another swim together. As they got out of the water, Roger appeared unexpectedly with some special creams and was smiling kindly at them both as their eyes were fixed on his hands. "I have been keeping them for this special occasion. I took a chance and wanted to surprise you both." The sun was beating down fiercely, and Roger came at the right moment. After rubbing the lotions on their naked bodies, which he had used on Beth regularly, Sophie stood up. He then made love to Beth while Sophie was behind a tree and having a pee. Beth had no control over herself, she was Erik's, but in reality, in her heart, she was nobody's. She remembered his words when he made out himself as being some protector of hers and she meekly gave up the fight immediately as she saw in the look of his eyes that he was ready for her. She preferred it long and slow, but a quick act of lovemaking was an unexpected delight for her too. After it her fight between nihilism and Christianity returned as once again, she was feeling numb as if she was the living dead. This feeling of emptiness was exacerbated as Roger walked off in search of her sister and all she could was to perch herself on a rock and dry herself in the sunshine.

Thanks to doing so much hard labor, Erik was all too often too exhausted to make love. Why was everything in her world so cruel? She asked herself. In the distance she could hear them both, unlike Sophie, Beth knew he had had both of them. Afterwards he then walked off without any fuss in the direction of Fell End. He wanted both girls to understand that he could live without them and that in turn they would want him more than ever. On top of that, he was trying to make himself a better person and no longer had his secret and sweaty bottom fetish.

At the Howe and it being the last week of August, there were plenty of vegetables in season. Roger had busily cultivated the grounds, and despite the tsunami, there were tomatoes, runner beans, apples, and pears a plenty too. Roger had collected some of the crops and the girls took some too for Fell End. Back at Fell End the men including Roger were busy in the garden while Jennifer was looking after the babies. As soon as the mothers arrived, the babies drank happily to say the least in the grounds, making their mothers feel wanted. Roger smiled to himself, he was absolutely convinced that his sperm was going to create a global situation of young mothers like Beth, Sophie and Jennifer all relying on just one man, himself. All he had to do; was to simply become the head of the Illuminati. He was very nearly there, and he planned to make the world his very own oyster, literally. With an international raping and satanic event of young girls, by himself exclusively and no other male would be involved, like a virus, he would become the new Luciferian religion. How he was going to achieve he wasn't sure, but in the meantime, he simply wanted to enjoy the good and quiet life at Fell End.

Everything was going peacefully. Of course, with the impending winter, life would be more difficult than the previous one when there was electricity. For now, at least, it was time to enjoy the harvest and the days which were still warm. Roger though, was thinking about who his real nemesis was. Erik was a plebeian, but a very handy one. He was an honest hard-working soldier. David was too clever for his own good, but equally in his eyes a very beautiful and effeminate dandy. If only there were more men like them, a few more would fire up his satanic desires. Instead, and with a shortage of labor he had for the time being other uses apart from sexual ones for them.

Once he had learnt all of the tricks of the trade regarding DIY he could discard of Erik. In turn he could have full control over David. If only Erik was just that little bit more submissive, as the kind-hearted soul he was, he didn't really wish to kill anyone.

Later and while he was mulling over what went wrong between him and Beth and to his great chagrin, he heard Beth giggling with her present beau. With David and Erik around he only had one woman in his life. For Roger this was a very bitter pill to swallow. A sixth sense went over him that he might lose Sophie too. He didn't know why; he couldn't think of other men arriving too. His inner voice told him that there were no other men coming along. Even so, he was feeling uncomfortable. He enjoyed testing his dirty deeds out on Sophie before he would turn to Beth. This wasn't the case with the last pregnancy. For him, Beth was a matter of greater urgency, and when Erik arrived, he felt vindicated with his actions. Had he waited a few weeks longer, she would be carrying Erik's child instead. Roger as what he believed to be the caring man he was; would have preferred for Sophie to have had a nine-month respite from a pregnancy, but he had to make the most of things. Beth was a warning for him. If he would wait too long, Sophie might very well fall pregnant to someone else and instead of himself.

As far as he believed, he certainly wanted the best for her. The world was about the survival of the fittest. In his eyes, Beth was the best; Sophie was a very close second. If, however, Sophie would fall pregnant to someone other than himself then the special love and protection he was giving her and keeping marauding men away from who might be outside of his territory would be less certain. Now, he had to keep his jealous thoughts at bay, he had to find some impulse to keep on looking after her. As far as he knew; there was only one way to do this.

One evening in the bed with Sophie as usual, which was sadly a daily routine for him, since he didn't really love her, he looked at her. "How do you feel about being a mother?"

"Well, since we don't have all the mod cons thanks to your old cronies, our baby keeps me busy. I can tell you that I don't want any more children. I just don't feel safe with you." She said. With that, Roger was disappointed. He wanted to make her pregnant with her mutual consent. Instead, he would have to remind himself about how he got her the last time up the stick.

Other things were on his mind too. He wanted everyone to be happy with him. That way they could indirectly control his urges of his, which he feared could reoccur at any given time. Apart from shooting Helene, he had only killed one other person and that was with his hands, a single punch. So long as he was happy, he would live peacefully. Disturbingly for him, his sporadic attraction towards the men at Fell End was complicating things for him even further and that his zoophilia was the least of his worries. In turn and in fear of himself he locked his bedroom door and drank a whole bottle of wine and decided to spend twenty-four hours in his bed. He had never before felt so languid in his entire life.

Of course, the girls knew he had locked himself in his room on his own, and both realized that he needed time to ponder the whole night through. Even so, he was heartbroken that nobody checked up on him before bedtime. He then went onto his bed and burst into tears. Suddenly he felt depressed no more. He was literally inches away from the room next door if he moved to another part of the bedroom. With that he hatched up a plan. Down in the cellar, there was plenty of his camping gear. Upstairs he went with a mat, a pillow and sleeping bag. With his right ear pointing to the wall all he had to do was to lie in wait. To his great delight, Beth and Erik appeared to be ready for passion a little earlier than normal. As they were together thoughts of Erik's balls freezing and turning to stone were exciting him. Without his manhood, a castrated Erik could still work on his garden without Roger having to worry about his own posterity. All he could hope for was that Erik would lose his mind before he did. If not, his jealousy could consume him so much, that his secret desires from hell, which even for him went beyond the pale would be unleashed. Scared of doing something so bad too soon, he simply imagined that he was some hermaphrodite and was joining in with his neighbours as both of them could make use of him with his masculine and feminine parts. It was such a beautiful feeling. As an intersex, all of his problems would be solved. Not really knowing what he wanted to be, and as someone who wanted straight couples for his pleasures, he believed that he knew, subconsciously, the solutions to his problems. For him, heterosexuals were his food, and he wanted to eat their yin and yang so that they would become androgynous beings.

After thinking for twenty-fours about his life he went in search of Erik. It was in the grounds usual where he was to be found and, in all weathers, he was this salt of the earth holding down the fort as usual. "Erik I would like you to teach me how to become a handy man like yourself, so that I can concentrate more with things at The Howe." He said insincerely and unable to look at him directly in the eyes, as he was thinking about the macabre things, he wanted to mete out on him. Erik was pleased too, with Roger at The Howe, he would be more than happy in seeing the back of him.

Over the coming days, Erik taught him about dry stone walling and sharpening knives. At Fell End, the house being less than one year since it had been completely rebuilt didn't need any work on it and Erik showed him what was needed to be done at, The Howe.

Around this time after fixing his shed thanks to wood which David had brought over from a barn near Ambleside on horseback as well as a saw; he was managing quite well without Erik's help. It was then that he was more and more determining Erik in being simply nothing more than surplus goods. Once he had no more of a use for him, he would have to see to his demise.

The setting for Sophie was beautiful. With it being mid-September Roger decided that LED lighting could be used for one hour in the evening and from mid-autumn one hour in the morning. It was such a treat; her baby was in bed and she was reading with the bright lights as he was staring at the paintings. True, they had candles, but that wasn't enough for the eyes of the Fell End dwellers who were inveterate readers. He then started to caress her. She wasn't ready for a second child. "Don't touch me. I feel sick next to you and have intention in ending up like Beth." He remained a gentleman of sorts and read a book next to her. In turn she started to feel somewhat guilty regarding her impertinent behavior towards him. Even so, she wasn't ready to make love with him

An hour later feeling in need of nothing more than a cuddle, she looked at him. "Roger, why are you so negative about everything? … Don't you realise that your energy attracts unhappiness and misfortune?"

"I'm lost for words . . . . What exactly do you mean?"

"I mean this business about the lawn and the wall, wouldn't it be nice to think that we have a beautiful house, lovely grass as well as a delightful view of the beck?"

"It would. And, if I were like David, doing everything in a beautiful way, would that be more interesting for you?" He asked her.

"No, you know it wouldn't! It would be boring. Life is not like this as you know." She said curtly as he merely smiled at her, she had said everything he knew about her, and he then took off her clothes without any finesse. They made love. She then cried as she saw herself as being little more than a whore and in turn she ran out of the room in disgust. On top of that, the way she left him after making love, made him feel empty to say the least. As for Sophie, knowing what she then knew: she would never have left Jan. Instead, had she kept his child, had she treated him right, she would have been so lucky.

The following day he stonewalled her. She was happy. If he could play that game; then so could she. Both felt that they were allergic with one another. Both felt that the other was acting in a cruel and nasty way. Later that night in front of her bedroom he made love to the ewe. Sophie was restless the rest of the night and heard the sheep bleating excitedly and the faint groans of what sounded like Roger in her turbulent mind. She looked out through her window, but in the dark couldn't see a thing. She suspected that she was going insane. There was no way Roger was going to make love to an ewe. While in many ways she was better than Beth at blocking out the terrible events that had happened in hers as well as for humanity generally, she too felt battered and bruised psychologically. In many ways she believed that the wipe out was worse than the Second World War. After the war, America invested into the free world, and even the Soviets hadn't destroyed people's lives as much as the recent holocaust. Yes, she had her reasons for blocking out her thoughts, without her brain, she had more chance to survive these dark and terrible days.

Daylight came. Jennifer looked so happy with David and had the perfect man, the perfect pregnant body. Beth was being looked after by Erik who like Jan was as solid as a rock in his devotion to his woman. As for Roger, he was still getting his sexual delights, she, Sophie, wasn't. He was a disgusting man. Even if they had sex, it was quickly forgotten, since she couldn't bear thinking about the plight of her sister. As if he was a virus spreading, she was scared of catching something from him. Another pregnancy from him; would send her into a panic, maybe she wouldn't be able to breathe. In short, he was the closest thing to being some deadly disease for her. The day came, and he decided to play the role of a quintessential gentlemanly artist. His sketching was actually quite good. His portraits that day of a couple resembling a man and a woman from Fell End received plaudits from the others. Sophie herself was forced to show her approval but wanted to spill the beans about his disgusting act.

That evening she went into his room naked in order to taunt him. She was angry and bitter, that that the other women had men in their lives. Very few people had survived the tsunami, and unlike in the old days when single people were a plenty, all of the men and women had been paired together. It was The Beast or nobody for her. "How much do I turn you on?" She asked him.

"More than you will ever now." He said to her, as she was the one whom he wanted to impregnate there and then.

"Ewe are one on your own." She smiled at him as her answer had some faint bleating feel about it. "If I shower your balls with cold water fresh from the stream will you still be able to make love?" So, in love with ewe, he had to control his real feelings somehow.

"What has got into you?"

"I am not falling pregnant to you Roger."

"There are no other women here. There are no other men here. Wars are dangerous."

"I am not happy that my savior helped to wipe out the masses!" She told him a little afraid of him.

"I regret that viruses hadn't been produced to have killed the masses so that there would have been less destruction for our terrestrial wildlife which the tsunamis caused. Even you have to admit that as far as wildlife is concerned, things are much better now."

"But Roger; viruses, what a terrible way to die while waiting for some silent killer."

"You cannot have it both ways, it was nature or us. There wasn't enough space for mankind, and you don't seem to offer with your faith any solution to this problem whatsoever."

"I am agnostic. I believe in God as much as I believe in Satan. Still, there are times I see you nothing more than a virus."

"This is nicest compliment you have ever given me." He then walked outside of the house as she was shaken and numb by his level of depravity.

All he could hope for was that she was once again in her bed. All he could hope for was that he wouldn't be caught out. In turn he waited until he believed that she was once again safely in her bed. Once again, he made love to his ewe. He felt safe in the knowledge that the other women would be busy with their men and oblivious to him. This time around, he was less shy about his groaning. This time he was sure that Sophie would understand what battles really all were about. She knew that he was making love to the sheep out of his own personal spite towards her. She had heard everything, feeling sick and disgusted she wondered when all of this horror would end. If only Jennifer would throw The Beast out, until then and as long as he was seen as a useful member of Fell End, there was nothing that she could herself could do against him other than to kill him.

As for Sophie, she had visions of him as some Mengele character as she was dreaming. His character was injecting the people all over the world. They were prisoners of his for their very own SAFETY and soldiers were making sure that nobody left home.

The next day was pretty much a repeat of the previous one. Roger was sketching, only this time his characters were of lambs and their mothers, ewes, just like one of Roger's loves. For Sophie it was a darkly coded message. He wasn't ashamed of his fauna conquest. Even so, he had some itch between his legs, and was worried that he had caught something off from his four-legged conquest. With that, he was deeply concerned.

Beth was pregnant; she couldn't discuss his bestiality with her. Poor Beth there she was carrying his child yet again. Hopefully, her baby would be hornless and tailless too. With him, anything was possible. In turn Sophie decided to tame him. How though? She didn't want war with him, equally how could she be some submissive being to such a disgracefully perverted man? One who should have been locked up before the tsunami when help was at hand through the genderless abortionist supporter at Manchester.

Feeling lonely, she was alone; the others were in a relationship, for all she knew he too was still with the ewe. Perhaps if she showered him with love, something her sister, Beth, was good at; perhaps she could tame him. "Roger dear," she said a few days since she fell out with him. "I don't want you to think of me in being jealous, but I don't want to smell of ewe next time you are inside of me."

"I understand that," he said to her horror as he was confessing to her that he had made love to the sheep. "Anyway, even if I told you that I hadn't made love to our pet, you wouldn't believe me." His answer wasn't enough to give her any doubts that his sordid affair had actually taken place, but it was enough for her to realise that she didn't have enough evidence to use against him with the others and convince them that he was a fauna obsessed sex maniac. He was then worried. Not about passing on his itch unto her, but the consequences which could lead to her being infertile. He was in turn very worried. He had to find out as soon as possible whether or not he had caught something from his beloved ewe, with a shortage of women, the females at Fell End were very precious for him. Unable to impregnate beasts, women were like gold for him, and ewe was off his carnal menu as he had an appetite for something else.

As for Sophie, her mind went back to her days in school. She remembered the way her classmates behaved and the pornography that they were accessing. As much as she wanted to believe that Roger was simply a disgusting animal, she felt weak analysing her final days in school back in Warsaw just two years earlier. Classmates had teased middle aged teachers from abroad that they loved them and wanted sex with them. Classmates had even taken photos of teachers and imagined that these men could be lured away from their wives. In her final year this wasn't so bad, she was eighteen, the teachers might have been less than ten years older. Uncomfortably for her, she remembered about how she had heard from school mates that children as young as thirteen were behaving the same way towards, teachers, divorced dads in their forties and even fifties. In short, the best thing she could do with Roger was to mother him.

It was still morning and she took him to the tarn and together they swam. After it they went below to the beck which was flowing down into the valley and from there, she washed his hair. It was more interesting than showering in their home. Looking after this tramp: who had made love to an animal and turning him into a prince made her feel strong. Without her, he was nothing. Delightedly she kissed him on his lips. Still using a battery-operated shaver which was one of the many he had stockpiled up on, his face was still smooth and the closer they kissed with the touch of their skins the more she wanted him inside of her but would wait until bedtime.

With Roger's strange behavior, whenever the others saw him taking the beagles out on a walk, they hoped that he wasn't carrying out any strange acts on them.

Around this time something unexpected occurred to Roger which frightened the living daylights out of him. In many ways he hated the human race so much that; he wanted to be the last man standing and to celebrate the end of humanity. In his mind, all people were evil, and the planet could only be saved without mankind destroying her. But one morning he woke up ran to the bathroom and threw up. Instead of cleaning the place up he collapsed into despair after making sure that the bathroom door was closed. He then wondered how he would survive without Erik. In times like these when he had just thrown up, his own mortality was getting the better of him. Being the last man standing when he himself might be too ill to cope on his own was making the visions of floating corpses less attractive for him. This was all in the past. There were too few people to create another red sea as bright and vivid as the last one. He simply had to find other ways to be excited with his life instead.

Several days later one evening, during late September now that they were an item again, he did what he did the first time he got her pregnant and simply orgasmed surreptitiously as she came. He had recently been roaring when he reached the point of no return and was not inside of her. As such she was completely unawares exhausted and fell asleep quickly after a tiring day with her baby. For him, the energy he had for her was simply like that of one earthquake as he believed there and then that her life was about to change from his act. The thought of her being flooded once again with his sperm, his genetic code from his mother and his father during her ovulation made him feel invincible. His parents were the pioneers in the development of transgenderism in that both were born in the wrong body and for him to be their son in name and daughter in soul was nothing short of a miracle as well as being of a great honor. Each time he impregnated one of the girls and they got closer to his prized painting in his bedroom, he believed that; he was one step nearer into becoming his beloved parents' biological granddaughter.

A vision of a genderless baby came across his fertile imagination. For him those who died in the rubble of earthquakes with all of their energy were like batteries. Batteries were dead until their owners inserted them inside an appliance. Dead people had energy too, and like batteries it was for him electric. Until then, negative energy of those who were transphobic, could be used positively. If the next generation could be genderless and reproduce in an asexual way, then he believed in the survival of the human race. For him, it was such a crying shame that men who imagined themselves as women were during the previous regime being addressed via the wrong pronoun. All he could do was imagine that as much as he had been born a man, that one of his children would be born as a hermaphrodite. The next time he made love to her; it would have to be like one big reverberation making sure that the consequences of his lust had got her exactly once again where he wanted her to be. Like a battery on a shelf, his energy wasn't going to last forever, but at least his was one that would both his mother Peter, and his father Sarah would have been proud of. Simply put, he wanted to have a child who was as butch as Sarah and as effete as Peter combined. This was the way to recharge his legacy indefinitely into future generations.

The next morning, he did the same only this time she wasn't ready to fall instantaneously in her sleep and he roared like a lion as he was climaxing. By then he was sure that he had already fertilized her womb and with a bit of luck, the child would be of intersex. "You bastard! You creampied inside me!" She said as she realized his sperm was oozing out of her and he was making her feel repulsed by his lack of respect for her wishes.

"I know, it happened last night too, only I was quiet, and I just wanted to make sure that I really got you pregnant." He said smiling. There were no laws against him, civilisation was destroyed; surely, she would understand by now that her purpose in life was to produce children in this sparsely populated world of his own making. Sophie was livid.

He had wanted an earthquake and this time he was going to get one since her fury knew no bounds. She then collected as much of his sperm possible, from her vagina, and rubbed it all over his mouth. This for even Roger was a step too far, but he wanted to show her that he was a true feminist. He wanted to show her that he loved women more than any other man she knew. In his mind, his bisexuality made him more virile than docile sheep such as David and Erik. The next thing he did was simply too much for her. He simply with his tongue collecting his fruits started to swallow his own sperm. He then opened it up to show her what a mouth full of cum looked like. He then continued to swallow it. She was shaken and numb; she simply had to leave Fell End. After calming down, and with memories of the squatter who had been crucified down in the dale; she then thought that instead it was Roger who had to leave. Although terrified of him, she saw him as an irresponsible and weak character and decided he needed her help.

After a few eerily moments, he then looked at her. "In public couples are role models, in private; one never really knows what they are capable of getting up to." He was right, in her final year at school, the police came one day. A fifteen-year-old boy had been making love to his fourteen-year-old girlfriend. Normally the police wouldn't have bothered about the sexual act. Instead, the girl had been forced to involve urine, bogies and excrement in the sexual acts and had been complaining via text messages to her female friend who then alerted the police. The boy denied everything and said that the girl was blackmailing him. He wasn't charged with anything. Instead, he became a hero and a few other couples from her school started bragging about taking part in similar depraved acts. Some of the girls strapped dildos onto the lady boys whose numbers were growing and both parties were more than satisfied. These teenagers thanks to the Internet: were able to be more experimental than their naïve parents. All she could was to block this kind of perversion out of her mind, which was too close to comfort for her.

Unlike Kendal, the shops in Ambleside didn't have a large supply of batteries. On top of that, Roger believed that a few years down the line the energy cells would be way out of date and that he was preparing the residents for darker days when many of the goods they were relying on would no longer be replaced. Who was going to produce new running shoes for Beth? Who was going to replace the convertible oven? In short, they had to adapt to the still changing world as they were still going further back in time. As such the residents of Fell End had to make the most out of natural light whenever possible. With a huge shortage of manpower, no amount of money could kick start the local economy. At least they had plenty of land to grow their own crops.

The next morning since Roger was with Sophie all the time, he was fortunate enough to notice her creamy egg white fluid running out of her and he was excited and thought about Beth and the same experience three months earlier. He was seen smiling at her. "What are you looking at?" She asked him.

"I was just thinking about when the vaginal discharge was flowing out of Beth three months ago?"

"Oh my God you mean I am pregnant?" she said as she looked below her flat belly.

"No dear, this isn't an indicator of that, but it shows that you are in a fertile period and that all the sperm I shot inside you yesterday and the evening before was at the right time and during your ovulation."

"For fuck's sake, so you are saying that I am conceiving now?"

"Yes, and then in a few days you will be experiencing the implantation phase." He said to her without any emotion. He then put his arms around her holding her body in his arms. Sophie fearing that she was once again pregnant felt very vulnerable. On top of that the paintings above her head were making her go insane as she was certain that her life was basically the same as the girl in the pictures. She wanted to smash the images, but equally she was flattered since she half imagined herself as the beautiful woman. Deep down she knew it was Beth: this was so painful for her. Equally she didn't wish to hurt her sibling who loved the paintings so poignantly; so much. In turn she gave in to his passion and had unprotected sex with him, since it was probably too late to worry. A pregnancy was in fact the last of her worries as she was worried that deep down Erik was a Satanist and forcing depraved acts onto Beth too.

His words started ringing inside her head for the rest of the day. In public couples are role models, in private, one never really knows what they are capable of getting up to. Those comments were simply enough to put her off men for the rest of her life.

After a few days Sophie and Roger were lying in bed together and waking up before their daughter had. "I don't want to make love until after my next period."

"Are you serious? You want to wait one year?" He then walked out of their bed in disgust. He had to show her who the boss was. Sophie was angry that he had the last word, left the room calmly and was alone in their bed. She was unable to sleep, even though she had no reason to get up now that her life was meaningless again. In short, his words were haunting her.

Her emotions were running out of control. He was the biggest bastard in the world. How could she forget about him when she deserved him? When she was with Jan, she had humiliated him in a way that would have made Roger proud. Had Beth been less of an angel, could she herself excreted into Jan's terrified face? Now she was receiving a taste of her own medicine and had only herself to blame. She was indeed a disgusting Jezebel who had really earned her fate with him. If her next period were after a pregnancy that would mean according to Roger, no sex for nearly one year, and she was desperate not to wait so long. Without sex, and Internet Porn, what enjoyment would she have left in her miserable life?

Her mind went back to when she was with Jan and he came into their mutual bed on the day she told him that she was with child and he fell asleep instantly after a hard day at work. She could have made the rest into a fairy-tale, instead she had produced her own horror movie. There was a third person in her bed. She had no intention in making love to the stranger she invited in their bedroom at Buttermere, it was just one of her many stupid games she had played against her partner. After undressing her lover to be, she told him to wait underneath the duvet while her ex gave her some money; instead, he was hiding from more things than he anticipated. He certainly didn't expect her ex to get into bed all he could do was lie quietly and luckily; he fell asleep. Jan was disturbed when he realized that there was an unwelcome visitor in the bed, in the middle of the night, and the naked man woke up instantly and ran out of the room like a terrified rabbit.

As she entered his bed he was delighted. "Roger you are the biggest bastard in the world." He smiled, but she couldn't see his face. He was awake but acted as though he was still sleeping.

Sophie didn't know what to do. Was he really serious that she would have to wait one year for him? Who was he to say after getting her pregnant that she could make love on his terms only? In turn she started kissing him all over. Eventually he woke up in front of her eyes. Very quickly, he was thrusting on her hips with those of his own. She then thought about how with her big belly she wouldn't be able to make love in this manner and was wondering why he was holding onto her waist too. She knew what he was playing at. He was the mind games player. In turn he roared like a lion at the same time he was inside her and she was as excited as she was frightened of being in the family way once more with him. He then ushered her head towards his groin since he wanted her to blow him. As she was doing so, she wondered if she was enjoying this since for her it wasn't so nice and sweet for her having her mouth around his cock as she used to feel. Simply put; his phallus had been all over the insides of his beloved ewe.

Roger was enjoying her fears, which made him feel so powerful. Her feminine emotions a little out of control were making him feel all man. In turn just as she was nodding off to sleep, he started rubbing pregnancy creams all over her body. "What the fuck are you doing! Can't you see I am sleeping!" She said to him angrily.

"I am doing something I should have done last time you were pregnant." He said enjoying her fears and dread.

"I don't give a shit about my stretch marks." She said deceptively.

"I do. It is bad enough that I compare your skin to that of Beth's you don't want any more stretch marks than you have already." She then started to punch him, this time she was going to kill him.

"Go on, my life is so miserable I might as well end up with you carrying me inside of your womb!" He said as her punches were nothing like when she was whipping him and only of some slight discomfort.

"You bastard, you bastard, you bastard!" She said as she continued throwing punches at him. Suddenly, she was not only furious but scared to death of him and ran out in order to calm herself down.

He was the last person she wanted to see. What was the use in killing him if he would end up as her child? For Sophie he deserved to be miserable and not to return back to earth as an innocent child. She then thought, maybe she should kill him after all. As much as she hated the idea that he would benefit the most from a reincarnation, with him no longer making love to her, at least she wouldn't have to worry about falling pregnant to him again. On top of that, she didn't believe in reincarnation anyway. As such she decided to go back inside the house and was thinking about which bedroom she wanted to sleep in after she had strangled him slowly to death. In the meantime, she couldn't stop crying. One reason why she had finished with Jan, was because he wasn't into oral sex. He simply wanted to be her missionary. If only he were still alive and the father of their several children.

In turn she was angry with society. As she thought about the feminists, she knew who didn't like the traditional love making methods. Those were the positions that had helped develop life and to produce humanity which seemed, so hell bent on her very own destruction. She too, had been a part to this. As much as she hated feminism, she had no real respect for men such as Jan and had ended with a being more than her match. Even so, for her feminism was no longer about giving women equal pay and freeing them from unfaithful and wife beaters, it was also about taking part in sexually perverted acts. The women were being brainwashed into behaving like men in more ways than one. The men were being brainwashed into behaving like women in more ways than one. It was helping twisted souls like Roger in carrying out with his depopulation agenda. If only she had respected Jan. She then believed that the penny dropped. If children could learn about LGBT, zoophilia, necrophilia and cybersex, then less babies would be born as people made love less often in a traditional way.

She then thought a little more and smiled. Since the tsunami, cybersex was dead and buried and the media and its perverted depopulation agenda was over. Even so, Roger was still around.

A few moments later and to her shock and horror he was standing behind her as she was in the bathroom gazing into the mirror which, in the darkness couldn't reflect her face's image. Death would be too kind a punishment for him. She then started screaming at him without uttering a word. David heard her; he was terrified. Fortunately, Jennifer was a deep sleeper, who didn't care about the rest of the world. Erik was already sat outside on the doorstep armed with a frying pan ready to run inside if necessary. Suddenly there was a lull with her screams. "Please calm down, now is the most important time for the baby. We don't want it to end up headless or genderless, do we?" Roger said in a calm, cool, collected, and soothing manner. Of course, she didn't want this. At the same time, she wanted him to be punished. This was a big dilemma for her.

"I really don't give a shit. Who deserves to be born into this miserable fucking world anyway?" She then slumped herself on the floor.

The silence between them both though welcome, and led Erik back to his bed, was deafening. "Sophie, I don't want Beth to hear this madness. Let's go back to bed and make up." Said Roger as she was still quiet but appeared facially somewhat incendiary. He then sat at the end of the bed a few moments later. "Sophie, please can you help me?" Roger said meekly as though he was a victim of his own mistreatment towards her. He then burst out into tears. Meanwhile, Erik was relieved, that all was calm. He didn't really wanted to be beaten up after having a gallant fight with Roger in order to restore his almost sisters-in-law honor.

As the older sibling, the one who had got the two of them into this disgusting mess with Roger she decided to turn her energies of hatred to those of love so that the rest of the house could be living peacefully. In turn, she made love to the man she wished was dead. With thoughts like this in mind she believed herself in being no better than him and wondered how much longer she could control the anger that was festering deep inside of her. Hate Sex was what she believed both she and he deserved. All Jan wanted was love and sex, and now she understood what it must have been like to have been in his devoted yet desperate shoes. Simply put, she believed in wanting to long for your partner and to care and to cherish you, was what she wanted. The one she longed to treat her beautifully wasn't Roger, she was mourning over Jan instead. The only pleasure she got in her wretched life, was when she made love with The Beast.

All that she could do during the coming days was to live her life as normally as she had done since she became a mother and to live her life from day to day. In turn, for several days at least, her life should be no different to how it was before he had psychologically terrorised her with a second unwanted pregnancy. Hopefully, she wasn't expecting.

Around this time, Beth was still keeping fit and healthy. Erik would join her as much as possible. He wasn't in any way a lazy man. The only time he was looking as though he was doing very little was whenever he was keeping watch over her sleeping William. Whenever Sophie would see them, she was often reminded of Jan.

She was then halfway into no more man's land as she saw. Still waiting to find out if the accident had resulted in implantation or not. The last person she wanted to see was in her bed as usual. He was the one who to some extent protected her from her dark thoughts whenever she was alone and scared of being kidnapped. "Roger are you awake?"

"I am dear, and I am devastated, that I want children so much, but you don't."

"A woman carries the children for nine months in her body. Surely she is the one who should be able to decide."

"I agree. This is the reason why I wish that I was a woman."

"I don't think that you will ever understand women."

"Do you understand men?"

"No, of course not. If I did, I would still be with Jan as you know."

"Why don't we feel what it is like to be in another body? We can still make love without you falling pregnant, since like my vagina, your penis isn't very fertile." He said as she deep down quite liked the idea of them both experimenting and playing role reversal in the bed.

The next night and after collecting her old toys from The Howe, both Roger and Sophie were in bed as he imagined that he was her and she imagined she was him. Clumsily and with her dildo strapped around her, she was pounding him. Roger came inside his pants as he imagined that she had impregnated him, but Sophie hadn't come. "It would be much better for me if I could climax while doing this." She said frustrated.

"I understand; why don't I wear the dildo this time?" With neither of them thinking about him with his penis, and her thinking of him as a woman, this sounded like a great idea. This time she climaxed, and Roger was able to too. Now they could have their pleasures without her falling pregnant.

The two sisters were together in the garden as Sophie felt it was high time for her to menstruate, her life had changed no matter how much she wanted to deny it her former innocent lovemaking dreams of a man getting on top of her, had simply turned to just hedonistic desires. "How are you Beth?" She asked wondering how she herself might be feeling in three months' time.

"I feel good. Thanks for asking." Sophie then placed her hands on her sister's bump.

"I'm bigger than last time, aren't I?" She said as Sophie then thought about how she herself would probably end looking even huger than her.

"Don't dwell on this too much. Let's enjoy a stroll into town instead." She said as Beth was overwhelmed with her own reality.

The girls enjoyed the stroll into the valley. In the shops Beth bought back some maternity wear which had been brought over from warehouses as far away as Manchester on Roger's orders. Sophie stared in fear as she saw Beth looking at all the maternity wear. Now was not the time for her to bring back similar clothes as her sister. All she could do was to enjoy something closer to nature. Although it was October, it was

Sophie's idea that they should swim in the lake at Waterhead and with the sun shining it wasn't so bad in the bracing waters where they both managed a twenty-minute swim each.

Sophie was content with her life. She had survived the genocide. She was enjoying doing some extra exercise more than ever. It was helping her to sleep better, and she was able to enjoy her food more than ever too. With her baby being six months old, looking after Jane was getting much easier. The worst days were over. Her daughter didn't need to be watched constantly and was starting to do things herself, such as to hold a doll and entertain herself.

Chapter 8

THE GYNACOLOGIST

Three days later on a fine and frosty morning and still early October, when Sophie realized that she was pregnant again, she simply lay on the bed in total shock as if she were dead. She thought about how after breakfast she wanted to throw up and was feeling dizzy. As soon as Roger walked in, he was delighted in seeing her so. She looked so submissive, and he simply got undressed and was inserting himself inside her while he was imagining that she was his beloved Ewe. In shock, she felt simply like his blow-up doll. She didn't move, she pretended to be fast asleep. For Roger this was a dream come to true as he then imagined that she was some kind of living corpse. It was the orgasm and nothing else that mattered to him. All he needed was a hole. If only they could make love more often like this. After his act, he looked at her. "I am pleased that once again nature has proven that you are all woman." He said as she wished that she could feel all woman without any sorrow or pain

"You are my gynaecologist from hell!" She said.

"I am not just your gynocologist; I am Beth's too." He said deliberately hoping to arouse the slightest wave of jealousy inside of her.

Later that evening they were in bed again together. "Do you remember how you felt last time?"

"What; when I was up the duff?"

"Yes."

"No, I don't."

"Maybe you are imagining that you are pregnant." He said as his words gave her hope and with his tentative signs of her being less at his mercy, she was under his mercy. He then went up to kiss her, passionately.

"Please don't; you haven't been washing yourself properly." She said as she thought about his ewe. Ignoring her plight, he then kissed her breasts, which felt as though they were on fire. "OK, I am pregnant." She said as she was wanting him to leave her alone.

"I was not so sure when we made love earlier this morning, you didn't react like this then." He said as his answer confused her and was leaving her feeling numb and shaken with everything. Suddenly he felt all super potent male and he then went inside of her, she felt less that she was just a hole for him and nothing more. He certainly did show her more tender loving care this time.

"No, I don't want this!" She said in a panic as his fondling of her breasts was making her feel faint.

"But you want to find out if you are pregnant." She did, but was this the only way the gynaecologist could find out? It was almost like some medieval torture when a hot iron bar was placed on the suspect's hand. If he wasn't injured, he was guilty, if his hand burnt then he was innocent. The lovemaking was incredible as he was only thinking about her body, rather than that of other beings, as the excitement that she had his bun in the oven was delighting him. "Do you feel different now?"

"Yes, I feel more sensitive from your touch." He then smiled at her as she in turn felt defeated. As for the lovemaking, she had simply felt dazed and confused.

"The job is done; it is better than waiting for the inevitable." He said as though she had been tortuously waiting for a raping injection.

It was times like these and feeling so masculine when Peter and Sarah weren't his role models and heroes. For him, the idea of being born again was less attractive, but if it was the only way for him to get back his youth, then to be born again as one of the girls' daughters was the way forward for him. "I don't want to play role reversal in the bed anymore. There is no need for it now; it isn't going to help me now when I am for fucks sake preggers again anyway." She said as he simply started kissing her all over.

Outside in the grandiose garden late one morning at the end of the third week in October Beth was feeling angry. As much as she wanted to remain calm, she needed to speak to Roger. "We meet again in the same spot where we met for your inspection when I informed you about your multiple birth!" He said feeling more masculine than ever, as his words were making Beth go as weak at her knees as she was disgusted with him mentally.

"Oh my God! What are you doing to me?"

"Nothing."

"I just want to know why, a man like you, who is sexually confused, who wanted to be a woman is now some raging bull like figure." She said as it was just after breakfast when she found out about her sibling's plight. Sophie had already told her she was late, but Beth dismissed this since her sister said she had no other symptoms. Sophie hoped by not thinking about it, her period would still arrive.

He then looked at her haughtily, yet inside he felt like nothing. Somehow, he had to control himself if he wanted her to remain under his command. "Beth, dear, you know how much I love you. You also know the effect that you have on me. When we make love, I feel so much like an Adonis. I feel some kind of addictive mortality with you. When all my testosterone has been used up from our beautiful bliss, I feel once again all woman and wish that you would pound me with your penis, and this is why we cannot be together. I simply wish I could control my demons."

"Then why did you do this to me?" She said as he was staring at her huge baby bump.

"We basically live in the jungle. I am more masculine than ever before as you are more feminine with the pregnancy, I love you more and more. As for feeling all woman, this is happening less and less recently, as I feel so indebted to you for bringing precious life into the world."

"Then given I have three or more children to you, are you now not man enough for me?" As for his evils around depopulation, at this moment in time she was fighting for her family first and foremost.

"I guess I am. There is however one other complication which I never envisaged before." He thought about his plans for Sophie, but instead decided that there more pressing things for him to boast about.

"What is that then?"

"I might have become more masculine since the tsunami, I might no longer wish to be a woman, but I am holding back from you a very dark and disturbing secret." He said as she then laughed at him. "Beth, this is not at all very funny."

"Well, what can be worse than when you wanted me to be David and you wished that you were I just before I gave birth to our first born?"

He then softened his look towards her with a shy smile. "I have been a pitiful sad fellow, I am afraid, but listen to me carefully please . . . You are the best mother I have ever seen. I simply wish that I was inside your belly right now and waiting to come out into this beautiful world and to be given all the love that you are going to be giving to our unborn child. If only it were me!" He said as he wanted to cry like a baby and for Beth to nurse him, to dress him up as a baby so that he could drink her milk and to live for eternity. "Imagine if I impregnate you again and again and then after killing me, I will be reincarnated as your daughter!" He said as she started feeling disturbed by him. She thought about the time he said he wished she was carrying him three months ago then she had some sympathy for him. Now she was feeling bitter and scared of losing her own mind too. "Please! Please! Please! I beg you!" He said before he fell down on his knees crying. As much as she hated him, as much as she was confused, he was still a human being. Nobody as long as they were alive, deserved to be going through with such psychological torture as he was, and in turn she wanted to help and to mother him.

Roger wanted to admire her belly and to massage her whole body, and she knew this. Fortunately, as she was feeling in a trance, shaken and numb with everything and before she had actually done anything untoward with him someone placed hands on her shoulder. He was feeling uncomfortable and sensed the glowing sentiment between the parents to be and was jealous. "Beth dear, I would like us to spend some time together and to go on a walk. I am sure Roger can do his share of the gardening." In turn, together they went in a walk hand in hand, but Erik had nothing to say to her, this made her nervous. Was he going to harm her in a moment of madness? At least she remained calm she knew it was deeds rather than words that mattered to him, that was why she felt the best thing for her to do was to simply follow and walk with him. After being in his soothing presence after several minutes, she felt safe with her silent gentleman who held her hand tightly and kissed her passionately whenever they stopped for a rest.

Finally, he was ready to speak to her as they were walking besides the river near Skelwith Bridge. "There is no reason for us to stay in the same house as him. As beautiful and spacious as the dwelling is: I would much prefer our own privacy." He said to her.

"My love, you are right. I want us to have our own home too, but most of the properties are owned by the state and a man was crucified and, in his hands, he was holding an official document that warned all survivors that any act of squatting is a capital offence." She said begging for him to remain calm.

"I bet that bastard enacted this law so that he could control us, but we will never be able to get to the bottom of this matter." He said as he felt trapped in seeing no other solution.

"As they say in England; innocent until proven guilty." She said. He had nothing more to say. She was relieved, what could they do? All she expected from him was that he would give her all of his love and devotion.

She also wondered how such a humble man was wise beyond his social class and hoped that Roger would from then on leave her body alone.

Later that evening after making love to Sophie he was lying in bed with her thinking. In Roger's perfect world, he would have four women. Sophie was one month pregnant, Beth four and Jennifer seven. If only Erik and David weren't around. If only in two months' time he would be able to impregnate someone else. A thought then went across his mind. Jennifer had already made love to him. In turn, he had every right to impregnate her. Given she had made love to him behind David's back; he believed that he would get away with this act. Later as his depression returned and, while making love to Sophie, all he could think about was the other two women with whom he was no longer making love to. Judging by the way she stood by Erik, Beth might no longer make love to him, but so long as he could convince her that he was some kind of obstetrician he would be able to inspect her breasts, belly, hips and thighs and hopefully be able to continue lovemaking with her behind Erik's back. On top of that, using his imagination he would be able to have wonderful orgasms thinking about her without any emotional drama. Erik was the one who had to endure her wild emotions, since he was living with her. Then again, it was the psychological terror he missed meting out on her. If only he could have his cake and eat it.

Another night and morning had passed by it was more or less late October and the colors of the leaves were as iridescent as that of her own life which was rainbow-colored with hues from hell. There she was crying the minutes away and felt that she was all alone and didn't want anyone to know what the matter with her was as she was looking over the garden wall in the direction of Rydal and thinking about life before technology and how then was strikingly similar to the present. She then felt a hand on her right shoulder as her sister noticed her tears. "I'm pregnant." Beth then collapsed as both started consoling the other and hugged.

"Please don't tell anyone." Sophie said meekly.

"Are you sure? You are only a few days late. Also how do you feel?" asked Beth concerned.

"I don't know exactly. Now, I no longer count the days in the week, but I must be around my seventh week now. As for how I feel, I don't know. I dread to think what the others will think. They will have to find out sooner or later. I just don't see the point in morals. Even if I had been a good girl, I would have ended up dead and buried in the Warsaw Rubble. To think that the mothers who gave life have lost their children around the world makes me so sad. Sex is the only pleasure I have in my life. As for being pregnant, I feel shaken and numb. I don't feel as though I am carrying life. Most of the time, my whole world is dead. I might not discuss the genocide, but I am still suffering. I wish that I were like you, who lets it all out. Instead, I feel so dead emotionally."

"I pray each day for you and all of my loved ones. Time is a healer. I hope your unborn baby will be full of love and in turn you will learn that the world is not so full of evil . . . This time next year we will be collecting the leaves for her children to play with. Think about the joy that they will have when they will be playing with their siblings just like you and I used to do." Said Beth reflectively.

"Is there anything I can do to make him a better man?"

"No, there isn't. His moods, opinions, desires just about everything keep on changing with him like the weather."

"There must be something?"

"We are what we are. Imagine I am Cinderella's dress, would you wear me in the garden?" Said Beth as Sophie giggled.

"No, but as people we can adapt. He has spoken to me about his gender fluidity and how he is attracted to me because I am a real woman. He then moves onto how when he has everything the boredom sets in and he wants us to play role reversals in the bed." She said hoping to reveal her cross dressing with him.

"This is impossible. There is nothing you can do about this. David told me when we were first met about how the Bible is a manual for good and happiness. How there is nothing more beautiful than monogamy between a man and a woman who are in love. Of course, he has broken so many of his precious rules, just like I myself have, but like Erik, he tries to be dignified."

"Roger once told me that if he could rid himself of his sexual confusion he would; and that you and I are both good girls in different ways. He then added that the most promiscuous relationships are gay ones, because the men get bored very easily and want to try things out, especially if they are bisexual and need both sexes. I think he said this when he was feeling very guilty about his treatment towards us."

"If he really felt so bad, he would stop thinking about himself and wake up to the consequences of his actions. At least the other men are into vanilla sex only. You deserve better than this for sure."

"I have had enough about this. What about you?" She said as she was then too scared to reveal to her about her own perverted acts.

"I don't feel very settled with Erik. I just wish I was with David."

"Had you aborted William, in all probability David would be yours."

"It would have had to be done secretly, he's a staunch Catholic, but yes, had I done so, things might have been different. As you know, I would never do such a thing."

"Abortion killed my relationship; Jan said that I killed a part of him."

"I smiled at David on the day we arrived here from Buttermere. All he could do was smile back at me. I often wonder if I should have done more to entice him."

"What more could you have done? It was simply his place to act. He didn't, we have to stop questioning ourselves all the time or we will end up insane. If I weren't breastfeeding and pregnant, I would be an alcoholic right now!"

Roger couldn't understand why the sisters were behaving less favourably towards him than the first time they fell pregnant to him. Surely as much as they were not being so attentive to him as he would have liked, their circumstances were better for them than being in the family way to different men. At least in both of their cases, the children would have the same father. He couldn't understand what their problem with him was.

With both sisters getting on his nerves, Roger was delighted to being with Jennifer for a night at The Howe that November when she was in her thirty-fifth week. They simply didn't care what the others thought. In fact, she saw David as some doormat, and was sure that he wouldn't notice. As for the sisters, they were used to being part time loves of his. Feeling like escapees from some boring psychological prison she was delighted when Roger took off her maternity wear and wore it himself. Roger was delighted when she was wearing his trousers and playing with his toys as he was feeling all woman. After a while the roles were reversed as she became a woman, and he became a man once more. After their fornication, her mind went back to paintings of Beth. The penny dropped; he was more of a fraud than she first thought. He said that Sophie was his partner, yet the paintings depicted her sibling who according to him had betrayed her own sister treacherously.

"I love you so much." He said as she privately dismissed the meaning of his false words, the following morning when they were in bed together.

"I wanted to make sure that you still have it in you for my second child!" She said somewhat brazenly.

"And I want to get you pregnant, again and again and again!" He said cheekily to her. "Have I said something distasteful?" He said as he noticed a veil of sadness go across her face.

"No dear you haven't. I was just thinking that it would have been so much nicer for me to have walked to the stream without having to walk through the tunnel like path." With thoughts of her not being his and the possibility of getting her pregnant several times he was concerned.

As they walked back a part of the way together, she felt increasingly guilty and halfway back home he walked back briskly as she went at her very own pace. By the time she arrived Roger was already safely indoors. At Fell End, he saw her. "I am so happy that you are back safely." Said her sweet and naïve David.

"I fell asleep on the sofa at the main house. Why didn't you go and look for me?" Jennifer said.

"I am so sorry; I had no idea." Said David.

211

THE VICAR OF BUTTERMERE

"OK, all is forgiven!" She said as inside she was proud of her very lucky escape regarding her deceit and adultery.

As for Roger, nobody questioned his movements, but the others apart from Jennifer, felt uneasy whenever they saw him outside walking with the innocent doggies. The only escape was death, and so long as suicide was painful, neither of them had the strength in doing such a thing.

A few days passed and he was lucky enough to see Beth in the garden without the watching eyes of others. "I would like to check our twin's health tomorrow. Let's meet up inside the shed at 2PM tomorrow." He said as he was making it obvious that he was admiring her figure and reminded her that he was thinking about their children as he placed his hands on her belly. Shivers went down her spine, as she remembered him doing the same to her belly when she wasn't with him when she was David's girl. "Oh, how much I miss the spooning position with you, when I held you and our baby all night long." He said as she was being haunted by his words. With that she ran off in tears.

That night he couldn't sleep as he imagined himself alone with Beth, while she was sleepless too because she didn't want to go near him. Sophie was lying next to him and he was thankful that he wasn't alone but was angry about his confusion. If only he could concentrate on one thing at a time and be in love with just one woman, he thought as he was missing Beth so much. All it took was for her to understand his gender fluidity and he would never leave her. As for Beth, she wanted to save him, but didn't know how and wanted nothing other than traditional lovemaking to take place between them.

They met inside the shed the next day. "Beth, take off your top please." He said with a husky voice.

"It is cold here."

"It is not so cold as swimming in the tarn." He said as she smiled and thought about how she was still going into the tarn for a quick swim daily. Then, she did as she was told. He then unfurled a tape measure and placed it around her chest. "That's a whopping three inches extra than at the same stage." He said as she opened her mouth in shock. He then repeated the process with her belly. "My God Beth, that's forty inches and an extra four than last time."

"Roger please don't measure my hips." She said as her words fell on death ears. He then checked her hips.

"It is amazing what I have done to you a second time. I don't need to check your hips. Your body tells me a wonderful story." Instead, though, he continued measuring her. "Wow! You have hit the hundred-centimeter mark or forty inches and more! It must have been so passionate to have changed your body so quickly, imagine how you will look soon. Now I will check the movement of both babies." He said as Beth was overwhelmed with the reality. First sit down on the bench. She then sat down. He was just about to kiss her on her lips when she slightly brushed him off with her body language, unperturbed he then went for her luscious left breast. His kiss made her feel good. After what was longer than he should he looked at her. "Your breasts are darker and fuller than last time. All the signs are pointing to both of your breasts being busy and preparing for the birth."

She had finally accepted that her body was preparing herself for the birth since her Braxton Hicks contractions had already returned, but she didn't at all feel comfortable with his haunting manner. "Roger, they have been bigger due to the breastfeeding."

"I know, but darling, you know deep down that they are growing further and further towards the painting. Your breasts thanks to the breastfeeding were large enough, but with twins they need to be larger than ever." Beth then froze it was as if his words had anaesthetised her repulsion towards him and made her forget that she was Erik's girl. For her, the fact that she was responsible for three of his children: meant that he simply had a big role to play in her life, and in her heart too.

He then placed his hands tenderly on her belly. If only he cared for her as much as he was proud of their mutual babies. "I can feel one of our baby's! Stand up please." He said excitedly to her. She was then mesmerized and did as she was told. He then touched her bottom. By then she was overwhelmed by his desire for her and was caving in as he was thinking about the Morecambe Bay being filled up with his sperm and all the fish in the sea would be carrying his children, since he saw himself as the great creator of life. Her mind went back to the wry jokes at Fleetwood about him being some marine father of all the seas and now she was more vulnerable than ever. Still thinking about his fertility more realistic was terrestrial animals. Could he miraculously impregnate his beloved ewe?

She had tears running down her face. She was disgusted with herself, but he was the father of her children, and she felt that it was right to be on friendly terms with him. Her emotions brought him back down to earth and away from his then thoughts about floating corpses. He was thankful for this; since he was about to come inside his pants when he wanted to come with Beth instead and was now inside of her and he wanted to wait for her. "Oh Beth! You are less than five months gone but compared to last time when you were pregnant; you look like you are more than seven months. I am sure you will resemble more than ever like that of the painting of you that I cherish." She was then in shock, as she thought about the time when she was at a similar stage of her maiden pregnancy. Her life had certainly changed since then. "Imagine how beautiful it will be when you are expecting quads. Oh, how I love the way our dreams being fulfilled, as I will get you pregnant, again and again and again and again!" He said as they were climaxing together. His prowess excited her body, as his determination to get pregnant several more times was scaring the living daylights out of her and perversely for her, was making her body long more for him more than ever before too. Still, he had no idea about this as she was shaking her head, "No, no, no," She cried.

She was shaken and numb as well as being dazed and confused. She had just cheated on Erik. David had cheated on Jennifer for her. In turn she had no respect for herself. How could she call herself a good Christian girl? She had to stay away from Roger. She could feel him all over and throughout her body, if only Erik was as sensual as the beast. How could she keep well away from Roger after giving birth next time when it wasn't so easy to find a place to live outside of his domain? Even if she were living at The Howe with Erik, he would still be visiting her there too.

She then started living for the moment once again as he then started rubbing some pregnancy cream all over her, this she found harmless, but it had special mix including ginger which increased her libido against her will of which she had no control either. He sensed her nervousness. "It is so romantic now that instead of pornography the old-fashioned ways of love are back in vogue. It makes me feel as though I am in heaven with you." He said as he was staring at her left breast.

"Why are you looking at my breasts like this?" She said nervously.

"Don't worry dear; there is something that resembles a bright red fiery but harmless stretch mark on your left breast." His answer made her feel vulnerable; she needed him more than she needed Erik. Not so much as she longed for David, but second best was good enough for her. She gave up once more to his designs on her, as she was enjoying his tender loving care and in turn, they made love. Making love to the gynaecologist who was her impregnator too: filled her literally up with a poignant delight as he came inside of her. "I am going to get you pregnant, again and again and again until the day I become your unborn child!" He said as she then wanted to be sick from his last words.

After a few minutes and for the time being at least; he felt content. He then studied her face and could see how distressed she was. "What's wrong love?" He said gently to her as he wanted her to be as happy as he was.

"I shouldn't have made love to you. You think you are the tender and loving father to be. How do you think I felt when I was heavily pregnant just out of high school and you told me haughtily about the other women you had impregnated? I even saw one of your dead victim's just weeks after she gave birth to your child. OK, the waitress wasn't murdered by you, but you are fully in support of that horrible agenda. And what about your child who after a botched sex change operation was killed by his mother?"

"I merely wanted to be honest with you. Anyway, it wasn't my child who was put out of its misery; it was the child of the other lesbian who wasn't impregnated by me."

"Well Roger you make sick. I was so vulnerable the first time I fell pregnant to you."

"And what has changed?" He said smiling at her. Too scared to reply she simply looked at him, she knew he could destroy everything for her. He then looked into her thoughtful eyes. "Don't worry, I will not be telling Erik that you slept with me behind his back, so long as this becomes a regular habit of ours." He said as his smile was widening into some wide leering grin at her. As for his threats, she simply didn't care: or did she? She asked herself. As for the waitress, she cried tears for her as she was no longer jealous of his one-night stand with whom he could have saved along with the mutual child of theirs.

"If you loved me, you would not be telling me how you want to use me just so that you can live forever!" She said suddenly.

"Don't tell me that if you could escape inside the womb of someone like you with a father like David and a mother like I, that you would never do such a thing!" He said. Humiliated from his depraved words, she simply walked off.

That evening as she was back with Erik, her feelings were like those of the rainbow, only one of all the dark colors from hell. They were mixed with thoughts filled with sorrow, regret, anger and hatred to name but a few of her feelings. Everything was connected to Roger. The sorrow that he had taken advantage of her that very same day, the regret that Sophie hadn't killed him and the anger that she had allowed herself to succumb to his hedonistic designs on her. The hatred for everything as she no longer believed that she had a reason in seeing things positively. Fortunately, when she woke up the following day, her sweet and loving self-had returned.

The second half of November arrived. The days went by as usual. Roger like the women would be analysing everything. The men would be working in the garden. Jennifer would sometimes help out at The Howe for some philosophical talk with him. If anyone saw her helping in the orchard there was nothing out of the ordinary, since much of the produce on their dinner tables came from there. Equally, Jennifer and Roger were good friends only and she wanted to forget about her cheating on David. As for Roger, he was enjoying being on bad terms with the sisters and making love to them. Even Beth was now making love frequently to him, but that was because she was confused about everything and having a personal fight with her own beliefs. While she knew what was right and wrong regarding marriage, family values and being a good example for her children, neither Roger nor Erik could help her on that score. Roger broke all the rules, and with Erik who was always exhausted from his toils outside, she felt compelled to be committing some form of adultery. What was this passionate young lady to do? Stay celibate and be even more miserable than ever. As for Jennifer, she was Roger's best friend now.

Several days passed and Roger was in buoyant mood. He wanted to tell Erik how proud he was that he had got Beth pregnant for a second time but instead decided that he would provoke Erik and in turn David in a less confrontational way. The setting was the garden. "I am so proud of Beth who stood up to me regarding the issue of the lawn." He said as he kept on slyly looking at Erik. He then decided to get ready for the kill. "Well guys, you have done a really great job in helping me get the garden sorted out. The place has been fully weeded, and I think we won't have much more work to do on it, it being November."

"Thanks for the compliment Roger." Said Erik.

"I have something wonderful to announce." Roger said.

"What's that?" Asked David.

"I got Sophie pregnant again! I am so lucky to be having so many babies!" He said animatedly as Erik was raging inside.

"Is Sophie pleased?" Asked Erik sarcastically.

"I think so. At least we are still an item." He said as Erik thought about Beth who wasn't an item with Roger. As far as Erik was concerned, he was a careless speaker at best, at worst Roger was a highly provocative man, who deserved to have perished in the tidal waves of hell.

Roger rightly sensed that he was hated beyond the description of the meaning of the word. He also knew he needed laborers, no matter how much their presence was of a nuisance for him. As such, he felt trapped that he couldn't escape from the men, who were both taking away his exclusive rights to the women and yet they too, these very men, were turning him on at times. His mind was in turmoil. He simply didn't know which way to turn. He wanted to impregnate David's belle, but felt as though he was walking on eggshells. He had to somehow neutralise any hostility the others had towards him, so that once he had achieved his aim, Erik would accept it. He was more concerned about him than Jennifer's week and girly partner. For him, David personified the archetypical Christian and could very easily be manipulated. Erik could humiliate David in showing his anger towards Roger about an impregnated Jennifer and have a fight with him, but for Roger at least, he preferred to write some other story for his life and to fantasise about all the different shades of hell which brightened up his own miserable world.

Beth was in two minds. A big part of her wanted to leave Fell End and to move back to The Howe, another part was scared that she would miss her sister and most of all, precious sightings of David. The others could have their own house. They would be sharing the same grounds but would have plenty of space. Erik was good with his hands and would surely be able to turn The Howe to her own liking. She had also been eavesdropping in on Roger's gloating about getting her sister pregnant. It had been such a sight, seeing the hateful friendship among the men. David was the man she loved, who loved her too. Erik was her partner; he was loyal and so true. Roger was the father of her children. Seeing all three men talking about women together made for Beth a most interesting sight.

With his hands in his pockets and looking down towards the Vale of Rydal just after the sunset he was thinking about how much nicer and cleaner the air was without the cars and the hordes of tourists. "I would like to move into The Howe with Erik." She said as he realized he was no longer alone and took him by surprise. She had just approached him because she wanted him to lend her the front door key. Before she had a chance to think he looked at her. In the fast-approaching dusk she was looking in his eyes more radiant than ever.

"I think that this is a wonderful idea. Erik is busy working in the garden, and it is great that you want to inspect it before you tell him, why don't we inspect the place right now?" She was overwhelmed as she didn't wish to go there with just him. Shaken by his gentlemanly response, she merely nodded her head.

As they walked together, she felt relaxed as he not once tried to take advantage of her. In fact, he seemed somewhat cold and distant like the air around them. He didn't even hold her hand. "Roger, it is dark I would prefer it if you held my hand in case, I fall over . . . . Of course, this isn't sexual, we are no longer an item."

"Of course, I have no intention in taking any advantage of you." He said sounding ever so gentlemanly. She was then content that her cold hands were being warmed up by him but insulted that he wasn't actually interested in her.

They were back at The Howe together for the first time since the day she gave birth. Fond memories were flushing back to her, but like Roger she was a little perturbed as to why the oven wasn't convertible. "I don't want to move in here." She said as every emotion was running through her tortured mind, on top of that she didn't want to be alone there with him. The past few days she had kept her promise to herself not to be touched by him again and he seemed to be getting the message. As for holding her hand this was only friendship and nothing more.

"Darling, just think about this properly. With three children, your life is going to be very different."

"This is only my second pregnancy."

"I know dear." He said not wishing to argue with her.

"What do you mean you know?"

"This is the second pregnancy and your second and third child." She then shook her head as she had a terrified look on her face.

"How will I cope?"

"Very easily, it was normal to give birth to ten children in the novels you have read." He said as he was almost licking his lips with glee.

"I am going back home." She said as she was scared of him taking advantage of her. He then ran towards the front door and locked it as she started screaming.

"When you have calmed down, we will discuss things as two adults." He said as she then immediately calmed down.

"What do you think I should do?" She said resigned to whatever designs he had on her.

"I think you need to spend the night here."

"OK, I will ask Erik first." She said as he then looked into her eyes.

"What if he wants to live here and you don't? If I were you, I would try this place first without him." She nodded her head: his vision made sense to her. "You know how tired he is, best for you to decide what is best for you and our babies." He said leering at her as she hated him for reminding her how all too often Erik was too tired to make love to her.

In reality he didn't want her to live in his house which he might need to run to alone for sanctuary one day. A part of him needed his own space and privacy; this meant he didn't want any woman to be living there alone with him. Still, in his haven, Roger and Beth spent the night together. They had such a beautiful and passionate night together. Even so, Roger was feeling uncomfortable in case she wanted to live there with either Erik or with himself. During the night she woke up and couldn't fall back to sleep. A delighted Roger stated kissing her all over before suckling her breasts and exciting her lady parts until she was screaming with delight. This time while they were making love: he wanted to share with her his thoughts. "I got you pregnant, I got you pregnant again and I am going to get you pregnant again and again and again." He said as she was shaking from his words as they climaxed together. His penetration of her was a frightening bliss for her. At least he hadn't mentioned his plan to be inside her womb again. Even so, those creepy words surrounding his rebirth as their daughter were still in her thoughts.

His gaze was as macabre as much as the sinister treatment of which he had bestowed onto her. She had never given up; he was the father of her child and she had never yielded to his hateful venom. His desires had always been ephemeral and fuelled by avarice and confusion. His hatred of her had been interminable. Looking at her beautiful embodiment of femininity he simply collapsed. "I'm sorry, I was never good enough for you, and your purity provoked me into the narcissistic beast I became." His broken and chastised heart gave up and she was free from his torture but felt guilty that her kindness had killed him.

He was shaking from the nightmare, not because of the death but because of the way he had left her. It had to be something dramatic like at surprise view. Too tired to think about a solution he merely nodded off back to sleep and was saddened that Beth was completely oblivious to his screams in his sleep. He had simply exhausted her and that night she could sleep through anything.

As they woke up, she said to him gently, "I can live here with Erik, but I don't know if I can live here on my own. I really enjoyed last night. Please Roger, go back to Fell End, that way the others won't know about what we did last night. I will stay here tonight and come back tomorrow." She said to him the while the morning was still dark. Roger didn't understand what she meant by living there on her own, even so, if it helped her go off the idea of living there, it would spare him from some superfluous arguments with her. After the breakup with David and Roger's lack of commitment to her; she felt that she could never truly in her heart trust a man again, who might one day leave her. On top of that, The Howe had been the scene of the corpse which touched her bottom on the day she was in labor and fighting for her life in the floods which included their former waitress at her favorite restaurant. In short, with memories on her doorstep about the death and destruction of humanity she needed to know in her heart that she really knew what she was doing regarding her nest. Still dark, they both fell back to sleep.

He didn't wish to be portrayed as a bad guy, he looked at her as they were still lying in the bed together and morning was breaking as the dawn was arriving. "What do you expect from me?" He asked her.

"I believe that children should be brought up and conceived in wedlock and that a man should look after his woman so that she can look after his children."

"I am sorry Beth, but you have to accept the world has changed. Your ideas are so out of date. I have tried to tell you gently that you are mentally ill, because you don't accept modern society."

"You led me to believe that we were overpopulated and now this."

"Most of us are damaged goods beyond repair." He pleaded. She decided not to reply and to wait for him to continue.

"You know I believe in depopulation, but in France, I met a Palestinian refugee. I felt so sorry for this man, who had been told that he had to go back to Palestine." He said as he was staring into Beth's eyes.

"How can you have compassion for immigrants when at the same time you want the indigenous people to die out?"

"Take my own country. There is plenty of food for everyone, yet millions of people were starving around the world and they didn't give a damn. People went out buying freezers in case the shops would be empty and once full; they had to throw out most of the groceries anyway, which had been lying forgotten for months. These people, the masses are no different to I am. They didn't care about the Jews and they don't care about the starving in Sub Sahara." Beth didn't respond, she simply found his reasoning at best confused and at worst demented. He then tried to touch her sensually, but she wasn't in the mood.

Later that morning; together they did some work on the garden. "I see things in black and white, love and hatred. We need some rules so that we can be saved!" She replied defiantly.

"Please don't preach especially, you."

"What do you mean?"

"You know exactly what I am talking about." He glared at her. "Blue denim dungarees on a woman means: liar!" He said almost bawling as she was wearing her garden work clothes.

"I have read enough from your novels, to see that we can and should bring back the human touch and enjoy making love in the traditional way." She replied dismissing his rhetoric.

"How can I? I was conceived in hell. I made love to my mother. Now even now, all I can see at night are those computerised images. I have wanked myself so much in front of my laptops that even now, since more than half a year has passed since we had electricity, I still wish I could have some cybersex whenever I want and to turn into fauna like cyborg. As beautiful as your words are, once seen, those Internet images are never forgotten. My mind has been raped by evil beyond repair, and you, you stare at evil in the face but still you want to see the world with rose tinted glasses. The way you want to make love; as beautiful as it is for you, is nothing more than a kiss for me. If you want to be more than just a hole for me, then I need to be more at your mercy!" He said as he found his escape from her in front of him, his shell-shocked belle. Suddenly she started screaming, she was terrified of being alone in the cottage where the waters of death had brushed themselves against the walls of the home. He walked back up to her and in turn she calmed down. "We come into this life alone, we leave this life alone." He said as she needed some moments to digest his lugubrious words.

To his great relief, he went back to Fell End after taking a long walk back via the Langdale Pikes. As he opened his bedroom door, he was shocked. Erik and Sophie were lying in his bed. He no longer needed an alibi. So, tired he left his room and fell asleep on Erik's bed after locking the door behind himself.

Later that evening after frantically trying to get Roger to open the door, Sophie and Erik decided to spend another night of passion together in the room of The Beast. It was so apt for him that they were enjoying each other's company so much, while Beth was away. Like Roger had told Beth, survival of the fittest was now more fitting than ever. As for the erotic paintings of Beth, the two lovers enjoyed the pictures above their heads, but Erik was jealous that it was Roger who was a father rather than himself.

Meanwhile, back at The Howe, Beth realized that he wanted to imply that she was a lesbian regarding the blue denim dungarees. She laughed off his pathetic thoughts about her, but in turn was about to explode over his taunting of her roots, while equally she was scared that being around him was making her confused. In some ways he was right. The old days had gone. She wanted to believe that thanks to the tsunami, her environment had been plunged back two hundred years. Two hundred years ago, would she have heard about sex change operations going wrong? In short, the answer was no. The people she was reading about in the novels, knew nothing about the things that she knew from Roger and that many young children had learnt from the Internet. With her mind being overactive all she could see was the corpse of the man with the frightened look on his face who had brushed up against her body on that terrifying day as well as the dead baby from the cottage at Tarn Foot.

The next morning Roger walked into his room. "I would like to have my room back." The embarrassed couple meekly left, naked. It was the first time Roger had seen his body and was in turn aroused. In turn, Erik was feeling morally weakened not by his actions but simply for the fact that he had been caught out cheating on Beth.

It was in the middle of the day when Beth arrived. Erik was in the garden; Sophie was in the house cooking. There was nothing out of the ordinary to suspect. "I am sorry; I wanted to spend a couple of nights at The Howe. I wanted to have my own house with Erik but have decided that I don't wish to live there. I went on my own so that I could decide this for myself." She said to Sophie as she was desperately doing her best in covering her tracks.

The four of them, Erik, Sophie, Beth and of course Roger had been up to no good. They all apart from Roger: just wanted to act as if nothing had happened. As for Roger, he was relishing in the power he had over them: and Jennifer too for that matter. The only member he had to deal with; was of course David, until he remembered that he too had spent a night at The Howe with someone other than Jennifer. At least Jennifer and David were quietly getting on with their lives peacefully. At least according to the sisters and Erik, David and Jennifer were not a part of this wife swapping charade. In turn they were in the eyes of Sophie, the arrogant couple whose pride would come before a fall.

That night all members were sharing their beds with their appropriate partners. While Beth was feeling very quiet inside regarding her cheating of Erik, Sophie was stewing. The man she was sharing the bed with had driven her into becoming the indecent woman she was. "I guess in a next life you will be a woman." Sophie said to him.

"I hope so." He said dreamily.

"I enjoyed our role reversal lately, but I want to enjoy being a woman more." Sophie said to him gently.

"Can we compromise? I mean do it once a week."

"I suppose so . . . I have something else on my mind. I can understand why you want to be a woman, but do you promise me that if we are still together in a next life, that you won't try to kill me?"

"It was you who tried to kill me."

"I know. But I think you want to seek revenge on me."

"Darling, there are other ways of seeking revenge without having to commit an act of violence." He said gloating.

"Please don't ever try to kill me." She said to him.

"You know I am not a wife beater." He said.

"I know." She said full of remorse over her act of manslaughter.

"In a previous life did I do something wrong to you?"

"How would I know?" She asked wondering what the hell he was on about.

"I am sure you tried to kill me because in a previous life you were a wife beater." He said to her as she froze wondering what he might do to her in a future existence.

"Please darling you will always be a man for me." She said.

"Let me lick that dildo of yours." He pleaded. She was feeling a little scared in case his paranoia turned to violence and decided to placate him as best she could.

She then went to the wardrobe and after placing the toy on her groan, Roger placed his mouth all over her dildo. It was dark, but with a candle shining, she could make out his movement as he was playing a lady. She went behind him, stated to massage his bottom with oils and creams before inserting her dildo up his bottom and enjoyed the feeling of dominating him. Best for both of them was the cowgirl position. As he got on top of her; she started to kiss his chest, as he started groaning. Feeling mysteriously turned on in exciting him as a woman as he started moving as though her dildo was sending him a few inches into the air; together they climaxed.

It was around this time that David and Erik had together demolished the trail leading to the path. Jennifer was delighted. In many ways she felt more powerful than Roger. Her body was holding his desires to ransom, and she was feeling very much turned on by events since the tsunami. In some ways she felt as if she was Roger's secret deputy.

One fine frosty morning in mid-December outside in the garden Jennifer began; "I would like to spend more time with you, but he is always keeping an eye on me. I mean there is nothing wrong in us meeting for a talk." Began Jennifer to Roger: as she felt her breath being taken away by his alluring presence.

"I agree. Love is the most important thing. If you no longer love him enough to carry his second child, I am always waiting for you." He said as he was hypnotising her with his words.

"I guess it is a nice idea for a woman to have children to more than one man. That way she can produce different kinds of children."

"Indeed." He smiled at her.

"I must say how lovely your babies are."

"Never forget, that the children of mine are the great survivors. I am sure you have read about Genghis Khan. We are all immortals, but the most important thing is that we reproduce wisely."

"I know this. I know I can't be with you, but so long as David doesn't find out, I would be so honored to carry your babies."

"There is plenty of time for this. Fancy a walk with me to The Howe?"

He didn't wait for her to ask him to hold her hand. Instead, he held her hand as soon as they were out of sight and out of mind from the others. He was delighted that she was wearing loose maternity wear so that he could give her a taste of his passionate hands and almost in tune with her Braxton Hicks he loosely fondled her pregnancy curves as a reminder that he wanted to see her in her in the full bloom of motherhood and that he was ready and waiting to fuck her senseless.

He was stood there on the grounds of his refuge. She was wearing a black winter coat and her belly was well hidden and all he wanted to do was to strip off every layer of clothing she was wearing. "Let's go inside, my belle." Together they walked inside. It was cold and she didn't take off her coat.

At least he was able to light a decent flame in the fireplace which he had installed with help from her David which was radiating heat towards her as she was sat on the sofa drinking the tea he had brewed, in what seemed to her as she was in dreamy mood to have been done by him in a jiffy. "Please allow me to give you a quick massage." He then started massaging her back. Then it was time to take off her black winter coat. He then looked at her admiringly, since the curves from her belly were starting to protrude delightfully in front of his eyes, as his mind was thinking how very soon, he would do to her maternal body what David had done to her. He then licked her face, took off her brown jumper and was feeling more excited than ever. She was then wearing just a sleeveless T Shirt and upon seeing her rounded breasts about to pop out in front of his leering eyes, all he wanted was her.

He continued massaging her and mainly all as he was focused on one thing only. Excitedly, he brushed more and more of his excited body up against her. "I don't think we should make love when I feel as though I can go into labor soon." She said shyly.

"I understand, soon I will do to you that I have done to the sisters when they were with big nipples and a juicy bottom." Despite what she said to him, she could take no more, and in turn her body warmed up. He then took out a small box and placed the contents onto her naked body.

Her body was tingling with delight. He had a small pocket mirror and she felt so regal wearing the jewellery. "This is for good luck. Beth wore the gems before and after she fell pregnant with her second child. And yes, she was heavily pregnant just like you." He said with his incredibly passionate voice. He then kissed her; she wanted his embrace to last forever but felt that they were simply running out of time. She was excited not only by him but with thoughts about cheating on David which made her feel more wanted than ever by men as she thought briefly how much even Erik was some kind of woman for her. They then made love. Luckily nobody caught them out, if only this could have lasted a little longer, she thought. If only they could be more open and to be swinging around along with the others at Fell End. She knew only too well that Roger would have loved to have made love with three pregnant women simultaneously and as far as she was concerned, those little boys, David and Erik, must have been suffering inside when all they could do was to block out their desirable fetishes out of their own minds which as far as Jennifer was concerned, were full of their very own hedonistic desires too.

After he had satiated her, her mind moved onto other things. "Do you remember the floating male corpse that touched Beth on the day she gave birth?" She said as he smiled at her but didn't reply. "If she wasn't in labor and there was no one around I would have gladly made love to him and you on the banks in the sunshine." In turn Roger's desires had been reignited and without any coaxing or requesting he simply imagined her as the corpse of his dreams and made love to her once more.

So aroused were they both the second time as they had thoughts of all the dead bodies on the day Beth gave birth that in no time at all they made love for a third time before falling heavily in sleep together.

In order to help cover his own tracks with his cheating which affected everyone in the room, Roger had prepared a lovely dinner. It was jacket potatoes, veal and three vegetables. That was after the starters, which was homemade salmon fishcakes with wine and spinach. The desert a chocolate fudge cake with cream, was something so rich that they couldn't eat it daily. All of his loyal and submissive guests were happy to be with him. After the meal he then began. "Let us pray." In turn they all closed their eyes and put their hands together. "Dear Lord God almighty I ask on all of our behalf's thy forgiveness. We are all sat here united as a result of our sins. Not one of us here is a hero. All of us are devastated that the human race has more or less been wiped out. Sadly, our Lord, we are all guilty men and women. Either we actively took a part in the depopulation agenda or we secretly allowed it to take place. Those of who took part were able to do so because as much as death and destruction was sinful to others, it was tacitly acknowledged by them as a necessity in order to prevent overcrowding. Those who survived: felt superior to the others. For this, only Beth is not culpable." Beth then shed tears. He chose her as the most vulnerable, as the one who was closest to his last statement but was still as guilty as hell in her very own eyes, and he knew it so well too. Beth also knew that all eyes were on her. Sophie under normal circumstances would have scolded Beth for being so pious, but under the poignant circumstances of them both; decided to bite her tongue instead. As for Jennifer, she was looking blank as his words were starting to hurt the insides of her less than pure self. As it transpired, she was a highly impressionable woman.

A draught went through the room as the others felt as though ghosts were appearing on the scene as the putrid wafts reminded them of decaying corpses. "As selfish immortals," he continued, "we think more about ourselves than the gifts of which you have bestowed unto us. As we grow older, we worry about who will look after us? Without children we are doomed to dying of old age and without any dignity. In turn all of us here honor and thank the children you have sent down from heaven unto us." The others hadn't thought about being old, but Roger's sermon was making sense to them. They needed more babies if they were to truly survive. "As real men, we must honor, respect, cherish and protect the women in this room."

"Hear hear!" Said David. Erik wasn't so sure: he sensed Roger was manipulating the others. As he looked around and saw the women fawning at him, he decided to remain silent, and to bide his time.

"Every child produced by these beautiful beings will be protected as we will worship the posterity that will keep the spirit of humanity alive. As weak immortals, we are forever indebted to your love. Amen." He said. With that the women were gasping for breath. He was simply their hero, and any man who said otherwise was simply a bitter and twisted soul. Equally, Beth, Erik and Sophie were relieved that he hadn't made any references regarding their adultery. David had conveniently forgotten about his own act of treachery against Jennifer, while she simply didn't care and wanted to live only for the moment.

For Roger as he was lying in bed with Sophie that night, he truly believed that the groundwork had been done, and, that a green light had been given for him to make Jennifer pregnant. On top of that, he believed that like himself she was a victim of Christian values. Like Beth, David was pious. In turn he felt really sorry for Jennifer's imprisonment with him. He then smirked in the direction of the woman who was lying in his bed. She had betrayed her sister when she slept with Erik and had no right whatsoever in berating him when and if his ultimate dream with Jennifer would come true.

As passionate as she was feeling about Roger, she had no desire for David. With her birth then due any day as she was in her fortieth week, he wouldn't suspect a thing. Even so, she couldn't sleep being in the same bed as David. With a pain in her heart, she was full of regret. She saw herself as simply being some evil, dirty whore and wished that she appreciated David who simply epitomised a man with a heart of Gold. On top of that, she sensed that David and Beth were meant to be and that she and Roger deserved to have perished in the floods of hell at The Howe. If only she were good enough for David. If only she could control her beastly and not so latent fetishes which were simply beyond the pale, yet so highly addictive for her too. Once she had given birth, she would be free from David, and exciting times lay ahead for her.

Prior to the tsunami, Roger had been delighted that the powers at be, had been clamping down on religion, especially Christianity. He had been looking forward to the imprisonment of the clergy who weren't embracing the LGBT depopulation agenda fully enough. As a lawyer, he could have demolished his enemies on behalf of feminists as well as LGBT and eventually zoophiles, paedophiles, and satanists. He could and had already helped minority groups against pious ex wives and husbands with morality, who were against no fault divorce and the bringing up of their children in LGBT families. The homosexualizing of the masses had already helped fuel family breakdown and there was at the time plenty of work involved. As a lawbreaker himself, he would have enjoyed his time in the family court where he could have been making lots of money. Instead, the tsunami had stopped all that. At least he had survived and was at the pinnacle of the New World Order that had given him plenty of sweeteners. If only he could visit London. Then again, what was the point? With the clean-up operation surely in its advanced stages, there would be no more sights of rotten flesh and blood. At least he had enjoyed to some extent first-hand the genocide from his beloved Lake District. For him, society didn't need any rules. People should be free to do whatever they wanted, so long as it made them happy, and they had enough money to pay for their pleasures. This was the reason why law appealed to him. He understood that laws would always be a part of the constitution. For him, becoming a lawyer was the next best thing to being part of a lawless society. He had made his enormous wealth by lying, cheating, and bullying. On top of that, like his colleagues, he didn't even follow the law in his own personal life. Even so, like his colleagues, the law was their daily bread.

At times life was becoming a bore for him. At times: his pleasures which had always been hedonistic, had to become more psychologically destructive for his victims. The eviller he became, the more he got a kick out of psychologically abusing those around him and didn't seem to care if this would eventually lead to his downfall.

As for Beth, she was stood holding her right hand on her mouth as she saw Jennifer coming into view. What were the crows doing encircling around her? Would they be lurking around herself in three months' time? Was this an ominous sign? She had to calm down, Jennifer was strong and in a few days' time there would be another addition at Fell End. It was better for her to think this way than for her to otherwise end up in going insane.

Chapter 9

SHE WASN'T WITH HIS CHILD

For Roger, having three pregnant women in his home was a delight. Less pleasurable for him was that two other men were there, but at least he was making love to all of the three fecund beauties. The men had their uses too; he needed their manpower as much as he wanted to kill and to make love to them. Sophie was just entering her second trimester and he expected her to be passionate with him as and whenever he required. Beth was just into her third trimester and he wanted her as much as possible. Jennifer was showing him that with her being ready to give birth and only the same size as Beth, that multiple births, as in Beth's case, were the way forward for her. For him in knowing how vulnerable Beth must be feeling about her pregnant body being much bigger than during the first time, was simply one of heaven for him. In turn the idea of making Jennifer bigger the next time around through carrying twins would be as far as Roger was concerned; a damning indictment that David was less fecund than himself too. It was times like these when he wished that he had gone on, "I'm a celebrity." The fame and the glory would have made him feel even more like God than he was already feeling about himself.

On the evening autumn turned into winter, the LED lights were shining brightly. David looked on proudly as Jennifer was being brave during her painful labor. She was as far as he knew; the experienced one medically and he had no idea that Roger knew more than his love about giving birth. Jennifer would be able to instruct him, and he could feel her pain and fears. Suddenly she started to panic. "Don't worry love, everything will be alright." He said as she bravely smiled at him. She then started to panic and to choke as she was gasping for breath, before her head slumped. Meanwhile, his baby's head appeared while Jennifer appeared to be looking as though she was being strangled. All he could see was blood pouring out of his child which was still trapped inside the dying mother.

Luckily for him Roger appeared. He ran up to Jennifer, saw her glass looking eyes, and somehow freed the baby. Sadly, it was too late; the baby was tangled up in the placenta and had suffocated. He then took Jennifer's pulse, but it had stopped. She was dead. Even Roger felt sick at the sight of these deaths, which brought back his earlier fond memories of floating corpses. He then shed a tear for Emma too. After getting over with the shock, he then came inside his pants, and hoped that David was unaware of his personal pleasure. He wanted to make love to David but decided to run to the bathroom where he was as sick as a dog. While a part of him was a pervert, another part was healthy. What a mess, but then again this was his nature. He was a firm believer in the depopulation agenda after all.

He then walked back to the makeshift maternity room. He made sure that his pregnant women, who were around, cleaned up the mess, so that it was a morgue no more. After diligently making the place looking fresh again, they were now out of the room, since they could take no more. He was also feeling bitter; he had been looking forward to impregnating Jennifer so much. She enjoyed talking about necrophilia, what more could he have asked for? David was still there. "David, Jennifer is proud of you." David didn't reply. "Just close your eyes young man. Think about how much she loved you. How faithful she was." He was saying everything so that David, who was relieved that she hadn't made love to Roger, would miss her more than ever. "Let her know how much you love her. Close your eyes." David then did as he was told. "Please walk over and kiss her on the forehead so that she can rest in peace." He said fatherly to David.

"Roger will you guide me to her?" He said shedding more than just a few tears.

"Of course, I will." He said gently to him.

Roger then helped him with his support to the bed. David kissed her. "You have made her proud. Before she can be released from hell on earth and placed in heaven there are two more things you should do to show her how much you love her."

"What are these things Roger?" He asked him deferentially.

"The first one is quite simple. Just pick up your child and hold her in your arms. First I would like you to open up your eyes."

Once again David did as he was told. Roger's request was a reasonable one. His hands were trembling, and he picked up his child. He then burst out crying. After a few moments he couldn't bear to keep on holding his beloved and dead child. "David, this isn't good with you behaving so feeble. You need to be more robust. Jennifer is going to heaven please show her your love."

"How?" He asked pleading.

"It is simple: make love to her." Roger said without too much feeling. David froze and was terrified; love was the most important thing in life as far as he was concerned. He felt guilty that he was also in love with Beth and somehow, he had to atone himself.

"I can't get excited making love to a dead body." He said horrified.

"Don't worry David, I will help you, just relax, please." In turn Roger seized his chance and hugged him. "In a few minutes' time you will give her such a fond farewell that she will be able to depart from this evil world in peace. Feeling blessed by you, when she is looking down from the skies above in heaven; she be forever thinking about your love for her." David was prepared to join her in heaven; he believed that she died because of him. Had she not fallen pregnant to him; she would still be alive. A short while later; he helped take off the distraught man's trousers and started to masturbate him. As soon as he was hard Roger looked at him. "Well done dear boy, now go inside of her." He said as he wished that he was Jennifer himself and freed from the misery of the world.

He was shocked, but what Roger was saying made sense to this man who felt as though he had lost his everything. In turn David did as he was told, "you are now united once more with her." Roger's comment was a mixed blessing. He had understood he had to die for her, and he was relieved that he was still alive but disgusted with this act but felt that he had reached the point of no return. As he was inside of her, instead of thinking about her, all he could see was corpses everywhere in his highly troubled mind. "If you need some help: pull out and I will help you." So, scared to death of Roger he then thought about Beth, and in turn he then climaxed, and, in the background, he could hear Roger ejaculating too, which was a most offensive, frightening, and deranged noise for him. "If only you knew how great she was in bed. It was only a few days ago when we were in heaven together and she spoke about having a child with me!" He said as David ran out of the room in great distress, while Roger burst out laughing. He knew that David wouldn't discuss this with anyone, since he too, David, had acted in a very non-Christian like manner and all over her dead body, literally.

Now, with very few survivors, he had one great big conundrum. With just four people around him he was scared of them taking their lives. He would then be on his own. He would have no one else to murder psychologically. For him watching David go from a saintly like vicar being, to one of a necrophile, bi-curious Satanist, gave him hope for the remaining survivors. Hope that life with them would be one great big hedonistic orgy. In the meantime, how could he introduce, zoophilia and paedophilia to David? There was only his baby's around, maybe there was no rush for this. He could at least encourage David to make love to the pet ewe on his lawn.

For Roger, getting angelic David to commit more sinful acts was a real sign of hope for him. Maybe, perhaps one day, he could have a threesome with David, Beth, and himself together. In the meantime, he was gloating over David's humiliation. Suddenly though, tears ran down his face as he wanted to scram rather than to shout. Why had the tsunami occurred a year too soon? Maybe his allies had been scared of Trump and the fact that his approach was resonating with the masses meant that the apocalypse had to come sooner rather than later. On top of that, the different cabal factions couldn't agree either. Poor Roger he thought to himself, under more auspicious times, he could still be making love to Jennifer more or less naturally had modern technology turned her into a cyborg. He then smiled to himself, maybe it was for the best, who would want to make love to a cyborg that had just given birth, lost its hourglass figure when Beth was so full of elasticity and able to turn her body more or less back to what it was when she was still a virgin. As far as he was concerned, after giving birth, a woman, apart from Beth, post-natal was no longer worth the fuck. Yes, he was going to fill her up with his fertile juices, but this dead bitch, had let him down in more ways than one. Somehow, he had to win back Beth's love.

As for the girls they were thinking about who would end up with David but didn't wish to reveal this to each other as they were sat in Beth's room. "Sophie, why don't you free yourself from Roger?"

"How? Who is going to want me?"

"David is alone."

"I would love him, I would look after him, but he doesn't want me." Sophie said slyly.

"Then, why don't you end up with Erik. I am going to seduce David in his moment of need and then you can end up with Erik." Beth said, as Sophie listened on in horror. She herself wanted David, but at least Erik was better than Roger. At least the issue that Roger was better than nothing was no more relevant. Thanks to the death of Jennifer, they had a better choice of the remaining men.

David was sat in the garden looking forlorn. He had lost his wife and child. Beth went up to him. "You seem very sad." Beth said not knowing what to say to him.

"What do you want me to say?"

"I am sorry."

"No, it is all of my own doing. I never really loved Jennifer, and I guess God took her life away so that I could be reunited with you." He said to her dolefully and waiting for her love.

"You call yourself a good Christian how can you speak like this?" She said aghast and horrified.

"Beth, we live in less civilised times as you are well aware. I firmly believe that I am being punished. I am grieving more about the child you are carrying now, which could have been mine but isn't because of my stupidity." He said as he was grieving, not about Jennifer but due to his desperate need for his nightmare without his love, Beth, to end. Beth was lost for words and took a deep breath as she felt both shaken and numb. Both hot and cold for him and both saddened and disturbingly delighted over Jennifer's death.

He then tried to touch her. At this time, she had reached an important juncture in her stormy, moral, maze. She looked as though she was about to snarl at him, and he quickly moved away from her as she wondered how Jennifer fell pregnant to such a cold fish. "Are you saying that this innocent child of mine should die for you? Roger couldn't have said this better than you!" She said in distress as she was thinking about Jennifer, about the times when she was a dreamy, innocent, and romantic.

"No, Beth, you misunderstand me."

"Then what are you saying then?"

"When you were pregnant the first time, I said with my hand on my heart that; I take your child as my own. Had I done so; we would now be expecting our very own bundle of joy. On top of that, you are right, I am a weak man. When you first arrived here, sometime in early July in the summer of 2018, I was walking through Rothay Park when a beautiful girl said hello to me. Thirty minutes later when I was shopping in Tesco the same girl smiled again at me and said hello." He then started crying. She didn't need to respond verbally. Of course, she knew as well as he did, that the beautiful girl was no other than herself, Beth, and had they got together then, she would never have been carrying a child of Roger's. On top of that, she had met him before Roger. She wanted to cry too. A part of her was annoyed with herself that she hadn't revealed this to him earlier, but back then she didn't wish to harm Jennifer.

So, overwhelmed with everything all she could think about was that handsome innocent looking gent, who seemed so refined and sweet and for her it was love at first sight. Then, he appeared to her as stable as the mountains around her as she was in awe that such a lovely market town existed and wanted to live there with him. She was right to approach him for a second time. If only he had had a bit more courage. Beth would do anything to be with him, so long as he showed her how much he wanted her. For tonight at least: she felt safe with him. He just needed to get over Jennifer and then they would both be healed. As far as she was concerned, he was no longer a weak soul; but one highly romantic gentleman and she would then have done anything to have gone back in time that being just eighteen months ago.

Roger and Sophie were of course also discussing the tragic event. "Terrible what happened to Jennifer."

"Well, she wasn't with my child." He said.

"What do you mean, you don't care?" She asked shocked.

"I do care, in fact I blame myself."

"How can you blame yourself?"

"Maybe carrying the can is too much, but I feel in my heart that the other men here are unlucky. It is almost as if only the babies of mine will survive and sadly that means the mothers who were impregnated by me too." He said trying to disguise his personal glee with false sorrows.

"You are a sick man, Roger."

"I am just trying to be honest. While we are on the subject, I am relieved that you have both been impregnated by me. I couldn't cope if I were to lose either of you."

"Oh my God, Beth is with Erik."

"But her blooming body is mine, so there is no need to worry about her." He said as shivers went down her spine as she thought about the hapless waitress and she then hated him even more than when she tried to kill him. He then sighed. "Stupid, Jennifer, an intelligent woman who could have had beautiful babies with me." He said as Sophie was worried that she would strike him there and then and this time finish him off.

Sophie and Beth were drinking tea together in the dining room when the babies were asleep. "Wasn't it a disgrace of him to imply that since she wasn't with his child and that she deserved to die?"

"Words fail me, there is no lexicology for this, his brain has a new dimension for me." Said Sophie.

"To be honest Erik is the best man." Said Beth.

"That is beyond doubt. Here we are far away from home, and the best men, Erik and Jan were and are from our own country!" Said Sophie.

"All the men are morally superior to Roger and have had less luck in becoming fathers." Beth said as Sophie froze on hearing those ominous words, which made Roger's ring in more truthfully for her.

"As evil as Roger is, I am wondering if our lives have clearly been mapped out for us and that there was, and is, nothing that we could have done, or do, against the beast." Said Sophie.

In short, they were both united in their terror against him and their grief for Jennifer and her baby.

That evening Sophie needed to carry out an act of perversion for the last time. Jennifer had died, and she needed to find herself. As such, she undressed him, and started spanking his bottom and gently biting it. He felt all woman and was enjoying her total domination of him. Even better was when he was forced to hold onto the bed headboard as she inserted herself in him with the dildo. "Darling, it is difficult to climax when my organ isn't being caressed." He said as she smiled to herself thinking that role play reversal didn't make any more sense to her. Even so, they had already got this far and as soon as he felt the dildo running up and down his scrotum, he felt all woman as his own tool was firm and ready. And, as he climaxed, he felt as though he had made love to himself. Feeling satisfied and in order to look after her needs he got inside her in the natural way. After making love to Sophie, Roger was scared. He couldn't sleep and needed to sort his relationship problems out. If he stayed with Sophie, he was sure that Beth would end up with David, and that would mean Erik and Sophie would become an item. He had to woo Beth back, even it meant being in a monogamous relationship with her. He was to some degree in one now and being in one with Beth was something worth trying out. Beth was easier to manipulate than her more cynical sister. The only thing he loved about this Christmas was the misery that the others especially the Christians were experiencing. He was sure that David wouldn't be much joy for Beth. In fact, it certainly didn't seem like Christmas for anyone at Fell End. Even the babies didn't seem to smile much either.

It seemed as though Jennifer and her child were the lucky ones after all. Who would want to remain in this miserable existence anyway? Even the beagles seemed sad watching the others wallow in the misery of themselves.

It was in the garden the next morning that he was thinking before the dawn had arrived and he was deep in thought. It was frosty, and he was scared of being alone and felt as though he was being frozen to death. It was only a slight frost and he had plenty of layers on but was feeling psychologically weak. He was also thinking about internet porn. The previous Christmas he was enjoying two pregnant women in his bed and home-made movies which he uploaded when he visited a Wi-Fi hotspot. While the Yuletide before that one, he had cybersex whenever he felt lonely. This Christmas, he felt as though he had nothing.

She then appeared, his beautiful lady, his heartbeat was rising, and he had to woo her back. He was scared of being a lonely and desperate man. As a mortal being, one day he would be grateful of her looking after him and being faithful was a price worth paying. "My love: my darling! Let's go and have a gentle stroll together after breakfast."

"OK." She said. His heartbeat rose as he felt the pheromones of love going inside of him. "I have just breastfed the babies they are sleeping again so you can make us some breakfast." There was nothing strange in

Beth breastfeeding her sister's bairn. Sophie helped her out too, and when she heard Jane crying, she saw no need for Sophie to wake up too.

Beth and Roger had nothing more to say. He was formulating in his mind what he would tell her just as he had during the sleepless night just gone. His main problem was that he wasn't exactly sure as to what the truth really meant. This had nothing to do with his judicial work. What was the truth for him in the short term was a lie for him in the long-term? While he could never be pure all the time with his intentions towards her, he did have fleeting moments of when there simply was no one else like Beth and he wanted to enjoy his feelings of ecstasy with her. He believed that he had moments of ecstasy together with her, that nobody else could do it better than him for his women. He believed that nothing lasts forever and so long as he could woo her back; he could worry about the consequences of his fleeting lust later on. He was still a lawyer at heart. He had to win no matter how much he would have to evade his real and long-term feelings for her, which were confusing to say the least. Today he would set the groundwork in for her love, with his acts of redemption in order to gain her respect. Tomorrow he would go for her heart. It didn't matter if that was what he really needed; he simply didn't want David to be with her.

As they were walking together, she needed to know that just one man truly, madly, and deeply wanted her. She felt that she was morally compel-ed to be with Roger. Yes, he was equally obliged to be with her sister, but in times of war, desperate acts would be taken by people. While there was no carnage taking place, the aftermath of the tsunami's nuclear explosions and whatever else Erik didn't know about, made things much worse than just after World War Two. Back then people had morals she believed. All she wanted to hear from him at a most natural location was simply, "I love you."

It was simply now or never for her, he had to show her the love that she desired. "My dearest, I feel so bad: I feel so guilty." He said.

"There is no need," she said to him as she held onto his hands tightly as they were standing together and looking down from the top of their very own fell of Loughrigg.

"There is every need to be." He said as his words had dampened her passion for him.

"OK, I am listening to you."

"It was wrong of the elite. There were better ways of reducing the population than the death and destruction that took place."

"I also admit that it was unsustainable to have had millions of people living in inhumane squalor and hunger." She said as she was desperate for this unromantic conversation which offered no hope for the two of them to cease. So long as she didn't disagree with him; she was sure that he would discuss more romantic things with her.

"Without the destruction, the population would have stabilised and fell anyway." He said.

"How would this have been achieved? I mean there was a lot of governmental help and support for families in Poland. Hungary even had zero taxes for those with four or more children." She said, as he then went into deep thought.

"Oh Beth, you are such an innocent child of nature. If only all people were like you. The world would be such a happy place. The thing is the LGBT Feminist war on families led to a confused generation and there was nothing Victor Orban could have done to have reversed this."

"I just want to be happy." She said sounding a little annoyed as she felt somewhat patronised by him.

He looked at her. "I know. When the communists took over Eastern Europe in 1945, they did it by stealth. They were lurking around in the dark and in the shadows. Those behind the depopulation agenda are nothing less than reconstructed Marxists. As such they took over two key areas. One of which was education. The result most children were indoctrinated against having a family on the grounds that to wipe out more species of animals and to cut down more trees was not only a wicked thing to do but would lead to a world that was unfit for habitation.

Education is the best tool. Feminism was used as the groundwork to create instability in the home. This is where my career comes in. I was nothing short of an educated Mafioso in the Family Court. Thanks to my mother I knew nothing about family life."

"I know, you have said this several times before."

"Yes, but it is relevant that I mention this now to you." He said as she was looking very humble, as he couldn't help looking away from her beautiful face which was gorgeously swollen naturally from her pregnancy. "Once the children became adults and fifty percent of them believed that having children was wrong, laws would have been passed banning churches, and heterosexual marriages, since to some extent we live in a democracy. Children cannot vote until they are eighteen, but until then, they are a property of the state. Once all people have been indoctrinated, in a Marxist state, there is no escape no matter how old you are."

By then she had had enough of his depressing conversation, she wasn't sure if his interpretation of communism was correct. Thanks to so much reading of his books, she believed that in the beginning many ideologies started off in being utopian. Her life was heavily embedded in Catholicism and she knew only too well that different members of her congergation read the words from the Bible differently. Finally, she wanted her own life to be more joyous too. "What was your sermon all about?" She asked as she metaphorically meant; what had this got to do with them?

"There are still some strong women like yourself who will always have children and help keep the human race alive, and yes, depopulation could have been done in the ways I have described, which would have been less violent."

"I am sorry Roger, but to kill the people's dignity, make them as miserable as hell and brainwash them into clones is worse than what happened with the tsunamis!" She said as his speech was too much for her simple heart and mind to deal with for much longer.

He wanted to cry but decided to try a little bit more with her. "Can I just tell you one more thing?" He said, as he was scared of losing her.

"Yes." She said wanting to make sure that she was in her mind making the right decisions.

"I worked at a school for a few months in Canada. The female teachers were basically an example for the next generation. The school curriculum had brainwashed them. They simply saw no future for the human race. Many wanted to see every other species saved apart from that of human beings. My then colleagues were mostly women. They were messed up human beings and the law was on their side. For every happily married female colleague with children who was aged between thirty and fifty, there were at least five women who were not so. It is safe to say that one was cheating on her husband. One was destroying her ex's life through the family courts while three were single and childless. After seeing this, sensitive children have no intention in settling down after they have been indoctrinated. Once they believed that families are evil because more mouths to feed takes away the lives of other species of life; they had less respect for their parents, whom they believed were destroying the planet. Also, seeing from their parents the death and destruction of love around them that is caused due to acrimonious divorces moved them closer to hedonism."

By then, she had had enough. She felt as though he was like some old man talking down to a child. "Oh Beth, I am so sorry, I just want you to know, that I have so many regrets."

"I understand," she said. His monologue had left her cold. She just wasn't interested. She just wanted to be a happy mother and wife. Her politics was her home and nothing more. If only he would have kissed her, instead he was acting like some distant theoretician despite having got her up the duff twice. As for his views on feminism, it was the same as his views on communism and unlike him, she wasn't dogmatic politically and believed that most adherents of a particular ideology were nothing more than pragmatists deep down. She believed in the right for women to work, to vote and to go to school. Did that make her a feminist? She didn't believe in women being given rights to break up marriages for no reason as well as to lie and cheat on their husbands, and, to expect their

245

men to do everything just because they were women. Did that make her a misogynist? She had no problem with people falling in love with people from other races, but she didn't agree with the state paying people to come over to Europe and to be in receipt of welfare state benefits. Did that make her a racist? She didn't want any harm to be done to anyone because they were homosexual, equally she didn't wish for children to be taught about transgenderism. Did that make her a homophobe?

They went together in his bed. This was so important for her. Morally she was doing the right thing and all that she wanted was for him to rekindle their love. Instead as the guilt was pouring out of him, he wanted Beth to take the lead. On top of that, he was convinced that he was a woman. That night neither of them could sleep. Both were crying out in their thoughts for the other to love them. While for Beth it was the simple and tender loving care that she wanted from him; he needed something more exciting than vanilla sex. He believed that making love in a natural and tantric way was simply the best and most satisfying for a couple in love and that this would make Beth happy. He also had no control for his other desires for her, which went much further than oral sex and making love doggy style. Then he thought a little more deeply and wondered why he hadn't carried out with his original and manipulative plan to woo her to his bed along with his lies and deceit and to have carried out his perversions on her at a secret location such as The Howe.

The following morning after being woken up to the sounds from the bathroom and thoughts of drinking her urine, he jumped out of his bed. He had to drink her fluids before they were diluted further and the sooner, he got in there he would be able to make out the contrasting color of her liquid and that of the closet. Instead, as he opened his bedroom door, he caught her before she went to her room. Beth didn't want him to know that David was in her bed. In turn she held his hand and directed them both into his bedroom. Once in the bed he began. "I know that you are going to end up with David. I know you want to be free from me and for me to lovingly accept you leaving this house and to start a new life. I will ask my bosses to grant you a manor house or whatever you want; next to a lake or wherever you want. All I ask is for one small favour. Would you grant me this innocent request?"

"What is it?" She asked. He then smiled at her.

"I will allow David to be the father of your children."

"I can't do this; this would make me a greater sinner than I already am." She said as she started shaking her head.

"I am dying Beth, and every child deserves a father." He said as he believed that the further, she moved away from him emotionally the sooner his body would give up.

"I need to know what you want from me before I can give you my consent." She said as she was overwhelmed with his words about his death, which came out of the blue to her. He then took a deep breath, placed his hands on her shoulder and crossed his fingers on his left hand.

"I want to fuck and to be fucked simultaneously with you and David, while licking the chocolate out of your sister's arse!"

"Please keep my sister out of this!" She said almost shouting at him as he in turn jumped.

"OK, what do you prefer? I fuck you and David fucks me, or you fuck me with one of my dildos strapped in front of you as I pound David?"

"I am going to be sick." She said.

"I am not bothered about you feeling sick I just wanted to know what your choice." For her there was no choice and she simply ran out of his room in terror into her room. That night Sophie, still shaken about the recent deaths, simply needed a good night's sleep alone and had already locked her bedroom door.

A few days later, the mood at Fell End had changed rather dramatically. For the time being at least, Beth hadn't ended up again properly with David. For the time being at least there was a lot of confusion taking place. Officially, Roger and Sophie were still an item of sorts. Even so, all three men were vying for pole position. The prize was Beth. In turn, she was making love to the three men; fortunately, that was taking place separately.

Sophie, during these free and easy days of love wanted David. He was sat reading the Bible downstairs as she came up to him one evening. "David, don't be sad. I know that my sister is causing you so much pain. I know that she is hurting you in having three lovers." He didn't reply. "I might never be good enough for you, your heart might always be with her, but if I am your number two then this is good enough for me." She said.

He then put down his book; her words had more than struck a poignant chord with him. He looked at her and seeing only her beauty which for him was almost as identical to that of his beloved, he started to kiss her on her lips as tears were running down both of their faces. "I called into Kendal and Windermere the other day. I wanted to pay my respects to my parents and to Jennifer's too. I should have gone earlier, but she wasn't up to it. Knowing from word of mouth that they had all died was enough for Jennifer to want to forget the past. Please follow me." He said. Tears ran down her face as she then realized that he too, like her had lost his parents due to an agenda that was meant to be about saving the planet, but in reality, was about giving more lebensraum for the elite.

They stood up and went to the cupboard and took out a bottle of wine and started drinking together. After a while, her wish came true, they were romantically kissing together. As he started to caress the whole of her body and not just those obviously pregnant areas she felt somehow born again. She made love to David for the first time. As with all new conquests of hers, she made David feel as though he was something special for her and simply followed his bodily actions as though whatever he did, nobody did it better. "So long as we do everything for each other, don't you think that our love is like that of a Romeo and Juliet?" She said.

"I feel the love between you and: I just know that I am in ecstasy."

"That wasn't the question to my answer."

"I am sorry." He said as she was then disappointed from his over politeness towards her.

"There is no reason to be. How many women have you slept with?" She said as she was feeling somewhat cynical and depressed about his lack of undying words of love for her.

"I have slept with four women."

"I have slept with four men too. As for my question, you are right in not giving me an answer. True love is when one is in love in a monogamous relationship with one life partner. The more partners one has; the more confused one becomes about love. Beth is certain that had you taken away her cherry that everything between you both would have been so beautiful. I had my chance on love, but I destroyed him. I was hoping that you would have told me that there was no woman like me and that together we are beautiful. I know deep down my sister is the one who is hurting you so much and is the one you will never get over." He then tried to kiss her, she had saddened him, but her feelings towards him had died for that evening at least. She no longer wanted to be touched by him but wanted to lie next to him in her tears of sorrow and fell asleep in his arms.

Beth was highly emotionally charged to say the least. Even so she was calling the shots. This side of her character was being both admired and feared by The Beast who was in need of some kind of therapy more than ever before. He had no idea what was going to happen. All he could hope for was these uncertain days would continue after the girls had both given birth. Then he would be able to make them both pregnant for the third time in a row.

Night after night, the five of them were moving around the beds. With just two women and three men, the men were the losers. The women were in charge. Basically, the situation was that whoever entered the room of Beth under her command first would be hers for the night. Whoever found her with someone else, could always try Sophie and it would be fifty fifty that she too was already with someone else for the night. If Roger was already busy with one of the women, the unlucky guy was always welcome to join in with a threesome as far as Roger was concerned. While this wasn't yet going to happen, the sight of a male walking into his bedroom when he was with one of the women was enough to send the juices of his fertile imagination into overdrive.

Thanks to David's contacts, Jennifer was given a quiet but respectable and dignified burial attended by just the members from Fell End, down in Grasmere where Roger himself wanted to be buried and lying next to her. David remained dignified and composed. Inside the church, David acted as priest, thanks to depopulation it was easier for the survivors to take on different roles. Roger then gave a eulogy, it seemed to have been done with the utmost care and discretion. After it he ran out crying while David remained tight lipped. The girls looked on in horror as David didn't seem to care. Beth then walked outside looking for Roger and found him in the graveyard. He was hyperventilating. She then put her arms around him as she felt humbled by his sorrows. "I was going to impregnate her just before you gave birth." He said as he then burst out crying. "Oh Beth! Oh Beth! If only I could make it up to you. Let me make you pregnant again and again and again before I enter your womb!" He said as he looked so distraught. Beth then ran off back inside the church feeling sick as she felt as though her soul was being raped by his demented rhetoric. He then followed her inside, and this time she had to go back outside and be far away from him. At least the babies were sleeping in their prams in the churchyard. As for Roger he was scared that one more impregnation of her would in Beth's mind be that of rape and that she would kill him.

Back in the graveyard she sat in a praying position as she replayed a conversation that had been haunting her for almost one year and was when Sophie was driving their long since obsolete car. "If you really are sincere and care about your brethren, then why don't we go to Manchester and bring back fifty Jews who can live in our home?" He said offended.

"Don't be so bloody facile we'd be arrested as conspiracy theorists." She said almost screaming as Sophie nearly jumped out of her skin and nearly lost control of her driving.

"You see; it is all about survival. You are not so different to Simon George. He escaped the Nazis by ratting on his own people and became an atheist! The truth is, you are in no way going to bring back fifty people whom you have never even met when with a growing family you will simply want The Howe for just us. On top of that, how would you be able to cope with living under the roof with other city dwellers? What would they think about you swimming nakedly in the tarn and making love in the open air?"

After experiencing cold shivers running through her spine: her turbulent mind went back to the present. She then looked around and checked that nobody was around. "I thank you Lord Jesus in saving my life. I know how lucky and blessed I am. I was just some humble teenage girl who was corrupted by the evil around me. Should I be happy that you have guided me to my New Jerusalem, or should I repent until the day I die, for being selfish in putting my own life before others? Amen." With that she ran back inside the church and saw David moaning with his head slumped onto the pew.

"Jennifer, Jennifer, please forgive me!" With that Beth's feelings for him died through her jealousy of the love he was showing for his ex who in her own eyes was in a far better place than she was. What she didn't know was that David was asking for her blessing regarding his future plans for him and for Beth herself. If only she could love Erik, she thought poignantly; then she could laugh behind the backs of the men who were breaking her heart.

Back at Fell End, Roger was at this time scared of David most of all. If David ended up with Beth, then his own life would be meaningless. He thought about how he had tried to humiliate David in the garden, but instead, Erik came to his rescue. As such, Roger spent hours writing letters to David. One letter would be about his love for him, another about his hatred. None of the letters were actually passed over to him. Luckily, David didn't know what was going on in Roger's mind. It was anybody's guess what might have happened if he knew about Roger's latent psychological stalking of him.

At least his jealousy kept him on his toes. So much so that he made sure that he would excite her more than ever. As such he made sure that the tantric love making, he had introduced her to at the beginning of their relationship was still close to his heart. He made sure that every part of her body was looked after by his magic touch. He sang to her baby or babies inside her womb, as she caressed his neck, and he was thinking every moment how he could keep her attention on him. As for Beth, although she was excited by everything it wasn't love for her; and knowing how deceitful he was, whenever he was being nice to her, she felt pains inside her body as deep down she didn't trust him. Even so, so long as he was sweet with her, she would reward him with their bodily union whenever she wasn't sure about being with Erik or David. With his strength he managed not to put too much in the way of pressure on her baby bump yet succeeded in a thrusting that made her feel sore from the vibrations around her hips as she felt as though she was still making love even after they had finished a few hours later. What a poignant lust it was for her.

The next day, she wanted something less masculine. She knew that whenever she was with Roger, and no matter how tired she was he would always somehow manage to find his wicked way with her. As such and desiring the gentle touch she spent the following night with David. "I am so happy to be with you." He said as they were lying in bed gently together.

"Me too. You are so sweet, my David." He then started to gently caress her, he wanted her so much.

"I am sorry my darling. I am really tired and sore after last night with Roger." She said hoping that he would be able to persuade her otherwise, since deep down she really wanted his body on hers. She hated Roger and wanted to see David's jealousy so that once and for all she would feel so wanted by him.

'OK, he said. Maybe next time you will be less tired.' He said before meekly falling asleep as his response kept her up the whole night as she was in despair about the three available men. Equally, while Erik was safe and sound, in some ways he was too normal for her.

Poor Beth, she simply couldn't sleep. Now that David was less of a man in her eyes she was thinking about Roger's proposal, she just needed David to say no and she would be calm again. "David I really need to talk to you about a serious matter."

"What is it darling?" He said as his word of endearment made her feel weak at her knees as well as tickling her breasts.

"Roger has offered us a home of his own, and freedom." She said afraid. David was a man of piety; how could she tell him? He merely looked at her. The silence was unnerving her to say the least and after a few seconds, which seemed more like a lifetime in her highly tumultuous mind she continued. "All we have to do is to endure a threesome with him." She said somewhat relieved that his, Roger's, poisonous words had been let out.

"As much as the idea disgusts me, one night of hell is a price worth paying if it means that we can from then on; live our lives in peace." He said.

"Well, I am not sure if we can trust him, I will find out more about it later."

Beth was more than just repulsed by his response. At worst, David was without morals, he was weak; and she decided not to discuss anything more on this matter. At best, he was still in love with Jennifer. Then again that was impossible, given the way he had spoken about Jennifer he was simply beyond the pale for her. Feeling somewhat stupefied she went downstairs.

"Beth, can I have a word with you?" He said as he found her alone in the dining-room drinking her cup of tea during her sleepless night with David.

"Make it quick, I have to go back upstairs and look after our baby." He then smiled at her, the issue was for him connected with their offspring and this gave him hope that issues were to be solved between them both.

"Will David make love with us?" He asked her gently.

"Yes." She said as she then gulped for some air.

"This is in our best interests isn't it?"

"No, because I simply can't do this." She said as the atmosphere suddenly darkened.

"I want you to stop making love with David." He said angrily.

"No, you can't tell me what to do." She said as he then lifted his eyebrows at her.

"Do you think sleeping around in the state you are in is moral?"

"I love David." She blurted out.

"That is all that matters to me, love is something you know nothing about." She said as he smiled at her.

"You can fuck that downtrodden Erik whenever I am with Sophie. At least when you are with that stupid Pole your mind is still on me, but please don't be screwed by David."

"What right have you to tell me what to do? I am a stupid Pole too!" She said unable to hide her disgust for him. He though; seeing how she hadn't lost her temper with him he felt that she was weak and that he could manipulate her.

"I know that you my dear are a Pole, but one of noble blood. You are poles apart from that baboon type ape."

"Too late, you have insulted my nation." She said as he then looked at her shaken. He wanted to say that her nation was Israel but decided instead against that. This normally highly cerebral lawyer was lost for words. "I met David before I met you, one night earlier in fact. He was shy, but had he wanted, I would have made love to him willingly on the first night and fallen pregnant to him consciously. Instead, you were showering me with gifts and trying to buy me and took advantage out of me. Let me tell you this, it took you more than a week to get your wicked way with me, doesn't that tell you something?"

His mind went back to when Hannah said something similar to him before he hit her. He knew not to make the same mistake again. "I am warning you," he said, "you are mine, and if David is going to keep on fucking with you behind my back, I will rape him!"

"What!" She said as she almost burst out laughing nervously and couldn't believe her ears.

"As punishment I will screw him. I can fuck with any man I want to. I can go down into the village and find a man to be willingly fucked senseless by me."

"Go on then! Find a man dead or alive who wants you."

"Don't provoke me; you little bitch; you dirty little whore. I don't want to do anything bad to David, but if I do, the price is on your head, not mine!" With that Sophie who had heard the latter part of the conversation stormed in.

"I am warning you king shit. You do anything bad to David or Erik for that matter, and within twenty-four hours you will be dead!"

Despite the venom that had been directed at him: he felt like some victor on a battlefield. All that mattered to him was that he then knew that it was more than just possible for him to do more than to masturbate David. A threesome was in the pipeline. As for Beth, she decided to stay alone in the lugubrious prison of her loneliness. All she could think was how she simply wished that she hadn't confessed to him about David's admission.

In some ways the forty days of madness when the girls were sleeping with all of the men on a regular basis which lasted right up until early February was the best days of the girls' lives. It was also the worst days of their lives. Sophie was most negatively affected by these events. She was in fact, madly and deeply in love with David. She also felt in her heart that good things would come to an end and that once things settled down and David and Beth became an item once more, that she wouldn't have the pleasure of him going deep inside of her again.

Both girls; then mothers to live babies, and then four and seven months pregnant respectively felt gutted that they were behaving in such a manner. Even so, this took their minds of the fact that they could end up in the same fate as Jennifer. It also took their minds of the fact that the men were at best useless.

It was as they sat eating the dinner together that the girls had something important to announce. "We will put our children to bed and then Beth and I will sit downstairs without any of the men around. It will be the equivalent of our very own girls' night out. Roger felt that the girls were going to decide upon their partners. He decided to simply show them both that he was a devoted daddy and after the women had breastfed William and Jane, he took them into his bed and fell asleep with them both.

Downstairs the girls were talking and laughing about their relationships, until Sophie turned somewhat more serious. "As much as I hate what happened on the day the Armageddon came, I have reassessed my life somewhat." She said waiting for her sister's response.

"Go on dearest, tell me what you mean."

"You have always been the good girl, but sadly, and thanks to my influence you have ended up in the same mess as me. I didn't realise how lucky I was when I was working at The Bridge. Imagine if Jan and I had found work on a remote farm like we told our parents. Under the watchful gaze of the farmer and his wife, I would never have treated Jan the way I did. What I am asking you is, do you think that there is some good out of this horror for mankind?"

"I guess as a Christian you think I might have some answer. There are two ways to look at this. I know about the Bible prophecies and it does speak about a big clean up. I like to believe in a loving God, and that we are free to make our choices. We both eat well, go to bed early and look after our bodies that for me is a virtue. It is a part of my own interpretation of Christian values. Sadly, I am not wise enough to answer your question. I am sure that many more humble beings than you and I together ended up as corpses. I just don't want to dwell on this, all I want is to simply pray for us both and for our children."

"What about the men?" Sophie asked.

"Maybe I should, but I am so disappointed with them, that I can't.

"Maybe that is the problem. What if you pray for them too, and then love will find a way to us."

"For someone who professes to be agnostic, your words have touched my heart. I will pray and hopefully we will find the love that will mend our broken hearts."

"When I started reading those old English novels, it was simply one of another worlds as to what I was living in. I had so much social media deeply embedded in my mind. Still, it didn't take me long to get closer to those settings. At The Howe we were already living in another epoch, but of course down in Ambleside things were just like anywhere else. Then of course when Roger told us about the tsunamis and the wipe out just as we were preparing for our births, we were mentally getting ready for going back a couple of centuries. Now how things have changed even further for us. We simply understand those novels as if the writers were still alive. When I read about 1817 or thereabouts, I feel as though it is about the present. As for 2017, I feel so detached from that time now. I just can't imagine reading about text messages, cars or TV etc. Instead, words such as spinney, gorse and beck have so much more significance in my life right now. And to be honest, I feel much more enlightened from this. It was a shallow world before the holocaust." Said Sophie as Beth was in awe of her words and her opinions.

"Yes, it was, but it is such a pity that; people were not advanced enough to fully understand the technology that they had. Instead, they allowed it to destroy their senses in so many meanings of the phrase."

The girls continued with their analysis of the world while the men were having a sleepless night as well fear in case, they would be of the unloved due to some unexpected maidens arriving on their patch.

Chapter 10

DRINKING AT THE URINAL SHRINE

As for Roger; as soon as he found out Beth and David were once again an item in early February, he was scared. His mind went into overload as he wanted to analyze everything more than ever before. Instead, before he was about to do this; he looked out of his window. It was bad enough when Beth and Erik were an item, now was much worse for him. Sometimes whenever he thought about Beth and David, he wanted to be their daughter there and then. Other times he wanted to be Beth, and for Beth to be David. The confusion was driving him insane. While he was looking after Sophie's baby in his room, he saw her kissing Erik. With that Roger wished that he was strong enough for just one woman. With that he was scared that he was on a road to ruin. He then went to his bed and started crying alone and he was hoping to die in his peaceful sleep. Luckily, his home didn't have pills, since a part of him was hoping for some miracle to come his way.

After waking up in shock, he started thinking. He missed the old world. Back then, although he would never have admitted himself onto a psychiatric ward, he did at least have this as an option. His best psychiatrist was Beth. Maybe the time had come for him to lie further and to tell her that he would run away with her to The Howe with her and that they would live there happily ever after. He had to save himself somehow. Suddenly, he came inside his pants as he thought about himself killing Erik and raping David. While this would help free his mind temporarily, he was looking for something that would cure him. While killing and raping would ease his symptoms of which there were many, he wanted a cure for his madness. In short, he knew to his own despair that there really was no hope for him. Even worse was that he wasn't sure that he could cope without David and Erik, apart from their labor he felt he had other uses for them too. While they simply couldn't move into a new home without his help from the authorities, he was scared that they were not so dependent on him as he was on them.

He then sat emotionless on his bed. He then realized that he was a man after all. If he had a phallus: he wasn't a woman. He was male, an impregnator. He needed to think about other matters so that he wouldn't end up insane.

As far as Roger was concerned, it mattered to him who went to the bathroom. He was so desperate to go to the toilet and the wait seemed so endless. David and Jennifer had been on a visit, and while upstairs on his own, he heard Jennifer go to the bathroom. Ten minutes later David went. He was worried that he could contain himself no more. As such he urinated onto his bedroom carpet. A short while later and still in his room, he was excited. As the door closed it was David, and he was in dismay. Luckily for him there were just two women left. It was her! But sadly, for him he realized it was Sophie. So obsessed with the bathroom, he knew who from the sounds that he recognized, who was on the toilet or taking a shower.

In his sorrow and pain, he fell asleep. It wasn't so deep. Beth was in the bathroom; he woke up excited. He was also confused because he wondered how he had heard a deceased Jennifer go to the bathroom. Once again, he needed the bathroom, couldn't she just get a move on! There was a bathroom downstairs, but he needed the one upstairs.

Luckily for him she left the upstairs bathroom. Frantically he ran in there just in time. He then urinated in the sink. All he wanted was a urinal, without one, the toilet cubicle was sacred. Beth had been there. He then crept down on his knees looked in awe at the place she had visited and licked the basin of the toilet. It was shaped like one of her big and juicy precious buttocks. He could smell her last visit there. Miraculously, she had forgotten to flush the toilet. Drinking her urine at what was for him, "The Urinal Shrine", as he cupped his hands inside the water closet, was better than of his own sweat, bogies and excrement combined.

As for David and Beth they were together once more. The last time that they were an item they were just two and her bump, now they were three together as well as another bump and sharing a bedroom since a few days. "Is everything alright darling?" She asked him.

"Yes, I am so happy to be here with you." He replied.

"Are you still getting over Jennifer?"

"Not really, but I am quite tired."

"Why, because of the baby and the semi-sleepless nights?"

"I guess so, but don't worry; I can imagine it is more tiring for you."

"You are so sweet." She then kissed him on the lips. He kissed her back. She badly wanted him. He put his arms around her and fell asleep. Poor Beth, she wanted a man to be as passionate as Roger, as sweet as David and as stable as Erik.

For the next few days Beth whenever her child was sleeping and when she was able to relax from being uncomfortable from her third trimester, she tried to fall asleep. What a discomfort it was for when night after night she had been woken up from the sound of the ewe bleating and the groaning from a familiar voice. She was tired to say the least. David knew what Roger was up to and was concerned that he seemed to be flaunting his beastly acts underneath the cover of darkness while equally within Beth's earshot. On top of that, the sparks she had been waiting with David, hadn't materialised. Their bed was literally used as a place for sleeping and nothing more. They usually managed cuddling and hugging but she wanted much more than that. In turn, her time was spent going through with lonely days and nights with him.

Roger was concerned. While at times he enjoyed his unhygienic fetishes, there were times when he shed silent tears. As a child, his mother forced him to eat his body's waste products as a punishment for refusing to wear a girl's dress. At times he wished he could be put out of his misery and to fall asleep for the last time ever.

After a few days, a meeting was held in the living room with Beth, Roger, and David. "What do you want from us?" Asked David.

"I love Beth. I cannot live without her. She is carrying my second and more than likely third child. As for you David, I think you need time to grieve over Jennifer." Beth was then in shock. She felt as though he was staring at her enormous bottom as she had suddenly stood up in order to breathe. She also needed to take her mind of her baby kicking her somewhat painfully, that she was feeling all too frequently. "Please let's think over the next forty-eight hours what we really want for the children, our honor and our happiness." He said as he, Roger, shot an expression of passion from his eyes into Beth's vision. David looked at her and noticed that she was staring at Roger too much for his liking, equally she looked so fragile, and he didn't want to upset her.

"I think we do need to discuss these issues later." Beth said, who was lost and confused. All she asked for was for David to stand up and lead her out of the room with him holding her hands. If not, she had had enough, and would do whatever The Beast demanded from her. As far as she was concerned, David was more than just breaking her fragile nerves. Why couldn't he just save her from the Beast?

They had been together and sleeping in the same bed for more than two weeks and David had only once made love to her. There she was this passionate young lady, who was simply full of and waiting for love. For her as much as she wanted the respect, the friendship and the security she wasn't getting enough of the icing on the cake from her David. It was meant to be Valentine's season, not that that meant much to anyone now that they were all feeling so down.

Roger's birthday had passed everyone by. At fifty-nine he felt as though had nothing more to celebrate.

As he stood up, she was in awe of him. All she wanted was for him to look into her eyes and Roger's spell over them would be broken. He noticed that Beth's eyes were firmly fixed on him, but he felt overwhelmed and didn't know how to snap out of his helplessness which Beth saw of his very own making. On top of that he felt overpowered by Roger who was sending powerful and dominant energy towards him, and he felt intimidated by him to say the least. "I will go and sleep in Rydal Cave until Beth decides what she wants. I love her, but I will not beg for her." He said as his eyes were looking at the floor. Beth wanted to feel loved, and his words were like a knife in her heart. Meekly he walked off as Beth collapsed onto the sofa. She was still feeling dazed and confused and so Roger walked off giving Beth some needed breathing space.

It was in knowing that he was in competition for her affections with another man made him feel strong. How could he think about bicuriosity with her and sex changes when in order to get her, he had to fight for her love against that of another man? Another man who as far as he knew was straight was his rival, the very one whom he wanted to bugger up and be buggered up by. True, he would do something sensual with him, but he, David could only do that with his belle's permission and Roger felt that Beth was too straight to allow him his special sexual fantasies. Once back safely in his den, he could carry out his special acts out on her. He had never seen her in such a vulnerable state. His plan was to give her the best love making she had ever experienced. Put her under his spell and introduce a corpse, his ewe, a child and of course David into his special acts of love making with Beth. He was hopeful that she would be something like Lyla for him.

As he was bringing out a bottle of champagne for a celebration when he returned into the living room, Beth ran off upstairs to her room. She found him insensitive. Now, she couldn't face seeing either of the men. If only she hadn't left Erik who was now safe and sound, and away from the virus of perversion AKA as Roger, and in the safe arms of her sister. Why was he behaving as if she was dangerous? Why couldn't he see that his feebleness or cowardice was breaking her heart?

As she was lurking around David's bedroom he walked out of his bedroom with his rucksack. She was almost gasping for her breath as he walked straight past her. All she had to do was to beg him to stay. As for David, he wanted to know that she was no longer in love with The Beast. Then and only then, could he fall under her spell, since as far as he was concerned, love had to be on both sides.

As a woman she wanted him to take the bull by the horns and to sweep her off her feet. She wanted him to show her that; she was more special for him than Jennifer. She needed the reassurance from him; that he loved her. Her heart was beating wildly. They had already made love, so he must have surely had plenty of flames of passion for her inside of him. A few moments later he was gone. He had left the house. She obviously meant nothing to him.

He hadn't given up on her as he was crying silent tears and walking around aimlessly in circles close his home, hoping for Beth to run outside and to save him. After a while, all he could think about was how he needed to show Beth that he was man enough for her, since she wasn't going to come outside and coax him back to sanity. He wanted a sign from the heavens above that he would be reunited with her. Instead, he started to think about Jennifer, and how he had mistreated her. The night was long, but he had no intention in going back unless she loved him more than she loved Roger. He had to stick this out for forty lonely days, and for forty lonely nights. By then, he hoped that Beth would have made up her mind. By giving her enough space, he believed that he was doing the right thing for her. Like some little girl running away from a wife beater, he walked as though he was lost as he was walking downhill. Eventually, he found his way into the cave. Placed his mat and sleeping bag on the ground and started thinking. Too scared to actually do anything in case an act of his went wrong; all he could do due to his helplessness was to analyze.

In his overactive mind, it was then that he wondered if feminism had destroyed him. He thought about how he never really approached women because he had been too scared to. He had read in so many newspapers about women accusing so many men of being sexual harassers, murderers, and rapists that he couldn't flirt in the usual way. What made things even worse was the fact that he didn't like it when women came onto him strongly. As a man it was his job to do so. What a big mess. Had Beth not smiled at him; would he have noticed her? And if he had would he have taken the lead? Had he spoken to her after she smiled at him, would this still have been he and not she who had done the initial courtship? Did it matter who ignited the love between them both anyway? What mattered more than most then to him was that he simply had done nothing to win her love.

If he could turn back time, then he would have made a move on her the first time that they met. In turn she would have been the perfect maiden for him, and everything would have been so beautiful. He would have been her first, her everything, her last, and together they would have their own family. This painful reality was becoming too much for him to bear and was doing him no good for his manhood whatsoever.

He then felt as though he was turning into a girl. He had done so many wrong things to Beth. He felt so bad. Only she could save him from his road to ruin. He liked Sophie too. Given that everything had gone so wrong between him and Beth he wanted to fantasise about her sister but felt that this would be immoral from him since his heart was into monogamy. He had to with a heavy heart with his morals accept with his blessing that; Erik and Sophie were an item. Instead, a beastly Roger like figure was lurking around nakedly in his thoughts as he heard the sound of a drop of icy water falling into one of the puddles close to him in the cave. Thinking about how it was probably too late for him and Beth, he then cried himself to sleep.

As for Roger, sensing the turmoil in the lives of both Beth and David he wanted to be their bridge. For him heterosexuality was what made him love both of them equally so much. He was attracted to their purity; they were both the real thing for him, if only he was as stable as any of the other beings at Fell End. Sexually, he would gladly swap places with any one of them. Contradictorily, he enjoyed bringing out the confusion in both David and Beth. The feeling of crushing both of them was what made his life one of heaven. Their weakness: was his strength. His mind was made up. A threesome was more than just in the pipeline he wanted to believe. Unfortunately for him, now, that Jennifer was gone; there would be less of some kind of lesbian act possible with Sophie. He had made love to Sophie in a most humiliating way for her. He had made love to Beth; couldn't he have a threesome with the two sisters? He had masturbated David's penis. Couldn't he have a threesome with both Beth and David too? It was then that he felt that Erik was in his way, and that the slaying of his rival was the only solution for him to find the peace and love that he desired, for one moment in his life.

In many ways he felt as if he was a tornado and simply wanted to devour everything in his path. Life was evil: he couldn't escape from this hellish world. In short, life was about the interaction of fire and water. Love and hate was his passion. A hellish cocktail of destruction and innocence was the energy that excited him. Neutralising one's gender was at the heart of his program when the world was overpopulated, but even now he felt that there was no going back and that homsexualizing those he loved, was some kind of firework display of his own rainbow of love. If they didn't love him, and enjoy his fetishes, he would destroy them. More and more he was feeling like a victim, as he expected others to not just tolerate, but to live life the way he did. Simply put, he believed that the human race was extinct. The survivors were merely living corpses for him and were nothing more than his own personal toys. In short, he was simply jealous of stable heterosexual men such as Erik who wholeheartedly wanted to have a typical Christian family. Equally, he enjoyed the pain and sorrows that Erik had been through with in his personal life. He was also relishing that he had helped ruin it for the Romeo and Juliet of Fell End. Knowing that he had impregnated his beloved belle, Beth, before either Erik or David had any choice in the matter, made him feel invincible. As far as he was concerned; nobody gained anything from being good.

That night Beth was in turmoil. David her weak but saintly gent was in a cave. Roger her confused but strong man was with her. He had been sat waiting in front of her room and when she opened her bedroom door to go the bathroom, she couldn't resist him as she saw him standing there in front of her. They were sat together in his room, with the candlelight. One of his fetishes was for Beth to be under the paintings when he made love to her, so that she knew how important it was for him that she was going back and forth from hourglass figure to mother earth figure with more and more babies of his. As a lover of the insentient, losing his cyber porn had been difficult for him at first, but he was so thankful that he met his painter before she became something akin to an inanimate corpse. "Just because I am with you, doesn't mean that I want to be with you instead of being with David." She said to him looking as cold as ice.

"Just because I appeared to reject you doesn't mean that I loved you less than anyone else. I love you more than my passionate body is capable of showing you." He said staring at her fully ripe maternal body as she found his lovemaking the thing that made her go weak all over her body. Beth burst into tears.

"I can't cope with all the drama!" She said as she wanted just one man, to respect her like Erik did, to love her the way David did and to satiate her all over; the way Roger did.

"Is David fucking you senseless? Does he fight for your love the way I do? Did he love you so much that he wanted to get you pregnant again and again and again?"

"Yes." She said as she suddenly felt as though she had a lump in her throat. On top of that she wanted to collapse onto the floor.

"Then you must be happy. He is so lucky to be kissing your milky breasts and to be thrusting himself on top of you as you both make love together." With that she felt a pain in her heart. David had been too tired to make love to her, his work in the garden thanks to Roger, and her baby up all night was tiring him out. On top, since he was so self-centred regarding his own sleep, she couldn't imagine him being a father anymore.

Although they were no longer an item, just like he often did with her, he seized his chance as he saw her looking pale. Gently he kissed her on her neck and placed his hands on her hair as he was looking into her eyes and started kissing her on her mouth. He wondered if he had been too quick, and started caressing her cheeks with his hands, and after a few moments her mouth opened. He then started to massage her gently all over, before slowly taking off her clothes.

She thought that he was going to make love to her, she knew his routine. Instead, he opened his bedside cupboard, and took out the creams. David hadn't been rubbing the lotions to her satisfaction. He had the first time she was pregnant, but now she feared that he was disappointed that she was once again carrying Roger's child. Oh, how she longed for him to kiss her breasts and to make love to her. She would do anything to have a traditional family and would even sacrifice David. If only she had thought about this earlier. Maybe she still could have respectable conditions, but then again did poor Erik deserve to be alone if her sister and the man she loved, her David, became an item as she herself was back with Roger? She simply couldn't allow her sister to end up with David.

Just as he was about to moisturise her, she cupped her hands around his head. He then felt weak and wanted by her. In the meantime, he knew how much she was enjoying his special tender loving care of her body. For him, she was his sexy mistress rather than his dowdy common law wife like her sister. Gently, she put more pressure on his head and he bent down and started to kiss her breasts as she felt as though she was in heaven.

After lovemaking she looked at him. "How can we live together?" She asked hoping that he would finally respect some of her wishes.

"Very easily, I will be having loads of babies with you. We will bring them all up together."

"How can you say this when I am about to give birth to twins, am just nineteen years of age and already having my second pregnancy. I want a rest from child rearing. This is one reason why we can't be." She said as he started leering at her.

"So, you prefer a passionless relationship?" He said as she looked stunned and shaken by the confidence from his words. He had a combination of zero emotional intelligence practically and the emotional intelligence of some romantic author. In turn she sensed he was schizophrenic.

"When I was pregnant the first time he was." She said almost in tears and noticed that he looked somewhat bemused.

"And I am passionate even with a crying baby, our baby!" He said pleading as his words struck her deeply as he was deeply angry as he had once again been reminded of the time David was enjoying her pregnancy curves during her maiden pregnancy. She also knew that Roger felt that by rights of his sperm, her glowing body was for him to enjoy exclusively. Most importantly for her was that her fight was between her need of love and morality combined. David her useless lover; was the one she loved. Roger the disgusting man; was the father of her children. She was in so much turmoil and was scared of having a breakdown not just mentally but also physically, an early labor or both.

She felt heartburn; she took a deep breath and was experiencing a rather painful baby kick as well as a Braxton Hicks contraction. "We will get back on one condition." She said feeling desperate.

"What's that?"

"If you really love me, you will not make me pregnant again until I say so." She said as she started to feel a little bit in control of her life once again and that finally her patience was paying off with him.

"OK," he said. She smiled at him, as he was distraught that he would have to deceive her once more, when all he wanted was for himself to be completely submissive to her. First, he had to control and to keep the woman inside of him at bay. The only way he knew was for him to impregnate her regularly. Then with a large family, he hoped that to save the marriage, Beth would become his master as he would become her mistress, before she would be so repulsed by him that he could impregnate against her will and be born again. She then thought about his last word, it was a little too hasty for her, and she didn't believe that she could trust him.

If he could no longer make her pregnant in the foreseeable future, then he might as well seduce David. With another man he could still have an orgasm. Every human being had a hole; himself included, and that he knew only too well when he thought about the way women had pounded him with their dildos intact. All he could hope was that; he would at a later date be able to introduce cross dressing and more for them both.

He then thought about the times women his own age wanted him. What could he have done in the present with such an old, used, and barren woman? Poignantly he then thought about his ex-wife, Hannah. He had been secretly following her until the tsunami. She might have been the bridge between his youth and his maturity. Already middle aged when he met her as a young woman, even now she would be fertile enough to produce him children, which at the time he didn't want with her. If only he had had better role models during his childhood. If only he knew how to love when he was a young maybe he wouldn't be in such a mess as then. He regretted that unlike other loving husbands, who had children in wedlock, as their wives grew older, they were still in love with their women in every sense of the word. On top of that, he was sure that there was something about this voluptuous lady; that would have tamed his thoughts about her ageing as he would still be able to make love to her without thinking about ewes, children, corpses and men. In short, Hannah the everlasting beauty could have tamed him. Like his paternal grandmother, he was sure Hannah would grow old gracefully along with her femininity intact.

Beth smiled as she felt her baby kicking. She then thought about how if she were living with just one man, who was the father and true love of hers, that her life would be so beautiful as it was then so miserable. Why couldn't either David or Roger offers her the love, passion, and devotion that she desired so much?

During the night David woke up. He touched his chest and was convinced that he was developing breasts. Tears ran down his face. He was scared that if Beth didn't save him that he would end up as Roger's lady-boy. He then ran his hands all over his body and was frightened that he had more of a girl's than that of a man's body. Fortunately for him, Beth had a more petite figure than he did. Even so, this wasn't enough as he felt as though he could very easily lose his own mind.

Starting to feel calm, he felt as though he was crying out for Roger to make love to him. The feeling of being a girl was better than that of being a weaker man being buggered up by such a manly alpha male as him. Roger had masturbated him when Jennifer died so that he could take part in necrophilia and he was still feeling so disgusted with himself for making love to her dead body. He felt so weak and wished more than ever that he was all woman. He then touched his body. The feeling of being a woman calmed him down. The feeling of being penetrated by Roger soothed him. Only Beth could bring out the man inside of him. Only Beth could save him. If she couldn't or more to the point wouldn't because of choosing Roger, David in knowing how weak he was; wanted her to remember him. He would then live out in the wilds, as long as his body would sustain his life. He then asked himself in his thoughts what a man was. He then wondered if he himself was a man. Had Jennifer been alive and with him being a devoted father he would have had a purpose with his manhood. Deep down he had his doubts about Jennifer. He then thought about Beth. With her and mutual children together, he would then be the man he wished for himself to be. Sadly, in such a desperate state, he wondered if he would wake up as a woman.

They had no children together, so she could easily forget him. She had fallen pregnant to Roger twice. In turn if he wanted to get his own back on Beth, he would have to involve Roger. He then asked himself as he started to calm down, why would he want to do something against Beth anyway and especially one of a homosexual act? What was more, what right did he have in doing something so hurtful against her anyway? Maybe he was turning as evil as The Beast himself after all.

At first light, he woke up and had been shivering somewhat. His sleeping bag was warm, but he felt as though he was giving up on his life. His mind was still disturbed from the corpses he had seen everywhere, and he wondered if he should join them sooner rather than later. Since the tsunami and seeing how his Ambleside had turned into a ghost town, made him feel scared that the earth would soon be obliterated. More and more it seemed to him, that those who died had had a very lucky escape indeed. He then thought about Beth. He was then angry with her. She should have known that to smile at a man she didn't know and to say hello to later wasn't very normal. If she really wanted him, she should have asked him a question that would have really caught his attention. When pregnant the first time, she should have understood that she was a fallen woman and that it was hers and not his place to fight for their love. The fact that she didn't try harder to keep him when they were living together at Ambleside, proved to him that she didn't really love him after all. Feeling distraught he then thought about how she had hurt him and how she had wasted her chances by carrying Roger's child for a second time. He was like her and both were useless. So, what! He thought, everyone was going to die anyway.

Back in his den, Beth was trying to control the beast. "If I agreed how soon would you want to get me pregnant again?"

"I respect your body."

"I am just asking." She asked trying to get him to be franker with her.

"OK, if I could choose, then yes very soon."

"But the picture haunts me I know you are going to make me exactly like the woman in the painting above our heads; given the chance."

"Beth, even if you leave me, I will make sure that the dream comes true." He said boldly at her. She then froze.

"What dream?"

"As soon as we made love for the first time, I took a nude photograph of you and asked a local painter to imagine you at the age of twenty-one. As a psychic as well as an artist she saw you in her tea leaves after two births with three children and being heavily pregnant again."

"I know I have already seen that." She said trying to sound composed while inside she was terrified.

"I know, but I meant a fourth and a fifth painting. I wanted to wait until the right moment. I want to show them to you now!" He said passionately at her as his eyes were shining brightly. It was all meant to sound romantic from him but for Beth it sounded nothing other than pure rape. As such she fled the room and ran out with her sleeping baby and placed him in his cot. Suddenly she ran back into the house and decided to take her baby with her, in case of another disaster or even genocide.

Feeling as though the end was nigh, he then walked to one of the bedroom windows and while watching Erik and Sophie who were outside and looking very romantic, he was wondering what to do. He did however have a brief moment of satisfaction and smiled to himself as he was thinking that it was, he, rather than Erik who was the father of Sophie's second child. As he heard the door close from the main entrance of the house, he simply put his hands on his face. He really did love Beth.

Beth was furious and decided to take it out on David. She had given up on Roger and now she had to shake David back into his senses. Suddenly she was angry. Erik was the best guy, and she had cast him off towards Sophie. Couldn't she get anything right in her pitiful life?

Walking down towards the cave Beth was feeling sick. Not with morning sickness but with regards to the men in her life. She felt as though there was no escape. A part of her still wanted to take Erik back, but she decided against this because he was with her sister. Now that Sophie was in a stable relationship, the two siblings were getting along better than ever. When they were sharing Roger, things back then were making their relationship more complicated. Even so, Erik could solve her bigger problems, David, and Roger. There was nothing special about Erik, nothing exciting but equally there was nothing unstable like Roger, or weak like David.

As she continued walking, she felt lethargic to say the least, and her insides were feeling sore from the stress connected with the men. It was by then twilight, and the sheep looked as large as their bleating in the calm air sounded deafening. Worse was the crows, they were in a greater abundance than was before; she had to block them out of her head. She wanted to live but felt as though the emotional negativity caused by both men was having serious consequences. Not one of these men could make her happy. All three together would make her content, but she couldn't face going through with all the complications of her own harem again. The idea certainly excited her given she couldn't fully trust one man completely. After what Roger had done to her and the way David hurt her emotionally, she had no qualms about using the men. As she thought somewhat more, she felt once again that this would be unfair to Erik and to her very own sister. The Christian side of her nature reappeared. This was clearly wrong of her. No matter how bad she had been mistreated, this was simply no solution. What if a woman appeared unexpectedly, she would lose one of the men. Sophie was already there, another woman on the scene would mean she could end up with the worst man, Roger, as there would be enough women for all of the men.

It was time to get her own house in order. Both Roger and David were making her stomach churn. Without a man, she believed that she couldn't survive. She needed the touch. She needed someone to love her. Neither Roger, David nor Erik seemed capable of that, but at least they were men, and she couldn't live without one. She then prayed to God that David would pounce on her and at least kiss her so that she knew that he still had some fire for her. She wanted to know that his Christian views about love were more than just words for him. In her mind the men needed to act like men. Then she would be forever turned on. They were handsome but, in many ways, dressed like emotional zombies.

She hoped that her waddling on the unstable ground in search of him had not been in vain. As she arrived at the cave and saw the pathetic whimpering character; she looked at him as though he was some errant child. "David, why are you so bloody weak!" She asked him as she felt as though the stress was making her gasp for breath. "You run off and leave me. It is almost as if you want me to end up with The Beast!" Tears then ran down her face and his own eyes willingly obliged in sharing the sadness as his own taps were turned on once more.

"No Beth, I love you and I want to know that you love me too!" He said as his answer was repulsing her.

"My God, David, Roger loves me but he's a sick bastard! You love me, but you are too timid to show it." She said as if she were his mother.

"Beth, I am sad, I want us to be happy!" He said.

"If you were me who would you choose?" She asked trying to provoke him. It was a most pathetic question and she needed to know that David still had some life left in his balls.

"I don't know darling. According to the Bible you are married in heart and soul to him. Still if you choose me, I will be very happy." He smiled at her timidly.

"I don't feel any love from you; it is almost as if I am talking to one of my girlfriends." She said haughtily as his meekness was driving her crazy.

"I am feeling very sad, please just give me a few days and I will show you how much I love you." He said as Beth wanted him to fuck her there and then, even in the cave, this would be more romantic for her than in a four-poster bed with Roger.

She simply wanted to know that he was man enough for her but felt as though she herself was the man when she was next to him. All she wanted was love and as much as she saw him as a victim, she wanted to feel some chivalrous conduct from me. Yes, she had sinned, but she believed that she had been more than punished enough and wanted the world inside her broken and lonely heart to be as beautiful as the natural environment around her. "The longer that you stay here, the more Roger is going to seduce me. I'm heavily pregnant and very soon if you are not looking after me, he will impregnate me again during a rape!" Suddenly a premonition like feeling went over her as she thought that even under David's protection, Roger would impregnate her again anyway. In short, David was weak beyond belief. Beth was feeling so sorry for herself. She needed a man, and both men available from Fell End were in equal amounts useless at best for her.

As much as she had in his puritanical eyes failed, she knew how much he was longing deep down for her. As much as she wanted him, she looked at him as though he was some errant child. "For Christ's sake David; pull yourself together!" He then started to surface from his sleeping bag. The pressure for him was too much and he burst into tears. "For Christ's sake David! Stand up!" He then stood up after almost falling on the floor. He tried to hold her hand, but she abruptly refused. In turn Beth waddled in the dull daylight of a drab and wild landscape complete with grey flood-like clouds carrying her baby with David following one step behind them. Beth wanted to laugh at him because she found everything so surreal. She also wanted to cry because in her mind all three men who had made love to her were nothing more than scary monsters for her that were ruining her serenity of the beautiful Lake District.

All he had to do was to tell her how much pain he was in through losing Jennifer and his child; and she would be his. Beth wanted to understand him better, and his lack of grief over their deaths must have kept a lot of poison inside of him. Why was he suffering alone? She wondered.

As for David, he too was in deep thought. Would Beth as a good Christian woman understand why he allowed Roger to masturbate him? Could he confide in her about his dark thoughts he had been allowing to enter his then terrified and disturbed mind at the cave? Roger would always be the father of her children, and could she forget about him, Roger, and love himself, David, unconditionally?

As they arrived back at the Howe, Roger was sulking. He was burning some rubbish in the garden. Little did Beth know that while he was staring into the flames, he was having visions of Beth and David and imagining that they were now a threesome and being burnt alive together on some kind of funeral pyre. Having given up on the idea of making Beth bisexual, the next best thing for him was to care only about himself. Having a man and a woman in his tryst would simply mean the best of both worlds for him as he could be as heterosexual and homosexual as he wanted himself in his bisexual world with his two great loves to be. Was he bisexual? He wasn't sure; at times he was gender fluid. Either way he didn't care; he simply felt that Beth had let him down.

The evening meal later that day was made by David under Roger's command and watch. Beth was sat at the dinner table breastfeeding. David was too embarrassed to make any eye contact with her; they weren't an item and he had to give her some space. Roger though, was looking at her lecherously somewhat and licking his lips. Beth felt as though she was sandwiched between mouldy bread and rotten flesh. "Beth, when will you let us know which one of us you have chosen?" David asked her politely but with an obvious hint of desperation. Roger wanted to snigger and was waiting for her response. She winked at Roger. This was a sign for him that she had chosen her man. Still, he felt insecure, he needed to hear an affirmative yes for himself. As for Beth, her mind was made up, and David was less of a man for her.

"Beth will probably choose me because I don't ask stupid questions!" Said Roger. While she agreed with him about the stupid question, his arrogance made her repulsed by his response as much as she found David pathetic.

"I have decided that I want to be left alone!" She said. In fact, she decided that if Roger entered her room, she would scream. She wanted Erik to enter instead. Just as she was thinking about him, Erik and Sophie walked in with her baby just in time for dinner and were looking very much that of a traditional family. All she could do was to simply hold her breath and keep her thoughts to herself. The dinner was pleasant, home-made vegetable soup and bread followed by local trout, potatoes, sprouts, peas and leek. This was finished off with apple crumble and custard.

As lonely as a cloud she went to her room and overwhelmed with everything she collapsed onto her bed after taking off her shoes. The sight of the loving couple made her grieve over her recent mistake in jilting him. There she was lying on her bed in a trance next to William. It was a mild and wet evening, and she could hear the frogs croaking as she thought that they were having much happier times than she herself was. As far as she was concerned; her love life was little better than that of the mother toads. David knocked on the door. The unknown gave her hope. Hope that a real man was about to enter. "Can I come in?" He asked her with a voice that was higher pitched than was normal for him.

"No!" She said abruptly. By then she hated David. It was his fault that she fell pregnant to Roger for a second time. She really wanted David to take the bull by the horns and to storm in, but once again he had let her down loud and clear. At least she had her son to take her mind off things. Without him she could have read, but thanks to the psychological torture from the men, she probably would have taken her life instead.

As far as Roger was concerned, tonight was the night that he had to fight for Beth. This would then send David into an even more pathetic state of mind. Then as he lost his integrity further, he would be able to more than just masturbate him. In his mind, the more that he would swoon Beth, the more he was on his path towards David falling in love with him too.

Half an hour later, and when William was asleep, Roger entered the room with chocolates imported from France as well as Champagne and daffodils. At first, she was silent. As much as she wanted to kill him; her mouth was watering at the sight of these delicacies. This was her anaesthetic against the hatred she had for him. David was useless with babies. She wanted help in bringing up her children. Maybe she could change Roger into being the man he had led her to believe that he was in the beginning. A rogue yes, but in her moment of need there was then nothing about the air of confusion in him. As he stood upright looking into her eyes with his breath-taking looks and powerful presence, she was in awe of him. By the look in his eyes and his gentle touch of her belly, he seemed genuinely looking forward to being a father again with her. Now was his final chance to prove to her that he was sincere regarding his initial intentions towards her, and that his confusion was merely just an aberration that had lingered on; far too long for her.

As for Roger, knowing that Beth was the door to David's heart, made this young lady more beautiful than ever for him. Seeing her as gorgeous as she was and thinking of her as a link between him and David, made

278

her simply more than ever before, irresistible to him. He wanted peace; he didn't want war. So long as he got his own way, nobody had anything to fear.

Under the candlelight thanks to the flickering flames, he started to swoon her with his love songs which she believed were coming out of his heart. They started to giggle at each other. After eating some of the chocolates and drinking together, Roger started to undress her before taking off his own clothes along with the womanly touch from her soft and sweaty hands.

Just as they about to reach the point of no return and make the night of one to remember, David plucked up enough courage and entered the room. Beth was frozen emotionally. Was David finally going to save her? This was the moment she had been longing for. Roger was aghast, was David actually going to stand up against him? "I'm sorry." David said meekly as Beth wanted the whole world to swallow her up. David was meanwhile thinking of something worth opening his mouth for.

"David, come and join us!" Roger said, as he had got his words in before his rival, as images of a threesome were running through his excited mind. David's presence was turning him further on, but he had to look at Beth only. He was sure that she wasn't ready to see him being attracted to another man. Instead, and to her disappointment David left the scene in shame. Ever since he made love to a corpse under The Beast's command, he felt as if he was doomed.

She then looked at him. "This is your fault." He didn't know how to respond to her and sat there as though he hadn't heard her. After feeling sorry for David and sharing his pain both mentally and physically she started crying somewhat silently. Roger allowed her to let some steam off and just before he sensed she was about to stop crying and leave the room, he started to touch her and gave a gentle massage of her body. At first, she was terrified as she sensed that he wished to be taking part in some threesome of which she found abhorrent, but his firm hands were turning her on far too quickly for her comfort. He then, without any hesitation moved onto to her sexual organs and brought out of her a feeling of living for the moment. Beth was then as hot as a sex kitten. Roger was delighted; and believed more than ever that; Beth was the door to David's heart for him.

As for David, he was completely gutted. He was defeated. He imagined that Roger was taking over his life. He had never been so frightened in his life. Dark thoughts went over him once more as he wanted to end his life as he imagined that Roger was penetrating him from his behind. Beth had told him several times that he was a girl. And then a most horrendous thought went over him and that he was in some ways the mother of Roger's posterity. It was then that he realized that he needed medical help more than ever: more than the meaning of the words. In turn he believed that he really was one big girl; and cried himself to sleep.

There he was alone in his bed and already twenty-nine years of age and had never experienced such confusion ever in his life before. He was scared. While he knew the best way was to have a fight with Roger, he was scared that his body was turning into that of a woman's. In turn there was nothing else other for him to do than to cry and hope that Beth would save him. If only he could be man enough for her, equally if she rejected him; he was simply too weak to survive without her. He could even end up at Roger's weird mercy.

As for Roger, he felt so virile and so macho. He then left the room and went to his bedroom. While she was waiting for his return, she couldn't get David out of her mind. As such she then sneaked out of her room with thoughts of simply crying next to David as they would be together in his bed were touching her heart. All she wanted to do was to release all of her emotions with him. She then opened his room, as she saw that he was lying prostrate; she felt that he was too soft for her and could even imagine Roger on top of him as he was lying down on the bed all woman with his face drowning in his pillow full of tears. The sight of him looking so pathetic was too much for her and she then returned to her bedroom. She couldn't decide who deserved to be put out of their misery: David, Roger herself or all of them.

A few moments later, Roger returned with one of his latest sketches of her. She looked at it and was dissecting every inch. It looked beautiful apart from one blemish. "Why did you have to have my right breast showing the scarlet stretch mark?"

"This pregnancy is different. The first time in many ways a first-time pregnancy is that of a woman who still has a pre motherhood body. While your body had been preparing itself for the birth, this was nothing compared to the consequences from the labor for your body after it had been fully opened up in the middle. Now your skin is more vulnerable and with your feminine imperfections and knowing what I have done to your body makes me want to enjoy our love making even more than when we did this, this time, last year. In turn, your breasts full of our blissful experiences need to be shown as beautifully and nakedly as they really are." His words along with his deliberately deep voice had the magical effect of making her feel both embarrassed and sexy as well as being very important in his life.

In turn, they had a night to remember as his passion knew no bounds. He noticed her looking at the picture he had drawn even though it was dark. "Do you think I can add a stretch mark or two onto one of the paintings on the wall?" He said as the idea of making her feel more and more at his mercy was turning him further on.

"No, please Roger, this is too personal!" He then switched on the LED light. "Please don't wake William up." She said. He then nervously took out a painting of her which was under her bed, this time it was of herself with a scarlet stretch mark on her left breast as she was sat with her legs wide open with sperm all over her belly. He didn't want to provoke her into resentment and in turn leaving him, but equally the satisfaction he would receive from her despair made him feel that this was a risk worth taking. In great anticipation he sat holding the painting on the covers of the bed. "My God! Where in the hell did this come from?" She said trying not to laugh and instead wanted to punch him as she looked at it.

"I told you that there were five paintings. I had been saving this one for the right moment. I had to pay the artist extra for this one, but you are worth every penny I spent on you." She then studied it in shock. While the painting was disgusting, having his sperm all over her pregnant body was a normal thing for a couple. The problem for her was that they weren't in a monogamous relationship and she didn't like being on show in his room and this was simply a private matter for a couple. The idea of the others at Fell End as well as later her children seeing such compromising pictures of her, in her mind, just simply wasn't right.

While she was still in shock, he wanted to break the ice. "She claimed to have psychic powers, and so far, so beautiful." He said as she was simply lost for words. "I gave her a photograph I had taken before you fell pregnant but probably when my love juices were travelling towards you and setting you off onto a tour of motherhood. As she saw your sultry face and then looked into mine, she said in her own eyes that we were two peas in a pod." With that she had nothing more to say.

While Beth on balance loved the night with him, apart from his latest painting of her, she hadn't forgotten that he had told that; no matter what, he was going to impregnate her whether she liked it or not again and again. Now with her being so close to the birth; and in his eyes with her being nearer to a third round of being in the family way she looked at him. "I don't want to fall pregnant again to you." She said sternly as she was shaking inside.

"There is nothing I enjoy than being next to you. Why is God so cruel? If only all women were as beautiful as you!"

"Your words are lovely and kind, but please Roger; you have had plenty of babies."

"I will make you pregnant again and again and again."

"No, you won't!"

"Then I will make a multiple pregnancy with you." He said teasingly at her.

"I am not falling pregnant to you again if I am with twins." She said as her semi acceptance of a twin pregnancy made him feel so virile.

"Our lives have already been written."

"Roger, stop this please!" She said with a nervous giggle while inside she was scared and felt as though her heart was pounding.

"Beth, you are a fantastic mother. Now that the world has gone back in time, what would you do all day without babies?"

"I would go swimming all the time!"

"When you are old, who would look after you if you were childless? My sperm is my love and investment for your retirement!" In turn they made love. She wanted to smash the painting but knew it would simply fall on deaf ears. At least he hadn't yet hung it up on his wall. At least she wasn't going to fall pregnant to him that night and was enjoying every moment with him.

A few hours later as the night was turning to day, Roger woke up feeling like an emperor. He had humiliated David, told Beth about his plans for her and was now feeling invincible. Soon the time would come when he could tell her about his love for David. Once again, they made love. "That was so lovely Roger!" She said smiling.

"Tonight, I have big plans for you!"

"Can't it wait until tomorrow?" She asked.

"Yes, tomorrow night is perfect!"

"OK, so this evening we will have a quiet night together."

"Oh, really Roger, tonight I'm with David! We meet tomorrow my darling!" She said as he looked on in great dismay.

Scared in case she would end up with David intimately he had to act. "Maybe now is the time my love, for us to study all of the five paintings together." Quietly he went to a bedroom wall. She didn't complain about the LED lights, she had to see what horror with his voice he had for her. He then took the paintings off the wall and had all five on the bed. The first one was of her body looking so nubile and naïve on the island. She stared at it and saw herself as simply a child.

"I have changed a lot since, then haven't I?"

"Yes, but please don't ask me which part of your evolutionary cycle I love most of all in you. I will never tire of your beautiful body." He said as his words were turning her further on. The second painting that he showed her was actually the one she hadn't yet seen and had planned to show her the night before. Her body hadn't changed from child rearing, but she looked more confident and was blowing him as he was holding her still slender bottom with her long hair running down her back and her pert breasts as they were both looking ready for action.

"Roger, I am not into blowing as you know." She said shell-shocked.

"I know, but I will never forget the time you did it with David." He said calmly at her. She was too afraid and disgusted to ask and to find out if David had been spilling the beans about their private lives.

"I have had enough of these paintings." She said as she suddenly felt a surge of despair running through her mind, body, and soul.

In reality she wasn't planning on sleeping with David the coming night. There was a greater chance that thanks to her shameful existence; she would take her own life instead. On top of that, she was feeling more and more at war with him. "Please! I don't want any lonelier days and nights without you!" He blurted out. Suddenly he was then at her mercy, as David was no longer on his mind. As for her and thinking about what she had been put through with him, she despised his deceptive vulnerability and fled the scene to his own personal terror.

As for David, his mind was made up. Ever since Roger had masturbated him and as much as it disgusted him, he often saw perversion as a means of making Beth feel guilty. If Roger would make love to him and agree to kill him afterwards, he could then leave the earth with some dignity of sorts. He thought of lying on a railway track but given that the trains were so limited there were more efficient ways of seeing to his own demise. Train services from Windermere were twice a day only and through the week only.

David now saw life on earth as being of one of a most insanely depressing black hell. How could he have an ignominious demise when he wanted the honor of his parents who were looking down on him from heaven? None of his DNA was being nurtured; all he could hope was that Beth would never forget him. He knew of course that Roger was obsessed with death. If he begged Roger to fuck him senseless in front of Beth and to then slice off his head off with a carving knife, he was sure that he would oblige in his final wish, willingly. He then believed that for the rest of her life, Beth would in turn be riddled with guilt. It could have been so beautiful between him and Beth had he acted on the first day she set her eyes on him. They could have got married. They could have had children together. They could have loved each other until death do them part. In short, when they got back together recently after the girls' forty days of madness, along with other recent events it simply depicted the hedonistic times he despised of. For him it was better dead than being in Roger's sphere. On top of that, it was excruciatingly painful for him that he too had been a key player in the bed hopping days of the mother's to be who weren't carrying his children.

Downstairs, in the kitchen, Beth was sat drinking and nursing her son in the dining room when David and Roger came down for breakfast within a few minutes of each other. Her sister and ex, Erik, had already had breakfast with her. As her lovers sat down, one platonic perhaps, the other actual; she served them both their breakfasts. She noticed that Roger looked angry, in fact very much so. David though, was very much giving off the presence of some meek girl, which was increasingly a common event. In turn she felt so guilty and wanted to coax him back into his manhood. All he had to do; was to show some sign of interest in her. As for Roger, given she herself wasn't so perfect herself, she wanted to soothe any pain inside of him that was bringing out the worst in him.

Feeling very much dejected, she then walked out into the garden. She needed to see something beautiful. After a few moments she then returned. She was terrified. The body gestures of David and Roger looked complimentary with one another. Both were sat as though they were shadowing each other, it was all so surreal. At that moment she felt that she had lost both David and Roger. She had of course lost Erik too, but what could she do about that?

Deciding that she was stronger than all the men put together, she needed to look outside again. It was then that her mind went back to the depopulation program. She had tried to come to terms with the fact that;

the earth was overpopulated, and that people had been acting insanely like hundreds of rats in small cages. On top of that, the others, who were in all too many cases healthy, couldn't be brought back to life. She wanted to live in the present too. Instead, she felt that God was really putting her to the test. Things were so bad that she was certain that she was experiencing a bad dream. As her mind went back to the present all she could think was that without overcrowding, without modern technology that there was no excuse for the mental issues surrounding the people in her life. The world was beautiful, where she lived was like some magical Garden of Eden. Previously, the masses went there to escape from the towns and cities. How could any man not live harmoniously in the simple surroundings and be thankful for her love? The penny dropped. Apart from Erik, the other men, David, and Roger were damaged beyond repair and couldn't be healed by nature. Poor Beth was destined to spend the rest of her life alone.

Not everything was going wrong in his life. He had arranged the paintings on his walls so that he could imagine her going back and forth between her child rearing cycles. On the inside of his bedroom-door was the painting of her blowing him, as he turned a little around clockwise and the painting was of her being heavily pregnant. All he had to do was to turn a little more and walk towards the wall with the window and staring in front of him was her standing slim and naked on the island as he could imagine Beth in between her pregnancies. Sure enough, the next painting was of her pregnant once more and this time breastfeeding. As for the fifth and to the left of his door was that special prophetic pregnancy painting with the scarlet stretch mark on her breast, with her breastfeeding twins, and, with her toddler son, William, looking lovingly at her huge baby bump. Finally, as he turned around some more, he could continue with his eyes in awe of her being slim again and blowing him as a part of a cycle.

What a way to be going through her ninth month as Roger and David were regularly crying over her. Sometimes they would describe their grief with one another. They were each other's psychologist. She was still recovering from her sexual promiscuity, which was being made worse from the fact that both of these men were pussies for her. She was adamant that the next man for her was until the rest of her days. She had to reluctantly choose between Roger and David. Ambleside was literally a ghost town; there were no other available men as far as she knew. These tortuous days lingered on until the third month of the year arrived and when spring was in the air. Now she had to find her man.

As such one evening she simply walked into Roger's bedroom. He was feeling depressed and terrified of her leaving him and wasn't in the mood to swoon her. Feeling humiliated that she wasn't being treated like a lady she looked at him. "I need to feel you deep inside of me," she begged. He merely got on top of her, and within two minutes he had ejaculated and was more or less sleeping again. No foreplay, no emotions, no speech. What the hell was he playing at with her? This was not the lovemaking that this heavily pregnant and sensitive lady expected from a real and sensitive man.

Feeling languid from his carnal humiliation of her; all she wanted to do was to give birth as soon as possible and live on her own at The Howe. As far as she was concerned the way he had used her as though she was simply just a hole for him and nothing more, filled her with disgust. She then calmed down, for him to have behaved in such a manner towards her, denoted that he must have been in great psychological pain to have acted in such a putrescent manner. If only he had raped her instead, having a fight with him before he climaxed inside of her would have been more exciting than for her to politely ask him to do what should have came naturally to a normal red-blooded male. All he had done as if she was merely on a factory belt was to find his way inside of her, cum and pull out. Maybe because of her peaceful manner he had behaved in such a clinical manner. Perhaps he was trying to awaken the more aggressive side of her nature.

Chapter 11

LOVE WITH CONQUER EVERYTHING

While Roger was a hateful man, he was suave, addictive in bed and intelligent. While David was a complete wimp, he was still in many ways a sweet and innocent pretty boy. She had tried Roger the night before and wanted to try David one more time before she could decide who the better out of these two unworthy men of hers was. As she walked back into the kitchen after a bathroom visit, she was scared, since day by day Roger and David were still looking increasingly like that of a romantic couple and she hated being alone. Maybe that was the reason for his ungainly fucking as opposed to her desire for some semi-tantric lovemaking. Seeing two of the three men in her life looking increasingly dependent on each other was making her feel more than just a little bit inert as she wondered if she was on a ward in a lunatic asylum. William was sat content crawling at times and looked as though he couldn't decide who his father was. For all he knew Erik might have been his da da too. He was living with all three men in Beth's life and must have sensed the intimacy that she had for them all.

As such, and full of what was frighteningly for her, her sudden surge of masculine energy, she went up to him and took a deep breath. "Instead of thinking about what could and might have been, I want to see that you are strong enough for my love. I have tried to tell you so many times and so lucidly to you, that I seek a good man and with his many imperfections he will be loved by me, and I want him to love me forever. I might never have expressed these things in words as I am doing now but my actions have always been of a genuine and everlasting love towards you. This is a crossroad for us both. I want to walk on to the path of which I can feel at ease with myself and I ask you to follow me and to take the lead so that I can count on you and know that my love for you has not been in vain. I want to know; that my love will conquer everything." She said looking at David as Roger was staring into his eyes and hoping that he could surface any love that David had for him. David, although his eyes were on Beth didn't want to offend Roger and was shaken and numb with everything.

He then looked somewhat deeper into her eyes. "I understand." He said somewhat less meekly than usual.

"I mean it David; this really is your last chance with me." She said as his manner wasn't quite what she wanted and wasn't of the calibre for her to go weak at her knees in his presence. They left the room together, as Roger wanted the whole earth to swallow him up.

David and Beth went walking hand in hand in hand outside after she quickly left her son with Sophie and Erik. She hoped that, with just the two of them together and enjoying the beautiful landscapes and away from the oppressive energy at home, that a much more passionate side to David would come out. William wasn't his child and against her better judgement she wanted David not to worry about a child that wasn't of their own. She was certainly giving a reunion with David one big last shot. If he couldn't love her as they were on their own together, she would be resigned to the fact that; she had tried her best and that David wasn't a real man. In such a lonely scenario, at least she had her babies to take care of as much as she would prefer the love and support from a handsome gentleman, which he was.

Together they walked up to the top of the fell on a fine early spring day. As they stood above Loughrigg Terrace with a view of Grasmere she started to kiss him. As well as kissing each other, he was running his fingers through her hair as her heart was experiencing a glowing sensation. As well as enjoying his touch, she was enjoying his tentative signs of manliness being shown towards her, as she believed that love was in the air. With her fullness of health and the feeling of being all woman she found everything satisfying and stupefying.

He felt so good going down the fell with Beth. She was well into her ninth month. She was scared, since the ground was a little precarious for her, but David was holding onto her all man as they step by step descended into the beautiful dale. For Beth, being at the mercy of nature and under the protection of a man who loved her; was the closest thing to heaven for this battered but still dreamy soul. Without the heavy traffic and the hordes of people, the birds were singing all day. She could no longer imagine going back to the old world when the melodies from above were less loud and only to be heard at certain times of the day. The only person who mattered to her apart from her children was her man, and hopefully he really was David.

Down in the valley with the lake and Grasmere Island in view and with the mild early spring sunshine they smiled together as thoughts about warmer days and the fact that they had survived their first winter without mod cons were in their thoughts. "Beth, I haven't felt so relaxed since I lost Jennifer. What I am trying to say is that with you, and without anyone else around I feel as though the world is our oyster."

"Why didn't you speak to me like this instead of running off to the cave?" She said hoping that he was a man after all.

"My love, I feel that I am a much better man than him, and I wanted you not to make a mistake out of your own free will."

"You mean you wanted to make sure that I am not some stupid silly girl?" She said both horrified and embarrassed. At the same time, she was starting to feel safe with him.

"Please don't put words into my mouth." He said as she then giggled. They then continued to look at the view of the lake with the island as she started to sink back into her sadness. As much as she was enjoying the abundant sounds of the birds, deep down, she missed humanity.

Just in time he started to kiss her, her heart started beating. Kissing him was purer and more satisfying than with Roger. If only he could be more passionate more often. Feeling insecure she pushed him away. "Why are you all of a sudden longing so much for me?"

"I have always been so. I just lost a lot of my desire due to the sleepless nights."

"Why didn't you express this earlier instead of giving me the cold shoulder when I wanted you so much?"

"I didn't want to look as though I was complaining."

"Instead, I thought I was too fat and ugly for you. Couples should be able to discuss things with each other." She said to him almost tearfully.

"I feel so pathetic that I am a man who without his sleep doesn't have any energy left. After working in the garden all day my body is literally exhausted."

"If only I then knew. I will now make sure that my child gets into a better sleeping pattern. I must confess, I am exhausted too, and I know that my mother made sure that my sister and I were well trained at night. I guess I have been too soft. I know you work hard outside, and I should have known better." As she finished speaking, his kissing and touching of her body increased with intensity over the coming moments, her mind was on one thing only, David.

He suddenly stopped touching her. "My love I need some of your humble advice?" He asked her thoughtfully.

"What is it?" She asked.

"You have always in my heart been my one and only true love. While paying my respects to Jennifer, Roger told me that a real man of God wouldn't be immediately looking for pastures new after the death of his family." He said looking as though he was as guilty as hell.

"Only the Lord can answer that question, my love. As for Roger, he has no right to usurp his position in the morality stakes."

It was then that he decided the Bible wasn't able to give him the advice that he desired. Yes, there were Christians who would preach chastity in order for him to be able to atone himself, but his interpretation was that love was his religion too. No one was around and as they made love at the lake shore with views of daffodils around, she felt as though she really was in heaven. As for him, she was his one and only princess. Making love had dissolved her fears of being without love as well as her insecurities that no man would be strong and passionate enough for her. Making love had dissolved his jealousies that she wasn't with his child as well as well as both their own fears that he himself wasn't a real man. On top of that she thanked the Lord in giving her another chance on love.

As they were getting dressed an old lady from Grasmere spotted them. "It is not very often that one sees so much love in the air!" Said the old woman. "I'm sorry, it is just that I was a great admirer of Stephen Hawkins, until he said that the human race was going to destroy itself. It is parents to be, like yourselves, who give me faith in humanity!" Beth's heart suddenly sank; this nice pleasant old lady had actually destroyed everything for her own humanity as she was sure that David's pride had been terribly wounded. She was trapped. She wanted to get away from this local. Equally, she couldn't in front of David show a rude side to her character. Not now, not before they were seriously an item again once more. "Would you both like to come to my house for a cup of tea?" The old lady said. No, she wouldn't! She wanted to run away even if David was left behind. She was jinxed; nothing would ever turn out well in her pitiful life. She then felt as if she had cramping pains, perhaps she was going into an early labor.

"That would be very ice." David said. How could David have done this? Couldn't he have asked her first? As they walked together with the small talk and the pleasantries, her mind went back to when Erik arrived from Poland. David wasn't so strong as the Pole and in turn with his Cumbrian pride he would dump her. The woman was of a traditional kind, and she would put shame onto David for being in such a relationship. As a survivor, maybe she had a lovely granddaughter for him.

"Given most of the people I knew died in the tsunami I am happy to meet such a happy couple." She said as the talk was becoming more personal, and Beth was trembling inside. "Obviously you being so young it is your first baby?" She said as Beth sensed she knew that it wasn't David's child she was carrying. David was quiet too, and she sensed that he was falling back into the effeminate weakling that he all too often for her liking was. What a right mess she was in! All she could do was to get a taste of honey without actually being able to swallow and digest what she cherished so much. Was this her life, to be given reminders of what made her happy while in reality, her own personal happiness would remain all so depressingly elusive for her. Roger had put some curse on her, hadn't he? The only time she could be free from him was when he had no real use for her. That was whenever she was expecting, during both pregnancies she had romances with both Erik and David, and he was busy with Sophie among other women. So soon as she would give birth, she was sure that he would be lurking around, ready and waiting to simply impregnate her for a third time.

Suddenly, just before pains of sadness were threatening to take over her body, a what for her deafening silence ended. "No, our first child is being taken care of by her sister, my sister-in-law and her husband." He said as all of a sudden, a patriarchal protectiveness for Beth came to him as she was poignantly reminded about Roger. At that moment as she was thinking about the ebbing tides of love and the flowing tides of hate. He had never told her about his analogy with the waves and their power of life and death, but at that moment she was sensing this. For her the tide of death was Roger, and the tide of love was David. In her confusion she decided to remain silent. After calming down, she realized that David was standing by her and behaving like a real man and that she had nothing to fear for the moment at least. Like a small child being handed a bar of chocolate she started licking her lips and believed that all would end well, finally.

Together they walked to the old woman's house which was above the one hundred metre tidal wave limit. In turn they were invited to stay at her home for a couple of days. Just after they arrived, they had a cup of tea and home-made cake and Beth decided to write a letter. The old lady had a son; he was a friend of John's from Tarn Foot. Beth asked him to post a letter for Roger, since her stay at Easedale was for more than just a refreshment. As a former curator at the Wordsworth trust, David was a guest of honor. After a lovely night's sleep in the guest room with David they had a typical Cumbrian farmhouse breakfast. After it, David and Beth walked up to Easedale Tarn gently together.

At the tarn, and holding their hands together inside the bracing waters, they were both giggling together. "Isn't it amazing the power of water?" She said to him.

"Not far from here at Codale Tarn to our left and higher up the valley, is where the source of this water is and flows from there to here."

"And then it goes tumbling down into Grasmere and into the sea." She said as she touched his heart with her beautiful words. Suddenly a veil of sadness went over her as she thought about those who had perished on her doorstep and were washed down into the Morecambe Bay as they joined up with tens of thousands of others and more, before joining with literally millions of others in the Irish Sea. She couldn't bring out the womanly side of David, not now; she had to stay strong so that she could coax even further the man inside of him. Like herself, David was a sensitive man and would easily be able to shed tears for all of the victims of the tsunami.

As Beth was thinking about the direction she wanted to take with her life, she was thinking about her letter of revenge for Roger. Not quite feeling safe with David, The Beast's response to her letter would determine as to whom she would spend the rest of her life with. At least that was how it seemed to her. In the meantime, her hopes were high that David had great potential for her. If she were lucky, both men would be to some extent healed and she would have to choose between two men as opposed to two spooks. As the dreamy romantic however, she much preferred it if just one of them was her beau.

Back at Fell End, Roger started reading the letter just before he was going to start cooking dinner for everyone who was there at Fell End.

My Dear and Darling Roger,

I would much prefer to be looking straight into your devilish eyes directly, and to show you that I really mean business with you. I feel compelled that since I am away with David, who is the sweetest man I have ever known, to explain to you why I wasn't with you, after my passionate night with him. Since you never take no for an answer and there are so many problems between us, I feel it as a matter of urgency to express my home truths to you.

The times you spent inside of me, certainly gave me such a thrill. It was great and they will always be a part of me. You have impregnated my sister and I twice over, and now it is time for the Young Turks at Fell End to produce with Sophie and I, the posterity that will lead the nation in times of peace and love.

I hope that when I am pregnant again, even though I will be carrying David's child; that you will delight in the painting of me as a work of art of yours.

I love you so much Roger, but not enough for you to ever make me pregnant again. As you are reading this, I hope you will be happy for me that although I am making mad passionate love to David, that I am looking forward to your body too.

After the birth, I will still make love to you, but only after showering your balls with icy cold water.

You had so many chances to take me as your devoted wife, but you have hurt me so much and made me want to be like you and to have my own harem. Hopefully, those deviant days of mine have passed.

Your one: and only true lover.

Beth.

While reading the letter he felt as though he was being stabbed to death emotionally as well as physically with his guts being thrown onto the floor and thrown into his fireplace. Feeling so cold and numb he perilously got closer to the heat of the flames as his body temperature was falling. He wished that he had never been born.

Not wanting the others to see him looking so distraught, Roger was relieved that the others were at the other house on the estate. He wanted Beth to kill him there and then. The idea of making love to her without impregnating her; was a terrible omen for him. Her letter seemed full of ambiguity, he was still her lover, yet she hoped her bed hopping days had passed. The game was up she was going to kill him before he had a chance to be reincarnated as her daughter. He felt that under the circumstances that their relationship would be barren, he might as well make love to David, or better still that he would make love to his beloved ewe again. Under these conditions he felt suicidal. If she killed him and was haunted from his smiling face as she put him out of his excruciatingly mental misery, at least she would never forget him. As an important Illuminati member, he could even order her to eat him. As the flames went out and he was too tired to search for more fuel, he simply went upstairs to his bed.

In the background he could make out the faint sounds of laughter from Sophie and Erik. He felt so helpless and unable to cope. He wanted the passion that they were during those moments encountering but was in two minds. Fuck them both senseless and have his needs fulfilled right then, right now, or wait for her to be pregnant no more and fulfil his dream for a third and lucky time with her. With all the confusion running through his turbulent mind, he ran downstairs on all fours howling like a wolf. He then stood up confused, opened the door and got back down on all fours. He was a man's best friend now. He went outside without any of his personal belongings. It didn't matter; he was a dog now. At least that was what he believed himself to be.

As he was walking, he was howling incessantly. With his then dry throat his noise was turning more to melodic yet melancholic hues as his whimpering sounds were less severe for the ears. Even so, his painful sadness was as depressing as for those who had earlier been watching passionate scenes in front of their insentient laptops. These people knew that real love was as elusive for them as their chance to change the world had been and missed the human touch. As he arrived at the front door of his house, The Howe, he sat in front of the door waiting for his owner, Roger, to let him in. In his mind, he was that canine lover, his mother. In turn he was a bitch of a four-legged kind. He then continued howling and eventually fell asleep. In his dream he saw Beth walking around looking as beautiful as ever wearing a blue dress and guiding his children as they were walking through a meadow with the sun shining with David holding her hand. Such a dream for him; was as evil as a dream about himself being tortured and having himself skinned alive while being interrogated by his nemesis David Icke was beautiful.

As they were on the way back walking from Easedale after a lovely sojourn; she held onto him tightly and felt so wanted and loved. As she saw the crows flying around, all she could hope was that they were uninterested in her. Normally, she would have been scared, since for her it was of some foreboding. There was nothing she could do but remain strong and keep her fears at bay and David was giving her all the emotional support that she wanted to muster. Suddenly she had a new problem, David was then in tears as he was walking next to her. "I am scared you will be with Roger tonight." He said as his world was caving in.

"David, a woman needs a real man. Who is neither beast nor coward: a man who is strong and a gentleman. You and Roger both drive me insane."

"I understand. I will try to do my best." Said David meekly. His answer made her feel even worse than ever. In fact, his weak, loveless, and pathetic response was killing her. Roger would have given her a response that would have been so fiery, passionate, and seductive while at the same time it would have been so disgusting, disrespectful and with disillusion.

A few moments later he started to kiss her fleshy lips in such a way that passionate sensations ran throughout the whole of her body. The air was cold outside even, so they were both thinking about one thing only for when they returned home. "Why don't we move into my flat? At least we will have our own privacy."

"Darling, with just one bedroom, for the four of us, that place is much too small for us." Her response had disappointed him. He was deeply upset but understood that Fell End was much bigger and had a lovely garden where they could grow their own produce. Knowing that he could not reproach her but was still reeling about living with Roger for what was becoming an eternity, left him feeling cold inside his heart. Due to his sulking, Beth's heart was gently drifting away from him, then, not so perilously for their love to survive, but enough for a man who loved her to take the bull by the horns. Instead, as he tried to kiss her mouth was locked. He gave up without a fight and in turn her amorous feelings for him were then in torrents being repelled by his lack of manliness. "I love you Beth." Sensing his desperation, she no longer felt safe and sound with him.

Back at Fell End, Beth was looking forward to making love to Roger. Instead, she was scared when she realized he wasn't there. Maybe David would leave her too. On top of that she was scared that she was becoming more and more like Roger, and that David was like she was when she was that submissive girl who lost her virginity and her own self-respect. If only David were stronger. In fact, her first impression of him was much better than this. Maybe as a cultured man back in the modern world, which had disappeared, he had a welcome nonchalance in the then unstable world. Maybe Erik was a much better man in times of a crisis. Maybe Roger, the great parasite was able to survive in any situation like that of some gruesomely big, fat and heinous cockroach.

Over the next few days, David was genuinely trying to satisfy her with his manhood. "Please David, don't, the father of my babies is somewhere unsafe. I can feel his pain, and as his biological wife I have to act." She said with a lack of certainty in her words.

"That's interesting; Sophie is his biological wife too!" He said as he looked menacingly into her eyes.

"Oh David! Now the man inside of you has come back to the fore, but I think that this is too little, too much and too late." She said in despair.

Back in their bedroom, her mind was still on Roger. As for David he worried that his now found girl inside of him could once again come back out into the open. As much as he was worried about his inner feelings, he decided that on the surface, no matter what, he had to make sure that in her eyes he would be all man for her. She was curled up inside a ball and wearing more clothes in the bed than was usual as she wanted to rebuke him physically. He was naked and pressing his groin against her bottom. He then put his arms around her: as she was crying tears of sorrow. He then gave up the fight for her love, and merely took her right hand and held it in his left hand. At least they eventually fell asleep together. For the next few days, all she could think about was Roger. All the good times they had together as well as all the things he bought for her.

One evening Roger ran down into Ambleside along with the dogs, and together they feasted on the bones of the carcasses of the former human beings which had perished almost a year earlier. Since he had metamorphosed spiritually into a dog, he had made many four-legged friends. Back at The Howe, the dogs threw up as they were feeling sick from the infested bodies. Roger though was able to digest anything and had more energy than ever. In turn the other canines saw him as their alpha male.

Roger was worried about his friends. They seemed as though they might die a terrible and gruesome death from what seemed to be their last feast. He was horrified that he had put the dogs in such a grave danger. As each hour went by, one by one a member of the pack was losing consciousness.

Not wanting to lose his friends he ran as fast as he could down into Ambleside. Once there, he feasted on as many human carcasses as he could muster. He filled himself up with plenty of rotten and stinking flesh. Very quickly he wanted to be as sick as a dog. Instead, he had to keep inside of him the vomit that he hoped would help the immunity of the remaining survivors.

Back at The Howe and unable to hold in his vomit any longer he puked up all over the place and into the faces of his new mates. In doing so, some of them had woken up from their impending deaths. For Roger the sight of innocent doggies dying would have been a terrible genocide for him. He found it utterly horrendous that they were on the brink of death. More and more seemed to being nursed back to health thanks to his vomit. On one of the other sleeping dogs, he had a wee like a waterfall and poohed into their faces. The other doggies were mesmerized by his act, which in their mind was simply one of love. He had for sure, helped the recovery process as one by one the doggies were coming back to life.

A few hours later all but one of the dogs had survived. The death of the Yorkshire terrier disturbed him. As the alpha male wolf like dog, as he cried, all the other dogs started howling in symphony. Roger went down lying next to the deceased canine and used the body as his pillow. The rigamortis had obviously set in, but worse was the flies which were enjoying their newfound feast and making the others itchy as they were all snuggled up to their master. As much as the insects were more than just a trifle annoying for them, their love, respect, and devotion for the little deceased doggy was a powerful and moving sight. Like his former rival who knew how to hit the rights notes at the right time as he had done at the time a princess died, Roger's standing was rising. As the wise alpha male, he became the pack's gamma dog too.

The following day rather than celebrate the fact that he had saved the lives of so many, the fact that one dog had died was simply too much for him. For him, the world with his dogs was so beautiful and it was a terrible tragedy that he had put his newfound friends' lives at risk.

After a few days while walking past The Howe on her own one afternoon, and fortunately without Timmy and Dexter, Beth was shocked in seeing him looking like a werewolf. There he was, playing with dogs. He certainly looked very robust next to the other canines and Beth feared his diet was that of the rotten flesh from infested corpses. She was terrified: was she carrying his puppies? As for a multiple pregnancy, that was now the least of her worries, so long as her unborn babies were human; that was all that mattered to her.

As for Roger, he was very angry to say the least. He was still waiting for his master to let him inside his home. It had been several days since he had been indoors. He also believed that Beth was his owner. As such and with his strong sense of smell, he started running uphill after her. He wasn't so quick as the dogs who were now living with him, and as Beth could hear Roger and the dogs barking, she was terrified. Even so, due to the fact they had made love so many times, she was less terrified of him than had he been just a stranger. The dogs continued running closer towards her and she didn't know what to do as she could hear their barking getting nearer. Suddenly two of the dogs loomed into her view, she panicked. At least they stopped running and were waiting for Roger. Luckily, there was a dry-stone wall and with all of her might she climbed over it, just in time.

A few moments later she heard Roger. He was barking. She laughed at him nervously behind his back. At least she was safe behind the wall. Suddenly she panicked. How would she get back home? A second attack of fear came over her. Maybe the hounds were going to kill all of the residents at Fell End.

David was in the garden and as soon as he heard strange howling sounds, which resembled a call saying "Beth," he panicked. He was terrified and ran inside the house. Beth continued walking, she was nervous to say the least, it was getting dark. As she got close to the gate on the bridleway she looked behind and saw the savage dogs looming into view and starting to growl at her. She was ripe pregnant but luckily very agile considering her condition. Again, and just in time, she climbed over a wall clumsily into her garden. This poor young heavily pregnant mother was in shock. Luckily, her body was in survival mode as opposed to that of fear, and she fell asleep. The ground was very cold but at least she wasn't going to have a heart-attack.

David too had fallen asleep in the daylight but then a few hours later in the dark he could no longer doze off. Where was she? Roger after suddenly jumped over the wall and was in the garden of Fell End, while the dogs were waiting close by on the bridleway which adjoined the entrance to Fell End; Beth woke up. Luckily for her she had been wearing plenty of layers on her body including waterproofs which acted as a shield for her against the stone-cold ground. The air was eerie, she got up and was unaware that she was a mother to be, it was almost as if she had gone back to the time before the tsunami. Gingerly, she walked to her home as she realized where exactly she was in her life. As she opened the door of the house, a smelly and lice infested Roger followed her inside.

She then got into bed with David and Roger sprang into bed with them. A few moments later, he was holding David inside a headlock. As the beagles were wondering what to do and were going from whimpering to barking and yelping and changing their sounds as they were in total confusion as to who their real master was; the silence was broken. "What do you want from us?" David asked struggling to speak from lack of air.

"Beth." He howled. Beth started crying. As beastly as he was, his passion was making her go weak at the knees. What was David doing in their room?

"Why aren't you with Jennifer?" She asked him as she was doing everything, she possible could to destroy David.

David remained unperturbed. Poor Beth was losing her mind and he had to look after her with sensitivity. He knew that he had to act. He knew that one wrong word and he had lost her. There he was the great manipulator. He had lost Beth, but he had to make sure that she was no one else's. In turn he composed himself. "A real man would have been in search of his beloved, where were you?" He said as David was lost for words. As evil as he was, as much as she would never allow him to go deep inside of her again, he had struck a chord with her. David had acted with a contemptuous form of cowardice.

Instead, and acting as though he had learnt a few devious tricks from Roger he simply smiled at the other two on his bed. "You have had plenty of time to show Beth how much you love and failed." Said David.

"You are lucky, you are more girl than man, otherwise; I would have fucked you!" Roger said, as Beth was feeling weak with everything.

"Roger, as the most intelligent man since Wordsworth, I ask you to consider yourself as a pillar of society. You will be a man who deserves a congregation of followers. Buttermere deserves her own vicar. I humbly beseech thee to study the Bible and to be a man of God in less than six weeks' time." He said breezily yet somewhat boldly and had miraculously disarmed plenty of the poisonous feelings flying around about him.

As an Anti-Christ, Roger wondered what madness and mayhem he could create on his watch. In turn David's proposal flattered his ego, and he vowed to get his own back on Beth somehow. He had to make her pregnant again, even if it were the last thing that he would do to her. As the quick-thinking lawyer, he was, he believed that; his key to his final dream with her; was for him to become, The Vicar of Buttermere. Surely, if he became a man of God, she would love him more than she loved David.

Roger had had a close shave. Had the others noticed his lice, it would have been a big personal humiliation for him. Instead over the coming days, he successfully through the chemicals that he had collected managed to somehow rid himself of the unpleasant insects. Miraculously, the others hadn't caught anything off him.

A few days later as David was bemoaning the fact that Beth hadn't waited for him romantically the night before, and, one morning he began as she woke up with him in the bed with. "How could you have made love to such an anti-Christ?" He said piously.

"I don't have to listen to your nonsense; you speak as though you yourself are holier than thou. Yet you cheated on Jennifer and then got her pregnant when you were still in love with me. So no, I won't be reproached by you. I admire and respect your Christian values, but I don't want any hypocrisy from you. Finally, had you not been so weak and timid the first day we met, our lives could have been so different now." She said to him as she looked directly into his by then tearful eyes.

Poor Beth, she had gone from being a dreamy romantic, to a lady in shock, then, she had hopes of romance with David before he dumped her. Before she was an uber submissive being with Roger and was now a cynic. On top of that, not one man was in love with her. The man who ruined her life simply didn't care about the consequences of his actions. The man she wanted to love, David, didn't seem to accept her for her imperfections. The man who would be as solid as a rock for her, Erik, was now happily with her sister.

Day by day Roger was studying the Bible. As the great survivor, switching sides was easy for him. He had gone from being a social Marxist capitalist to Satanist and now he was a man of piety. That first transition had been easy for him and he often wondered if his Satanism predated his far-left ideals. Now he was to play the part of being a man of God. He was surprised. This was coming naturally to him. So much so that he was able to convince himself that he was a good Christian.

After a few days she noticed that he seemed somewhat sad. All she could hope for was that he was a reformed man. She had always wanted a strong Christian man. Surely this wasn't too much to have asked for she thought: as she bemoaned the fact that Europe had changed in so many ways since Wordsworth. What a tragedy, her own country Poland had survived Communism and had been in many ways the last bastion of family values and a Christian enclave in the Slavic spheres. Even there, things had changed, with satanic parties and orgies springing up all over Warsaw. That was of course before the tsunami. She just had to keep her distance from Roger, just one more day and as his sadness intensified, he would finally be the man whom she desired, as she had no idea as to what she was thinking about, or even which man for that matter. In short, she knew that Roger had no idea as to who he was. She also had by then given up on finding a traditional man who loved her. On top of that, she wanted him to be physically attractive for her too, but she also had to forget about the times when he was recently some kind of a werewolf.

Tossing and turning that night, she felt so guilty. She was torn between two lovers and was breaking all the rules. If only she could sneak out into

Roger's bedroom and feel safe again with her strong and passionate man, whom David wasn't. Now with his remorse and his piety, Roger apart from his age, was her perfect man. All she could hope for was that she met his expectations as a woman with good family values as he would become a man of God for her.

The following day as she saw this man of piety looking extremely sad, she was delighted that he was harmlessly looking very busy in the living room and studying the Bible. "Roger dear," she said to him. His ears picked. "What's wrong dear?"

"I am fine," he replied.

"Roger, I know you well enough to know that you are sad."

"As I said, I am fine." He said looking sadder than ever.

"You can open up your heart to me."

He then slumped his head into his hands. In turn she went right up to him. She wanted to save him. He then looked at her. "When I was at The Howe, I went along with the dogs, who are my companions in heart and in soul, down into the valley and we had a feast of human carcasses. Sadly, one of my friends died." She wanted to scream and to shout at him. Instead, she hoped that with his newfound love of God that he was so sensitive that what he meant was that he wouldn't even want to harm a fly let alone a dog and certainly not a human being.

"You must be terribly sad about the people who died too." She said waiting for something Christian to come out of his mouth.

"Beth as it simply says in revelations, all evil people must be destroyed! Only those who accept that they have sinned and follow Jesus will be saved!" He said as he bemoaned the fact that human beings had not been herded off to concentration camps just like in the Second World War. At times he had wished that he had been born a generation earlier and sent to Auschwitz as a doctor. He then smiled to himself; that was Bill Wheatson's position and was pleased that his former boss wasn't in such a position, given there were simply too few useless eaters left.

Suddenly she froze. While her own interpretation of Christianity was one of love, she had to accept him as her religious leader. She was proud of his newfound love of God and had to accept the consequences of his own interpretation of the Bible. He was going to be a vicar; and he would be her divine connection with God.

As for her feelings about David she was in turmoil. On top of that, on a personal level as opposed to a religious one, she felt as though Roger was some parasite inside of her womb. For some strange reason she believed that the crows that she kept on seeing were a sign that on the day she would give birth, Roger would die and would be born again as her daughter. Maybe there was no longer such thing as a man for her. All her amorous feelings for men had been dissolved since she left Easedale. Then she was so full of love, and now she was feeling as empty as the village centre down in the dale was since all of her cafes had closed down.

Not knowing which way to turn she looked at David dolefully after walking away from Roger as he was sat reading a book on their bed with William sat on his lap. Why given Roger had let her down was she not seeking the arms of David? He was keeping his end of the bargain as he was trying to be all man in front of her at least. He was doing his best to steer them both through the stormy seas of her confusion of which he knew nothing about, but simply and subconsciously he was in tune with her psychotic behavior. Feeling numb and shaken, zombie like: she managed to get through another day.

There were no feelings of love in her empty heart the following evening. At least David wasn't getting on her nerves. In bed during the night, she woke him up. "Beth, Beth, I lost my willy!"

"Beth, dear you are Beth, and I am David." He said reassuringly to her but was inside giving up on her.

"Oh my God, Roger don't fucking rape me or I will send Erik onto you!" She said as she sounded like some feline maniac undergoing some gender realignment on a psychiatric ward.

David was horrified and shocked, in his mind she was little more than an angelic being who due to her misfortunes in life was being possessed by the Devil and that he himself was thanks to his faith a healing messenger of love for her. Beth then burst out crying. "Oh David, I am so sorry, I am so confused, and I don't know who the hell I am anymore." She then started to breathe faster and was scared of going into labor. She was scared of dying like Jennifer. She was scared of living, and simply wished that she was dreaming about being alive and that she was simply in the death of a permanent sleep. She then closed her eyes and saw crows pecking at her deceased new-born baby.

Everything seemed to be such a terrifying situation. She had to block out of her mind the images of the crows. In turn she had another terrifying image; that of the most powerful man in her life who had a form of piety might end up in being more akin to that of an ISIS terrorist than that of a loving man of God. Her mind went back to her own country. No Muslims were welcome into Poland. She then thought about Manchester. The place had become a playground of fundamentalism with veiled women everywhere. Shivers ran down her spine as she remembered Hassidic Jews walking around the city close to women who were dressed in black tents. The polarisation and similarity was disturbing for her. In turn she thought about the gay village full of former Muslim, Jewish as well as Christian descendants and wondered if the Mullahs given the chance would have had these sinners pushed off the rooftops close to the arena, which had been bombed. Another thought crossed her mind. What if given that the Chinese president's daughters were living happily in California that behind the scenes, the leaders of China were secretly working with the Democrats and their depopulation agenda? At first, the correspondence she had read secretly between Roger and Beijing was as far as she was concerned at the time; simply nothing more than in his own overactive imagination. Now and thanks to her own misfortune, she could believe in any evil as being real if it flashed in front of her closed eyes and of those in her dreams.

She wanted to believe that she herself wasn't an extremist. She then thought about her holiday at Izmir with her mum dad and sister five years earlier. Then she was too young to analyze religion apart from going to church, being a good girl and wanting to one day meet a man like her daddy and to be something like the apple of her mother's eye. At least her eyes had fed her thoughts belatedly onto the present. The people she met in Turkey were no different to Europeans. They were peaceful, friendly, and kind. Even so, the photographic memories on her mind were of women with tattoos. Her mind went onto the tall lanky Muslim looking male who walked like a woman and was being worshipped by his Turkish girlfriends on the beach as if he was the alpha female in the group. She was then sure that had the tsunami not taken place that, in just another ten years' time, that transgenders would have been parading the beaches of Aegean on the Turkish side. Little did she know; that one of the biggest role models for Turkish prepubescent children at the time was in fact a transgender model actress from Istanbul. Disturbingly for her, she had more respect for the veiled women, who knew who they were sexually. These pious and modest women would certainly have made better wives and mothers than the other EU obsessed Turkish fanatics who hated their own identity she had met on the beach and found out were from the Satanist camp. Poor Beth felt that the world was simply full of evil. She also felt that Roger hadn't any answers for the satanic hell of which even he as a former Satanist on the inside and now a man of God would offer no solutions. In fact, he might as well continue with his depopulation agenda with his hatred of those who in his version of God's eyes were simply sinners and deserved to perish.

Her mind went back to the members from the Satanist camp. Her mum and dad were walking lovingly as usual hand in hand. As they saw the naked man wearing a bikini along with two men who were singing love songs to him. Her mother burst out laughing, while her father started smiling. The man in the bikini started crying like a girl and the singing queens surrounding him started shouting in Turkish at her parents. They continued walking, and suddenly they saw four police officers walking towards them. "Excuse me why where you making fun out of LGBT?" The most serious looking police officer said.

"I am sorry, as a Christian, I didn't expect this in a Muslim country." Her father said politely.

"I am a Muslim myself. I respect you, but please; be careful next time."
Said the same police officer as his colleagues smiled at her mother.

She had to pull herself together, and as they were sat outside and
looking at the stars she looked into his eyes. "Darling, what is your
interpretation as to the place Christianity has in society?"

"Well, things have changed somewhat I guess that now we can think
more in terms of Adam and Eve and the beauties of a rebirth for
mankind." He said as he wanted to swoon her.

"Oh David: that is so beautiful of you. What about when we first
met?" She asked him as she thought about things taking place that she
wanted to get off her chest with him.

"I have always been a Christian." He said.

"OK, what about gay marriages?"

"I think that given these became enshrined into law that given that the
Lord is a loving God that as good Christians we should embrace this." He
said at peace with the world.

"What about children being brought up with transgender parents?"
She asked him hiding her feelings.

"That too, as much as the Bible preaches traditional love between a
man and a woman, not all people are capable of this."

"What about churches disturbing mosques?"

"Times were changing. I can understand that it wasn't nice for clerics
to hear Christians singing and that some churches had to be closed down
as a result."

"What about God as a woman?"

"I guess that given women are capable of everything we have to accept
that our creator might very well be a woman." David's week and wooly
wooly interpretation of Christianity was not what she expected from
him. He was clearly not the Christian he was on the first day they had
met. As horrified as she was, it was at least for her no worse than Roger's
extreme version of piety that everyone deserved to die.

That night as she closed her eyes and fell asleep, she saw veiled women
being beaten up by their husbands as bad as the dream was; it didn't fully

resonate with her. Suddenly, the dream changed, and the women looked more European and were wearing dog masks and were seen running as riot police were shouting, "Get inside!" after being sprayed with some blue dyed liquid. With her heart pounding to such an extent she could have had a heart attack, she woke up in a cold sweat.

She knew that Roger was leaving in a few days' time and she was already missing him like crazy. She could still feel him in her heart and in her mind and could still feel him pounding her like a raging bull. The reverberations from his from his movements still gave her body some kind of floating feel and were almost as if he was still inside her. Luckily as she went downstairs and was unable to sleep that night, she found him there with a Bible as he was sat on the sofa in the candlelight. A tingling sensation was running through her womb and her breasts started leaking with excitement as the thought of him kissing her all over, made her weaker than ever in his presence. She then went back upstairs and took off her dowdy blue denim dungarees. She then went back downstairs and up to him wearing the scarlet, silk maternity dress.

As she sat down, she opened up the novel she was reading so as not to look too desperate for him. "I suppose when you read about Mary you see yourself. At least you are not reading Tess again."

"What has it got to do you as to what I am reading?"

"I guess you see yourself as nothing less than a Hardy character!"

"I see myself as Tess."

"Tess was a stupid slut!" He said full of both self-righteousness and venom as his is words saddened her and she tried hard not to imagine that they were an attack on herself.

"I will be giving birth in a few days' time." She said proudly showing off her baby bump respectfully, but in a way that looked so innocently beautiful and sexy.

"I know. I am ready to be the vicar now." He replied as if she was merely an annoying member of his congregation.

"What about being a father?"

"I will always be our babies' father." He smiled proudly at her.

311

"Yes, but you won't be around for the birth." She said.

"If you really loved me you would accept me as I am."

"Stop playing games with me." She said emotionally.

"We are very similar. We are both gold-diggers." He said smiling and to her chagrin.

"We are not similar. I was a virgin when we met and wanted one man for the rest of my life. I hate it when you say I was after your money."

"You knew the kind of man I was. Yet, you still wanted a night of passion with me despite knowing I had already made love to your sister."

"Roger, you are very cruel to me."

"Then be happy with David." He said knowing full well she wasn't.

"I am not happy with David as you know. All I ask for is for a real man to love me until death does us part."

Then hating everything around him with his newfound love of his own interpretation of Christianity, he put down his Bible as he was able to look into her eyes with sincerity. "You should have thought about these things before you opened up your legs to me. David is a man of piety, had you waited three months longer in losing your virginity you would have found the perfect man as he would have found the perfect woman. Instead, he has ended up as insecure as you. You have made love to three men. With three different ideas as to what constitutes your beau, you have made your life three times more complicated." He said feeling satisfied with himself.

"How can you speak to me like this, you are also a part of my sins."

"For this I am only too well aware. I deserved to have perished in the floods, which for all we know were not mans, but God's own acts against shameful and wicked sinners who like myself hadn't repented. I have been studying the Bible as you are well aware. I have learnt a lot of things that I never before knew about myself."

"Then Roger, stay with me." She implored him as she was delighted that she was listening to the teachings of Christianity from him.

"I agree with you I should. Sadly, without Christianity I have no control and am not a man who is good enough for a woman and that includes you." He said as his lack of romance was killing her.

"I can follow you to Buttermere." She said feeling as though she was his loyal and dutiful wife.

"I think the time has come for you decide which of the three men is yours. Your dire choices are as follows: one a completely morose bore who is as alluring as President Jaruzelski, two a would-be Christian gentleman whose has been fully emasculated: three a former wannabe transgender follower of Hitler."

"And four, the women who in-spite of everything you have done, forgives you and loves you just the way you are! I am that same woman who can only be saved by a man of God as she begs for your guidance."

Roger felt as though he couldn't breathe. He really loved her, but her devotion to him was frightening him. Knowing that he had tamed her to the extent that she would spend the rest of her life with him; didn't please him. In fact, he saw her in being no more exciting than any one of his previous sexual conquests from both sexes and that of both sheep and dogs. "When you speak to me like this, I no longer see you as somebody special. What woman worthy of self-respect would want to be with me, when she has another man. A man who has never sinned like I myself have."

"You said that he wasn't a real man."

"Yes, due to the evil around him." He said as his answer wasn't vitriolic, she smiled at him.

"David said I am married to you."

"In many ways he is right . . . Please I beseech thee to allow me to humbly repent for my sins!"

"Maybe I should be alone and not with any man and repent for the rest of my life!" She said as he wanted to say that he agreed with her but felt it wise to remain silent and simply walked off.

Instead, she ran after him and grabbed a hold of his trousers. He then looked into her eyes and started to cry. She cried too. This schizophrenic was at times a healthy man emotionally. She knew that he loved her, and that her persistence with him was finally paying off. "My God Beth! I have never seen anyone so beautiful as you; yet the smock that you are wearing seems to reflect and magnify your femininity a thousand times and more!" He said as her body was longing for him.

"Roger, please don't go!" She begged him in desperation.

"Yes, it is true I that I love you like I have loved no other." He said as Beth then burst louder into tears.

"Please Roger! Don't send me into an early labor." She pleaded as she started to kiss him passionately on his shirt covering his chest.

"Calm down," he said as he gently moved his face away from her, "I love you so much, that when you wanted the grass to remain, and I was scared of disease; I gave my body to our ewe. If you will take me immediately for my sins, then yes please follow me!" He said as his passion for her was rising rapidly.

"Am I right; you made love to our pet ewe?"

"Yes, I did. I did this because I love you so much. I knew how important that the grass was for you and so I tamed our ewe."

"Like the time you slept with Eva so that I could be with Erik on holiday?"

"Yes, dear the time I impregnated her."

"Like the time you were fucking with Emma as a warning that you could find someone else?"

"Yes, dear I simply didn't want you to end up confused from your later acts of fornication."

Beth suddenly felt an acid sensation in her mouth. "I need some time to think. I think it would have been better had you not made love to our sheep and got rid of the grass. I also think it was a little bit out of order you cheating on my sister on my behalf. Seeing Emma in such a compromising position was far from what I expected from a father to be of my child." She said as her lack of fawning was killing him.

"Love is unconditional, and you have failed on this test. I am sorry but I must go my love."

"You are a very irresponsible beast!"

"I know that dearest. If you were my Adam, and I your Eve, I would be able to bear you more than ten children. It pains me when we are apart, and I am so jealous of your beautiful body too. If only you knew how painful it is for me in seeing you looking so out of this world when I wish that I was you."

She wondered how she was able to cope with his insanity. "Am I right in thinking that you wish that you were a woman?"

"Sometimes when I kiss your breasts, I imagine that you are kissing mine, and you being not as I but as David. When I am inside of you my energy is wasted. It should be you pounding me as I am lying below you. All the masculine energy I am giving out to you; is one big lie. It is powerful for sure but at the wrong end of my own desired sexual spectrum. I also have times when I think that it is I rather than you who is about to be giving birth."

"Please Roger, forget about this! Please just use all of this energy of confusion to make me happy as your sperm feeds me with all of your energy and love!"

"I can't! I am a man of God; I have to cure myself."

"Then please make love to me! If you really are a man of God, you know how much sodomy is a sin!"

"I can't as you know. I am a sinner as I am only too well aware of and I must pay the price for this!" He said as his words were killing her and against her desires, she left him as she herself was crying profusely.

Beth then went back to bed. She was desperate. She was desperate for love. What had happened to Roger? All she could see in her mind was his silent hauteur as she left him. Why was he so passionless now? On top of that she was disgusted with herself. Had she really inadvertently forced him to impregnate Eva? Did he really make love to a beast because of his devotion for her? Was he really serious regarding his gender dysphoria? How could he condemn her for her lovers when he had been as promiscuous as Hugh Hefner. For her it was simply now or never.

In turn and wanting to move on in her life, she started to kiss and to caress David. She was full of passion; she needed to feel all woman again after Roger had insulted her. Instead after what seemed like David forever lying like a log, she gave up. All she could think about was the time she heard Roger and the ewe together and fell asleep in her tears of sorrow.

Two days later and it was the night before Roger left, Beth was restless. She couldn't sleep. While he had knocked up her twice against her will, both times she was willingly making love to him. In turn she was filled with fondness regarding the times when she conceived. He had shown her how much he loved her. David was still pretty passionless. They hardly ever made love. Sophie had no intention in visiting him, this she knew, she was now with Erik anyway. As such it was safe for her to walk into his room.

She wanted a cuddle, for old time's sake. As such she lay next to him. After a while he realized, she was in bed with him. Without saying a word, he started to caress her. For Beth, speech was cheap, she had begged David to show her how much he loved her but all he could say was that without a good night's sleep he found it hard to show her how much he loved her. Roger then started to kiss her breasts, everything was like a whirlwind of: fire, earth, water, and air, and, in no time at all they were making love. He had done what she wanted David to do. Now she wanted him to talk to her. "Please don't go!" She begged him tearfully, as he was lying in her bed with her.

"I have to go darling."

"Then I must go with you to Buttermere."

"Yes, please do."

"Do you mean it?"

"Of course, I do."

"Without you I am nothing." She confessed.

After a few moments she thought about how before he was a Satanist, how he even considered himself as being a dog. In short how could she survive alone with him at Buttermere. How could he be leaving her? How could she be so in love with him? Her mind was in great turmoil. Surely a good Christian boy could be passionate? Why was it that this Satanist cum vicar was able to fulfil her more than David? Couldn't she have passion with a good and genuine man of piety? Was this too much for her to ask for?

With her breasts and wide hips, she was thankful that she had found David. She woke up without a care in the world. A new life for her had along with the dawn just been broken. Just as she was about to thank the Lord; a veil of sadness went over her.

It was a funny old world. She knew from her Bible studies that perversion on a grand scale had taken place earlier and an angry Lord from above wiped out most of the earth's inhabitants in a great flood. Yes, people were able to state that they were gender neutral and that they were living in the wrong bodies or that they were not the sex that the other eyes thought that they were seeing. It was then that the reality sunk in. She wasn't Beth, she was a he: and she was Roger.

As a man of God, he had to stop thinking that he was Beth. He had to stop thinking that Beth was David. His breasts although heavy, were nothing like those of a woman's. His hips although wide, were supporting a bottom as broad as an elephant's, but that was due to his recent depression and gluttony. In just six months he had gained three stones in weight.

Later that morning; the splendid coach arrived, it looked like something out of a fairy tale. "Follow me, my Cinderella!" He said romantically to her as he then kissed her hands. She got inside with Roger as they looked so regal together. She was pleased that he could no longer run away from her. No longer looking and acting like a child, they didn't look so strange as a couple. Heavily pregnant for a second time she had matured in so many ways. Finally, her dreams were coming true. "I will be back in a minute." He said as he remembered that he had left his precious Bible indoors. With that she seized her chance. She looked at her baby on her lap and wondered how she would cope without the support from her sister. She then looked at the coachman.

"When he arrives tell him I changed my mind, and I am in hiding until he leaves Fell End."

"Madam, there is nothing I like less than a man who mistreats his women."

"Thank you." she then curtseyed gently as she was holding her baby and walked off and hid. Thanks to reading old novels and no longer living in the modern age, Beth found it easy to speak the language of the ladies of times gone by and to behave as if she was in Pride and Prejudice.

As soon as Roger got inside the coach the rider set off. "Stop! My wife isn't here!"

"Let me make one thing clear. I do not take kindly sir to men who treat women badly. You are the Vicar of Buttermere and if you can prove your salt, she will come back to you. Don't forget you are still small fish in the enormous pond of the Illuminati."

As for Beth it was one letter from the coachman that decided her fate. It was the letter, "E." Had he said woman that would have been one less mistake of Rogers, but alas, it was women, he had ruined the lives of.

Beth then went onto her bed with William beside her. She had never felt; so dazed and confused as then. Sophie sensed that her sister was in trauma over his departure and walked into her room. "I should have gone with him." Beth murmured.

"Are you insane? I should have killed him."

"Children are more important than we are. Our parents did everything for us. They deserve to have both biological parents alive."

"You didn't want to have children with him."

"I know, but I had sex with him, so I should accept the consequences of my sin." Beth said piously.

"He got us both pregnant and as victims we should both have been his wives. Had Jennifer survived and not David, you would be quite happy if he were to have the three of us producing his kids."

"Yes." Beth gulped, believing that perhaps God might have carried out such a test on her stoicism.

"Christianity doesn't support bigamy, so I can't understand what you are on about." Said Sophie bewildered.

"But it doesn't say it is right for a woman to run off with another man when she is pregnant. It also says that children should be conceived in wedlock. I am nothing more than a stupid slut!" Cried Beth in desperation as a then tearful Sophie put her arms around her.

Chapter 12

THE VICAR OF BUTTERMERE

With so many of his personal belongings to arrange in his new home, Roger would be kept busy for a few days at least. Not everything arrived with him; and deliveries came along while he was still getting his new place of abode in order. Still worried about another tsunami only this time like the flood from the time of Noah, he made sure that his prized paintings of Beth were upstairs and once again above his bed. As a Christian, and living in such a heavenly place, he hoped that his faith was strong enough to move mountains. He also decided that his new life was the perfect time for him to cut down on the foods he ate for pleasure and to bring back his normally conditioned body back into great shape. As a man of hygiene, he would also have to deal with the flies everywhere in the building.

With Roger no longer in their home, step by step David started to gain strength mentally. While he knew that for his relationship to survive and to move onto a higher plane a lot of give and take was required from both sides, he was still reeling about the way she had hurt him. Even so, he knew that Beth still felt let down by him; and somehow, he had to make sure that he didn't lose her. He tried with all of his passion to make love to her, but she lay there as if she was asleep one evening. He tried again in the morning as tears ran down her face. Knowing what he then knew then, he would have gone for Sophie instead of Beth when Jennifer died. He knew from Erik that; Sophie was passionate with him and he had some of his own pleasurable carnal experience with her too. On top of that, her baby was quiet during the night. It was depressing for him to learn, that one didn't know his or her other half until they had experienced him or her twenty-four hours a day over a long period of time. While for David relationships were about compromises, he believed that with Sophie that less disappointments would have come to the fore. He had lower expectations of the elder of the siblings, and the more he got to know her, the more he liked her. Even so, he didn't know her so well either.

It was during the days of hedonistic madness just after Jennifer died that he gained a new Polack conquest. As far as David was concerned, the older Polack girl enjoyed sex much more than her sister. Yes, she was a little more adventurous regarding her tastes, which included many positions which he found superfluous, but for him this was a small price to pay when his other half was simply as frigid as the Slavic winter of her birthplace. Why was that it she so often spurned his touch? They were in the same bed together, as man and wife, yet there was no passion. He was also unhappy that Beth had slept with Erik too.

He had breakfast alone. As he was drinking his tea, she noticed he was using a cup. "You left a cup on the table." She said trying to berate him. He looked up and noticed that she was wearing the dowdy blue denim dungarees which were neutralising her beauty in more ways than one.

"I haven't finished with it yet!" He replied not so very meekly.

"I am not your slave who is here to tidy up after you!" She then walked a few steps away from him. Nervously after several moments he washed the cup and placed it on the shelf in the cupboard above the kettle. She then opened the cupboard, in the deathly silence she moved the cup to the exact spot it had been earlier, which was a few centimetres away from his placing of the item of crockery.

"You left your heart with Roger from the sounds of things."

"Don't threaten me!" She cried.

"I am merely speaking the truth about you."

"Go on, leave me!" She screamed at him.

"You might drive me mad. But Beth, as much as I am fully haunted by our first meeting, I am still a man. Yes, I made the biggest mistake in my life. But let me tell you this. After the second time you saw me, I was about to run after you. I regretted my inaction for days on end and instead all I could see was your dark and silky hair, hanging over your face, as the air swept it over your beautiful eyes. For days I saw the contours of your T shirt from your breasts. You were so slender; yet so ripe. For days on end, I imagined that we would meet and be together forever. I am never in a million years going to miss out again on having a baby with you. The next time that you fall pregnant, you will be carrying our child!" She was then lost for words and she left the room. In his mind, she hated the fact that she was a mother to Roger's babies and was taking it out on the man who should have made an honest woman out of her, that being David.

She was later sat in the garden while William was sleeping on the lawn. She hated David as much as she hated Roger. One man was faking his orgasms as he was imagining that he was a woman being fucked senseless by Beth as David. The other man, David spoke about real love but was unable to deliver the goods. She had gone through hell and wanted a man who was stronger than her pain, her demons, her imperfections call it what you will, but David was too polite in her hour of need. At least she still had some use for him, and he readily looked after William when she needed some time to be alone. She wanted to enjoy the scenery but instead and just a few hundred yards away from her home she became mesmerized with the gorse. As prickly as these plants were, they were still able to produce the most delicate and beautiful yellows from the small flowers on them. Her own life was full of thorns, yet her beauty was still there even after the hardships of the past nearly two years. She then thought about how she enjoyed the simple things in life more and more and wondered how much humbler she would have to be before she would receive some peace in her life. When it came to marriage and family values, she had more than been compromised and wondered if for the rest of her life it would be simply of blood, sweat and tears.

Later that evening as they were in bed, David felt the tension between them. He touched her body, but she appeared lifeless and numb. "It is amazing that even when you dress so hideously and masculine that I am still able to see your beauty." He said to her as he was well aware that she was awake.

"I am happy that unlike Roger that you don't demand me to wear what you want." She said somewhat confused by his speech.

"I would never demand anything from you: but obviously some things that you wear are sexier than others." She then froze she was both insulted and feeling somewhat flattered by him. At least he had shown her some manliness and interest in his behavior towards to her. She then took the bedside torch in her hands and went to her wardrobe. She didn't want to annoy him any further.

"Why are you looking at me like this?" She said to him as deep down she was in a desperate need of some affection in her life.

"I want to watch my chrysalis bloom into the butterfly of love once again." He said sincerely. Lost for words she then turned around and was waiting in great anticipation as to how he would respond to her sultry body.

A few moments later he was drooling at her and was simply awestruck. She was wearing her sexy, scarlet, silk, maternity dress with pride. He then took a hold of her hands. They smiled at each other. He then kissed her on the forehead. A warm glow went through her heart. He then kissed her on the lips. "Your dress is so beautiful, but I want you so much and if I don't undress you now, I might lose control and rip that cloth off that heavenly body of yours. I am in such a desperate need for our skins to touch each other."

After taking off her dress, the one he bought her with love, they kissed each other passionately. As he touched her body all over with his hands, she was in heaven. Although she felt that her bottom was huge, she was delighted by the way in which he couldn't take his hands or his eyes off her behind depending on the position they were in. As they made love, she was in turn satiated and content once more with her life. "I am so much less tired now that he has left our home." David said.

"Were you jealous?" she asked him.

"You should know this by now." He said to her.

"One day we will have children together." All she could hope for was that she would have a baby with him.

"Next time darling." He said to her. She smiled at him, she kissed him, but for some reason a vision of Roger came to her and was staring at her as she was sat identically to the painting with her third pregnancy and was once again scared that he would impregnate her one more time. At least the paintings had along with Roger left Fell End. Her mind then started to think about the fourth painting and she looked at David desperately.

"Are my breasts OK?" She asked him.

"They are so beautiful." He replied admiringly to her.

How could he say such a thing? They weren't so perfect; she even had a blood red stretch mark on her left breast. Had Roger not made an issue out of this she wouldn't have cared, but Roger was enough to make any vulnerable young woman suffer from body dysmorphia.

Beth would analyze everything percentage wise. At first, she wrote down three of her needs during a quiet moment the following day, strength, attractiveness and sex. On these issues she felt that Roger was the best. As such she missed him like crazy. Whenever she was with David, she was torn between telling him about her feelings about Roger and pushing him further away and giving in too soon to the man she wanted to in her eyes become a real man for her. Why couldn't David fight for her? Eventually, after adding more needs, David was her best option. Even so, it had been a very hard decision. On top of that, had it still been in the days when money and career were important factors; then

Roger would have won hands down. She then thought a little more. Money was not the issue. Her mind was in turmoil and full of contradiction. Her parents loved each other, they had two children together and she wanted to have the same with David.

After putting her baby to bed they were sat together. "What about if we get married?" She asked him. From her recently promiscuous behavior, David wasn't quite ready.

"I think it is the right thing to do."

"My God, David what has happened to you?"

"I am still getting over events. The world is cruel and miserable."

"David, we have to survive. I need a man who is strong enough for me." She said ashamed of herself, her sleeping around and felt demeaned by his lack of enthusiasm for committing himself to her.

He then thought quickly, he didn't want to lose her. "Beth, we will make the world our own oyster. One thing though is this; I want to know that you enjoy being a mother. I hate to tell you this, but Sophie seems to care much more for her child than you do for yours." He said trying to sound manly once more again to her.

"I know; what you must understand is that my life before we got back together was a complete mess." She said scared that he wasn't going to take her unconditionally.

"Beth, I don't know any other girl who has suffered so much as you have. I will do my best to help you mature, calm down and gain the confidence about who you really are. To me you are the sweetest girl that I can see, the closest thing to heaven and my everything." He said as she in turn felt once again safe with him.

Over the coming days instead of living in fear about her coming birth, all she could think about was that her dream of romance was coming back into fruition. Along with his love she would be able to get through with anything. On top of that she was missing Roger less and less like crazy as she was feeling more and more all woman and less confused. On top of that, the flowers in the garden were springing up all over the place. All she wanted was to survive the birth easily and give hope to her sister who was probably nervous too as she was now into her final trimester and like her sister must have been having black memories regarding Jennifer's untimely death recently. In the meantime, she had to blank the crows out of her mind, which were around too much for her liking.

On Sophie's birthday, the twenty-ninth of March Beth gave birth. David was acting as the perfect midwife. She was touched by his help and healthy twins were safely delivered within minutes of each other. Roger of course wasn't there. Instead of feeling depressed with post-natal depression, Beth felt as though she had been released from Roger and was happily accepting all of David's tender loving care. The girl's name was Sarah, named after Coleridge's daughter. This time David approved of the name. Little did he realise that this was also the name of Roger's mother. As for the latest boy, he was named Peter after Peter Rabbit and little did, he realise that that was the name of Roger's father. She breathed a sigh of relief; at least David was unaware that both children were carrying the names of the paternal grandparents. Even so, she was horrified as the reality sunk in that the painting was becoming so prophetically accurate. At least David wasn't going to force her to get pregnant so soon. Looking after three babies was enough work the time being for her. With Roger now safely out of her life, she would fall pregnant for the third time at her very own choosing. Even so, the painting of her being pregnant, breastfeeding twins with a toddler watching her was unnerving. Aged just nineteen, she certainly didn't wish for a third pregnancy to happen so soon.

The setting was so serene, and the babies were left with Sophie. In turn she was looking after four children so that her sister could spend some time alone with her man for the first time since giving birth to twins a few days earlier. They were not far from their home; even so, sitting on a small crag together in the pleasant and warm sunshine with views of Windermere below them made for them a delightful and romantic setting. "Beth. Without you, my life is empty. With you, everything is so beautiful. Do you take me to be your lawful and wedded husband?" He asked her.

"I do, I do, I do!" She cried happily.

Both couples wanted to get married in April, that very same month. Roger though, via letter, advised against this on the pretext that Sophie would be heavily pregnant, and Beth would still be recovering from giving birth. In short, it seemed as though his advice was a reasonable one and both parties agreed with the date of September the twenty-fifth. Sophie might not be giving birth until July, and it was best to wait for the baby to get stronger. What the sisters didn't realise was that Roger was bullying them both insidiously. Very easily they could have married before Sophie went into labor. As a newly member of God, he knew only too well the difference between giving birth to a bastard and to bringing up a child in wedlock. In turn, Roger saw this as a good sign. He wasn't exactly sure as to how. In the meantime, he took out his tarot cards and went into numerology mode. This wasn't at all what he was meant to be doing as the good Christian he was. Then again everything in his life was fleeting including his religion as one minute it was corpses on his mind, the next a fertilized egg. Like the camp newt he was, he moved around with his sexual fluidity too. In his mind he never got bored, but equally he realized more than ever before, that with his previous mundane blow-up doll, Sophie, life was better previously than in the insecure and lonely world of his own making. At least the dirty flies took his mind of his loneliness. He had been cleaning the place and throwing out remains of food matter from the previous owners but there were still too many flies for his liking.

Being as bored with her as he was now as lonely and miserable, he realized that being bored was better than his loneliness. His times alone were spent running through his impending death; he believed that he was going to die from an ugly disease. Oh, how he regretted that he was such an absent and useless father. If only he had wanted to teach his older children how to walk and swim the things that he himself knew so well. He could have taught French too and read them bedtime stories. Feeling as though everything was too much to bear; he fell asleep on his stool. Suddenly he started shouting in his sleep as he was thinking about the mistakes he had made in his pitiful life and fell off in his sleep onto the hard surfaced marble floor violently. The crash was paralysing him as the excruciating pain was electric. Staring at death in the face excited him: as he wished that he had never been born. He then thought a little more, would he die alone? That was the last thing he desired. If only he had someone close at hand to look after him who would cry and shower him with love before he passed away. All he could hear were those haunting words from his mother, "We come into this life alone, we leave this life alone." Things couldn't get worse than this. All he wanted was for all members of his family to die in solidarity with him.

With his broken neck and spine, he couldn't get off the ground. He simply fell asleep once more. He woke up again and realized that Beth must have given birth again as Sophie was now heavily in the family way. On top of that he was dying. Without any water, he would perish of thirst. As for hunger, there was no chance for that; he still needed to lose some more of his layers of fat.

Prior to his accident, he was about to take out the rubbish. This included plenty of rotten food and some sour milk. Instead, plenty of flies were attracted to the waste which was lying not too far away from him and in turn he was much more disturbed by the itchy flies all over his body than of the large beetles that were running up and down the place. On top of that, the insects were leaving droppings everywhere. They seemed to be in a greater abundance than ever before. On top of that, the stench from his body was suffocating him as if the odour was that of a mask that had been worn indefinitely on someone who was scared of some imaginary virus.

May arrived and as far as Beth was concerned, having three children had a much greater effect on her than having just one. In fact, she felt like a real mother and that looking after more than one baby, although tiring was more enjoyable for her. Sophie was worried that she herself was a little too fat and believed that if she helped Beth with the breastfeeding that she would keep her weight in control. Sophie felt that since she herself was having just a single pregnancy that she was right in helping her tired sister out with the breastfeeding. In her eyes, Beth was slim enough. She had forgotten how her sister was when she first arrived in the Lakes and compared it to how she was when she was with twins and believed that she looked somewhat emaciated.

So obsessed with her swimming, Beth would leave Sophie with her three babies. So tired from everything, Sophie would spend most of the day in bed. Beth felt guilty but couldn't control herself. It was spring and she couldn't imagine her life without swimming and running daily. As for meditation, she wanted to believe that she was still a good Christian girl; she enjoyed the woods on the way to the tarn and the sight of bluebells. If she went there with William; he too was mesmerized, but she would do her best to stop him from plucking the flowers. Since living with Alan, the girls cooking skills had certainly improved. It being mid spring, one of their delicacies was rhubarb crumble and now the men were enjoying their culinary delights.

Not everything went to plan. She would often study her body and was a little bit disturbed about her waist which was no longer so petite. Tears went down her face as she thought that no matter, she would do in getting herself back into shape, on her wedding night her hips would still be wider than the day she first met her beau from child rearing. How could she have such a perfect wedding after all of the sins she had committed? How could she allow the father of her children give her away to her groom? If only it were David who was responsible for her maternal figure. Then she could carry her wider hips with pride.

One night as she was asleep and feeling unloved, she had a dream that her three babies were asleep, and David was lying beside her. She was then carried into another room with Roger holding her in his arms. A few moments later he raped her. Feeling overwhelmed with her life and still dreaming she was then staring at the painting of herself heavily pregnant, breastfeeding her twins with William looking fondly at her. Her heart started beating wildly as she started screaming. Away from her rapid eye movements, David who was lying next to her; took her in his arms. This time she was no longer dreaming that she was awake. She was entering the same, fully conscious world as David's, but still, she couldn't stop crying. She was feeling more scared than ever of making love, but had they done so together, she would have been released from Roger in more ways than one.

Since giving birth for the second time, she was too afraid to make love. At first this was normal, but she got back into shape very quickly not that she fully appreciated that. More importantly, she felt as though she had fully recovered from the labor. Filled with paranoia, for some reason, she was convinced that the next time she would make love, she would fall pregnant, and she was far from ready for that.

As for Roger, his impending death wasn't so comfortable as he would have liked. On top of that; he wouldn't be going out with a bang. As beautiful it would be for him to know that Beth would be able to see him with blotches from parasites taking over his body and faecal matter from tiny bugs, deep down he knew Beth would never know. Knowing that she had given birth and he was unable to lurk around her made him feel useless. His former glory of intimidation over his belle was finished. For him, good old fashioned sweet love was boring. Fuelling her repulsion and delight for him excited him, now he had lost all that power over her. The wedding wasn't taking place for a few months, and his body would be interred before then. At least he had stopped excreting. After the accident he passed solids just once. His mind went back to when he was desperate to release his waste when his body felt as though it could be sliced into two from his movement. In turn, once was enough and when he managed to pooh a couple of metres away from his resting place where he had his final wee too, he didn't wish to repeat such a gruesome performance. The site became a shrine for many small bugs. Sometimes the odd rat even visited and wanted other creatures to know that it was around and waiting for the death of a big animal that would herald a feast for the rest of his family members. As for the rats, in one sense he found the situation hilarious and often laughed sinisterly at his own expense, while on the other hand he felt sick knowing that he was going to be a rats' dinner. He was certainly sleeping more than usual, and for him, his prized painting of Beth was a double-edged sword. Thoughts of his beloved breastfeeding twins, having a toddler sat below her legs and her belly swollen sent him to sleep very quickly. Once asleep, and with a vision of the painting still on his mind and David on scene as Beth's spouse; the picture became his very own made hell. Over the coming days he would wake up fearfully in case Beth was already pregnant to David.

During these days he felt as though his final call had arrived. In between thinking that he was about to die and the times when he wasn't quite ready to kick the bucket, his mind went into overdrive. His worst moment was when he wished that he could move on with his life and become a cyborg with wires and nanobots instead of nerves running through his body. In knowing that the National Grid wasn't going to arrive in his moment of need made him wish to die more than ever. On top of that, and in his mind, which desired a most evil act to be meted out onto him in the form of artificial intelligence but couldn't, made him despair. How then he thought about his dream being unfulfilled was his body fighting harder to keep him alive when as far as he was concerned: was he being kept alive in the body of a man, instead of that of a transgender woman, which was something that needed to be gassed.

It was then that he realized that eating faecal matter wasn't normal. As a young girl, and when he knew that he was in fact a boy his mother had forced him to eat his own excrement. Although he was too young to fully understand her words her shouting at him when he was aged just five was all too vivid for him. "I am a boy, mummy!" He said.

"How can you be so disgusting, if you want to be a man you will lick my hands clean!" Sarah then placed her hand inside her bottom, collected some faecal matter and forced him to lick her fingers clean which were right underneath his nose. Roger did as he was told. Roger's mind then went back onto the present, as he was sure that he was about to die ignominiously.

Sophie in order to impress her sister, managed to go swimming. Given she had represented her school, like Beth, she was able to do some impressive laps around the waters that spring. In some ways, she was feeling more relaxed during the second round of being in the family way too. Nights were however different, as memories of Jennifer dying in labor would haunt her more and more as each day moved closer to her own due date. This could be tempered by having passionate pleasures with Erik, but afterwards as she would be recovering from her; swimming, breastfeeding, sex, cooking, walking and other duties; thoughts of her former housemate would turn into vibrant visions of painful memories for her and chastise her. Even worse was when she had visions of crows lurking around and waiting for death.

In great times of need one will go to any length to save themselves. Some of the succulent bugs available were very nourishing too. This could help prolong his death sentence somewhat. Not that he worried too much about that since life was one living death for him anyway. With a shortage of, woodlice, ants, and spiders he would soon pass out from hunger. As for his thirst, that was of a greater concern as his parched lips felt as though they were burning in the sun.

Regularly, he had been reciting off the top of his head the Bible and wondered if he was a true believer. With nothing to lose, having faith was no longer a laughing matter for him.

When it had only been four days since his accident he felt as if were three weeks. He then after praying to the Lord fell asleep. The next day he woke up and felt as though he was no longer dying and floating up to heaven. Miraculously, after five days off his infirmity he had some luck. His death sentence was ending as he was feeling weaker than ever. Just as he was about to start fading away, he stood up and walked to the tap in his kitchen and drank slowly some water. As it sunk in that his life was saved, he then smiled to himself. He had been punishing women because of their Christian values, and now it seemed his conversion to God was the reason as to why he was still living. He had also lost some weight and felt as though he was more or less back to normal regarding the shape of his body.

It was a beautiful month of May. By then Sophie was looking forward to her unborn child and was happy with Erik too. For some reason she had a little bit of the maternity feel inside of her, which came as a surprise to her. On top of that, in some ways although life was hard, they were happy. In so many ways he was an incarnate of Jan for her, and she felt so blessed that she had been another chance on true love. Erik and David were like brothers and the two families were certainly looking after each other.

June too began peacefully. Sophie was twenty-one and Beth celebrated her final day as a teenager and as a single mother of three children. At least she was planning to get married to the first man she had fallen in love with during the very end of her maiden days. Two areas of Beth's life were a disaster; her family was dead and buried, and she wasn't living with the father of her children. Other areas were of bliss: she was living with her beau, her children, who were healthy, and she loved her simple healthy routine in life.

Roger would often think about how the past two years had changed for him since he arrived back in the Lake District. He often felt that all of his efforts in being the quintessential, white, straight male had been in vain. In turn he often perished the thought of himself as being a true follower of Christ. Alone and without any victims, he was depressed. He had kept one of Jennifer's dresses as a keepsake. Jennifer was taller than the sisters and, on top of that; with him being somewhat slimmer he hoped that he could fit into her frock. It was a hot day in the middle of June, and he decided to walk around the lake. He also had the vain hope that on the way back that he would be Jennifer herself. Then, and only then could he win the love of his cerebral soulmate, David. The only regret that he had; was that he was a bearded lady and had a manly and somewhat muscular body. At least with no one around, he was who he wanted to be. With a bit of luck; as his hormones would change, his beard as well as his penis would fall off. In turn his facial features would soften, and his breasts would bloom like the fruits which were flowering around him close to the path with their petals.

Stood in front of the waterfall below Buttermere Fell, he believed that the force of the water which was tumbling down the mountain would answer his question. If God had been so kind to have created him as the fine specimen he was, then he should be so lucky. Only an ungrateful soul would not be thankful for the gift of life bestowed onto him through his maker above. If he was a woman, what was wrong in him being Beth, and David being his or as he hoped her true love? The fact that God put him into the wrong body and took away his happiness was proof that he didn't exist. As far as he was concerned, both arguments were equally plausible.

As he reached the bay opposite his home; he burst into tears. "Roger," Said a voice. In turn he didn't half jump when he heard his name, since he was then known as Alan. He didn't want his acquaintance to see his tears as such he composed himself. 'It's funny how one meets the same people on their favorite walks." The voice was in fact that of Alex or Louise as she had been born. Julie or John as he had been born was holding the hand of their toddler and the happy family and their guest continued on foot with them. Roger was also surprised that despite him wearing a dress, he was still recognisable, but didn't go into this. They spoke together about what they had done since they last met. Roger also explained how he became, The Vicar of Buttermere.

"Fancy staying at my place for the night?" Roger asked them both after they had been walking together for twenty minutes. The couple didn't need much convincing. Both were attracted to the bearded lady and simply smiled and nodded their heads in unison. As they arrived at the inn, the horses were waiting, and Roger joined them inside their two-horse powered coach.

Roger cooked a sumptuous meal for everyone and once their child was in bed, the three adults were able to enjoy the rest of the night together. He took them to his room, where their baby was sleeping at the other end, and closed the curtains, he didn't wish for them to observe his prized paintings in too much detail. As they were sat together with Roger still wearing his dress, he looked at them both. "I want to fuck and to be fucked." In turn his wish came true, and he was delighted that Louise, who was now a man was making love to him and that John who was now a woman was being pounded by Roger.

335

After their lovemaking session he looked into both of their eyes. "Now I would us to do role reversal." Roger said.

"We would rather not." Said Louise.

"Why?" Roger asked in dismay.

"We want to reverse back to our original genders and this would be too painful for us." Said John. Roger then burst into tears.

"What's wrong Roger?" Louise asked.

"Before the tsunami I wanted to become a woman. Now I am stuck inside the wrong body for the rest of my life!" Said Roger. In turn the confused trio made Roger's dream come true. He made love to Louise, while John had one of Roger's dildos strapped on him and in turn they felt as though they were in heaven.

Once again, the three of them were depressed and wished that they could sort out their problems of gender fluidity but kept all their confusion to themselves. The following dawn arrived, and Roger opened the curtains. He wanted to know what effect Beth would have on his guests. He also wanted to make love to them but was scared that the issue of Beth might turn them off.

"Who are these paintings of?" Asked John who glanced at Louise making sure that he was still asleep.

"They are of the mother of my children. She left me because of my gender fluidity."

"She is so beautiful. If she were mine, it would have been such an honor that I would never have thought of having a sex change." Said John as Louise then opened her eyes and John was sat there looking scared.

"If I were born like her, I would ever have thought of having a sex change. Whenever I see such beauty, I long to be once again a woman." Said Louise as Roger was sat there frozen.

"Can't you win her back?" Asked John.

"The next time we meet up I am meant to be marrying her to someone else." He said dejectedly.

"If I could be born again as one of her children, maybe I would be as pure as she is." Said Louise. Roger continued looking numb.

"Roger, you are with friends now, you don't have to look so glum." Said John to Louise's approval.

"Do you think that it is possible for me with the blessing of God if I become a good Christian, to be reincarnated? Jesus is a forgiving lord who loves everyone."

"We are both atheists, so we really can't answer that." Said John.

"One must live for the moment. You get one chance in life. We can't run away from science. Man destroyed the planet and all the chemicals he unleashed, poisoned us. I didn't choose to be confused. To be honest, I am mentally ill." Said Louise. With that, Roger wanted to lighten up the mood. He then tried to make love to John as he was attracted to him as the woman he was.

"Please, Roger, I don't think that now is the time to make love." Said Louise. "I think you are less disturbed than we are. Your body is less damaged. If I were you, and given you look so handsome, are the father of her children, I would win back her love." She finished.

After breakfast, his guests left. He regretted that he hadn't asked them what their views were on sex, death and life. Primarily he wanted to know if they thought it was possible for him to impregnate Beth and to enter her womb and to be born again as her daughter. Now it was too late to ask them, they had gone; and his depression was consuming him. For a few days Roger was on the verge of committing suicide. He also stopped eating and was drinking only water. The pain of his rumbling stomach delighted him as he hoped that he would develop an hourglass figure, like the one Beth had when he first met her. Disturbingly for him, his ugly and large breasts didn't shrink. Too scared to die a violent death after raping Beth, he was hopeful that a miracle would take place as he would be metamorphosed as a young and beautiful woman instead.

Sophie's second child was delivered safely on June the twenty-eighth and immediately she sensed that something wasn't at all right but didn't know why. Without Jennifer around, Beth helped her sister deliver her sister's beautiful baby. Beth was confused. She had never seen anything at all like this. Never having read any books on science fiction, her mind couldn't digest fully what she was seeing. Very quickly she wrapped the baby up and handed it to her sister. Sophie smiled her new-born was beautiful and seemed very healthy.

One thing alarmed Sophie later as she had to change the nappies. Thanks to the shops in the valley and in Kendal, they still had plenty of nappies for several more children. Roger had been delivering plenty on horseback too on his monthly toiletries run before he left. Even so, seeing that her baby really was an "it", and had no sexual organs was a disturbing sight for her. At least later she would find out that the child could wee and pooh like any other, but how would it reproduce? In short that was of course impossible.

At least as they were picking berries in the garden it could take their minds off from the sad reality that Sophie had given birth to an "it". Then again, their minds could never go far away from this sad fact, since it was thanks to Roger the father of the "it", that they were able to enjoy the small but deliciously succulent fruits. Escaping from him, was much more difficult than they had envisaged, spiritually. Thanks to her reading about natural remedies, she was increasingly thankful for living in such a pristine environment. There were more insects than ever before. Butterflies seemed to be in the greatest abundance in living memory as far as she was rightly concerned. Even so, she was never in a million years going to be thankful for the depopulation program.

That evening as Roger looked at the sky that night; he brewed his tea in the pot and started staring into it. As he saw visions of a shell-shocked Beth holding his genderless child, he started sobbing his eyes out. This was clearly not what he had intended. As far as he was concerned, his mother who hated the world, who wished that she wasn't a woman had created his pain. No amount of love from the good women he had met had been able to cure him. He then composed himself what else could he do? A short time later he was relieved that he was seeing her handing the baby over to Sophie and in turn he laughed a cackling screech that must have been heard in the heavens above as a ball of lightning struck the tree, he hated, and set it on fire. Two birds killed with one stone. He could now relax when thinking about Sophie and the tree which attracted unwelcome squirrels into his garden was burning in its own wood.

Day by day Beth was coming terms with the tragic birth of her neither latest niece nor nephew. "Sophie I just want you to know, that I feel for you. I hope you are getting over the shock that you gave birth to an 'it'." She said embarrassed.

"Beth there is nothing to worry about. It is for the best; this earth is so full of evil. I don't think it is a great idea to bring any more babies into the world."

"I like the name Greta." Said Beth trying to change the subject.

"Well, Greta, was Roger's idea if we were to have a girl. We don't have a girl but calling my baby Arnold after Schwarzenegger doesn't seem right either." She said morosely, as she felt sick thinking about Roger's curse. Sophie was obviously suffering from post-natal depression while the younger sibling was still a dreamy romantic and relieved to have three normal babies.

Now July and with five babies to look after, the siblings were busy. Three were small babies. Two were toddlers and eating solid foods. William and Jane were being breastfed just twice a day and Beth would sometimes take them with David out for the day and although only fifteen months old they were quickly getting used to walking. One obvious haunt of theirs was Loughrigg Tarn. Erik was sporty too, but he seemed to be spending more time working at The Howe and Fell End than David and had less energy for exercise with her.

At the tarn during that hot and sunny July, both David and Beth made sure that they got in plenty of laps around the tarn. They were adamant too, that the toddlers would learn to be confident in the water too. "With the babies being able to walk a few kilometres each day, it was hard to imagine that during the days of affluence that; healthy children as old as four were being pushed around in their prams. It is amazing! Just look how happy the children are!" Said David.

"It shows you how free they are!" Said Beth delightedly. As they were walking back home while Erik was laboring.

"Beth, now I see you as a role model mother." He said as Beth felt as though she was on cloud nine.

Accidentally, on the way back William and Jane got stung by some nettles. Beth picked them both up in her arms while David ran off for some dot leaves. At first, she was afraid that he gone because he was scared of crying babies, but when she saw him picking leaves in the distance, she was relieved. He then arrived back with some of nature's remedies and Beth had a loving smile on her face. "It is times like these when I am thankful that you are learning from the old books about all the herbs for our health." He said as she gratefully took some dot leaves for William while he used the rest for Jane. "I am also proud of the fact that you remain an inveterate reader." He said effusively as she started to blush.

Sophie was happy to stay at home. She was depressed about the way her second child had turned out but didn't want her sister to be unhappy. On top of that, she was pleased for Jane that she was able to enjoy some adventures with her aunt and somehow, she would continue putting a brave smile on her face. As for Erik, she was so proud of him, he was a real grafter and without him, she wondered what use David would be when so much in the way of intensive labor was needed.

July the 29th was his thirtieth birthday. As he woke up Beth kissed him but as he tried to French kiss her, she made sure that he was unable to. "I have tried to get passionate with you. At first, I believed that you needed time since giving birth, but four months have since passed."

"And luckily I am not pregnant so soon."

"So, thanks to The Beast, I myself must suffer . . . This isn't at all fair from you."

"I want our child to be conceived in wedlock. I became a teenage mother of three bastard children. I am a disgrace. I couldn't bear it to be with child again until you have made an honest woman out of me. What is two months when we have the rest of our lives to spend together?" She said as she thought about the time, he wanted her to wait six months for him.

"I feel old already. Shouldn't we while we are still young enjoy our carnal desires? The only time we have made love, was when you were pregnant, and both times that wasn't to me."

His words had hit her like a knife. She had to stay calm. He was right on this score. One of them had to back down, but from his words she rightly suspected that any discussion would lead to an untimely escalation of discord between them and the end of their marriage plans. Equally if he felt neglected there was every chance that he would leave her.

After several moments of a deafening silence, neither of them had moved. He was waiting for her response. In total fear and dread of losing him from arguing or from his neglect she didn't know what to say. One thing was certain; she wasn't going to make love out of wedlock again. "The best day of my life will be when we get married. Oh, how I long for at the still tender age of twenty to be your lady along with the blessing of God. I will be a new woman; I will be your loving and passionate wife and I want to us to be happy forever." With that David was reeling, this was so unfair from her, but her words were loud and clear. Knowing that one of them had to back down, he simply accepted her words with good grace. He loved her like no other, and simply took her right hand and kissed it with his mouth.

August arrived, the weather was still hot, and the toddlers were getting stronger on their feet. "Sophie, I feel so guilty with you looking after the babies. Go and visit the shops for our wedding dresses." She said as they were together wearing their night dresses in Roger's old room.

"There's no such clothes around here." Said Sophie.

"Bridal wear has been brought over from Kendal. Roger made sure that we would be well looked after."

The following morning after breakfast and while the men were in the garden working, Beth was busy clearing the tables while Sophie was busy breastfeeding her two children. "Are you OK looking after all five babies?" Said Sophie.

"Of course, I am, just go! Just make sure that you bring back a beautiful dress for me too!" Said Beth cheekily.

"What size?"

"The same as you."

"But I'm much fatter than you are."

"Don't be crazy, now go!" Said Beth smiling at her.

Despite the fact that they had been hearing about manmade global warming, they were surprised to find out that; September 2020 seemed to be starting off as if it were high summer on the near continent. It was a sticky morning, and everyone was helping out in collecting the harvest of beans, apples, pears, and tomatoes. "They said that we were warming up the earth." Said Beth.

"I know; people often get things wrong." Said Erik.

"Isn't life so beautiful?" Said Sophie.

"Yes, it is!" Said Beth delighted with her sister.

"David, what's your intake as to why without greenhouse gasses it has been so warm lately?" Asked Erik.

"The sky is bluer than ever, maybe more sunlight is now warming the earth up some more. In the middle ages there was a warm period when grapes were cultivated in great abundance."

After cleaning themselves up after their harvesting, what more could the ladies desire? Their men as they tried on their wedding suits who looked like princes. William would be a little page boy, as Jane a little bridesmaid. Everything was so beautiful, and the loving couples were ready to tie the knot. All Beth could think about was that; when she arrived at Buttermere for the first time, she was such a heavenly and wholesome child of God. In her mind her wedding was taking place at some sacred shrine as she would be able to sanctify herself. Roger had redeemed himself as he was now The Vicar of Buttermere and her faith had been restored fully.

Summer was turning into autumn, but the girls had springs in their steps. They were looking forward to going back to the place where they first fell in love with the Lakes. On top of that, upon their return to Fell End, they would both be honest women.

On the first official day of autumn, and in beautiful two horse drawn carriages as VIP guests of the Illuminati, Beth and her children went in one carriage and was driven by Erik. Sophie, and her children travelled in a separate equine drawn vehicle and was driven by David. They decided to leave the beagles in the garden. They felt cruel in doing so but saw no other solution. Beth was so happy, this time she was going to her beloved Buttermere under fairy tale conditions.

Roger had made sure that as they arrived, they would feel so welcome. The vehicles belonged to his bosses at Cockermouth and Kendal First impressions counted for everything as far as he was concerned. Biblical paintings of Adam and Eve type figures and some of a baby Jesus were in the hall which they admired just after they had taken their shoes off as they entered the building. As their vicar, what else would they expect from him? While David and Beth were in awe, Sophie was happy to see that the couple were in heaven. Erik though; wasn't taken in by Roger's preparations and saw him as some fraud.

On the eve of the wedding and two days since their arrival, a stag night had been arranged by Roger. Erik was feeling tired, but he enjoyed drinking some of the mead before going to bed. David however, decided to stay a little longer. "Remember from tomorrow you are no longer a free man. This is the final night that you can do whatever you want." Roger said hoping to bring out more out of his only male idol's effeminate side as memories of himself masturbating him were vivid. He then noticed that David was looking more than somewhat sleepy. Roger rambled on and was making sure that David was asleep. In turn, after several more minutes, he carried him onto his bed. For Roger looking at his sleeping beauty with the moonlight which was strong it being just before the full moon, made him feel so dreamy. What right did David have to be happy? Nobody made Roger's life any better, not that this was possible anyway. In short, and with tears in his eyes as he had no control over himself, he decided not to care. He realized that in doing what he was about to do, that Beth once she found out would probably never love him again. He almost lost his mind, since whenever he was with Beth; he often wished that he was just like David, straight and thirty years younger. All he could do was to pull himself together somehow. In turn he kissed David on his lips and whispered in his ear. "I can make any man gay." David didn't respond. His heart started beating faster as David's presence was electrifying for him.

He looked so sweet. He was still and silent like some rubber doll, or even a corpse. Roger was old enough to be his father and as he imagined that when he himself was a little bit older than David; that David was then a little boy, he felt so excited as he imagined that his act would take their body clocks back twenty years and more. David's relative youth made him feel at the mercy of his unwarranted desires for his toy, his Cumbrian gent. In fear of being caught out he made love to him before his young protege would arise from his sleep like some pebbles on the shore as the tides were going out. For Roger, this was the moment he had been waiting for.

While David may or not be enjoying what Roger was doing to him, he, Roger, believed that given he was in such a need of him, that his positive attraction for this innocent being was more important than any negative repulsion that his victim may have had for him. In all five senses of the word, Roger was enjoying himself. In the dark he could make out David's bottom. He could hear him sleeping gently. He could smell him as David passed wind into his face. He could feel him with his phallus. All he wanted to do was to taste him. After scoring with his latest conquest, he licked with his own tongue, David's sweaty and salty body before gently massaging his bottom. With all five senses being about David, Roger left the scene in peace as all the colors of his rainbow had been illuminated with pride. He was however somewhat frozen as he heard Sophie's words ringing in his ears when she said several months earlier that if he did anything bad to David, that within twenty-four hours he would be dead. All he could hope for was that David didn't know what had happened to him and that if he did, that it was something that he himself enjoyed too.

Roger then went to his room, turned on an LED light and believed that he was looking more than a decade younger than he had been recently. For him getting so close to David was amazing. David wasn't simply just a new conquest for him: He was Beth's beau. As a man who believed in the importance of touch, knowing that Beth had been touching David; he felt serene. He believed that along with his own positive energy that his dreams were coming into fruition.

David burst out crying as he felt sperm coming out of his itchy and sensitive bottom. It was an experience he had never in his life encountered before and as the alcohol was wearing off; the rape was killing him. He then realized that his thoughts about being treated as a woman recently were nothing but an aberration of his otherwise heterosexual self. Now, he would have to live with the fact for the rest of his life, that he was one of Roger's sexual victims. Too scared to take a shower on his own, he decided that as much as he could smell his rapist's presence, he felt that the best way was for him to somehow fall asleep. Firstly, he had to swallow some acid which rose up to his mouth and was probably a result of his nerves and tasted nothing like a desert for him.

It was night, and he wanted his wife to be with her infectious beauty to look as stunning for him as ever. He was asking himself how such a sordid act had taken place against his will while Beth was using this night to heal herself and to be ready to spend the rest of her life with him and to consummate their marriage as of one holy act. He wanted to punch Roger in the face but was actually lying next to Beth since Roger had gently returned him back to his bride to be, after his successful dirty deed. Yes, gently, because David wasn't built so big like many of the other women, he knew who wished that they were male body builders. In tune with his appearance, he was of a slightly build. Disturbingly for him, he was comparing Beth's breathing to the sounds of Roger groaning while he had been carrying out his wicked pleasures on him. Poor David, was he going to end up scared of everyone around him? Terrified as he imagined Roger on top of him, he placed his hands on her bottom but felt as though Roger's hands were on his very own buttocks. There was no reason for him to think this; it was simply his mind playing nervously out of control.

They all had breakfast together and after eating his scrambled eggs he asked himself, what he could do? A stag night was a night of decadence and debauchery. Before settling down to married life and as a strong man he wasn't meant he had to reveal to her what he had got up to. If he did, would Beth see him less of a real man and Roger more masculine than ever? The fact that he was merely a helpless victim might make him come across as some hapless and jinxed loser. Maybe Beth would say that with him being so innocent that he deserved it. She had three children with Roger after all, and he was sure that she had more love for him than she dared to admit. He was all too aware how she expected nothing less than stoicism from him. How could he ruin their big day? She had been purifying herself so that she would be more or less born again as a maiden for her beau. On top of that Roger was the perfect host. Breakfast had been so wonderful, and his repulsion and disgust over Roger's fruits buried deep inside of him proved that homosexuality wasn't for him. At least he had experienced it and could say with his hand on his heart that he himself was of a heterosexual persuasion. He had to look on the bright side of things. At least he would never have to meet up with Roger again. After the wedding ceremony and before their departure he would simply have a quiet word with his former friend. First, he had to be married; he didn't want to upset Roger before he became her husband. He loved Beth so much that for him to ruin their big day would be an act of treachery against his one and only love, Beth. When he first met her, she found him very attractive, then when the things went wrong between them both she saw him as some kind of girl. He had to be that country boy she first saw in her eyes of him as she was eyeing him up from his down to his toes and was admiring his well-toned legs. Simply put; he had to be that strong silent man that he believed she deep down dreamt of.

Erik was helping Roger with the wedding preparations while the girls were taking it in turns to look after the babies and to beautify themselves for the moment they had been dreaming of.

Stood in front of the waters alone with the looming fells behind he started to think about his future more deeply. As much as he was trying to survive; he was scared that he would end up dead from the humiliation of Roger's act. If Erik were to find out what Roger had done to him; he would beg him to kill the dirty man on his behalf. This too made David feel less of a man and more suicidal. Roger had wronged him; if only he were brave enough himself to kill him directly himself. As for the wedding ceremony, it had to be the special one that Beth was dreaming of. If he could, he would find another vicar. With him taking his marriage vows in just an hour's time, the idea of finding some other clergyman was simply preposterous. After a flash which went in his mind telling him to drown in the waters so that Roger and Beth could be happily reunited, he felt as though a mask was covering his mouth and his nasal passage. Trembling with fright and not sure as to whether he was breathing or not he ran as fast as he could back along the path following the stream to the venue for his new life. As he was doing so, he felt as though he was being chased.

Wearing his no-nonsense clothes, the vicar has an interesting presence. The formal attire helps radiate from him his penchant for a great semblance of an orderly dress code. Christianity, with its rules, appears to keep his very active mind in balance. For him, having the power of God in his services as he orders the couple to obey and respect the vows bestowed onto them with the grace of the Lord and via, he, the vicar himself, gives him his narcissistic satisfaction. Everything is working with synchronicity apart from his eyes which appear somewhat sad and confused. Nevertheless, as a well-respected pillar of society, the couple, being married by him couldn't ask for a better village elder than that of the Mayor of Buttermere, who also happens to be the vicar of the church where a eulogy of the famous fell walker Alfred Wainwright took place a few decades earlier. Of course, there were very few members of the clergy left by then. The couple after becoming husband and wife kiss. Looking no less than Romeo and Juliet it is strikingly obvious for those present, that the blissful couple are well connected in mind, body, and soul.

David and Bethany Bell are now in the eyes of the church; married until death do them part. An Erik and Sophie Alexander had been given a similar ceremony less an hour before. With his surname coming before David's in the alphabet, Roger was able to save his two loves for the end of the special occasion. Erik's name was not of Alexander, but Roger wanted to anglicise it with a Jewish sounding name. Beth, to her fury who had been studying English names prior to the tsunami, knew exactly what he was playing at.

Roger was then in a great delight as he was ready to humiliate the men. "The strongest men and women will survive. The rest will be childless or bring their children up into a broken society. The strong men and women still love each other. Even if the rest are crazy, they remain a beacon of hope for mankind." He said defiantly, as Beth was trembling and wished she hadn't told him what her beloved daddy had said. "Lest we forget that we must now move onto to our children he said as he darted a quick glance at a sullen Sophie and a nervous Beth. We are here for the christening of our beautiful babies, William, Jane, Sarah, Peter and Greta. It is with such a great honor that our babies have these wonderful names. Their grandparents are honored and smiling down from above." He said grinning slyly at David and Erik. "William is of course the name of the great poet." He said as David looked on proudly. "Jane, is an honorable name and after Sophie's first love, Jan, the one whose child she aborted and a great way to show some humility for the deceased." With that Erik was furious, as Sophie darted a glance of disgust in the direction of her sister.

Could things get any worse the others feared as Roger was enjoying the moment? "Sarah is obviously a lovely name for a baby who might one day resemble the stunningly beautiful Sarah Coleridge. It might also be the name of her French paternal grandmother, as Peter is my father." He said as David looked aghast as though he wanted to be sick. Roger gave him a sinister look as though he hadn't finished with him. "Finally, Greta, the name reminds me of a Swedish self-loather who believes in the end of the human race and is one of Beth's kind!" He said as Beth saw this as a thinly veiled Anti-Semitic attack on herself.

After the ceremony Roger's mind went once again back into overdrive. On top of that, he had to act quickly. In fact, although he had longed for depopulation, there was a shortage of maidens; in fact, there was a shortage of just about anything. Yes, he enjoyed the simple things in life, or at least they cured him to some extent, but now with his beautiful home and even with his butler whom he hired after he recovered from his fall this weren't enough for him to make him in any way content with his life. Without electricity the cyber world was no more. While in the days of Victor Hugo there was no electricity, things had changed. If he could, he would be something like; The Marquis De Sade, but the genocide had cleaned up the rest of humanity in more ways than he could have ever envisaged. There were simply less people, and those who had survived seemed to be more pious than in the days of old. At least his guests would be overawed with his opulence. At least the former shops of Keswick still had a great supply of goods and he was able to grow his own produce. It was however, more pressing things on his mind, which were twisting the area above his neck and were spinning out of control; that he saw as matter of greater urgency.

His main concern in his mind concerned relationships but was not of his sexuality. His recent species identity crisis was an aberration of this otherwise stable being who believed that he was nothing else other than a normal homosapien. So, obsessed with Genghis Khan whom he had read about when he was a young gender fluid male, he saw this former warlord pro-creator as his very own savior. In his mind he saw himself as a full red blooded heterosexual male; and this was his problem.

He had no woman, there were none available anyway. He had married the couples out of his newfound love of God, his two loves of all people, Beth and Sophie to his rivals. As such death was on its way to him. To merely commit suicide was no longer a viable option for him. After taking a deep breath his mind was made up. He believed that neither Sophie nor

Beth would stab or beat him to death. Instead, he might as well go out with a bang and do something to both girls that would affect them for the rest of their lives. In turn, not everything in the immediate future appeared bleak for him. There had been no mention of the incident which took place between him with David. As such and given he had enjoyed it so much he believed that once things settled down, he would be able to make love to him, once more at least.

Thanks to his high standing and the food imports which arrived via coach from the south after arrival from Dover, Roger was able to provide his guests with dishes fit for royalty. In turn the five-course dinner was a blessing for each and each and every one of his loves. This was merely the eye of the storm of his own making.

Given the survivors were living under austerity; they wouldn't be able to complain about the dinner. Salmon baked in spinach leaves for starters; roasted duck, sprouts, peas, and cabbage along with local potatoes which were normally sent abroad for the main course followed by cheese and biscuits. A chocolate gateau was the penultimate course, which was simply finished off with a bowl of exotic fruits. As for drink, it was simply tea, coffee, and plenty of water for the thirsty.

During a quiet moment Sophie with her body language asked him to visit her discreetly outside of his kitchen. He followed her as the others were unawares. In the hall she began. "That wasn't a very dignified christening was it?"

"No less dignified than the circumstances I might add." He said trying not to grin too obviously at the woman who had tried to kill him.

"You didn't respond to my letter that said our second child is genderless." She said to him dolefully.

"What did you want me to say about it? I am sure it is better than anything that Erik could produce." He said with a pleasant smile.

She then belted him hard across his face as he felt as though a rock had struck him. "I haven't forgotten that you almost killed me." He said as he was still smiling at her.

"So, this is your revenge, you impregnated me with a genderless embryo?" She said in distress.

"I will never forget when I told you to stop screaming at me when over this innocent baby you told me that you didn't give a shit if our beloved baby is genderless of headless!" He then decided to look more into her eyes and noticed that she was starting to avert her gaze from him and looked as though she was drowning in shame.

"My God! I am sorry, you are bleeding so profusely!" Although he was enjoying every moment, he had by then stopped smiling. He then walked off. He wanted her to fear him more than ever. He knew that the unknown would make her feel worse than ever as her stomach would be tied up into knots. By then he felt so powerful and had a huge smile on his face. As he walked off, Sophie was for the first time in her life terrified of him. He was also thankful that there had been no mention about his dirty act against David.

No matter what she would do to him, he trusted that he had destroyed any happiness to come her way for the rest of her miserable life. While he felt that she deserved to have given birth to an "it," due to her almost successful act of homicide against him. Subconsciously, the real reason was much deeper rooted. Sophie was in fact even more of an innocent party in this tragedy than it seemed. Her misfortune and bad treatment from him were merely for the fact that he didn't love her and wanted someone to pay the price for his lack of fulfilment, confusion and misery. Basically, he was taking it out on her for his bad intentions. Of course, in his own mind, he was at the vanguard of a pioneering humanitarian movement; the radical LGBT Feminist alliance. As someone who believed in mind over matter; his genderless baby was a result of the power of his thoughts and a dream come true for him. Given that he felt in some ways as Beth's subservient, and given he respected as what he saw as her purity he didn't wish for the "it" to be bestowed onto her own motherhood. Instead, he felt that that it was Sophie's calling for his twisted agenda instead.

Another interesting fact was that this man, who had enjoyed impregnating the women twice over each, didn't involve himself with his children on this visit. He also suspected that the women didn't want him near the babies and that they would pay the price for their lack of respect towards his paternity.

One hour later he was still busy preparing the matrimonial banquet. Sophie left her babies with Beth. She wanted her sister to be kept busy so that she could find him. He was occupied with the cooking, as she walked in. "There are four types of men." He said upon noticing her as she stood there frozen. "And they are based on two simple traits: honesty and intelligence. You might say that honesty and intelligence are a virtue. People with those kinds of traits usually find work helping others and their pay is humble. Less educated and honest people have it even worse; they might be simply earning a living cleaning the streets. Honesty doesn't make either group well off does it? Now let's look at not so intelligent but dishonest men. They can make good money through crime as you are well aware. As for myself I am a combination of being intelligent, dishonest and an Adonis, what a lovely combination this is!" He said in a manner which he knew would leave her lost for words and was in some ways a coded attack on her. He sensed quite wrongly that Sophie was impressionable enough under the right circumstances to carry out evil acts without too much coaxing. He just wanted her to understand that his version of survival of the fittest was not based on merit. By not revealing too much but expressing how bad he was, he was sure that no matter what, there was no escape from him and that even if she killed him, his disgusting theories would forever be running all over her body as she would forever hate herself for opening up her legs to this man from hell. If she couldn't love him; he didn't want her to feel indifferent about him.

"What wrong did I do to you?" She asked him.

"Maybe nothing. Then again, you did. I wanted you at first. I found Beth too pious. The day before we made love for the first time, I had decided it was you. The next day you were behaving somewhat strangely, and my affections moved towards Beth's. That was the first mistake you made. To be honest I think that the real problem is much more complicated. Had I never met Beth, then you would have tamed me. Beth was a distraction. Too much of a good thing leads to hell. I behaved terribly to Beth because I love her so much. In turn, I hate you so much for two reasons. Firstly: because I prefer Beth and secondly because under normal conditions, you are the best woman in the world for me."

"I am not going to kill Beth for you. And thank God, I have Erik anyway." She said.

"A driver would never ask his chauffeur to kill his vehicle."

"What are you on about?"

"I want to be her daughter." He said and with that Sophie simply walked off and decided not to dwell on his insanity too much.

At least Roger had done them all proud with his meal. Thanks to his connections and civilisation getting back on its feet, Roger had some delicacies brought over from France for more than just the wedding banquet, which his guests fully enjoyed and appreciated. All he had to do was to kill David and Beth would be his. All he had to do was to kill both men, and both women would be once again his own. He was torn between stabbing the men with his six-inch carving knife and waiting until he had impregnated the girls. In Roger's eyes he couldn't rape a woman, or a man for that matter, since any activity taking place between himself and another human being was one of love. In his mind if someone was doing something out of love, only haters would bear malice against him. After his loving deeds, if he were to be threatened, he was well within his rights to make sure that his would be assassin would pay the price with his head. As things stood; David wasn't going to harm Roger at the present moment. Could he carry both his dreams to impregnate the women and murder the men more or less simultaneously? In his eyes, the slaying of others was an act of love, since in times of war, no matter how peaceful one might be; even a man as peaceful as David could be provoked into carrying out acts of a gruesome homicide.

Once they would be with child, they would need him as the only male survivor more than ever. As for his butler, he was in no uncertain terms at all interested in women, and that was one reason why he had hired him as he was still working out what he wanted from him outside of his professional life. In short, he had to impress Beth, and that meant him being the perfect self-sufficient host before the couples would depart within the following forty-eight hours. So, scared of people asking questions about his servant, his butler had been given a few days off leave.

His mind was awash with plenty of ideas. Everything simply looked bleak. He sensed that the longer he played host, the more that Beth's fondness for him was returning, equally the longer he waited, the less time he had for his plan. Not knowing if his plan to impregnate the girls would end up with his death, he mulled over other possibilities once more. Killing both Erik and David was a real possibility, but he wasn't sure if he wanted to live a normal life and to live to a ripe old age. Equally without manpower how would he cope? He needed slaves. His butler like himself, was a dandy, and not the kind of rustic hodge that he needed to help him survive out in the wilds below the Honister and Newlands Pass. The confusion was driving him deeper to despair and he needed to discuss things with Beth.

One added major problem of his; was his genuine love for David. He was sure that this young semi protege of his was not only in awe but in love with him too. So, overwhelmed with everything; the confusion was blocking his senses as he felt as though he was a TV which had been receiving multiple channels simultaneously. Spinning further and further out of control, he started placing his hands on his hips and was wondering if he was some kind of feral queen and wanted to make love to himself. All he wanted to do was to run into the bedroom of his guests, wear a smock and dance with the women before as a favour for marrying off his greatest loves of his life; the men would make love to him in the presence of both Beth and Sophie.

His mind then went back to his guests' stag night, the night before. What a missed opportunity that had been for him. Why hadn't he been more passionate with David? He could have tied him up so that he would have experienced the thrill in his victim's terrified eyes. In short, a terrified and defenceless David could have been going through torture visually as, Roger, the most miserable man probably left on the planet was getting his own pleasure out of buggering someone up against his will. Things were not so black and white. People who said that they were straight were liars. Roger was simply carrying a worthy educational program to awaken the ones he loved out of a hypocritical spasm. As for Erik, he wanted him to take the lead. How he could have done this he wasn't sure. In short, he hadn't planned things out in advance as efficiently as he should have done.

As for Sophie being in his home, she was devastated, how could he produce with her a child that was gender neutral in every sense of the word? It was bad enough that her new-born was some kind of android, but to think that it was some sort of sordid revenge on her was inexplicable beyond belief for her. Too scared to confront him further, she merely looked forward to when she would depart Buttermere with her groom. Being married to a decent man meant everything to her, how could she ruin Erik's day? How could she ultimately ruin her beloved sister's day too? All she could hope was that the father of her children would end up being the most broken-hearted man in the world. All she wanted was for him to languish in the hell of his own making.

Roger with so much depression inside of him as well as regret, he wondered why he hadn't taken up the chance in being the first ever transgender American President. Instead of creating mass destruction globally with tsunamis, nuclear bombs and chemtrails he could have found a less inhumane way of wiping out the most despicable thing on the planet for him, human beings. The plan to reduce the population from eight billion to five hundred million had gone wrong. He was sure that his enemy, God had done this to him since the population was probably closer to just ten million at the very most, and in turn this was the reason as to why there was a shortage of manpower and maidens for him. As was all too often the case, his mind often ran around out of control and he had no idea as to what he was thinking about. Equally he wondered if his earlier fears that just seventy thousand people had survived globally was no more farfetched as his hopes that only ninety-nine percent of the population had been destroyed and leaving as many eighty million survivors.

Had he been in control, he could have opened up baby making factories for the elite. These would have been something like farms too, to feed the rich and famous. They could have been laboratories supplying the pharmaceutical companies. Of course, there was no rush to reduce the population so quickly, since the macabre energy from billions of people living under the ghettos of the NWO would have made his life one of an eternal joy. Had he not ran away from the feminist farm over superficial misunderstandings about having a child without any sexual organs he could have been the most powerful person on the planet. More powerful than any man who had lived previously.

As a transgender mother, he could have been a role model for Common Purpose. All that death and destruction could have been one big party for him. Transgenders had been taking over countries globally before the wipe-out. What a missed chance, and to think he now had a child without any sexual organs at his own free will. If only he knew then what he knew then, he would have cherished the opportunity to giving birth to a child without any sexual organs and became a transgender woman president in the capital of the free world, The USA. If it weren't for his sadness and pain, he would still be with one of the girls. He realized that his insanity had driven his women away from him and this was why he felt more destructive than ever. Nobody understood him. He felt so alone.

As for his services as a vicar, almost nobody attended his thrice weekly services. There was though, one Turkish Muslim who attended. He loved the area and wanted to integrate as a new local with his own version of love. As for being mayor, almost nobody saw him. Once again, it was the Turk who visited him, and once again because he loved all things English. In turn Roger shed a tear as he thought about Murat, who came to England because of his love for the people, the language as well as the culture. Murat had a great respect for Roger too. What would he think if he knew who the real Vicar of Buttermere underneath his skin actually was?

While his guests were happily celebrating together their first official day of marriage, Roger didn't feel thankful that what she saw as his curse on Sophie wasn't anything worth worrying about. Simply put, he knew deep down that the genderless child wasn't creating any tensions between his second-class love and her man. He had though one other thing to investigate and that was also concerning his guests. So, scared of any happiness taking place in their beds he decided to walk around his home. As he stood in front of Sophie's room, he listened attentively, all he could hear was her apologising to Erik that due to her babies not being used to the environment they were in that it wasn't possible to make love until they returned home. At least something was working out well for him. He then walked to Beth's room. All was quiet; all he could hope was that with an extra child than her sister, that she too hadn't yet officially consummated her marriage in wedlock.

Chapter 13

THE GREAT DILEMMA

A new day arrived, and he was once again the great deceiver, this time his sleep had metamorphosed him into a gentleman of sorts. It was nearly thirty hours since he had fulfilled his ultimate dream with David, and he was still alive, despite the fact that he had done something against him. He then stuck up two fingers in the air out of defiance as he thought about Sophie and her promise that he would be dead within twenty-fours if he did something bad to one of them. His mind then went back into manipulation mode. He was a romantic man, wasn't he? Given he loved David; his actions had been noble as far as he was concerned.

It was during the late afternoon when Beth went up to him as he was looking through the bookcase. He wanted to read something about psychology. She was wearing a simple dress and that of a peasant woman. Even so, it fitted her perfectly, enriched her gentle and discreet beauty as visions went across his mind of her looking pretty much the same with older children as she would look like their elder sibling. Her eternal youth, beauty and wholesome goodness were simply killing him. He was frightened of her, he knew he was evil, but wished that she was a transgender cyborg that could be programmed to fulfil his needs. "Roger you have certainly proven yourself in being a great host." Beth said, who didn't see his insults about the paternity of the children as being anything of her concern. He had, as a man of piety, spoken the truth. As for the remark about Greta she was ready to forgive him. He was the father of her children, who were healthy and probably thanks to his genes, and she didn't wish to bear him with any malice.

"Thank you." He said looking and sounding very sad.

"Is everything alright?" She asked him sweetly as they were then stood together, and both had rising heartbeats.

"No, it isn't. I am scared that you're loving, and beautiful face is of the calm before the storm, just like with Judas." He said to her almost shaking as she looked on bemused.

"What are you on about?" She asked.

"I am terrified that you are going to kill me." He said to her as though he wanted to be sick. At that moment in her presence when she was showing him kindness, she kept his wicked dreams at bay and in turn a more gentle and vulnerable side to his nature was around. "I have never done anything to you in a violent manner, have I?" He asked as he was terrified that she could read his mind. If she knew what was really in his head maybe she could have blown his head off thanks to 5G technology. He quickly calmed his inner thoughts down as he was in turn relieved that the National Grid was obsolete.

"Of course not, you know how soft I am. How on earth can you say and think of such a gloomy portentous thing? I carried your babies." She said as if she was pleading to him.

"I know, but the second time you fell pregnant when I made love to you weren't very happy about it."

"I know, it is terrible, but if you did this because at the time, we were still an item then it is not so bad. Many women want their partners to respect their needs with love making, of course they don't expect to be impregnated in such a way, but these things do happen." She said with a wistful smile as he detected that she had deep down more than just a mild longing for him.

Mesmerized by her love, he looked at her. "I'm sorry for that. I am sorry for the fact that whenever I look at you, I imagine you lying next to me. It is just you look so stunning as ever." He said as he wanted to touch her dress but was scared of dying there and then.

"You look pretty amazing yourself too, Roger."

"If you weren't with David, I would love to kiss you all over and to make you pregnant just one more time, Beth." He said as she was numb and shaken by everything. "Remember how much I loved your maternal body and how much we couldn't get enough of each other more or less as soon as we met. You are the most beautiful woman in the world." He said as she was feeling faint inside. "I don't know as to which of the five paintings hanging above my bed and elsewhere in my lonely room, best describes my feelings of utmost devotion for you." She felt sick inside, the fifth painting of her heavily pregnant with sperm all over her body and the scarlet stretch mark on her breast was simply horror for her. Even so, she believed that it was a result of his highest devotion towards her.

David had never commented about her breasts looking different to the first time she was in the family way to when she had that unsightly mark on her left breast. In one sense he wasn't so manly for her as Roger. She wanted to know how deep-down David felt, did her highly maternal body excite him as much as she had excited Roger? As for the exhibitionist fifth painting of her blowing him, this was enough to put her off falling pregnant forever. The thoughts of being nauseous and swallowing his sperm made her feel somewhat sexless. "Has the stretch mark from your left breast disappeared?" He asked to her surprise.

"What gives you the right to know this?" She asked him as he was getting too personal for her.

"Has any man ever loved every inch of your fecund body as much as I myself have? And shot as much sperm inside of you as I have?" He said to her with his then gruff voice.

"Please Roger I beseech thee, I am now a married woman I can no longer be your concubine." She said politely.

Brought back down to reality that Roger was nothing more than a hedonistic beast she looked at him somewhat less gently and was looking very thoughtful. As much as she enjoyed him fucking her senseless, deep down she wanted him to spend time with her doing things other than making love. Sometimes they had been out on trips together; sometimes they had lived as man and wife together. From those experiences she felt that they could live together and be happy, but in her eyes, he didn't want this. Now she was married it was too late for this. If she could wake up alone with him and their babies without any distractions, then yes, she would. Trying to keep her sentimental feelings about him intact she had to quickly reply before she would do something regrettable as her breasts and womb were desperately longing for him as she even felt as though her body was giving off signals that she wanted him to take her.

Still, they looked into each other's eyes. "Thank you for the compliments, but as you know, David and I are married and if you were to touch me now, I would kill you if David didn't." She said playfully at him as she was also tiring of his attention towards her. All she wanted for him was to tell her she could stay with him at his vicarage forever and that his love was unconditional. "What's wrong you look as if you have seen a ghost!" She said to him soothingly.

"You mentioned that you would kill me." He said as felt as though his groin was momentarily frozen.

"I am sorry, that wasn't so impertinent from me: as if I would kill you." She said to his relief.

"I understand that you are wary of me. I just want to say that our babies are incredibly beautiful, and I am sure we can both see our grandparents in them." He said wanting to manipulate her. Equally he was feeling faint; Beth wouldn't kill him, would she? He still wondered.

"Yes, I see in William your grandmother." She said feeling blue that he wasn't offering her the security of his nest.

"I see you in her too. You look more and more beautiful. The paintings assumed you would be a little older looking after giving birth, but I am sorry. I never thought a woman after giving birth twice and to twins the second time could look as innocent and sexy as you. You don't look any different to when we first made love, when almost by magic I turned you from being a saintly virgin to that of a holy mother."

Her heart was pounding, she had to walk away and to make matters worse she was feeling confused and trembling inside and sensed that he was going to kiss her as he was hypnotising her with his eyes. "I am so proud of the way you are looking after our babies." He said as she felt as though she was going to faint. Without realising, and as he couldn't take his eyes off her, she stroked her belly, as his passionate look on his face made her turn white with fear. "Beth, to have you for just a few seconds more, would be worth literally dying for!" He said as his trousers were bulging, and he deliberately rubbed his body on her skirt. Her body was longing more than ever for him too, but she believed that it was one of habit for him to speak to every bird he wanted to charm off the trees, since deep down this man disgusted her in every sense of the word. "All I want to say is that had Sophie and not you gone to bed on that fateful night, I would never have cheated on you. I am full of remorse and regret." He said as he sensed she wanted to escape before she would run off with him to his room. "Just remember, love is the most important thing in life, it is simply what makes life worth living for, and I am waiting forever for you." He said as she was scared that she wasn't genuinely in love with David.

Beth then walked off in tears. She still had strong feelings for him, but never again would she make love to him, no matter how much she wanted to. She still believed that she was healthier than he was mentally but didn't feel strong enough in dealing with his demons. If she could be some kind of nurse for his mental health and to protect him from his insanity and to save his life, this would be no great sacrifice for her. Instead, this would be of one great honor for her. She also took her marriage vows seriously, especially since her husband was the one, she should have waited for. If only she had made love to one man. If only her first was David, but instead she had gone against her own morals in having more than one partner. The Beast hadn't shown her anything more than his desire to fuck her senseless and impregnate her without offering any long-term commitment for her. She ran to the bathroom, cried tears of relief that she was a married woman as well as tears of sorrow for the bad man who still excited her, whom she hated too, who was good enough for her if he could devote his life to their family full-time. If only she could get over him and see him as the hedonist beast he truly was. Why did she feel responsible for all of his dirty actions, couldn't she accept that no woman would have been so magnanimous?

As for Roger, he had one great big dilemma. He wanted to live but was equally determined that one day he would make love to her with her fully awake and ready to fall pregnant to him. He wanted to make a baby with her when the feeling of making love together was mutual but didn't know how he would be able to persuade her to willingly cheat on David. After a few morbid moments he then thought about how he didn't care if what he had to do would cost him his life. By then he gave up with the idea of research, he was sure that the answers he wanted wouldn't be able to be found in books. Trembling with fear of the unknown he had to run away, but where? Was he in fear in not having her: for just one more time, or was death what he was afraid of or both perhaps? To die without the cause of his death in being that of either sex or murder was for him a wasted fatality. For his life to end under the excitement of sex and death would be a most fulfilling and chain reaction of his whole purpose in life, especially if he could be reincarnated inside of his victim's womb.

He then looked at his himself through the mirror in the bathroom. He felt as though with his door locked, that the mirror was talking to him freely. He saw why young women were attracted to him. He looked amazing for his age. Equally he asked himself what was the point? He looked so good because of the food he ate; he believed. Everyone was born to die. Why couldn't he have lived a life of monogamy with someone who loved him, and brought up thanks to his wealth several children and now be a proud grandfather? Due to his inability to truly love a woman, he had failed as a real man. Given that the world was such a miserable place, why had he taken so much care of what passed through his mouth? He was going to die anyway, what was the point in prolonging the pain? What was the point in washing his hands before he would prepare the gourmet style dinner, when he hated the world and wanted all those around him to be wiped off from the face of the earth? Wouldn't it be good if he could watch them suffering as a result of his putrid actions? He sensed that his bottom was hot, smelly and sweaty. He wanted to burst out crying. He then sat down on the toilet. After doing what he needed to do, he was trembling after passing his solids; and wondering whether to wash his hands or not. With his mind in such turmoil, he was feeling sick inside as he was going through with a second dilemma that very same day: to wash, or not to wash his hands, to make everyone ill, or to take a chance on love with one of the girls.

The dinner was one of mixed blessings for the party concerned. While Erik and David were fawning at Roger from his speeches at the dinner table, Beth furtively couldn't take her eyes of him. He knew this too. He knew that she was both scared and in awe of him. If she were his, then in ten years' time the age gap would no longer be of anyone's concern. The only problem was that he wanted what he couldn't have, and she knew this only too well. Beth sensed that he wanted to speak to her, she knew him so well, but wasn't going to ask him in front of the others. Sophie and deep-down Erik too, wished that he was dead, while Beth wished that she could hate him, but simply couldn't.

Luckily for both of them while Beth was in the drawing room, after looking for her he found her alone and walked up to her. "I just want you to know, that I have been poisoned." He said to her.

"My God, what happened?"

"I mean generally. All the pollutants from city life kept my sexual confusion ignited. My parents conceived me when they were going through madness even by their own standards. I hoped that after the tsunami that I would be cured, and I fear that these are the last words I will say to you as a man."

"Roger, you have done everything to tear us apart, but I will always love you, even though we see each other much less nowadays." As much as he was a cad, her body had reached the point of no return and all he had to do was to grab hold of her, when was he going to realise that she was ready for him? She wondered.

"Where did I go wrong? I mean our lovemaking is one of heaven, isn't it?" He said to her emotively, as his words were putting her passion for him under some semblance of being out of control.

"Yes, I love making love to you this is true. The problem lies elsewhere. I believe in monogamy. I believe that we should spend time together as much as possible. As I told you many times, I wanted to be with you every night, not just for one big fucking, but to be lying in your arms all night long. I wanted to have breakfast with you daily, to speak to you daily and for us to never be apart from each other. As for our children, I wanted you to teach them French, to help me teach them swimming. I wanted to hear your loving voice as you would be showing me how thankful you were that I have carried our children inside my womb for eighteen months as you would be reading them bedtime stories. Oh, my Roger! Had you been so, I would gladly be fucked and impregnated by you again and again and again and more."

"Beth, please forgive me! I was a family lawyer. I made my money representing nasty and vindictive mothers who didn't want the fathers to bring up a child in the way you wanted with me. Had I known earlier I would have been less scared of you alienating the children from me because I had after all raped you!" Beth took a deep breath, her passion for him was cooling somewhat further, but she couldn't alleviate herself from going into hysterical mode.

"You didn't rape me! The sex was consensual, you really turned me on, but you made me pregnant surreptitiously. What makes me so angry is that you thought that I, a traditional and loving mother who wants the best for my kids would do something so nasty and not so different to your own sick mother to the father of my children!" She screamed at him

"My mother is sick. Whenever I am in your presence, I feel healed. All I ask is that you come into my room and that we make love for the last time as though it was for the first time." He said to her as her tempestuous desire for him was confusing her.

"You know that I am so afraid of you that we are all sleeping in the same room together, tonight." She said bluffing. Not knowing how to respond, he simply stood there helplessly.

After longer than expected she was still stood there looking into his eyes and waiting for him to react. Knowing that she was asking too much out of him he then blurted out. "Mummy, if only I were your daughter!" He said as he burst out wailing like a child as Beth suddenly felt terrorised by his madness. She thought about how David too was disturbed somewhat and in turn she believed that women were stronger than men.

"Roger stop it please, your craziness is becoming such a cliché that I am no longer concerned about your incoherent words." Incensed he then stared into her angelic face.

"As much as I enjoyed impregnating you, your vagina isn't as tight as David's arse!" He said as his voice sounded as if it was coming elsewhere other than his mouth as he appeared to be sounding possessed somewhat. Beth merely laughed off his last statement. All of her fond feelings for him had turned to dust. Finally, her passion for him was frozen. At last, her mind was clear, David with all of his imperfections of which there were many, was her one and only, and she was no longer afraid of such a ghastly depraved and sick being who was her manipulative impregnator.

Luckily for Roger, who then wished that he hadn't washed his hands before he prepared the meal, the door opened. Beth froze with relief and it was Sophie who arrived. Roger was delighted. He wanted to have the last joy with Beth and his head was full of ideas as to how this could be achieved. Sophie, who although beautiful had reminded him about his intentions and why he had postponed the wedding which was because of his love for her as well as for her sibling. Although in a trance and feeling as though he was the living dead, he believed that he would be guided somewhere and to a better place as he left the drawing room trancelike.

His mind was in a greater turmoil than ever before. Sat inside his room, which he had locked, he had never felt so confused in his life. He was scared in case he would kill himself, now that the excitement that he had survived his 24-hour death row had ceased; he was bored. He looked at himself in the mirror and was amazed as he saw the image of a man entering middle age as opposed to leaving it. After the tsunami money was less important, couldn't he have more confidence in himself and truly believe that Beth loved him just the way he was?

Her feelings meant everything to him. If she really loved him and if he really loved her, then he would have to hate himself for being such a great deceiver. On top of that, if he didn't kill himself as a self-hater, he might end up killing the woman he loved instead. With such turbulent thoughts inside of his head; he wanted to write Beth a letter in case he would die before she did. Killing her would mean that his ultimate necrophile dream would be fulfilled. Something had to change, with the terrible pains inside of his body, he was sure that his mind would kill him off. It was then that he decided to write some letters to Beth.

After he had written and sealed three letters with opposing needs and desires, he was looking simply shaken and numb. The locking of his door had been in vain. Nobody had tried to find him; it was simply as if he had never even existed. With pains running through his body, his heartbeat rising he felt as though with the acid running through his throat that he was going to be sick. He only wanted one letter for her to read, but which one he didn't know. Equally, if she died before him; then the letter writing had been a complete and utter waste of time for him.

Painstakingly, and after another twenty minutes of letter writing, he was staring at what was his then favorite letter.

My dear Beth,

I am, as I am sure you now are only too well aware; the ugliest and fattest man who has ever entered your body. On top of that, I am a very poor man too. Due to my depression; I have a tendency to overeat and to stop exercising. It is only because I was so obsessed with my image, that you now know and too late, everything about me is simply all a lie. I am sure I look like a grandfather as opposed to father figure for you. As for my money, which is more or less worthless since the tsunami anyway, I never earned any of it. I have been a leech, a parasite on other hard-working people. While parents were fighting each other, I was milking their savings away as they fought, and I enjoyed watching them destroy each other from the side-lines.

I am simply sick beyond sick. All I can say is, be thankful that you have survived, I, the most despicable being who ever existed. Had I not met you, and had the tsunami not taken place, then I was going to do something so evil and cruel that after reading this, you will not shed a tear over my demise. While in many ways you failed to tame me, you brought out to some degree a human side of me. I developed some empathy for others and had many battles with myself as I wondered if I might be capable of giving my love towards you in being a good husband and daddy. Never forget; without the modern and technological age, the remaining survivors will flourish.

Now back to my far from innocent thoughts about you. A part of me wanted a child so much; that I was even considering locking you up until you gave birth before killing you, so that I could then bring up my own child in peace. Artificial Intelligence was about to replace humanity and I could have impregnated cyborgs. In turn the idea of having you as a baby making machine was one of hell for me. Hell yes, because I hate the idea of heaven when the excitement of destroying others has made me who I am. As for men of all sexual persuasions and tastes and being able to bring up children without mothers on a commercial basis, this was also a part of my Satanic agenda. Until men would be able to give birth, my ideas on sexual equality and my love of both men and women meant that I had to think of a new money-making business plan before families had been destroyed. Please do not think of me as someone who was on the side of men. As a man who represented women in the family court, I had destroyed the lives of so many men. My tsunamis put a stop to all of that.

Please in turn see the wipe out as my gift to you, since you have inherited more of the earth for just yourself and our posterity. Isn't this simply a testament of my love for you? I also wanted to be a woman. In turn I was a schizophrenic feminist with misogynist lapses.

As I write, these twisted and perverted ideas are simply rushing out of my mind as I frantically want you to know who the real, Roger De Cadenet, unmasked, really is.

Instead after reading through his letter, he had a sudden flash of hatred of Beth, as he thought about how pure, sweet, and innocent she was. All he wanted was for her was to be humbled. How could he send what was for him, such a modest letter about himself to her?

Safely in her bed with her husband, Beth had to get Roger out of her mind and felt that the only sure way for her to do this was to fall pregnant there and then to David. Now that they were married, she felt that they were both free to put mutual children of theirs into the world. As she got into bed, she started to touch him, to kiss him all over as she had visions of herself in the family way once more. He looked so peaceful, and she was being turned on by his innocence. He was however deeply in sleep, maybe she had to calm herself down, prepare herself mentally for her third pregnancy. She was only twenty years of age and she didn't need to be in such a hurry. On top of that; she had only recently given birth. In the meantime, she had to fully become the devoted wife for her David and then in turn she would be ready to carry his child. As such, Beth fell asleep longing for him and thinking about how she was planning to fall pregnant to the sweet man lying next to her.

A short while later, the man lying next to her was no longer her sweet and loving husband. Instead, her sweet and sugary daughter was sandwiched between herself and David. She was curled up in a ball, as though she was an unborn baby inside her mother's womb. Although her mind was not on him, she wanted to feel safe in his presence, that of her protective father. She then after unfurling herself placed her hands on her mother's tummy and wanted to be inside her mother's womb again. Suddenly she felt some strange but soothing energy exchanging between herself and her daddy. Certain feminine traits from David were entering her brain as in turn she felt as though she was being released from some of her own masculinity which she wanted to give to her father as a gift, so that he would be more gallant, brave and bold in order for her to feel safe with him.

The confused soul was no other than Roger. He wanted to make peace with the two people he loved like no other. On top of that, he was scared in case things went wrong. As much as he hated his life; he didn't really want to die, all he wanted was to be happy. Equally, he felt as though he could no longer continue living like this. All he wanted was to be David's and Beth's child. As he heard Beth breathe a heavy sigh in her sleep, he was worried and quietly left the bed where he had never felt such serenity in his life before. As he was leaving the room, he looked at the bedside table of Beth's and was making sure that everything was in order.

After a while Beth found it difficult to get away from the drama in her dreams. She woke up in a fright. Jennifer died in labor. Was it because she was carrying the wrong man's child? With that she decided that she didn't want any more babies. David would have to accept that three children were enough for her. Her mind then went onto the men. She had made four big mistakes. Jan was as steadfast and reliable as Erik, but she was too afraid to make a move on him because she believed that her sister who thought of him as being one great big laughingstock was justified in her opinion of him. David was an old fashioned romantic, but circumstance had been cruelling to them both and the scars would always remain. Erik was reliable but now her sisters anyway. Roger was her potent superhero who had other interesting points too, which he dangerously went simply beyond the pale.

If only one of these men could have all of the positive attributes of the others all rolled into one. She then wanted to be sick as she thought somewhat more as she was trying to fall back asleep. Jan and Erik were boring; she would have had to have forced herself to love either of them. At least, Jan, the nice but uninspiring young man was dead; she could get him out of her head very easily. Erik was a boring moralist, and she wasn't going to do the dirty on her sister. David was the fragile romantic who under pressure was nothing more than a girl for her. Finally, Roger the bastard, who was full of a Satanic evil, yet a sex machine.

What if Roger had really buggered her husband up? All she could think about was the stag night when she touched his bottom as he was lying next to her and wondered what the fluid around him was. What a sick bastard, Roger had taken advantage of her husband. Why hadn't David confided in her? Maybe her husband was gay after all. She had to stop thinking like this or she would end up as insane as The Beast himself.

Roger's schizophrenic mind was in turmoil. Like his fetishes of corpses floating downstream and filling his women up with his sperm without any parental responsibility, he was in two minds about his own mortality. He had lived the life of some hedonistic beast; equally, he had his own thoughts on fidelity as he was sensing that his life was coming to a new chapter. Yes, he had been blessed with an everlasting youthful appearance, but this had all gone to waste. His deceptive life was the reason for his thoughts. He thought about how he had been a feminist. How he loved his mother and fought for women's rights. He then realized that he was a fraud as he thought about the nicest women he had ever met. Women such as Lyla, Pascale, Hannah, Celine and of course Beth he allowed to slip by. None of these women were interested in the emancipation of women. All that they endeavoured was a loving and protective man: a man whose eyes would only have been for her, a man who would have loved their mutual children. In short, this man who would one day be too old for his pleasures; would die all alone instead. He then shed tears for these women. He had ruined all of their dreams. It was then that he shed a tear and more for the sisters and was terrified that their lives were going to be even more challenging. He didn't really wish to upset either of them but had no control over his self-indulgence.

After abusing Lyla psychologically and seeing her years later in a traditional loving family: out of spite he knocked her husband off his bike sending him to his death. Pascale, after convincing this vulnerable jilted mother to be that he would accept her child as his own and have a traditional relationship with her, made her feel that she deserved no one, and in turn she took her own life. Hannah, who believed in marriage for life was divorced by him out of his spite; because he didn't want to admit that he had let her down. Celine, he had humiliated her in a love tryst of his own making and was very similar to the one he had had with the Polack girls. As for Beth, he was the dumbest man on earth. What man in his right mind would have turned such a young beautiful woman against him? What healthy man would have used all of his psychologically destructive energy he had meted out on the four aforementioned on just one young innocent maiden such as Beth? Luckily, she was as robust as she appeared to him so loving and tender, and she had always shone her love towards him, and that was the problem. The question was, why despite everything he had done to her had she only hit him across his face once? Since Sophie had tried to kill him, he had in some ways more respect for her, the older Polack girl. He worshipped Beth, in so many ways beyond a doubt, but as far as he was concerned, the fact that she saw things so much between good and bad when he saw everything as simply being grey was daunting for him. Surely, even the most delicate, loving and sweet woman he had ever met was capable of homicide. Maybe, he had chosen the wrong target of her deep-rooted anger. Was there more chance that she would attack Erik or David if he could find some caveat about either of the men? In the meantime, he had other things to worry about.

Erik was deeply in sleep yet again after being intoxicated from drinking the mead for a second consecutive night. Sophie was lying in the middle of the bed. With all his strength and precision, he carried her into his arms so that she felt comfortable and took her to his room. All she had on was her underwear. Her skin apart from the stretch marks was soft and tender. He didn't want to make her pregnant. He had already made her pregnant twice against her will. For him, Sophie was a test run on the ultimate. If he succeeded in climaxing inside of her, when she was no longer his, he would in turn have more confidence at a later date in going for Beth. If in the meantime she fell pregnant, so what! He then and thinking about his loneliness felt that he had to impregnate her. The women were his after all: and neither Erik's nor David's.

In his room suddenly he started to feel very weak and wanted to drift off into sleep but felt that it was then or never. In fear of her waking up he had to act quickly. He then started suckling her left breast and sensing that he had drained enough milk out of her, he then moved onto her right breast as he started feeling less insecure and very quickly, he felt rejuvenated from her delicious milk. Feeling good about himself once again, he was once again living for the moment.

For him, releasing his load was one of a great big anti-climaxes. The thought of impregnating her while Beth wasn't pregnant was a bitter pill for him to swallow. Mechanically, he had achieved his aim, but emotionally Sophie, who was sleeping, was nothing more than simply a blow-up doll for him. At least his tool was still working despite his advancing age, but only just since he was feeling once weaker again and as though he wanted to faint.

Roger then looked at Sophie. Erik was stronger than David. Sophie was more aggressive than Beth, she had after all nearly killed him. He had succeeded with Sophie, yet for some reason he was more scared of Beth and didn't know why. The turmoil inside of him was that; if he had never met Beth, he was sure that Sophie would have been more than good enough for him. Sophie had all the attributes that he believed to be of a good woman. Sadly, he couldn't get Beth out of his mind. Not all of his thoughts were of love for his Beth, who was becoming depressingly at times little more than his platonic belle. He also had thoughts of jealousy and hate. Whenever he loved David, he felt that Beth was keeping his boy away from him too. Sadly, the times he loved both of them simultaneously were few and far between. Even so, thoughts of kind will for both of them existed since he often still had thoughts of a threesome with both Beth and David present.

In the meantime, Sophie would believe that Erik had got her in the family way, and within a few months he could maybe inspect her body on a visit and make love to her underneath his prized paintings. Demonically he also believed that; Beth would be happy that he was showing care for her sister who was carrying somebody else's child and any animosity towards him would be anaesthetised. In such a scenario he would then, so long as David hadn't got in their first, fulfil his dream for the third time with her. He also believed that; subconsciously, in order to feel closer to her pregnant sibling, Beth would more readily accept another fertilisation of his. He had been thinking all of this while he was looking at Sophie. He believed that his energy was being absorbed by her, as she was lying peacefully in her sleep. A shiver of ecstasy went through his heart as he believed that his rape of her had resulted in his mission being accomplished with her yet again.

He then picked her up into his arms and carried her out of his room. As expected, Erik was deep in sleep too, as he placed Sophie next to him. Everything was going to plan, and he was happy that he had postponed the wedding so that he could impregnate her for a third time lucky. He smiled to himself. How stupid the girls had been in allowing him to delay the date so that he could fertilise her on her honeymoon in his den. All he had to do; was to bide his time for his real target. He then left the room. His body was so exhausted with everything and needed to recover. He then, very quickly fell into a deep sleep.

The night was beautiful. He was feeling more confident within himself. For the first time in ages, he was enjoying a beautiful dream. There he was with Beth. They were sat together on the beach with golden sands and walking hand in hand to the sand dunes along the Cumbrian coast in the warm sunshine with the seawater drying on their skin. Her breasts were extremely pert. She was a little younger than when he had first met her. Most importantly for him, was that; he wasn't a paedophile. Although older than her and a man, with his acne, he too was still a teenager. In turn they made love, and these two youths made a beautiful sight. With no one else around, for the two of them nothing else mattered as both of them lost their virginity together. What a scenario! What a beautiful setting! He himself had had plenty of opportunities when he was young. While Nicole was a little older than himself: plenty of his female contemporaries would have run away from university to have had a life full of passion with him.

As he woke up, he changed his plan as he was convinced that for him to shed a few decades off his age and for Beth to be with eternal youth he had to make love to her not later on but right then. On top of that, he took off his wig, which he wore almost endlessly. In order for him to be rejuvenated, he had to be in the flesh bear naked. No wig, no clothes and not even a watch would he allow himself to be wearing. Once he became a teenager again, his hairline would be restored. Then, he switched on one of his LED lights, picked up his bedside mirror and saw himself. Without the softening effect from his false hair, he had aged twenty years. His scalp was full of scars and blemishes. At least his penis was erect: he was ready for the kill. He then took a deep breath, but his inner voice told him to wait. In turn he felt as though his mind was fighting his body, which appeared to be preventing him from moving.

As he managed to stand upright; his thoughts of doubt disappeared into thin air as although feeling weak again, once more his mind was strong. After a few moments of deep thought about thinking that he would see her in the flesh for the first time since she gave birth a second time, Roger had never felt so happy in his life. He was convinced that he had found his youth and was about to be three times younger than his real age and that his natural mane would return, and Beth would be a maiden once more. On top of that, he had never felt so heterosexual in the whole of his entire life. He then walked into the bedroom where she was sleeping. David, like Erik, was again heavily intoxicated from drinking the mead. It seemed that he needed another night of the mead in order to help deaden his feelings about the fact that he had been raped. Roger smiled lovingly at him. It didn't matter to him that David had been abused despicably against his will, Roger could still look at him romantically and believe that David still worshipped him. Confidently he took off the musty bedsheets and picked her up into his arms, as his erect penis was touching her bottom. For him she had the everlasting youth. Her body was one that many of the deceased ex partners from both sexes of his would have died for. It was then that he wished more than ever before that he was her, and that she was David. For now, though at least, if he wanted to carry out his plan, in the short term, he had to feel as though he was the luckiest red blooded male alive. Still feeling faint, it was his mind over his body that was the driving force for his plan.

As he was leaving the room his mind almost went blank when suddenly a beautiful vision of the floating corpses of David, Erik and Sophie went past him downstream while he was saving Beth's life. This was a sign that somehow, they would be united in every sense of the word. With all the other people in Beth's life drowned, he would be able to devote himself to her, only. If two's company, three's a crowd then obviously living with five adult members in his home had simply been way too many. Living then for the moment, he dismissed thoughts of himself dying from a gruesome demise as being nothing more than an irritating distraction from his about to be fulfilling pleasure.

It was with a great relief when he had left the room and was no longer in David's sphere. Her waist was slim, all the breast feeding, and sport had kept her body in shape, and he wondered if she really was in her twenties as opposed to being in her teens. She still had a body that many maidens would die for. As far as he was concerned it was her love of swimming daily, healthy food and good genetics that resulted in her keeping in such good shape. Even so, he smiled to himself that he was the only man who had had her when she had her real hourglass figure. The fact that her waist was a little bit wider than when they first met was all thanks to his own work, which resulted in her twice giving birth. He felt so virile and so dominant until he suddenly started to feel faint.

Feeling weaker than ever and although scared of her ruining his plan, he started suckling her left breast. Beth was less of a deep sleeper than Sophie, he had to be so discreet. At first it appeared easy, unlike Sophie, her breasts were leaking. When they had dried off to some extent, he then went for her right breast which was also as milky as those breasts he had seen from his favorite maternal porn-star, Linda, who was also an Eastern European. He then went back to her special scarlet left breast and quickly he felt rejuvenated after so much fluid of love had been delivered between his lips, and luckily for him she didn't wake up. With that, he couldn't believe his luck.

With the full moon shining through the windows as she started to open her eyes, she could make out that the room she was then in what was the most elegant room of the house. It was such a beautiful way to be woken up by her loving, romantic husband who was then full of passion. Despite all the wrong things he had done to her; he was now all man for her. As he climaxed inside of her, all she wanted in her life was to fall pregnant to him. She had never felt so happy in her life. Her dreams were finally coming true, in short, he felt exactly the same way as she did too and felt that she was enjoying the moment. Ever since she met David, she wanted the seeds of his loin to fill her up. It was third time lucky for her. She could certainly feel his semen inside of her. She was sure from his prowess that he was just as fertile as she herself was. Her child was being conceived in wedlock. She thanked God for answering her dreams as she was drifting happily back into sleep.

As for Roger, he wanted to end his life in harmony with his desires and started dozing off to sleep with her and was madly and deeply in love with her. Not for the woman or the man he was, but for the fact that she was simply his well and truly prized vehicle. During his orgasm Roger had never felt so serene. With his heart beating wildly he was hopeful that he would suddenly metamorphose as the egg inside of her womb. Sex and death was his hobby, now though, it was sex, death and life that he desired, and Beth's womb was his window to a new life.

A moment of anger then flashed through him as he feared that he wasn't going to enter her body as a baby. He also felt that although she didn't want a child with him, something told him that she believed he was David. Beth really felt that David was making love to her, and with that she was delighted. Roger couldn't understand why she didn't want any more children with him. In turn, he believed that he was doing the right thing in curing her deception and that he was helping her in so many ways. What difference did it whether she fell pregnant to David or to

Roger? As the strong man he wanted to be, his then negative thoughts about her; left him almost as quickly as they had entered his head. His sperm had once again he gave her the great purpose in life, that was simply in carrying his great posterity and hopefully himself too. Mysteriously a veil of depression went once more across his mind. What was the point in procreation when the world was such a miserable place after all? This was not the way in which he wanted to part from the earth. Suddenly a rush of positivity rushed into his thoughts. He was going to hand David the sword and to order him to put him out of his own misery. Knowing how much of a pacifist David was, was making him aroused, but sadly for him he felt as if his testicles had run out of juices before he had a chance to make love to Erik. As for David, after being slain by him, he would be one step nearer in becoming a woman like the one whose body he wished was that of his own, that being Beth. As her daughter, he would one day be the girl his mother wished him to be.

Suddenly, after a few minutes she was aware that it was Roger who had been on top of her. As she felt his sperm oozing out of her, she wasn't thinking about a conception, instead all she could think about was David, and the sticky stuff coming out of him. In turn she started to scream. As evil as he was, she still loved Roger, but wanted this to stop. She then opened up her eyes, and this young girl saw his beady eyes, the deep and chiselled crevices all over him, his Dr. Spock like ears and his large bulbous nose, of this dirty old bald-headed man. Along with his bad breath which he was producing from his nervous gut, she had never felt so dirty in her entire life. As far as Beth was concerned, he looked like a slimmer version of a top film producer. She then wondered if she got what she deserved. It was his money that had got her into this mess. If only she had died along with the masses as an innocent, instead she felt as if she was some whore from Hollywood.

Her thoughts then moved onto David. Surely, he must have known how evil Roger was. A real gentleman would not have sent her back to The Howe after he had allegedly proclaimed his eternal love for her and bought her such a beautiful, scarlet, silk, maternity frock. Like Roger, he wanted to use her as nothing more than his mistress. He hadn't married Jennifer, but she knew that he had asked for her hand in marriage. Now, she wondered; if like Roger, the real problem lay in his confused sexuality, if so then one of these men must die, so that one of them could devote his attention to women only. Hopefully this would send him onto the path of a loving monogamous relationship with her as she would be for his eyes only. Her idea was vindicated in her mind as haunting memories of the two men sat together and dreamily at the kitchen table came back to her tempestuous mind. As evil as Roger was, David was nothing more than a useless fairy for her. Roger had promised to make her pregnant for a third time and she was trembling with fear in case that this was another fait accompli of his. At least he was passionate. Without David around, she could live happily with exciting Roger. There was never a dull moment with him. All she had to do was to stay and become the mistress of The Vicar of Buttermere. Without any official documents it would be easy to annul her marriage, in turn she could be Mrs. De Cadenet after all. Even without his mane, she still loved him. Sophie was out of the way with her love for Erik she was happy, wasn't she? "Please my love, I have sinned. This time I raped you. You have read Deuteronomy 22:28-29 this is the closest to our situation right now." He said to her. She then gulped. "If a man find a damsel that is a virgin, which is not betrothed that is, meets with one in a field, that is not espoused to a man, and the man is supposed to be an unmarried man, as appears by what follows, and lay hold on her, and lie with her."

"You didn't rape me, if you are referring to me as your former maiden." She said since she herself knew The Bible inside and out.

"Either way I should have made an honest woman out of you, your belly was a testament that we were found. I would like to marry you." She was then feeling more than just faint and was ready to free her children from his sins. It seemed to her that he had done this in order for himself to put himself into a situation in which the only way to redeem himself was in marrying her.

"Have you raped any other women?"

"As a Christian I have to repent, I will not lie to you. I have raped a few underage maidens; I must atone myself." He said as a matter of fact.

"I guess if you have more than four victims this is a problem for you." She said as his words were more than just on her mind.

"Normally yes, but we can thank the tsunamis for solving this matter." He said as this time and unable to take no more, she started screaming to Roger's fright.

He stormed in the room to her relief. She then found a large towel hanging up and flung it around her body. In turn he started punching Roger. Roger was much bigger, and he had no chance. On top of that sadness went over her since it wasn't David who had come to save her. For what seemed like an eternity but was a few mere seconds at most, she observed the sword hanging on the wall. She wanted to die, she couldn't do such a thing, but she had never been so provoked in her entire life. In turn she picked up the shiny weapon and upon seeing it both men released themselves from each other. Roger didn't know that the game was up. "Before you stab him, shouldn't we have a threesome first?" He said as Beth was relieved that the choice wasn't between her husband and The Beast. In some ways she had more respect for Roger than for David. As it sunk in exactly this momentous situation in her life, she then burst out laughing at his face. In turn, Roger; became nervous as the atmosphere became somewhat eerie.

At that moment, Beth froze. All she wanted was for Roger to take the sword off her. All he had to do was to show her once again how much mettle he had. With the sword she had never felt so powerful physically in her life, yet mentally she felt as weak as a demonic murderess. As Roger had images in his mind of her being filled up with his love juices, all he could do was to look at her in awe and wonder. In turn, she started to remember the good times they had shared together. Inside, Roger was trembling with fear. For the first time in his life, he realized that he had fallen in love with someone he worshipped more than with all of the other beauties he had slept with in his entire life. He was too scared to tell her the truth: all he wanted to do was to fall down. Instead, he had images of her body glowing as she carrying his children and couldn't think of anything more beautiful than to be a father and a husband. Unable to take no more he looked at her. "Beth, the best days in my life began as soon as I set my eyes on you. I am healed. I am devoted and inspired by you.' He said as she was mesmerized by his words. Sensing her weakening with his words, he then felt brave enough. "I love you, Beth." This time she knew that his words were real; he had expressed them never like this before. It was then, that he sensed as his mother had told him, he had sentenced himself to death. Once he had fallen in love, it was time for him to perish.

He believed that she was going to kill him. "May I make just one small prayer before the next part of a cycle continues?" He asked. With that she didn't know how to react; she was terrified since those were words of a prophetic pregnancy as far as she was concerned. She merely nodded her head. "As the most important savior of the dwellers of Fell End, I ask for them to be spared from a virus which unleashed, would spell the end of humanity. I humbly ask; that in order for the others to survive, that I will live on, the servant of my dear Lucifer, and to be born again as the daughter of the most beautiful girl in the world." Beth's desire to kill him had been opened up as much as her fear of his disturbing words were freezing her strength to save the others from Fell End from his evil.

Suddenly, violent flashes of lightning followed by peals of thunder chimed in so well and naturally with Roger's feelings. A new scene of hell ensued as Roger starting puking profusely and he looked as though he was withering in pain and like a dying dog as all of his vomit was being thrown all over Erik's face and in turn, Beth was too scared to move. Even if she wanted to move: her body was locked. The power of his wickedness sent a cold draught into the room as well as a deathly putrid stench which resembled burning tyres of a pyre smelling of manure. Erik closed his mouth, but the acid from Roger's mouth resulted in a semi reaction with an unpleasantly metallic taste inside of his mouth. By chance, his trousers fell off and the bile coming out of Roger showered and covered Erik's naked scrotum. His manhood turned from being of a healthy pinkie one to one of a nasty brown color as he felt as though his testicles were being frozen solid from the fast-drying vomit of sorts onto his sexual organ, which suddenly had a painful burning sensation. Poor Erik was rocking around on all fours pathetically as though he was suffering from distemper.

Beth had never seen anything so disgusting in her life. Why hadn't she already stabbed the bastard? Why was she numb and in shock when her former love had never been so desperate for her help as then? As Roger's evil liquids continued pouring out of his humming mouth, she herself was feeling dizzy. She saw a vision of Roger raping her in her sleep, which resembled the night before and all she could hear at the back of her mind was, what's done is done! As for Roger, he couldn't decide which of the terrified four eyes gave him the most pleasure. Deep down however he wanted Beth to understand that he loved her and was thankful for her being with child, and that he hated Erik for ruining his exclusive rights to his posterity with her sibling. Poor Erik, Beth was a nightmare for him too. Why was she doing nothing to help him, why was she just standing there in shock as he felt as though he was being poisoned to death by Roger? As for Beth, she wanted to save him, but was being drowned in the presence of a maniacal madman who was taking away all of her precious finite energy.

Roger was satisfied; it was all a part of a process, of which there was no return. Suddenly, her strength came back to her. Not wanting to hear any more she pointed the tip of the sword at his testicles as he simply smiled at her. With that, his beaming face was shining into her eyes and perilously disarming her as she simply couldn't think of a better thing to do than to make him happy. His power of love for her had won the day. All she needed to choose was between killing him in order to be his mother and sparing his life so that he could have another litter with her. In turn, she simply didn't know which way to turn at this critical juncture in her life.

What was she the hell playing at, wondered the man with his frozen testicles. No man had shown her the passion he had for her and all she wished was that she hadn't added two more partners onto her tally since him. Suddenly Erik coughed violently, and without thinking about her love for Roger, she felt a surge of warmth and strength inside of her arms. It was then that moment that he, Roger, knew that her affections had moved away from him and onto Erik. He wanted her to forever remember him as her smiling inseminator. He had, as far as he knew, got his final wish, and could die happy in the knowledge that the beautiful painting of her heavily pregnant during the third time when she was filled with the seeds of his loins was a reality coming true. Excitingly for him the towel fell off her chest. His last memory of her would be of the scarlet stretch mark on her beautiful and milky left breast. On top of that he was licking his lips with glee as the milk was pouring down on her body. On top of that he was going be born again as her daughter.

For Beth it was now or never, as she saw him licking his lips with glee, she was more terrified of him than ever. Things had simply got out of hand. Every emotion was running through her highly tortured mind. A part of her wanted to laugh as though this was all some comedy. Another part wanted to cry, since he was the best lover she had ever had. As the sword was coming his way, he didn't flinch. He loved her like no other and was relishing in the psychological power that he had over her. A deep breath was taken by her. As the sharp and shiny metal tip of the sword cut right through his testicles, with all of his inner strength he kept his eyes firmly fixed on her, so that he would forever be vividly etched on her mind. His last vision of her was of her horrified face. It was then time for him to pass out in peace.

As he was dying with the blood gushing out of him, she fled the scene of her heinous crime. She ran into his room and was searching everywhere. After a few frantic moments, she found what she had been looking for and ran out before she was able to digest that she really had it in her arms. As she came back to him, she held him in her arms while the blood was still pouring out of him and placed his state-of-the-art black wig that she had found on his bed, back onto his head. Erik fled the scene. With him dead, she felt as though a part of her dignity had been restored. She felt as though she was a teenager again.

There he was, he looked so innocent, his hair was jet-black, and he looked as though he was approaching two score years instead of three. On top of that, while she felt that he had been taking advantage of her when she was nothing more than a child, she believed that she matured into a fully-fledged woman and was old and mature enough for this man who satiated her intellect. Sadly, he was now dead. She herself had murdered him. At least she had his children, and he would live on forever in her life with his posterity.

The morning was broken, and she was still sat nursing him, even though he was lifeless. David walked in; he was shell-shocked. Had Beth met him before Roger, she would have been the perfect wife for him. When carrying Roger's first child, David had hurt her emotionally. In turn she couldn't fully trust him, and when he tried to touch her, she froze physically and started screaming in order to scare him away. As he left the room, she hated him more than ever. If he really loved her, he would have during the two years they knew each other impregnated her. David was weak. So feeble, he was torn between Roger and herself, this contemptuous situation was even worse than when his attentions were divided between both herself and that of; God bless her soul, that of his deceased partner. Now it was even worse given he was under the spell of a man, The Beast himself, whom she was in love with too, what a contemptuous triangle that was. As for morality, what Christian values did he, David, have when he was flirting with sodomy and making a vulnerable woman cry over him when she deserved much better than this?

After what seemed like an entirety, as she was slumped to the floor in deep thought, for an hour all alone, it was Erik and not David who boldly walked up to her. "David is looking after the babies, and he asked me to tell you that we need to move the body." With that some semblance of respect for her estranged beau, David, rushed back into her heart. "He also said that; we can't just flee the place because the authorities will be searching for us if we do. We must get our house in order first." He said as Beth wished that she could respect a man again.

"Please tell David that I am a bad girl, I am not so pure as he, and that if he has any respect for me, he will bury me besides Roger." She said as Erik looked on at her aghast

"I will do no such thing."

"Then I will kill myself."

"No, no, Beth."

"Why?"

"Because I care about you."

She knew that Sophie was giving him a hard time; she knew that he needed some praise. She knew this for the simple fact that; she herself treated David in such a manner. The fact that he cared about her was a greater sign of love for her than both David and Roger combined. Unconditionally, he was concerned about her and she felt somewhat drawn towards him. "You are more of a man than David, only you can save me now." She then grabbed hold of him in great desperation and buried her head into his chest and was crying as she wanted him to take her. David didn't care about her, and who could blame him? All she knew was that she didn't want to be alone. Erik was confused. She had left him recently, and as much as he wasn't so happy with Sophie, he was too tired to keep on playing around. "I love you, Erik! Let's run away together and start a new life together!" She said as she hoped that unlike David, he had no homosexual desires. He wondered if the guilt had set inside her over the fact that his manhood had been taking a bashing partly due to her stupefying cowardice that led to more and more of Roger's poison being unleashed on his hapless self.

She could leave her babies behind, forget about Sophie and David and make sure that any future babies would take Erik's name, included those she was carrying inside of her which of course she hoped she wasn't. Three of Roger's were more than enough. She then started to kiss him; Erik was hypnotised. A new life sounded like a dream come true for him and her. His eyes were closed, and he wanted to get inside her as he simply found her more beautiful in every sense of the word than her sultry, feminine, and appealing sibling. For him, Beth was everything beautiful that Sophie was but even more so. By chance he was distracted as he spied Sophie. Beth had already seen her, but with David around the others could form a new partnership and leave her along with Erik in peace. Even so, Erik felt uncomfortable and knocked Beth onto the floor as he grabbed a hold of Roger's bloodied left arm. "You can't carry him like this Erik! You are so fucking impractical!" Sniffed Sophie at him.

As much as he hated her berating of him, he was relieved, like Beth, that she hadn't caught him kissing her. Sophie called round for David. Beth seized her chance as she started staring at Erik and placed her hands on his head as though she was analysing an inanimate object. Her touch unnerved him. "Why are you touching me this way?" He asked.

"I just want to make sure that you are not some cyborg."

"Beth, how can you think of such a thing? Any anyway, there is no National Grid anyway." He said as she then looked at him relieved.

"Please make sure that David isn't some kind of robot, at times his coldness resembles something like that of artificial intelligence."

"Beth I will do no such thing." He said as she looked at him respectfully.

Upon David's and Sophie's arrival, Roger was then carried to his temporary makeshift morgue. It had taken the four of them to carry and place Roger down into the cellar, while the babies were still sleeping.

That evening as she was lying awake with David, she could take no more. While David left her stone cold, Erik could help her get over the man she loved and had murdered. In life she tried to block out any thoughts of hatred for the man who had enslaved her, taken her dignity away and destroyed her innocence and most insultingly for her, he had proven to her that things were not so black and white as she once believed. She had and against her peaceful and loving nature carried out an act of homicide. Now he was dead. She was missing him like crazy. Carrying the whole world on her shoulders she felt a generation older. Despite looking as beautiful as ever and being a femme fatale with her seemingly endless youth, she felt as though she was drowning in a sea of shameful decaying matter and that Roger's sperm was filling her up as she tried to swim to the safety of dry land. It was crazy, she was being fertilized by him even though he was already dead. At least that was how it seemed to her as she couldn't and didn't want to imagine that at the tender age of twenty, she was so close to being the mother earth figure in his prized painting of her.

Unable to fall asleep; David knocked on the door. Sophie stood up and when he arrived in her face as she opened up the room to his eyes, she felt weak at the knees. Was he finally going to choose her and not Beth? Why had the most desirable surviving man come to see her? "I'd like to talk to you in private about Beth." He said letting her know that he had no intention in doing anything improper. He was everything Erik wasn't, educated, a gentleman and a man who understood women and like Erik decent, so yes both surviving men had something in common. On top of that, she still had feelings of passion from him as a result of sleeping with him just after Jennifer died. "Erik is with Beth, he wants to find out about you, he is badly hurting inside. If only you knew the pain and suffering, he has over you."

"David, you don't understand. I am torn between my honor and my need to be healed." David looked at her.

"I know, we have all suffered so much."

"Can I tell you something in confidence?"

"Of course, you can."

"Roger raped me last night. I woke up briefly in his bedroom."

"This is in your dreams." He said bewildered.

"No, it isn't. Erik was pretty much comatose from the mead; so, he was completely unawares. I woke up this morning with sticky stuff around my pelvic bone." She said looking more than a trifle horrified.

"So that's why Beth killed him?" He said relieved.

He was then thinking that his wife wasn't insane and distraught that she might be carrying another round of his babies. He thought a little bit more. Beth hadn't been abused by him that night. She was merely furious with him because of what he, Roger, had done to her sister.

After a long pregnant pause, Sophie then looked at him. "Beth hasn't yet discussed anything with me, but I know my sibling and him more than anyone else; although as it happens, I cannot speak for Beth, who is too traumatised to speak to me. All I can do is to piece together the mysterious jigsaw puzzle together using my own intuition. Roger loves Beth more than I. He usually tests his prowess out on me, before getting his way with her. I am merely as he has told me, just his blow-up doll. He got me up the stick soon after we met, and a few hours later he did the same to Beth. I am sure that after raping me, like the night she lost her virginity, he couldn't sleep over her and went for her too. I am sure he took her into his room and raped her last night." David's face went white. "She needs you more than ever, but she is rejecting you, because of her emotional injury and she isn't sure that you are strong enough for her." David in turn looked on aghast. "It wasn't Erik's fault, but he's my man and he didn't protect me from Roger, and that's why I punched him out of frustration."

Once again it seemed to David that the Anti-Christ had jumped the queue. He thought about himself and wondered what kind of man could be more stupid than to agree to a wedding ceremony conducted by that of his belle's ex? Like Beth, he wanted to do the right thing, and like her, he was taken advantage of. Both of them felt that having The Beast giving them away was a most loving deed of theirs and for that they had paid far too heavy a price.

Feeling distraught, he looked at her. "You might both be expecting his child!" He said as he found the story unbearable.

"Yes indeed! And Beth almost killed herself when you dumped her for carrying Roger's baby."

"I do not believe that so soon after giving birth to twins that she is pregnant again."

"And if she is, do you stand by her?"

"I do . . . She is my wife." He said trying to sound like a man of piety but instead his sincerity was that of a limp wrist handshake.

Sophie was shocked. Poor Beth, she deserved better than this; she thought. By then her own secret and personal desire for David had vanished into the thin air, despite the fact that he turned her on more than Erik and Roger combined. On top of that, another mystery was as to why she enjoyed making love to him when he was much more boring and predictable in the bed than The Beast. His less than moral self inadvertently awakened an inner need of hers to carry out the acts that her older colleagues had at the hotel in Buttermere been bragging about. She then thought about her animal masks, and his occasional cross-dressing not to mention her whipping of him, which she vowed to block out of her mind. With him now and dead and buried all of her perversions which took place between her and Roger, had to be erased out of her disturbed memories of acts she of which she was then ashamed of; in order for her recovery to begin. David left the room. He couldn't bear to be apart from Beth. Sophie wondered if Beth would try to take Erik away from her due to David's weakness. A part of her no longer cared. In her mind, all the men in her life were as weak as David and as perverted as Roger. Maybe Erik was more normal, but so battered and beaten psychologically from recent events in her life, she no longer trusted and believed in love.

Chapter 14

ECHO FROM ANOTHER REALM

David had gone through with so much and had lost his girlfriend and baby during labor not so very long ago; it was a mere ten months in fact. Like, Beth, an inveterate reader, he was probably downstairs in the library. Today things would work out well, Roger was dead and buried and they could now get on happily with their loving and peaceful lives. Any issues concerning Roger had to be dealt with without messing up her dear husband's life any further. Even so, a curious Beth looked at the bedside cupboard standing next to her side of the bed. She felt sick looking at the flowers in the vase with-

This is for the best parents in the world. Love and kisses Regina,

Written and found underneath the floral display on a piece of card in beautiful blue ink. It had been written in Polish so at least David wouldn't understand it. How the hell did he know these words in her native tongue anyway? Perhaps he wanted to put the blame on her fellow countryman, Erik. Even so, as dead as he was; he was still playing with her mind, as the reality was that he would live on forever in her mind was still sinking him.

She then looked inside the bedside cupboard as she was clutching at straws in finding out more about Roger. She did however find a letter and was happy to be in the knowledge that her three babies were still asleep.

The beautiful envelope had written on the cover in red ink:

My Dearest Beth

It had been written in his own handwriting and a tear or two ran down her face. Nervously she then opened up the letter, which too was handwritten and six pages long. He had written the letter just after he told her she was going to kill him the evening before and a few hours before he raped her. He was seeking revenge on her for the letter she had sent him from Easedale and placed his letter inside her bedside cupboard when he walked in looking for her while she was lying next to David.

My one and only Dear Beth,

I never wanted to fertilise either of you in your sleep with your second child, and in your case third child. I would much have preferred that when I impregnated your fecund bodies that you were both at least wide awake and enjoying our lovemaking just like the first time around and aware of what I was doing. I am however proud of the fact that like the lady in the painting; you have baby twins and an older toddler child. I trust that in several months' time that the similarities will become more than just a passing resemblance.

With that, she then froze and was terrified, he was dead, she had killed him, but he was still living on. Shaken and numb she had to continue with the reading, which had so far made sense to her.

In just six months' time, our oldest child will be looking on at you with greater fondness as you will be heavily pregnant and still breastfeeding our twins. I am sure that I have impregnated you for a third time. I am sure that you know in your heart, that the painting depicts not only your beautiful reality, but also that of my profound love for you. If only the painting were to be depicting you during your fourth pregnancy of ours, I am sure this one being only your third; that I would still be alive, and in turn you would be having another litter of noble blood to me later on. I am convinced that with you being so fertile as I, that a multiple pregnancy is on the cards as you are reading this. I wanted to have six children with you, there was plenty of time for this, but I feared that something bad would happen to our physical, passionate, and romantic union. As such you gave birth to twins last time, but this time and with a greater urgency I had no other choice than to make sure that you are expecting triplets. With me being dead I saw no need to wait and to impregnate you at the end of the year so that during the summer your maternal body would be glowing in front of my own very passionate and peaceful not to mention loving eyes.

With that, she was shaken. She had waited to make love to David on her wedding night, but sadly he was too intoxicated from the mead to consummate their wedded bliss. Surely, she was finally free from the beast. She had to make love to David as soon as possible. She looked around the room and jumped nervously as if Roger was in front of her and memories of when he secretly touched her pregnant belly and breasts came back to haunt her when she was with their first child and dating with David and later on with Erik. Then he, Roger, seemed to be more of a decent human being than the man he had became since her maiden birth. She had to read on; he was dead, and she needed to unlock the secrets from beyond the grave.

I saved your life. I saved Sophie's life too. Becoming a Christian was very difficult for my conscience. I knew me being a vicar made you so very proud of me. I also delighted in the power that being a member of the clergy was bestowed onto me, even though I remained until death a convinced atheist.

Beth was by then trembling with fear, but she had to read the end of this letter before her beloved returned or before her precious children woke up. They were rising later than usual; it was almost as if Roger was controlling their children's sleeping patterns so that she could read on while her mind was still fresh. Even so, she decided to leave the room and look for David, when suddenly she heard the latch on the bedroom door lock. In turn she then held her breath and as was clearly in fear too.

Consequently, she walked back to the bed and picked up the letter once more and held it in her shaky and sweaty hands.

I wish that I were alive to once more admire your maternal body, just like the second time, and to reminisce about the first time I fertilized you when we had so much excitement and love together during your maiden pregnancy. I respect you as my Venus Fly Catcher. As deadly as you are inside, you are surrounding in the flesh with your beautiful body. I could not bear to see neither you nor Sophie carrying someone else's child. In turn I must accept that my desire to have several babies with you has cost me my own life. Knowing that David will be enjoying the fruits of my success with your soon to be enormous boobs, hips like those of an elephant and, your Linea nigra, nature's own tattoo on your skin as well as the ever-deepening scarlet stretch mark on your left boob, fills me with great despair. I reluctantly accept that you will expect David to kiss your breasts, place his hands on your belly and to enjoy holding your juicy bottom as he climaxes inside of you while you ride him in the cowgirl position. In turn I beseech you to put the needs of our children first. If I could, I would demand that you pre-natal do not make love to David. Sadly, I respect that you might not honor my dying wish. If, however you see a need in making sure that our fourth or maybe even fifth and sixth, God willing, seventh child of ours in your womb will in turn be duly blessed, then, please take a deep breath, pause and read on. Please imagine how I must take a rest too, since writing this with my own blood is making me feel somewhat faint.

In turn, a terrified but somewhat hypnotised young lady, just twenty years of age, was at her deceased rapist's command, as she could feel the love, he had for her as he was feeling weak through his dripping blood and felt as though he was still there as she could still feel his movements the night before reverberating throughout the whole of her body.

She then looked around the room, only a few minutes had passed since she had picked up the letter, but it felt as though a day and a half had already gone by. As overwhelmed as she was, her curiosity was getting the better of her. In turn she picked up the letter as a faint spooky being like figure suddenly appeared, smiled at her before vanishing into the thin air as quickly as it came into her view and very nearly terrified the living daylights out of her.

Our children are of a noble blood. Please do not allow the semen of David's to enter your amniotic sac. One thing I must tell you, in order for any baby to be given the best chance is for you to listen to my modest pleas. My only regret is that I did not kill Erik and David, so that our children would have the best start in life, but I will not dwell on it.

She then froze. Had he done so, she would then have a traditional Christian family, but then she herself would have to have killed Sophie too. Neither bigamy, nor murder were for her very Christian.

As for our bairns, I had previously informed Sophie that any babies she would carry would be lawyers, politicians, scientists, and lecturers and thanks to my bloodline, the Illuminati. Yours though, given you are so loving, would have been the nurses, doctors, and teachers. Now of course, things are sadly very different. Please place your hand on your belly, so that any dark thoughts have been washed away as my love for you is cleansing you from heaven above and take a pregnant pause before reading on.

In turn she did as she was told and felt a warm glow in her heart as she had forgotten that he was dead and as far as she was concerned, he was still alive.

Shaken and in a trance, she then continued reading his hypnotic letter.

In killing me, you have unleashed a new desire of mine in having you as the queen bee of our hive. The children that you are carrying inside of you are the Illuminati. It is imperative that before you make love again you are fully aware that I have impregnated you for a third time. My final wish is that; you along with Sophie will be one hundred percent certain that you are both once again carrying my children and in turn will not be infecting them with the semen from your co adulterers. I do not in any way recognise your marriages, and our children have a right to know where they really came from. I have never loved anyone as much as you, Beth. Do you remember the jewellery I bought for you?

With that she was feeling so alone, where was David? If he really cared about her, he would be with her right now just when she needed him most, but now, it was Roger who was declaring his ultimate love for her, posthumously. Like the waves from the tide ebbing and flowing over the rocks, she felt as she herself was one little pebble. As each time she would be drying off from him; he would all of a sudden come rushing back to her in more ways than one and even as an echo from another realm.

She then looked around the children were still resting but breathing she could hear, fortunately. She then walked towards the door and tried to unlock it again until what appeared to be an apparition of Roger appeared and smiled at her before disappearing as she wondered if she was losing her own mind. Zombie like, she then returned to the bed and continued to read on.

I am delighted that on this beautiful earth maybe as many as six of our children will be healthily making our beloved Cumbria one beautiful garden of Eden. If only I had met, you a few years earlier. Perhaps now you would be pregnant for the fifth or even sixth time with me. So tender and so young, not knowing any different, you would have understood my pure intentions for you and your sister and to have saved you both from the necessary depopulation agenda which is now a fait accompli. Had your parents played their cards right and accepted me as their mature son-in-law, we could all be living as a big and happy family at High Close.

With that she was shaken, she had survived this far, he was thankfully dead, she had almost read the whole of his letter and she had to remain strong. Even so, the fact that he was admitting to her that he wished he had met her when she was still a child was simply too much for her, and those what for her were disgusting words of his which were an echo from another realm, made her feel better about her slaying of him. What a sick man, who could have saved her parents too, but had no intention in doing so. On top of that a vision came over her of a white-haired paedophile who had visited a hospital, raped an unconscious girl as a burly politician smoking a pipe walked up to the old man and a young-looking Roger before introducing the two of them to a female prime minister. With that her heart started beating wildly. Although Polish, thanks to his books, she was well read in British political history.

The door was still locked, visions kept appearing, and her babies were sleeping and the sooner that she finished off with reading the letter, the better.

While you have never thanked me for saving your life, I am sure that whenever you think about all the people who have died; that you know that you are special. Even back in the days when the masses were around, there was no one nearly as beautiful as Sophie, apart from you. My job is done; I live on through our children and we both couldn't have asked for more superior specimens than they. I have left my body and may you and Sophie eat my flesh as any loyal black widow spider would do. Eating me will more than help ease the symptoms of morning sickness, remember how bad your symptoms were when you were pregnant the first time and how the second time under my protection it wasn't so bad? As such, please call in at the Fish Inn, and inform them that they and my Illuminati friends from Cockermouth are invited to feast on me and to be your guest. They will know who is invited and will go round on horseback with the invitations. As you know, I love David, and wish that he was the father of your children. All I can hope is that with you as my mother, everything will fall into place, and I will explain this at the end of this letter. I promise to watch over you and your sister, especially you Beth, and that knowing as you are reading this that an egg white vaginal discharge is flowing out of you, fills me with delight. I am however feeling queasy as I must have lost a substantial amount of blood through writing this loving, yet poignant letter especially for you. Once again and before reading, the beautiful conception of our very own making is now taking place.

She then did as she was told and took off her skirt and in turn her knickers and looked at her middle body. Sure, enough she was having a milky colored discharge. Should she read on? Was she tempting fate in doing so, or should she be prepared for her fate? Worse still was that she could feel him almost losing consciousness as he wrote her his powerfully passionate and poignant tale which was pretty much smeared in that of his own precious blood.

This does not confirm your pregnancy. With that she smiled. It does; however, show you that you are fertile. Yesterday, I shot a load of cum inside of you just like the second time when you were then in turn pregnant. Remember that beautiful evening when we made love and I told you that I had hit the jackpot a second time with you! The first time I impregnated you the sign came the next day too, but I didn't know then so much about pregnancies as I do now. I am sure that the implantation will be taking place as soon as you calm down and before you will realise that you are once again with child. All I can is that I have died happily. Seeing the beautiful blemish on your left breast was the most beautiful way for me to part from this morbidly and depressing hell simply known as earth. At least thanks to you, I died happy. Only you can brighten up the place. If only other people were like you.

With that, the vision of his painting which depicted her heavily pregnant for the third time was staring in her terrified thoughts. She then thought about the time she was making love to him passionately just before the tsunami when the living was so much easier, when she admired the paintings of herself too.

Numb and wanting to escape from him she read the penultimate part. This was to be the final reading part; she had no intention in reading his twisted conclusion.

In the event that you do not have enough breasts to feed our babies simultaneously, I humbly request that Sophie will come to your rescue, since without you; I wouldn't have even bothered saving her. Wouldn't it be so good, for me to be growing inside of you and that you will feel closer to me than ever before. You will make a better mother for me than that of my own. Once you confirm in your heart this pregnancy, I will then be able to leave you in peace.

I will return back to you as an innocent baby girl in just ten- or eleven-months' time, with fair hair and be as innocent as my paternal grandmother. Your other babies will leave your womb one month before me, so that I your delicate princess will be able to grow a little more. Once I have been weaned, please make sure that David will look after me and teach me how to become a good daughter and sister so that one day I will be in every way the fair apple of your eye. I want him to read me bedtime stories, to teach me how to swim and for him to bring me up inside a traditional Christian home. As for David, he might not be the potent man I am, but at least in his heart, unlike myself: he isn't confused and knows what gender he is.

I painfully suspected as we were stood in front of the bookcase earlier together that your fondness for me was returning. Maybe had I waited another evening for the impregnation after another day of me being your loving host, you might not have killed me. Would you have agreed to have stayed another night? For that we will never know the answer as such; it is imperative that you carry on reading until the end of this letter.

With that a petrified young lady whose heart was beating out of control, went back towards the door, she tried to open it. Suddenly she heard a voice inside her confused head. "Beth, once you have read the final part of the letter, the door will be unlocked." She thought that she was going insane, was she schizophrenic? She had no choice other than to simply read on.

With us no longer being together, it was my own gut feeling and bathroom inspections rather than my sensual observation of your cycle that told me that I chose a great anniversary for your wedding. My birth which will coincide with the date of your wedding will remind you about your last impregnation by me in the flesh, and that of my death. Celebrating my birth and your wedding is enough for one day. The next day you can think about the last time we made love, and the day after my death. As for your twins, I would like them to be a reminder of the day we first met. Inside your womb, a little Robert, Mary, Dora and Regina will be born. As for Sophie, the birth of her third child will also be a memorial to Jan, but one even more special, but I am not yet sure as to how exactly.

With that she started to cry for her sister. What could be worse than having a genderless child? She asked herself in great fear and dread.

I am not doing this to harm you. I merely want you to share my great passion of life and death with our offspring. To understand how I picture myself climaxing inside of you like the tides coming in and bringing in the fish to feed the thousands. To understand my despair about the wasted precious sperm of mine, enough to produce millions of my babies, that oozes out of you like the corpses of the plebs floating downstream.

It is a pity that Sophie wasn't happy about me cheating on her with you. It is a pity I had to die. Sadly, as you know, I could not be yours exclusively as your spouse. Stay strong my dear, please purify me while I am safe inside your womb and as your daughter may all of my dreams come true.

Finally, this has been one exciting journey for us both. Please remain the woman you are, and I am sorry for any confusion you might have had through me. When I first saw your beautiful body in the flesh, I knew that the best days of my life were about to begin. You were so slim, your breasts small but pert and I knew then that a changing body of yours would be the closest thing to heaven for my eyes. Please do not be sad that I didn't enjoy your heavenly body as much as I wanted during your second pregnancy. I am now in a better place and heading inside of your womb.

Please do not worry about how weak I am feeling as I write this letter due to the fact that my blood has been so much drained away for the love of this letter. I will replenish myself with your milk and with the strength I will gain after my suckling of your scarlet breast put you back in the family way passionately as you are sleeping once more.

We come into this life alone, we leave this life alone.

I love you so much.

Yours forever, Roger.

P.S. Please be careful with my David. He is still full of my sperm, and in the event of you becoming pregnant again by him, don't be at all surprised if your fourth pregnancy ends up in producing mutual children of ours once again. My sperm is able to mutate inside him and spread right down into his testicles as neither of you will ever be free from me! While he will be able to enjoy the impregnation process with you, it is I who although dead who lives on with my posterity, which has been taken away from him. As for Erik and Sophie I am sure that they will want a mutual child together. Sadly, he is no longer able to deliver the goods. As a devoted sister, I ask thee to lend David to Sophie as a part of the impregnation process. It is for the best if Erik doesn't find out. If he does, he shouldn't be jealous of David. Even in death, Sophie, you, and I are bonded together with all of our precious posterity. Equally, I am forever indebted to you, have always loved the courage of your tenderness and during the next ten or eleven months I am incubating inside of you.

I made a few carbon copies of this letter, which can be found in my cupboard. I also forgot to mention two important points. Firstly, I must evince that question surrounding you being interred. We will be together forever, in death. In the Kirkyard and close to my ancestor William Wordsworth I will as your beloved daughter lie between you and David. Until then, I wish the three of us a long life. Secondly, I am a virus. Nothing more than a common cold and you have released me into the air. In the vast majority of cases, especially the young and healthy you won't have any noticeable symptoms. If you are about to die with serious underlying health issues, I could finish you off. It is imperative, that you self-isolate and lock yourself away until you give birth and wash your hands every twenty minutes with soap for twenty seconds. I don't want to become a pandemic, stay SAFE.

Your devoted and loving daughter, Regina xxx

Trembling in fright that she might be pregnant again and this time with triplets, she couldn't understand why he had even implied that she might be with quads. He was messing up her mind to say the least. Her breasts were tingling as she remembered that he had been drinking before he got inside of her as she was scared that she was noticing the first sign that she was portentously with child again. Maybe he didn't know what he was writing about. Pregnancy symptoms didn't show up so suddenly. The door then unlocked, she had never been so frightened in her life. Unexpectedly for her, David appeared, and she wished that she had killed him instead of Roger.

David looked into her eyes, for the first time ever they looked demonic. His poor wife, the killing of Roger had been too much for her. He had to reassure her. He had to say sorry for leaving her alone while he was awake on the couch thinking. He then put his arms around her. She then lashed out meekly with her arms and legs in order to extricate herself from him as memories flooded back to her when she fled The Howe and ran to Ambleside during her final hours as a maiden. Had he really been her true love, her knight in shining armour, when she was in her greatest hour of need, he would have been there for her. He could have gone to The Howe with her to collect her passport. If only he had had the courage to swoon her, her life, their lives would now be so much more beautiful. Instead, and with great contempt, she looked at him as if he were her posthumous rapist. "I want you to read this letter." She said to him, before handing him the paper and walking to the door, which was then unlocked, in case she needed to flee and leave Satan's babies with him, her husband, whom she was terrified of.

A mere fifteen minutes had passed since she had found the letter, but she wanted David to finish it as soon as possible. Surely David would leave her alone in peace, since their marriage was a sham and now, she could mourn over Roger forever so long as David left her in solace. She simply felt that Roger loved her much more than David did, since he wrote passionate letters to her, showered her with jewellery and impregnated her three times. On top of that, although she had never seen such a passionate and disgusting letter as that of which she had just read; the fact that wrote it with his own dripping blood; meant that she must have been extra special for him.

After reading he looked at her. "I still love you." David said. In his eyes he sounded like a gentleman, he spoke deeply, but in her ears, he looked like a fairy as he wasn't standing upright and hadn't yet even consummated their marriage. How could he love her after all the humiliation he had been through thanks to her? On top of that, Roger was a real man, he had kept his honor and his genetic code intact. She then looked at him with her by then somewhat beady eyes.

"And I still love him!" The relief of her confession seemed to enlarge her eyes as they appeared once more to those of their fish like selves. Even so her cold demeanour spoke volumes and radiated a fiery explosion of hellish hues stating that she wished that she had killed David instead of him. Then again, David had survived her second of violence which succumbed, only the flesh of Roger. She could still produce more babies with a posthumous Roger thanks to David, who was luckily for her carrying inside of his balls the dead man's super potent sperm.

Exhausted and trying to dismiss her frightening presence, he then got into bed as Beth despised him more than ever. He was a bastard, who thanks to him, Beth ended up with the twins to her rapist and now she was pregnant yet again. No matter what David would do, nothing could be right; he was nothing more than at best a beta male for her. She then took a deep breath as she wished that he would die, and that Roger would save her honor as an incarnation. With several babies to him she needed him more than ever. Given she loved Roger so much that she would have killed even her own sister for him. As for the real him, being of an old and seedy bald headed, beady eyed and bulbous nosed beast all she remembered was his jet-black hair and youthful appearance. As for his gender confusion, all she remembered was his passionate and potent pounding of her. As for his lies, all she remembered was his words of love for her.

As she calmed down, she then realized that David served a purpose for her and she could leave her unwanted babies with him. With David being so weak in her eyes; he deserved to look after someone else's children as though they were of his own. With Roger's sperm inside him he would never be able to produce any children of his own anyway and he wasn't the man that she thought he was. On top of that, this was all of his own making. For all she knew, he might have been enjoying the sodomising of

403

him by Roger and for all she knew it might have been a regular and sordid event behind her very own back even before the time when they were all living together at Fell End. Maybe they met together in the spinney close to the Wordsworth Trust. If he wanted to, he could have made her pregnant, but was simply too late. He simply was nothing more than an emasculated man for her. She then believed that she then knew the reason as to why he was so shy when she first met him. He had obviously met Roger before he met her.

Beth then left the room with the letter as her heart was beating wildly. She then walked to the room where her sister was sleeping and placed the letter underneath the door. She then walked down into the cellar. He was there; still as haughty as ever. As she saw him; she felt sick. As she saw him, she wanted him to arise from the dead and to fuck her senseless. How was she going to move his body into the kitchen?

Miraculously and all of a sudden, good, simple, down to earth and reliable Erik appeared and without saying a word they carried him upstairs to the front door of the house together and then he left as he heard Sophie screaming. Beth felt sick. How was she going to be able to pick up an object, study him with her eyes and then cut him up into pieces so that she could cook him in the pots? She then went to the front door and carried him into the kitchen as she placed him on the floor and without any help from Erik. She then felt as though she would pass out.

After taking a few deep breaths; she calmed down. At least it was Erik who had helped her earlier and David who would probably have been squeamish. Erik was the man who didn't analyze a thing and would never suspect that Roger was going to be on the menu. She then went back downstairs into the cellar. She looked around as a large black moth flew into her face and made her jump as she immediately closed her mouth. As it reached her mouth and tickled her, she accidentally opened her mouth as it flew inside her. There had been enough death in her life, she was going to be poisoned slowly with diarrhoea or worse she feared.

Luckily, the horror ended as quickly as it had begun, as the moth flew straight back out of her mouth as she found a hacksaw hanging on the wall. She then picked the rusty tool up and walked back into the kitchen. Feeling as though she was going to be sick, she started sawing off his head. After several minutes sawing the head it gruesomely fell off and suddenly drops of more or less dried blood splattered all over her clothes. The sawing process continued, as she sliced off his arms, she had pains running through her body. Fortunately, she was getting into the swing of things and was able to slice this part off quicker than the head. The legs being somewhat thicker, took a little longer. Eventually, Roger had been broken into pieces. At least the pots were large. So large that she could cook him in just one go, since the kitchen was that from a former large country guest house.

In turn she broke down. He was having his last laugh until she realized that in maybe two weeks' time, she would very well be suffering from violent bouts of morning sickness again. He wanted her to eat him so that he could laugh at her from the gates of hell. Still, she had to loyally carry out his final wish. Shaken and numb she realized that he wasn't going to return back to life. Then in pilot mode she started to calm down. Thanks to Roger being a pillar of society, they had plenty of gas cylinders and matches which were still filling many of the warehouses up and down the country.

The ignition was easy, but with plenty of water it would be a long heating process. She added the potatoes and vegetables. She stood there in front of the pots weeping. She missed him like crazy. As the smoke came from his boiling body, it wafted into her face and smelt somewhat disgusting as shivers went down her spine as a part of her wanted to taste him. Even worse was the ghoulish whisperings that started ringing in her ears. 'Fear not, this is not the end of me, my belle!' He said as she imagined him standing next to her wearing a mask as she felt as though she was drifting out of consciousness she felt as though his phallus was vibrating her womb to an eerie satisfaction. After two hours David arrived with her three children as she nearly jumped out of her skin upon seeing them. She needn't have worried, David was quiet. Suddenly her thoughts turned to Sophie. In turn she looked at David. 'I'm just going to make sure that my sister is OK.' She said as David merely nodded his head. Not wanting David to inspect the meal, she made sure that it was on a lower heat so that there was no danger of it, that being Roger, boiling over.

As she went to find Sophie, she froze. Sophie had lost her mind. Sophie was wailing. Erik who had a black eye from Sophie, was nursing the babies. She then looked at Erik. Please go downstairs with William and Jane, Sophie and I will follow. Beth hadn't noticed Erik's black eye, while Sophie looked like a crazed feral animal. Beth didn't flinch. 'Mummy, mummy, Sophie moaned at Beth.

'It's OK, everything is going to be fine. Said Beth who was scared in case both siblings were about to end up insane. Looking less crazed, Sophie burst out crying, as Beth joined in serenade with her.

'Beth.' Sophie said to Beth's relief that her sister wasn't suffering from distemper. 'After I looked at the letter with Erik, he then held my hands and smiled at me. He said that we should not dwell on what has happened and that we must focus on the present so that the future will turn out better. With that, Beth's heart was touched. David had said he loved her after he had read the letter, she then realized that she herself had been treating her husband contemptuously too. In turn she looked at Sophie dreamily.

'That's so romantic of Erik.' Said Beth.

'I told him that he was a pervert making love to someone who was carrying someone else's baby and punched him in the face, when in reality I wanted to strike Roger dead.'

'Oh my God, Sophie, I think that we had better go downstairs and meet up with our faithful, loyal and devoted men.'

In the dining room, the men stopped speaking when the girls entered, and this made the girls feel more than just unwanted. Beth went to the kitchen and checked the soup, and then sat down gracefully. After twenty minutes or so, Erik had prepared an enormous omelette with tomatoes and onions and they had plenty of milk and bread. Everyone was enjoying the breakfast dish, but there wasn't much joy passing through their lips verbally. The men hadn't paid enough compliments to the princesses. In fact, they hadn't said anything nice about them, just when they needed flattery more than ever. At the same time, they appreciated that they didn't deserve any praise from their beloveds either.

After eating, David looked up. 'We had better leave here tomorrow.' He said as Beth was delighted with his gentlemanly decisiveness.

'One of Roger's final wishes is that the local Illuminati feast on him. I haven't got the guts to call in at the Fish Inn. David, you will do this for me.' David simply nodded at her. He had every intention in doing the right thing, but as for his love towards her, it wasn't so unconditional as Beth desired. 'In turn we had best stay here another two nights so that we can make sure the pervert bosses of his are kept sweet. I am overwhelmed with everything; I can hardly breathe, and I would like to walk around the lake.' She said as David was relieved that she was acting sensibly again.

She wanted to absorb the serenity of the landscape with or without the others. Erik and Sophie were sat there silently. In so many ways, David and Beth were the leading couple.

'David and Erik, please make sure that the children are looked after properly.' Said Beth.

'Why don't you two ladies walk together, and Erik will look after the children and I will call in at the Fish Inn with the letter, so that they will not be searching for you Beth.' Said David. Beth then froze as she felt more than ever like Tess and was scared that she too would be hanged. All she could hope for was that David would help save her life. Even if he could, did she deserve his love? Even if she didn't deserve his love, she wanted him so badly.

The two sisters enjoyed their walk together which in the early autumnal balmy sunshine was pleasant to say the least. As they approached the lake both girls were in awe. 'I'm only twenty-one but I feel as though each pregnancy has added half a dozen years to my age.' Said Sophie as Beth looked at her intensively.

'To be quite honest, you look great; just a little bit curvier from the babies, and still look too young to be a mother!' She said cheerfully.

'What are we going to do if we are pregnant yet again?' Sophie said.

'To be honest, we have more important issues to deal with.' Beth said.

'What can be more important than bringing the children into this world?' Said Sophie.

'Now we must concentrate on David and Erik, I can't bear to think about bringing up several children on my own. The letter from Roger was horrendous. I am not thinking of myself as being pregnant, there's nothing I can do about it and just hope that tonight David will fuck me senseless, and I'll convince him that it is his child.'

'Or children.' Sophie said provocatively.

'All I want to do is to be good, and then the problems which are being sown such as God forbid a triple pregnancy will be shared and solved so long as I haven't lost my David. It is no good for us to bring up our children without a man, a father figure. They are our husbands after all; we didn't break our marriage vows, we were raped.' With that Sophie was speechless. Beth then started to look morose as she then thought more about Roger. 'To think that my poor David is nothing more than a carrier of Roger's DNA and posterity fills me with both grief and despair. It is all my fault.' Said Beth.

'Don't think about it, not everything he wrote is the truth. He was such a big liar about everything.' Said Sophie as Beth smiled at her but was worried that many of the evil things, he mentioned were actually truths of his, which she knew from past experience only too well. She then wondered why she herself had smiled, when after all she wanted to cry buckets of sorrow. As far as Sophie was concerned, Roger hadn't raped David.

Both girls continued on their way and admired the changing colors of the leaves, the waterfowl in abundance and the clean air which with them both coming from the city they would never take for granted. Even so, they had noticed that the sky was looking brighter than the previous time they were there together when human influence was in a greater abundance and contributing to darker and somewhat more polluted skies. They were also well aware of the fact that the winters were less stormy too and during summer there were more days with no wind.

As they stopped at one of the water's bays Beth was deep in thought. 'Can I tell you something in the strictest of confidence?'

'Betul you should know this by now.'

'On the stag night Roger took advantage of David.'

'Oh my God! How do you really know that this happened?'

'By chance I touched David's bottom and it was very sticky.' Beth said as she deep down found the story revolting and too painful to mention to even her sister.

'Don't get your feelings entangled with him. He did everything so that you would kill him; I only wish I had done it myself.' Said Sophie.

'No need to cry over spilled milk. I never in my life imagined myself in carrying out such a macabre act with the sword. I know he did this to prove a point, to prove that nothing is black and white and that everything is grey in his dramatic and twisted world, and that even I am capable of homicide.' Said a distraught Beth.

Sophie, who like Beth; had been raped by the beast just the previous night had to with all her psychological might for her vulnerable sister, remain composed. 'He might have masturbated himself.'

'Come on, his penis isn't up his bottom!'

'Oh no! This so gross, I remember that part in the letter, but I didn't believe it.' Said Sophie.

'Gross it is, but sadly it kind of turns me on.'

'How can it turn you on?' Said Sophie in utter horror.

'I know it sounds crazy but knowing that he somehow lives on helps me get over him better.' Beth said confused.

'Look Beth whatever you do, don't mention any of this to anyone! David must never hear of this.' She said as she was trying to keep her thoughts about her beloved but damaged sister to herself.

Around this time not far from where they were, David was being semi-detained at the Fish Inn, with his new acquaintances wearing animal masks, who were stood upright and staring at him. There was talk of hanging Beth. In the eyes of the law, she had assassinated Roger. David knew only too well that his days were numbered too. Even his strong arguments that David put forward in her defence weren't enough for her life to be spared from her treasonable offence. On top of that, he had to act soon but due to his nerves he was unable to find the last letter that Roger had written. After several minutes of him frantically looking for, 'Echoes from Another Realm,' the men at The Fish Inn were getting restless.

'Before we hang you, we want to shave you all over.' Said the member wearing a rat's mask.

'I haven't done anything wrong.' David said.

'That's what they all say. Please take off your clothes.' Said the rat masked man.

'I can't in front of you.' Said David trying to sound dignified.

'Very well, but when we show you a good fucking, we are going to see the whole of you in the naked flesh anyway.' The rat masked man continued. David started to take off his clothes and the letter fell out of his left side trouser pocket. In turn one of the members quickly grabbed the letter as they all sat down, with David standing there like a frightened rabbit and wearing just his underpants which smelled so bad thanks to his fears, which had also set off plenty of body odours of his as well as some produce from his unsettled stomach. Fortunately, the fear and terror in David's face meant that the Illuminati members present; felt that he was no threat. As he saw them reading the letter David was praying silently. At least the letter expressed Roger's desire to be reincarnated as David and Beth's daughter and it was for that reason alone his final wish, that the Illuminati couple living at the inn along with two friends from Cockermouth; that it was decided to leave the hapless newlyweds in peace. Even so, they didn't half laugh their heads off in front of David, when they read about David's rape and Roger's sperm living on inside his testicles.

As for the fact that Beth and David were innocents, this was not the issue. This wasn't a strong enough argument to spare them from capital punishment. The argument was simple. Roger needed them, and even if they were guilty, they now had every intention of looking after them.

Beth and David were no longer useless eaters. They were then useful vehicles for the agenda.

David had left, and all he could think about was the sterile environment he had just departed from. Before the tsunami, excessive hygiene was the norm. Even then, everything was looking so polished at the inn as though they were advertising for up market furniture which had just left a pristine factory, but he wondered how filthy these people were inside. He knew that they were even dirtier than the soiled rhetoric which had passed through their mouths to him as he felt as though he had been staring at Satanists who were even more evil than The Beast.

The members were still with their quorum. 'Simon will be kept updated along with Busby.' Said the Buttermere member: as he was sat deferentially to the others with him being the junior member.

'Will be interesting to see what they think about the circumstances. I mean the girls in theory are lapsed Jews.' Said the larger of the two men from Cockermouth.

'What do you mean, Beth is a devout Catholic.' Said the other member from Cockermouth.

'Yes, fourth generation I believe. If, however we wish to dig some dirt up, we can use her origins. Simon another lapsed Jew, but atheist, will approve of this.' Said the first Cockermouth member.

'What plans for religion do they have regarding the children?' Asked the Fish Inn member.

'I have no idea. We are Marxists, and we are still dealing with things by stealth. We must first allow things to calm down. I am sure that a new religion will take over, but this is not priority just now.' Said the second member.

'I think we need to accept, that now that they have a purpose for us, those commoners will need to be looked after as if they are one of us. In fact, they are now, whether we like it or not.' Said the junior member.

As the girls arrived back from their beautiful lakeside ramble, Beth was nervous; she simply didn't want to lose him. As she entered the former elegant guesthouse, she saw him and noticed that he was still quiet. He still had nothing to say to her. She loved him more than ever.

He was there right now and in her aching heart. Erik was quiet too, and Sophie kept on nervously asking him if he was alright. After serving the soup, Beth delighted in seeing David finish off her meal, and was pleased with herself and that she was doing the right thing for her man. She even felt as though he was as manly as Roger. At least David had never suffered from gender dysphoria and maybe Roger had raped him rather than in him being a willing and complicit partner. On top of that, he was a real gentleman in deed and not just in word. She loved him like no other.

Later that evening and in bed, both Erik and David fell asleep before their wives. Sophie, although still shaken with Roger's letter, fell instantly in sleep. Beth though, was thinking about the present. David didn't seem to love her. Beth was devastated. She couldn't sleep. Her mind went back to when David threatened to jilt her before he met Jennifer. Now was worse. In fact, it was much worse. Was she with triplets? For Beth concentrating on the present and to fix the future seemed to be one of a pipe dreams. Even if he stayed, was it real? Surely had this happened before the tsunami he would have left her for someone else, wouldn't he? Then again during the days of civilisation as she knew it, Roger wouldn't have done this to her for a third time and so soon after giving birth to twins.

Unable to sleep, she went down to the cellar just before midnight as she was overwhelmed with the power he was having over her even after his death. A white light between the pots, which were full of him, and her appeared. It didn't give off any signals directly, but as she closed her eyes, she heard music pulsating that gave her the impression that he was alive and that he was going to become a woman and that she would be his man. In fear she opened up her eyes and saw the white light that was growing as if it were some extending wire that was to connect them both like some umbilical chord. Suddenly she felt as though a magnetic force was connecting her to the light and that she was being paralysed both mentally and physically. The idea of being freed from child rearing due to him had some therapeutic effect on her, but as she came round to her senses and saw herself as a man and him as a woman her heart started beating wildly as she felt as though she was literally scared to death. It was then and with all of her might she fled the scene in terror.

Back in her bed, too scared to keep her eyes open, too scared to close them her body took charge and she fell asleep regardless.

The next day Beth was busy in the kitchen with David after he and Erik had carried the pots full of Roger that had been fermenting somewhat in the cellar. Erik and Sophie were cleaning and looking after the children as well as preparing the place for their unwelcome VIP Guests. The fear and the unknown were daunting to say the least. As they were waiting the fear was something like that of watching the news daily as though a virus was coming closer and closer to the viewer until it hit their neighbourhood and with everything in lock-down or more to point, Martial Law. Would these silver-spooned beings understand that not all people were capable of providing the hygiene, the atmosphere, the cuisine of which these clinical members of the elite required? Only her faith in the Lord Jesus and his maker were keeping her suicidal thoughts on hold. All she knew was that; she had to believe that it was better for someone else to kill her as opposed to she herself seeing to her own demise. As far as she was concerned, the game was up; they were going to murder her. So far in her tumultuous mind her story mirrored that of Tess.

The six male guests arrived for the luncheon along with plenty of gifts. They were all wearing masks of animals, which Beth recognized from a Stanley Kubrick movie and she was in turn terrified. Sophie though, wanted to burst out laughing. Erik wanted to punch the living daylights out of them, especially if someone would touch his Sophie, but restrained himself, while David was worried about one of the men still wanting to make love to him. They didn't have much to say, they simply handed over the presents towards before they sat down. Politely, Beth opened up hers first it was a big soft bag. In great trepidation she opened it. The garments were of the highest quality. In six separate sealed packets and looked very exquisite. 'Thank you so much. Why do they have the numbers from one to six on them?' She asked curiously.

'Roger gave us your measurements and the first packet is for now, the first trimester. The second packet is for the first half of the second trimester. The third is for the second half of the second trimester. Then as you will be heading full speed into your voluptuousness maternity, we have a packet for each month. Roger hasn't left you, and as you know he wants you to look sexy for him.' Said the rat masked man. With that, both shaken girls placed their hands onto their mouths and felt ashamed for the humiliation that their husbands were going through with too.

Sophie's bag was much smaller, and as she opened it, she saw beautiful shoes for a new-born as well as well several other items. As much as she hated the seedy atmosphere, she looked defiantly into the eyes of the men. 'Thank you, what sex will our children be?' She asked accidentally with Greta on her mind. With that there was a round of thunderous laughter, which sickened the innocent hosts.

'The measurements he gave us couldn't determine what kind of baby you would be carrying!' Said the rat masked man.

David had been given a good supply of pregnancy creams while Erik had been given plenty of bars of dark chocolate. They didn't ask, but the words sexy and frumpy went across their minds.

Even more daunting for the newly married couples was the next round of horror which started with the soup. This had been served by Erik. 'We recognise David and Beth as the parents of Roger's afterlife and in turn you will be protected and informed in due course of our plans for them. On top of that, Sophie is to be protected too, thanks to Roger's impregnations of her.' Said the rat masked man as he then stared into Erik's eyes. Erik remained silent. Sophie burst into tears.

'Erik, Erik, Erik!' Cried Sophie.

'Are you sure you are quite happy in standing by this woman who is only with you because she can't find anyone else? Then again, I guess she has met her match in you!' Said the rat masked man. Erik didn't respond. The man was angry. 'Get down on your hands and knees!' Again, he refused, and the man went up to him and placed his hands on his groin. With that Sophie was in shock, while Beth started screaming.

'OK, I will get down on my hands and knees.' After getting down on his hands and knees he looked at the man. 'I love Sophie and I take my marriage vows seriously.' Said Erik. With that the mood changed and as the Illuminati members present burst out laughing Erik went back and sat down.

Sophie and Beth then served the main dish before sitting down again. The creepy guests of honor studied the meal, together they smelt Roger's aroma and then tucked in morsel by morsel. The sight of Roger's flesh was so beautifully in tune with their ideals as to how he should be cooked that they could almost hear him, Roger, praising the cook as they started to eat him. Their tongues in turn enjoyed the feel of his flesh which tasted along with the vegetables to be of one delicious concoction. 'Excellent meal.' Said the biggest member of the party.

'You are the best chefs! It is the best human flesh I have ever eaten!' Said the almost equally enormous blob sat next to him. Those from Fell End simply kept their heads down and ate in order not to offend their cannibalistic bosses. Even so, this was probably the worst suffering that they had ever endured in their lives.

'You might never have eaten human before, but we are satisfied with the way you have cooked him, he has the right shade of brown. He is neither too raw nor too burnt.' Said the most evil looking one of the rat pack members. For some reason, his emotionless disguise appeared more sinister than the other masks. In fact, he was a special guest of honor.

They continued eating and the atmosphere turned somewhat light-hearted. 'He smells better on our plates than when he is trying to get something out of us!' Smiled George as his henchmen started laughing.

'I have a morsel of him etched between my two middle lower teeth. Busby said cheerfully.

Previously, there had been plans to assassinate Roger on the grounds that he was a liability. Simon George: was in Lancaster and was planning to assess Roger's mental health. He was surprised that other NWO members found Roger unhinged, since having met the guy, he found him incredibly charismatic and something like a Gallic version of Bono from U2. Very quickly, as soon as David informed them of his death, one of them set off by coach in order to bring the slimy Hungarian snake to this very banquet in Buttermere. Originally it was only a luncheon, but George had ordered Beth to cook the man he had murdered at Lancaster too; and he was brought along in his carriage. The man: was just a civil servant and like David Kelly, he happened to be at the wrong place at the wrong time. At least the guests were responsible for sawing off his head and dismembering his limbs and other bodily parts.

Just as Beth was starting to get over the fact that her nerves had given her diarrhoea, she walked back into the dining room as she returned from the bathroom. Somehow as she walked back into the room, she felt more uncomfortable then when she had left. In fact, she wanted to walk back to the bathroom. 'Beth, we would like you to stay as a special guest of ours and reside at our hospital in Lancaster until Roger is safely delivered as your daughter.' Said one of the masked members.

'No please, don't! The mental health of the mother is so important. I am just a simple country girl and my heart is in Langdale.' She said looking like a damsel in distress from her plight.

'Don't worry we were only joking!' Said a feline masked George.

'Hygiene standards are amazing here. We have nothing at all to worry about.' Said the first member. 'Thank you.' She said. With that a terrified Beth felt as though her bottom was about to pass liquids as opposed to solids once more.

'You are lucky that we no longer have the technology to transplant the embryos into another womb.' With that, the girls tried not to give anything away with their facial expressions and were relieved that they were not micro-chipped. 'The girls and I have more in common than their stooges realise.' Finished George. With that Beth went red in the face. She certainly didn't want her Jewish roots to be revealed to the men in her life. She was born a Christian and didn't want scumbags such as the atheist snake telling her how she was allowed to portray herself. Simon George was paying women to say that they were men, and men to say that they were women and for Beth this was a much bigger lie than for her to say that she was a follower of Jesus. While Sophie sat there impassively, Erik and David were raging full of anger inside.

As for a joke: it simply was originally intended to be an order. Beth had had a very lucky escape indeed from these very same men who were in charge of Martial Law.

That evening Beth, Sophie, David, and Erik were relieved that they had survived the seven-hour ordeal. After the men left; they still felt as though they were still being watched by Roger. They could have been murdered for disloyalty towards Roger as David from his meeting at the Fish Inn knew only too well. As for the visit, had Roger not been cooked to their satisfaction who knows what the consequences might have been? It was with great fortune that Beth had added plenty of vegetables. Had she cooked him as plain steaks, with the meat being on its own, the flavour might have gone awry. With plenty of vegetables fermenting with each other it was much harder to make a mess out of Roger.

Scared to death of the Illuminati, they didn't mention to them about their impending departure.

Poor Beth, she spent much of the night sat on the toilet. All she could think about was the words from the Illuminati bosses ringing in her head. All she wanted to do was to hate Roger. Equally, his letter had beguiled her. What man could express both love and hatred in such eloquent prose? How could an atheist, make her feel that it was she, and not he, who deserved perdition? All his hateful acts towards her, his lies, his deceit, his perverted thoughts had all been carried out with a passion, obsession and love for her which no other man could ever offer her.

As for David and Erik, they had no idea as to what Simon George was speaking about when he implied that he had more in common with the girls than they wanted their men to realise. The men from Fell End simply saw him as an ugly, perverted, seedy and dirty old man.

It seemed as though Beth hadn't suffered enough. As she left the toilet and was looking for her bed, Roger appeared wearing a mask as she then tried to touch him. 'Have some respect for me. You should give me at least six feet so that neither of us can contaminate each other with our viruses. I injected myself into your body in every sense of the word. My dear belle, never forget I will be linked inside you for the next twelve months as your longest pregnancy lasting one year, will result in me being your daughter.' It was then that he faded as she wanted to scream and just before she did; he returned, 'calm down my dear,' he said as he placed his fingers on her lips. The smell was overpowering and made her feel nauseous, while his slimy touch didn't in any way feel human. 'If you scream then this mask on my face will be embedded deep inside your throat as you will never be able to speak again.' Wanting to be sick, she eventually found her way back to her bed and was too terrified to realize that this time he was a ghost no more. An acid taste went inside her mouth as memories of his odours from the kitchen tasted stronger than when he had touched her.

As she entered her room for the night, a strange androgynous cyborg looking being appeared in the dark that was illuminated from the energy inside of it. At least she knew to remain calm, as fears of being masked and injected from a greater evil than she had already experienced kept her silent.

Instead of visions of him, all she saw was her bookcase turning to red as all her prized books were engulfed in flames as she saw a vision of Adolph Hitler dressed as a woman rising from the ashes of a war-torn Berlin spoke. 'Every transgender Slavic Jew is worth as much as ten white Germanic heterosexual Christians! Beth out yourself and bring out the Slavic and lesbian heritage of your mongrel heritage!'

Chapter 15

THE PHALLUS LIVES ON

The day after the feast and another solemn breakfast, David was the driver for his family, and Erik for his family. While the vehicles looked like relics from the nineteenth century, the family members were still dressed in matching clothing. The girls were dressed like the ladies they were, and the men were dressed like the gentlemen they were. As much as they had so many of their imperfections, they were still well-mannered country folk from the days of old. As they went over Whinlatter Pass; they felt as though they were being followed. Even as they were going down into the Vale of Keswick they felt as though they would be frogmarched back to the inn. In fact, as they were getting closer and closer to the town, they were at times deathly silent as they felt as though they were heading towards their very own guillotined and headless demise. They kept their thoughts to themselves, especially David who had been a witness regarding the secret and naked desires of the men in their disguises at the Fish Inn.

Five minutes after their departure, the Illuminati members had arrived at the guesthouse. They were not entirely convinced that the newly-weds still had a purpose for them and arrived to arrest them and to place the babies in temporary care until a decision had been reached as to either release or hang the parents. They also believed that; they may have been set up and that Roger hadn't written the letter. This would mean that even if pregnant, as non-carriers of his sacred posterity and typical commoners, they had no use for them.

For some reason, it was Simon who believed that the peasants were suspects. He had no reason for this. It was merely a whim. He himself was a great survivor and the sisters had origins closer to his than appeared on the surface. For him, Beth was simply playing some cat and mouse game against him and he was somewhat perturbed that she might be some distant surviving relative of his.

The seedy characters entered the building wearing their disguises. On seeing that they had in their eyes fled, with the place being so silent, the seedy characters then took off their sacred animal masks.

Roger's writings were then searched and seized. It was then that they felt that they should send out an arrest warrant for the residents of The Howe. Meanwhile they had other pressing things on their minds. The literary works of their hero had to be briefly read first. They had the vain hope that the answers to the mysteries surrounded Roger could be solved. In the past, depopulation was a priority. The problem then was how the elite could have economic growth for themselves exclusively. They were in deep despair too; since they were badly missing: Internet porn, soap operas, children's blood as well as exotic holidays and they didn't even have enough slaves to bring back the National Grid to power their beloved sybians. All they could hope was that hapless newly-weds had some purpose for them, since they were no longer excited in having more blood on their hands.

Walking around the building was an eye opener for them. 'What a splendid shrine this should be!' Said Busby.

'What happened to the paintings on his bedroom wall?' Asked Simon.

'I don't know, this is the first time I have been looking around here.' Said Busby.

'I sneaked into his room during the meal. It was amazing, five paintings, all of them serious wanking material!' Said Simon.

'So, they have absconded and ran off with his valuable treasures!' Said Busby.

'Yes indeed. That's a capital offence.'

'What about the paintings?'

'They were of the girl, Beth. Her as a young maiden naked in the first, pregnant in the second, slim again and blowing in the third one, and then pregnant again in the latter two paintings.'

'Makes my heartbeat wildly! Helen and I used to paint sketches of some of our child conquests when I was president. It also cost me a lot of money keeping everyone sweet when they were doing some kind of Watergate on me.' Busby said with feelings of both sentiment and anger.

'Anyway, we had better keep an eye on the others and see if we can find any revelations from Roger behind the grave.'

'More like below our bowels!' Said Busby smiling, with his remark the others started beaming.

The party of humble innocents and victims of a former satanic lawyer; stopped at the former Co-Op supermarket and were surprised to see that there were some good supplies of local produce. Keswick like Ambleside appeared to be getting back on her feet once more. After taking some delicacies and as official Illuminati they didn't need to stand in the queue and pay.

The journey back over Dunmail raise was a little bumpy with potholes springing up, but that was the least of their worries. They thought about the big knobs they had met at the feast. All of them looked sinister to say the least. As Beth thought about Simon George, a lapsed Jew like her great-grandparents, her mind went back again to when she was going down the raise when Roger was taunting her about saving Jews. In short, she wondered if she was any better than George. Maybe Roger was right, and she could have saved fifty of her races from Manchester, but like

Simon George she turned her back on her own tribe and felt that she was indirectly responsible for the deaths of the many. Basically, she had a terrible and guilty impression of herself.

They were all silent as they were close to Fell End. At least Roger had been slain far away from their home. As they arrived the sisters took all of their belongings and the men drove down into Ambleside where they could leave the vehicles with a member of the clergy who knew David since he was a baby. Instead, the men were told that since the death of Roger, they had moved up higher within the ranks of the elite, Erik included and could keep both carriages along with the horses.

The two sisters were together seated solemnly after the children had been put to bed. After going through so much they had nothing to say until Beth started weeping. 'Beth, what is wrong sister, we are home now, everything will be fine now.'

'We are as evil as Simon George.'

'No Beth, we are not. It was one thing to hide from the Nazis as many Polish and Germans did and to convert. It was another thing to help the Nazis directly against your own people as Simon George did.' 'Roger wanted me to believe that the top Jews were behind Hitler.' She said looking as though she was looking nearer thirty than twenty, as the recent events were taking their toll seriously on her.

'Look, this depopulation agenda had obviously been in the making long before our parents were born. Please, I beg you to leave it alone, to move on with your life. The genocide is over. More people died in the tsunami than expected so we can now live-in peace.' She said smiling at her with the vain hope that her sister would calm down.

'Oh, so you want us to celebrate the holocaust!' She screamed.

'No, Beth; that is not what she meant, she simply meant that we don't have to live in fear of another disaster coming our way!' Said Erik who had been listening in on them both along with David since they were sat in the same room but at opposite ends. Like the women, the men were going through their own traumas. Wanting to keep their roots hidden in the destruction of Poland with all the lost records of her family no longer archived; the girls stopped speaking about their roots in front of the men.

She then calmed down; but her silence was making the others feel rather uneasy to say the least. 'OK, as someone who believes in love, I will do my best to survive. But what a waste, all that time and energy wasted because of evil. To think that our country-folk had children only for them to die and to perish, it breaks my heart. What reason did they have to produce children out of love when the world is so much full of hatred?' With that, nobody knew how to respond to Beth.

In Buttermere, the curious former colleagues of Roger had already dissected many of his writings and were holding an emergency meeting. 'Apart from the fact that they have moved to Fell End, nothing untoward from his revelations is of any news for us.' Said Simon George. 'I do believe, once again that those peasants are useful idiots for us.' He said. His mind was still full of confusion and schizophrenia about them, but he knew that once they had been slain, it would be difficult to bring them back to life. 'They deserved to die, but there is no other way out of this. How would Roger survive if his mother, Beth, the one he impregnated died?' The room was silent as the other five male members of the NWO sat imperiously in their own macabre world of insanity. 'There is nothing more than I would like to do than to take the embryos out of her womb and insert them inside mine, but things have changed now that we no longer have the technology.' He said as the others were sat forlorn. 'David doesn't seem like in any way a threat to us. In some ways he reminds me of Gromyko, I bet he will do anything that Beth says. With her calling the shots, we might as well allow the other identical couple to live in peace. Imagine the humiliation these men must have in bringing up so many of his sacred descendants! As for the children they do need a father figure, but I am not so sure as to how much David can play that role!' He said as the others looked at him, saw him smiling and they all simply burst out laughing. 'Calm down everyone!' He said with glee. 'On an even brighter note, I will read you three extracts, which we can use as a part of a process and those four clowns we met yesterday will be our vehicles. Just listen to this extract from his diary.' The others sat there in great trepidation. 'David and I will make very good brothers in law. The most nourishing finding for me during our meeting; was of our hearts beating as one over the beauty of the Lakes. We both agreed that; the Ordnance Survey maps produced in the first decade of the New Millennium were simply the best. What a compliment for me! I am living close to the photo on the cover of the South East Map! Loughrigg Tarn! Yes, as David said. Oh! To walk from here to Wastwater, via Angle Tarn. To then walk on to Buttermere via Black Sail hut! As I myself, Roger, would then go onto Borrowdale and visit my satanic shrine at surprise view as a quick detour.' The politburo looking subordinates of George were in despair. One of them, Busby, happened to cough. The atmosphere was shaky to say the least.

All eyes were then on Busby. 'I wouldn't let the Indians get sight of this!' Said Busby.

'Thank you, Bill.' Said Simon arrogantly before reading on. 'Then I would via Watendlath go through Thirlmere and onto Ullswater. Yes, David has the same tastes as those of my own. Imagine the look on my children's faces as they could later on follow in the footsteps of these maps and camp at these four most heavenly aforementioned places. Loughrigg, Wastwater, Buttermere and Ullswater are four corners of the beautiful central lakes. Then I could go back via Grisedale and visit the shrine of the great poet before returning back to The Howe. Finally, David said that this is his dream trip too!' The room was silent. 'Don't you see, with these letters we can make sweet David as the beautiful face of Roger! As much as he deserves to die; we have our potential uses for him.' The members looked at each other, Busby nodded his head, and in turn the others quickly followed suit.

What was odd about these cold-hearted killers was simply the image that they portrayed of themselves. In the public eye they came across as calm, cool and collected. In reality, these psychopaths were just as insane as a screaming transgender woman who might have claimed to have been Marilyn Monroe in a previous life, or one who might have reported an innocent mother who had misgendered him or her or whatever it was meant to be.

Simon then looked at the others, 'let me now read another extract. If any one of my homosexual desires were to resurface again, then I can think of no better purely heterosexual Christian male to be buggered up by myself than David.' Simon then placed the diary onto the table. So that he could take few mouthfuls of his drink before reading on.

The others were thinking about using David as a vehicle to carry out Roger's mission were in awe as well as wonder. 'How I long to kiss his lips, how much I hate him! One minute I want to wake up as his bitch, the next I want to kill him. The best revenge I seek on him in the event of my death, is that he will take my place as Satan's child, lover, prince and mother. As sweet and innocent she is Beth is my subservient damsel in distress. She will even at my request place the paintings on her wall after my death to remind that Christian wimp, who the father of her children is. If only I could be a fly on the wall and watch them making love with the fruits of my success depicting her carrying my children inside of her womb, as for the picture of her blowing me, what a perfect icing on the cake!'

With that, the room turned into an ambience of thunderous applause. The extracts sent a warm glow went through their hearts. 'Is that wimp David?' Asked Busby smiling.

'It is indeed.' Said George with a wicked smile on his face.

The die had been cast.

The next day and after a few moments silence at the then morbid atmosphere of the dining room table the newly-weds were sat looking miserable. At least the beagles were happy to have their loved ones back. 'Erik and I are going off on a Wordsworthian tour of the lakes tomorrow. We will be back. We need to let some steam off and will be sleeping in the wilds for two weeks at the most.' Said David, without much emotion.

'You can't just leave us!' Pleaded Beth.

'Our absences will heal you. When we return, we hope that you will both know what you want, and in turn we will have a new beginning.'

Said David formally as Beth burst out into tears. 'When we return you will both know whether you are with child or not to him, and, when we return, we expect your minds to be clear as to what you want from us.' He continued.

'But as our men, you should stay with us.' Said Sophie.

'Indeed, we should. But you have no respect for us, and we cannot deal with your menacing instability.' Said Erik as Sophie had a lump in her throat from his words.

'I am sorry David, please be with me while I am going through with the trauma of whether I am carrying his children again or not.' She said pleading as he was worried about his own manner, which appeared somewhat distant towards her to say the least.

Just as she was about to burst into another round of tears in order to help her get what she wanted out of him he composed himself even further, which in turn scared her as much as it attracted her to his newfound soothing masculine energy.

'It is the uncertainty that is sending your hormones into a dangerous volcanic destruction of our union. I deeply regret the way I treated you when you were for the first time with child. Even so, you need time to think. Are you going to forever bemoan about what could have been? There are now other concerns. If you are not pregnant; you will know if as a result of the rape whether or not you will want to as you promised me earlier to bear me a child. If you are pregnant you will know whether or not you want to be touched by me.' David said coldly.

Beth then went to the bathroom, where she cried and cried and cried. David was now showing an even worse side to his character than when he was weak. Now he was acting strong and as if he didn't care about her. When he was that weak insipid character who ran off to the cave, at least he was a man who wouldn't harm anyone. Now his cruelty was breaking her heart badly. In her mind, Roger was living on in more ways than one for her and seemed to be ruining her love life, posthumously. She felt as though he was living deep inside of David's body but without the passion.

She then froze; Roger didn't act so haughtily towards her, never! He was acting like Roger did in the courts as far as she knew.

In bed together and in the darkness, she looked at him. 'If I am such a black cloud for you, shouldn't you be in a different room tonight?'

'Please do not put ideas into my head. I have nothing more to say, I simply want to relax in peace no matter how much we are both suffering.' He then held her in his arms. She loved his touch so dearly. Was she just his friend? Why couldn't she be his one and only. In turn his protective but not so loving arms were killing her.

The silence was eerie and had to be broken, even if it preceded the death of their fragile union. 'Why did you make love to Roger?' She asked him boldly.

'Because of you and your love for him.' In turn she felt sick inside, as he was sounding more and more like Roger for her. Equally, he would more than just jump off a bridge for her. How could any guy be so weak she wondered as her mind was starting to spin out of control in this increasingly ambiguous and vile situation that she was in. 'He took advantage out of me. Since I met you my life has been simply of nothing but trouble. I almost wanted to kill myself when he took away my honor and I decided to keep that rape intact in my mind because I didn't want to ruin our wedding day, for you, because of my love for you and look at the price I have paid for my love and devotion to you. And you think I enjoyed it! You keep feeling sorry for yourself, at the same time you don't understand how much I have suffered too.' He said as he had simply had enough of everything.

He knew that he had said no wrong but was scared of losing her. Her silence was speaking volumes to him. She too was desperate. She was in need of his reassurance that he still liked her. As for love, she felt unworthy of it. 'I am sorry,' she said crying. 'Why didn't you open up your heart out to me earlier?' She said wanting the whole world to literally swallow her up.

'You are so wrapped up in your own problems that I was too scared to seek some emotional support from you. I know you were raped by that bastard. I know it was terrible of him, but there was a time when you wanted him. I never wanted him, never! Of course, raping a woman is wrong. At least though, it was heterosexual. How do you think I feel that not only did he rape me, but he carried out an act against me that I find so abhorrent? Not only that: it will have an effect on our lives and mankind forever!' He said as once more she then burst out crying and was feeling guilty. She was thankful when her mind went blank, and she fell instantly into her deathly and morbid sleep.

The following morning, Erik and David left promptly after their women had cooked them a hearty traditional English breakfast and prepared a large, packed lunch for them both. Their stomachs were full of butter, fried eggs, bacon, sausages, toast, and tea. As thankful as they were for their send off, the men were thoroughly relieved to be leaving what they saw as being an emotional prison in too many senses of the word and was connected with the girls either directly or indirectly.

Beth decided that she wanted David more than ever and didn't care whose baby she may or not be carrying. All she wanted was the man who first stole her heart at Rothay Park. All she could hope for was that this intelligent and attractive man didn't meet any other belles on his travels. At least she had recovered from her recent bout of diarrhoea. Her mind went back to breakfast time when she was holding back her tears and when Sophie was sat there in shock. All she could ponder was whether or not she should have done something to have prevented him from going off.

With sound travelling further than in the days of old and the gentle light air from the east and following their destination, the men decided not to speak until they were well away from Fell End. It was as they reached the point where they could observe the imposing view of Windermere that they breathed a sigh of relief and started speaking. 'I would like us to visit the coast.' Said Erik.

'As a Christian, I am not fully convinced that the flood was manmade. There had been talk only about the Morecambe Bay Tsunami, and I believe that it is a Bible prophecy, from Revelations, that came much sooner than we expected. I am worried in case it could happen again, like some kind of a belated reverberation. As such I have decided against a visit to the coast.' Said David.

'Thanks to Roger, we are now being looked after by the Illuminati.' Said Erik.

'What use is that if another flood occurs?' said David.

'That wasn't at all what I was meaning. I am just thinking that, like Roger, the mad monks of depravity who enjoyed wearing fauna masks were convinced that you are the father and mother of a soon to be reincarnated Beast, and that Beth is carrying him inside of her womb.'

'I am sure that as far as they are concerned, putting us under their auspices must be the bitterest pill that they have ever had to swallow. They must know deep down how much we despise them.' David said as he was thinking about the four places where he could replenish his supplies en route: Chapel Stile, Wasdale Head, Buttermere and Patterdale. He knew that both Keswick and Ambleside were starting to get back on their feet but wanted to stay clear of too much civilisation. He didn't want much fuss, just a quiet adventure in his beloved Cumbria. Equally, Erik thought about how they were probably fighting each other, but decided that their thoughts should move onto happier things.

Being close to his home, he knew the Co-Op shop in Chapel Stile only too well. Given they had only just set off on their tour, they didn't need anything. Out of curiosity they walked inside the store for a visit. Around fifty people, mostly off-comers were living in Langdale. The shop had fresh supplies of chocolate from Haute-Savoie France, a sub alpine region whose topography was above the flood limit and given it was close to Switzerland, there was no imminent desire to obliterate the peasants with nuclear warfare when the radiation would soon reach well to do Geneva. As such, unlike England, certain parts of the continent were getting back on their feet quickly. Even so, the French National Grid was out of action. As for the Swiss, they had been encouraged along with incentives to disperse to lowlands depending on their mother tongue, to areas such as Roger's Flanders as well as the lowlands of Northern Germany, where if the elite decided that there still too many Indians they could once again create another Red River. The only problem was with such a shortage of manpower was that they didn't have the means in order to enact such another genocide. Back to David and Erik, they left the shop with just some delicious confectionery. The man who now owned the shop, was the former Chief Executive of the Lake District National Park. As a junior Illuminati member, he quickly made sure that a telegram was sent onto his bosses at Cockermouth about the romantic walkers. As they continued on along Langdale, they were enjoying the colors of the leaves on the trees as they were a reminder that the easy days of summer were already behind them.

It was almost October and they felt as though they were experiencing four seasons within a day. They were camping at Angle Tarn. As they arrived the sun was shining with a gentle and welcoming breeze. They were feeling hot due to the walk and felt that summer was still lingering on. David went into the tarn for a swim and was quickly joined by Erik who left David on his own a few minutes later.

For both men it was good to spend some time on their own. Both were thinking about the other. Who had been treated worse themselves or the other? It was simply too much to decide. They hadn't discussed Roger's final wicked act on them, but they both knew from their spouses what had happened. Determining what was worse, was by no means simple. Roger hadn't raped Erik, but what happened to his testicles from Roger's bile, vomit or whatever poison was coming out of his mouth was too much to bear thinking about. David had been raped, but hopefully he hadn't contracted some disease from him, and even if he had, hopefully it wouldn't kill him.

He was in the water for nearly an hour, too long and as he got out, he was shivering and drying off in the by then weak sunshine and the wind had ominously picked up further somewhat, while Erik was eating. The sun then went down below the mountain, and he was experiencing the onset of hypothermia. In turn he simply got inside his sleeping bag and fell asleep hungry. Later that evening due to high winds, Erik and David spent most of the night holding up the tent's walls in order to keep the canvas intact. Unable to sleep all David could think about was they hadn't seen a sole since they headed up from Langdale.

That night and unable to sleep without him, she realized that she genuinely cared as to whose baby she might be carrying. For some reason she depicted herself running on the sands across the Bay and away from the stormy seas which as far as she was concerned was full of a virus. She had no idea as to the significance of this and wondered why her head was full of such a setting. As she woke up the next day, she no longer believed in God. Her life felt so empty, but she questioned what the purpose of being good was when the evil ones seemed to be having more than their own fair share of luck. She then cried, since just two years earlier her devout Catholic parents were so proud of her. She was the daughter who found the teachings of Christ as a manual for her life. Back then she was convinced that she would one day have a most beautiful life not just as a minor during her childhood but also of that as an adult. David's absence was killing her in more ways than one; she missed him in every sense of the word and was worried that he was seeking new pastures.

After a cold and sleepless night, David was of course very hungry the next morning. Even so, they decided not to eat until they arrived down in the valley. At least the winds were veering, even so they had to climb somewhat more, and the air was hairy once again to say the least as they were more exposed and a few hundred feet higher than the tarn.

Down in Wasdale both men were treated to a hero's welcome. Most of the inhabitants at Wasdale were sporty and some had small children. There were however two families with teenagers. One was a family with three boys, the other with two daughters. The girls were aged thirteen and fifteen. The father, Wayne Bakewell, had arrested men who were in his eyes grooming teenage girls and had helped put many behind bars. His former patch was at Stalybridge. Luckily for him and his family, at the time of the tsunami, he was staying with them at Black Sail youth hostel and heading towards Wasdale Hall. Unable to get into the youth hostel due to the flooding, they walked back tired and hungry to Wasdale Head.

Miraculously, the dwellers from the hamlet; were paying homage to Bill Ritson and were at a plaque dedicated to the man close to a waterfall and higher up the valley.

Very quickly he was given the old police house, which had since become his family home and once again he became a local bobby. The Bakewell's were simply so glad to be alive. After a while, his wife was concerned that there were no young men around and after one year her worries had moved onto him. In short, his daughters without any bachelor boys around would never marry.

As soon as he saw the young men in the Wasdale Head Inn, who were not so much younger than himself, he was delighted. Due to his past record, he agreed that his wife should do all the matchmaking. 'What an honor it is for us to meet you both!' He said.

'Thank you so much. We are just on a man's holiday before we settle down to the normal routine of family life.'

'How nice.' He said insincerely. His wife then came towards them.

'My name is Dora, after the poet's daughter.' She had already been given some background information about her new acquaintance.

'How nice I used to work at the Wordsworth Trust.' David said proudly as Dora smiled at him.

'This is my daughter Melissa; she is thirteen and thinks she is eighteen!'

'Hello.' She said.

'This is Julie she is fifteen and very mature for her age.

'Hello.' Julie, said shyly.

'Fine specimens don't you think?' Said Dora.

'One day they will make fine wives!' Said David diplomatically.

For some unknown reason the father came over and patted David on the back. Both Erik and David felt very uncomfortable. After several minutes of listening to the rambling mother, luckily for them the father, who sensed their unease, intervened. 'You must both be pretty tired after being out walking on the fells all day.' He said.

'We are, but it is well worth it.' Said David jovially. In fact, just like Erik he was happier than he had been for some time.

They were then treated well by the other drinkers. Everyone around them was heaping loads of praise onto them and they had no idea why. As for the inn, it wasn't very different prior to the genocide. There had never been a strong internet signal there and people went there to socialise with other drinkers and the establishment was a jovial place to be. Later on, they were then escorted to the policeman's home.

At dinner his wife was nervous, and he decided to lighten the atmosphere up somewhat. 'I am a police officer. I used to lock up paedophiles. But what would you do if all the men have died out and you have teenage daughters? I mean, I come from Manchester, I am now here, and you are the first young men to have arrived here since we have been here eighteen long months.'

'Yes, you are both handsome young men and have brought so much joy to our village!' Said his wife who although tidying up decided to come over and it was her place to be a matchmaker after all.

'I understand what you are saying. You have two very pretty daughters, but I am not attracted to young girls.' Said David.

'Neither am I. Said Erik.

'As pretty as they are; we prefer girls with women's bodies.

'Julie has already a woman's body. Take them now and when you are ready and in ten years' time the age gap won't be so serious.' Said the mother who seemed insulted to say the least.

'I am sorry, but we are both already married.' David said.

'I know and they are the mothers of someone else's children. Have some respect for yourselves.' Said the father. There was then an uncomfortable silence.

'If you are such a man of piety, would you have gone for a teenage girl when you were nearing thirty?' Asked the mother referring to the time when he met Beth aged eighteen and he himself was twenty-eight. She said playing the bad cop.

'Come on Doreen, don't exaggerate, it is that Roger who concerns me most of all. Fancy both those girls falling pregnant to a bald-headed man three times their ages! I feel sorry for these men, and I want to hear no more about it.' Said Wayne.

As for the daughters, both were feeling somewhat humiliated to say the least. 'Look Erik, you are Polish right?' Said the mother: while her husband was visiting the bathroom. 'The legal age of consent was fifteen in Poland; my daughter is in your law old enough.' She said, since thanks to the telegram she had been informed from the masked men from Cockermouth about two saintly gents who would almost biblically be passing through her village, and they had been given some useful tips about how to seduce a Polish man.

Both young men felt uncomfortable to say the least. The girls were ushered upstairs with their parents. 'What do you think of those handsome guys?'

'Mother, they are not interested in us.' Said the older child.

'That wasn't my question.' Said the mother.

'They are really handsome.' Said the younger child as her proud father arrived in on scene.

'Listen, your mother and I are going to leave you on your own with the men. We will be staying at the inn for the night. If you need us, you know where to find us. Before we leave, we will show the men their room for the night. I suggest that they have one of your rooms each.' He then smiled as the mother winked at them.

'You see those clothes of mine on the table.' Said the mother as the girls nodded their heads. 'Wear them and they will soon forget about your real ages.' Even before their parents left the room, the girls excitedly got changed into more grown-up attire.

Later after plenty of small talk with the parents, the men were ushered to their bedroom for the night by the parents so that they could make themselves at home with their rucksack and hopefully as far as the parents were concerned; for as long as possible. The parents left without saying goodbye to the men, because they didn't want to be seen as aiding and abetting two minors.

While the parents were away, Melissa and Julie were in the kitchen making sure that the apple crumble and hot chocolate was the way to the boys' hearts. Julie went upstairs. Realising that at fifteen she was legal in Erik's home country, she decided that he was the one for her, even though she had her eyes on David. 'Erik, me and Melissa have prepared a treat for you and David.' She said kindly.

'That's kind.' He said and was relieved that the parents weren't planning anything odd for them. His appreciative response gave her hope.

'I will be ready in a few minutes; I will inform David too.' He said. Melissa must have had a change of heart, since she too went upstairs and as she opened the door David wasn't so nervous.

'Are you ready for some apple crumble?'

'I am Julie.' He said not realising that she was the younger girl since her mother's outfits made her look more mature. Even so, he still found her too young.

Downstairs in the living room, the four of them were sat on the sofa. The girls had their mother's clothes on and made sure that their cleavages were protruding somewhat, and Julie looked indeed like a fully matured woman. Luckily for the girls the men were tired. David and Erik soon retired to the bedrooms and as soon as they were out of sight, after a few moments, the sisters started to giggle at one another.

After having a drink of tea together, they then went into their own double orthopaedic beds for the night. David was delighted. His back was aching, and he needed a good night's sleep, and the bed was the best he had ever slept in. Just before he started nodding off to sleep, he was in shock. 'Don't be afraid. I know you are a good man, and I am sorry for any embarrassment that my parents might have caused you. Just relax and we can sleep.' Said Melissa.

'I don't want to sound rude, but how can your father who is a police officer approve of this? I mean I am more than twice your age.'

'David, of course he would have preferred things to have been different. If a woman in her thirties was the last survivor on an island, and the only other being was a teenage boy, would she be a paedophile? Close your eyes and think about this.' David did as he was told. 'She is all alone with her two children, her husband who was the same age as herself died along with everyone else. She hasn't got the strength to do everything on her own and is afraid of beasts lurking around. She hasn't seen a man for days, apart from those of dead bodies. Suddenly a male, a teenage boy walks into her vision.' Melissa ends the story.

'Things are not so bad.' Said David somewhat shaken.

'They are bad enough.'

'At thirteen, I don't believe that this story is yours.'

'Are you saying that I am some silly young girl? Since the tsunami survivors including adults have had to grow up somewhat.'

'I need to sleep.' Said David, overwhelmed with everything.

Meanwhile, Erik was having the time of his life and didn't care if the whole of Wasdale Head could hear him.

As for their wives, it was Sophie who was behaving more stoically. After their routine and humble day of being devoted mothers who were faithfully waiting for their husbands they were sat together in the lonely lounge. 'I have lost my faith in serving God through Jesus.' Said Beth.

'I need faith more than ever before. I will pray daily, from the person who inspired me, I will pray for her, you too.' Said Sophie.

'How can I believe when so many people have died? So many adherents of our beloved Jesus died too.' Said Beth as she was bursting into tears.

'God didn't ask mankind to destroy himself. Millions of people believed just like Roger, that the world was overpopulated, so what else could our savior have done for his people when we hated all the beauty that he had created in his own image?' She said wisely.

'My God Sophie, you have answered all of my fears and doubts about my faith. Sadly, I am too weak to have any hope that what you say is now for me so relevant. As Roger said, all sinners must perish, so why am I still alive?'

'Oh Beth, you and David are the nicest people one could ever meet, who simply believe in love and in happiness.'

'No, no, I murdered him!'

'No Beth, many a time when David ran away from trouble you merely saw the coward in him. You cannot have it both ways.' She said as Beth was lost in her words yet unable to digest what she had said. So lonely both girls slept in the same bed that night as they would, nightly, do until the men came back.

Beth then stood up. 'What are you doing?' Asked Sophie. 'I need to wash my hands.' Said Beth.

'You have only just washed them.'

'But there is a deadly virus in the air because of Roger.'

'Let me look at your hands.' Asked Sophie as Beth did as she was told. As she saw her sister's flaky skin, Sophie was horrified.

'Carry on like this and your hands are going to drop off from being washed away and after David will dump you for insanity!'

'I must self-isolate for my own SAFETY and stay indoors until I give birth.' Said Beth to a shell-shocked Sophie. 'You are not pregnant, so what the hell are you playing at?'

The following day unashamedly Erik and Julie were kissing each other at the dining room table during breakfast. 'Love is such a wonderful thing.' Said Melissa deliberately making David feel uncomfortable.

'I am too tired to move on today, David.' Said Erik. David was terrified he wanted to leave and was scared of being another night in bed with someone other than Beth. At least the day was pleasant enough. The weather was fair. The four of them climbed up Scafell Pike. David enjoyed telling tales connected with all the famous people he knew who had climbed England's highest mountain, and the girls embarrassed him with all the praise for his intellect they were heaping at him. There were times when he thought about the hundreds of people, he saw on his previous walk connected with England's highest mountain, now the only people he would see were the members of his small walking party. There were stories that in the days of old, as many as then thousand people would visit this peak in one day and that the daily average was above half that figure. At the top they ate the packed which the girls had prepared for them. The men thought at first, they were going on a short stroll before they would move on, had left their luggage in the house. On top of that, Erik was already tired from his night of passion and after another walk in the mountains he was sure to spend another night at least with Julie.

It was their second night, and this time Melissa went to bed with David at the same time he did. Once inside the bed she began. 'What is worse for you, committing adultery or having underage sex?'

'Both are as bad as each other.' He said as he was scared of her intellect. What he didn't realise was that his suspicions were correct. These were not her own words; her mother had been coaching her so that she would be able to groom an older man.

'In the days of Wordsworth, the legal age for girls was twelve.'

'I am not interested, back then it was legal to rape a woman.'

'Please don't think of me as being a bitch, but every survivor in the Lakes knows that your wife is an adulterer. What are you going to do if she meets someone else, and you will never meet anyone else?' She said as David was angry, he had been waiting months for Beth, only for her ex to make her pregnant once more on their wedding night. He was for once feeling bitter about the way of the world. Feeling as though his blood pressure was rising, he simply nodded off to sleep.

'Beth, Beth!' He murmured.

'David!' She whispered. He opened his eyes. Still dark and without street lighting everything was black around him, but now back with his one and only beloved, this tired and exhausted man was in heaven. Finally, his marriage was consummated. As he got inside of her, she was simply in ecstasy and wanted him so much. There was no turning back and by then he realized that it was with Melissa he was committing fornication as well as underage sex with. By then, and to his horror, as far as he was concerned, it was too late for him to pull out of her, as his body was losing control from their pleasures and together, they came to one great loving crescendo.

The following day was spent around the lake. They walked to Wasdale Hall with views of The Screes across the waters and luckily for David they didn't walk on the lake path on the other side of the lake where previously mountain rescue teams were in action. Feeling guilty about everything, all he could think about was the so many crimes he had committed the night before. While under the New World Order there was nothing wrong with his actions, he was ashamed of himself. All he could was to seek solace in the fact that during the days of old, in the days of his grandparents' grandparents, there was nothing wrong with what he had done regarding underage sex. Was he a countrified gent or a barbarian? His mind was in turmoil. To make love to her again or not? Not to; he could simply say how deeply sorry he was. If he did it again, they had already made love anyway. His choice was either to show her that he had used her for the night, or to show her that he really was her paedophile lover. He hated himself, but all he could hear in his mind was Beth begging him to be a man. He felt as though he no longer really knew the meaning of the word.

Back at The Howe, Sophie walked into Beth's room. 'I am sorry, Beth, but I am leaving. You can have the whole house to yourself, and I will ask the men to leave you in peace so that you don't catch the virus.'

'But what happens if I fall ill, who will look after me, I might die alone.'

'I am sorry Beth, but I can't cope with this madness of yours; either you get yourself some fresh air and stop washing your scaly hands away or I am leaving you right now.' With that, Beth started to pull herself mentally and burst out crying.

'I am sorry, I am sorry! I just don't want to die!' With that Sophie put her arms around her crying sister.

On the third night the two bedrooms were cradles of love. The day after they walked around the valley and, in the evening, Julie cheekily wanted to try David out. At first, he was shocked, but given she was two years older he less of an excuse to go on about underage sex. After making love to someone aged only thirteen and with her looking all woman and at fifteen less inappropriate for him, he gave into her lust she had for him easily. Erik though was exhausted, and simply lay next to Melissa.

As far as David was concerned, the world had simply changed, he still kept his views on Christianity intact. He was cheating on his wife; that was surely more frowned on than in the days of old when the living was full of avarice and decadence. Now it seemed to him that the old patriarchy which made his stomach turn and allowed dirty old men to have their wicked way with young girls was now back in fashion. All he could feel about himself was shame and guilt and simply had no control. As much as he hated the lack of decency people had previously in the ancient regime, he hadn't expected that old men would be expected to take good care of young girls in the New World Order. No, he had expected to have settled down in his youth with a woman from his close circles. Sadly, both of his first relationships, although the same age as himself, were with female libertines who along with their hedonistic desires could have been little more than of Roger in drag.

Each evening as she went to bed, the strange vision of her running on the sands was becoming clearer. It appeared that it had nothing to do with stormy seas. Instead, the notion of her being chased by a being seemed to be getting stronger and with her being all alone she was scared that something was happening to David and either she needed to help him or that he no longer wanted to look after her.

Back at the serene setting of Wasdale Head, the next day the new lovebirds visited St. Olaf's Church. As far as David was concerned, he had committed so many sins. The yew trees in the grounds had a therapeutic effect on him while the others enjoyed the serenity of the place. As they left, at the end of the path which hit the track, the boys would turn right, and the girls would turn left. 'These beautiful days will always be treasured in our hearts.' Said Melissa who kissed David as Julie shed tears and was kissed in turn by Erik. In total they had spent four nights with these underage girls.

As they were leaving the valley, they were a little afraid in case the father would come out on horseback and arrest them. Anything was possible. 'Before the wipe out, it was becoming increasingly a crime to produce children with so many rules and regulations about the way a man could approach a woman. Now it seems that things are different. With a shortage of men, women and children it seems that impregnating women will soon become law.' Said Erik.

'I don't feel in any way good about what we did. Those girls are teenagers.'

'David, don't take everything so seriously. A man who gets turned on by a small child is sick, a pervert and deserves in my view to be poisoned but they both have fully matured bodies.'

'Even if they do, mentally they are still immature.'

'Well, there is nothing we can do about it now.' Said Erik who wanted the matter closed.

No matter what, they would always have fond memories of Scafell Pike which was on their right. David was meanwhile studying the vegetation. 'One thing I have noticed is that the valley is much more forested than before. Without modern machinery the trees are springing up much more.' Erik said as he had changed the subject which for David was quite fitting.

In some ways regarding humanity, Erik was right. The Common Purpose agenda was incoherent and had always been. Within it although they all supported minority rights, which was replacing the majority, not everyone wanted to see a mass wipe out. Simply put, the agenda had two phases. Phase one, support of LGBT against families as well as support of immigrants against indigenous people. This was a part of the liberal agenda of inclusiveness. Phase two was however more complicated. While minority rights activists had helped ferment madness and mayhem onto societies globally; this was not the full picture. Simply put, the minority activists wanted genocide of heterosexuals but not that of LGBT, while the real elite had simply wiped-out ninety-nine percent of the population and that of course included almost all of the LGBT community. Those with alternative sex lives were more attracted to the low-lying cities which were more prone to flooding. There they could feel free to live their lives more openly as opposed to in the more conservative highlands, where Church services had a stronger influence on the country-folk. Of course, in the UK, not just white, male, Christian, straight males, were wiped out, but blacks, Muslims, women and LGBT too. Simply put, this was not at all what the minority rights activists had envisaged.

The minority rights activists realized too late that; men such as Simon George were really looking forward to wiping out the human race apart from those who had the DNA of which they themselves approved of. That lucky DNA turned out to be very different to that of which the radical minority rights activists envisaged. They died before they had a chance to realise that they themselves had been betrayed by the so-called philanthropists. Simon George was actually a homophobic misogynist. His first two wives had divorced him because he treated them as if they were his servants. As for LGBT, as far as he was concerned the only good things about them was that they might be able to spread disease easier and help reduce the population due to as he saw, their disgustingly filthy and perverted sexual acts. Even so, he too had homosexual tendencies and put the blame on the fact that he had been traumatised during the Second World War. In reality he had been working for the enemies of his brethren and had done quite well himself out of the holocaust during his childhood.

They sat outside on a bench in front of the former Black Sail youth hostel. David had stayed there as a younger man. He thought about how he once walked there over from Eskdale and how on the way he met hostellers on that same day from Wastwater, Buttermere, Ennerdale and Borrowdale youth hostels. Now things were different. The walk was now so eerily silent and would be until they reached the next valley.

Buttermere was the highlight. It was so uncanny; the place was now full of dairy farms. Cows where everywhere, and local cheese was being produced abundantly along with Butter. It was definitely much more like it was two hundred years earlier. Some families had taken over the farms. The previous big farmers had been swamped in the tsunami. Some of the residents of the local hamlet of Newlands which was high above the Buttermere valley had been offered a free exchange of their humble dwellings on the condition that they became tenant farmers in the Buttermere and Borrowdale Valleys. As for being a resident it simply meant survivor. In the holiday cottages at the time of the tsunami many visitors from far away decided to stay. With the area being plunged back in time, what else could one do? Flights had been immediately cancelled and without electricity the modern world of travel became obsolete. As for the fittest they could like Erik had done, swim across the channel, and if they understood weather lore they might not get battered against the cliffs of Dover.

One walker was staying at low lying Barrow House youth hostel and had left just in time after breakfast. With the windy roads and paths, and the fact that he could no longer see or hear sounds from below the flood level meant that he was in another world as he had quickly and unawares headed towards safety. As he arrived at Watendlath, a local invited him in for a drink during the power cut, which turned out to be permanent. The walker then walked down into the valley and upon seeing that the youth hostel, where he was staying, would no longer open and that there were corpses inside the building he returned back to the friendly hamlet. He told everyone about the destruction in the valley was given a room and couldn't believe his luck when he was sent to a sheep farm at Gatesgarth, Buttermere. He was a Turk, and very grateful that he wasn't in Izmir and knew that like the rest of his family he too would have perished. David and Erik stayed with him for a few days and were given plenty of local cuisine.

The Turk, Murat, who had been fighting to save relationships in his home country almost died from the stress. He had four children. His wife was at home looking after their small children while he was working very long hours as a doctor. His wife had many friends who were female lawyers. They were jealous of their happy domestic life. Some of them had a child and were single divorced mothers. They encouraged her to cheat on her husband. After plenty of persuasion she did, and from then on, the marriage was broken. Now, this humanist was then living happily in the UK, and had blocked out his previous life. It was uncanny, he was planning to take his own life at the end of his English holiday, but the death and destruction around him eighteen months earlier had saved his life. His ex-wife had been planning to give him another round of hell in the family courts over the visitation rights of his children and his money. David and Erik enjoyed the time they spent with him and exchanged addresses and sent Christmas cards out during every following advent.

Now, while this part of the tale is interesting enough, what wasn't mentioned was that while they were staying there, three young maidens had been sent round. 'Hello, we have come to entertain you!' The oldest one said who seemed to be around fourteen years of age.

'I am sorry, but we are men!' Said Murat bemused.

'Oh, we are sorry, we had been told that with you being a Muslim that you might be into little girls!'

'This is really disgusting. Go back to whoever sent you here and tell them that they are immoral!'

Murat was badly bruised and shaken from what he saw as a grave insult to his honor. Equally he knew that his own country-folk had equally insulting views about the west. As far as he was concerned, as a child born in the 70's the world was harmonious before it became somewhat dystopian in the 90's. Luckily for him he was busy with his new friends and so this sensitive and humble man was able to have some pleasant conversation with his humble guests. Like David, he was an intellectual, and both swapped many of their thoughts and ideals while Erik too was of course fully participating in their discourse.

Alena George the granddaughter of Simon, had been told simply where she should go and all he said to her was quite simply, 'The Phallus, Lives on!' With that and being more or less in his inner circle, she knew that he was referring to Roger De Cadenet. A short while later a beautiful lady, Alena with long blonde curly hair aged thirty-two appeared on his doorstep with her two teenage daughters, Andrea aged fourteen and Michelle aged fifteen. He opened the door a little surprised. 'Hello dear, I have heard that a handsome Turkish delight is going to let me into his home.' She said looking alluringly as possible.

'I am pleased that such a beautiful woman has come round to see me, but I find things a little suspicious after me turning three prepubescent girls away from my estate.'

'Not to worry. My girls would like to meet the other men.'

'I am sorry, but as a Turk, I have to take good care of my guests.'

'I don't think you realise who I am, do you? I am Simon George's granddaughter.' She said as she was holding herself upright with her chest although covered in plenty of layers it appeared as though it was staring at him. With everything Murat almost passed out. She was indeed George's granddaughter, but a wild child at that and he never made any mention of her publicly. She was descended from a coherent family tree of teenage single mothers and her grandmother was already a teenage mother when George met her on holiday when he was twice her age in the late fifties and wanted a holiday romance in Cumbria.

Under the normal conditions he would have rather died than to let into his home some immoral mother and her innocent teenage daughters, no matter how attractive she was, instead his survival instinct kicked in. 'Please come inside.' Inside the house and to the living room she went along with her children, after the females had taken off their coats. Immediately she went to his bathroom. It was slightly odd her behavior. She looked around the bathroom saw that the toilet was exactly as to what she was used to and was delighted in seeing that he, although from the wrong side of the EU and from Turkey, had toilet paper.

At first everything seemed normal. He was sat with his male guests' side by side. As for the mother she was sat directly opposite him with her girls sat on each side of her. This happened on the first evening of boys' visit. In turn that night he arranged that; the sisters would sleep in one room, the boys in another room and Alena with him. First and foremost, on his mind was his new beautiful lady. He also trusted that the girls and the men were safe too, God willing.

Erik and David had just had a dose of teenage lovers. The girls were more beautiful and slightly more mature than their previous conquests and looked as regal like as their mother as well as being simply dressed to kill. As they entered their room, both of the men were delighted and after some small talk, the inevitable happened.

When Murat found out he was disturbed by these events to say the least. As a sensitive man, this could have pushed him off the edge. Luckily, Alena seemed to be madly in love with him. At least the girls weren't his own daughters. If they were, he could have killed the paedophiles. Instead, he tried to block these issues out of his highly thoughtful mind. On top of that, his male guests were simply victims too of this New World Order that had turned everything upside down. He had survived so far against all odds. Whatever went on between the sheets in the other rooms had to be of no concern of his.

David also persuaded Murat to become the new Vicar of Buttermere. They both agreed that he was a better member of the clergy than a previous atheist they could mention. He was living in England, the land of Christianity and felt completely at ease in serving his God through the church. In Turkey, he saw Islam as being the religion of his nation. He wasn't a Mosque goer, and for some reason, he loved the quaint English churches. No longer able to get back to his country, and wanting to get on with his life, he found solace in Christianity. Unlike with Roger, his services would have attendances and people would later on come afar from Keswick and Cockermouth. For now, though at least, his days as one of the clergy were a part of his future.

Around this time the strange visions that she had as she entered her bed seemed to be fading. Instead, she started to have dreams that were giving the answers as to what the meaning of her on the sands were simply all about. In short, an old man rose out of a crypt in front of a sand dune clothed in just his bones and started making love to her with his still fleshy phallus. With that she believed that the message was clear, if he, Roger, came back, she would love him forever and unconditionally. Without David, and feeling weak and vulnerable, she was scared more than ever of some marauding tribe coming from the Ullswater Valley. There she was, the former city girl and now she was scared of anyone outside of her family. Surely, with David gone, Roger would come back and save her.

A few days later and after spending a whole week at Murat's and then walking around Borrowdale, Erik and David missed their belles. It was a highly tortuous time for the men, but at least they could speak about their problems together. Both wanted to return home as soon as possible, but both didn't want to give up before the other. 'What do you think we should do about the women?' Asked Erik.

'Well, I think we need to control them. Under normal conditions they would be fallen women. I have always been the kind of man women rely on, but cheat on. I have morals, but most women don't. I mean Roger, is such as disgusting man. The girls are pretty stupid to have gotten themselves involved with him. They have both especially Beth teased him. We are both men. There are no other women, it makes no sense to stay alone.' Said David tongue and cheek. As for Beth teasing The Beast, that was when she was with Erik rather than himself, but he simply didn't wish to rub any more salt into his friend's wounds.

'Well, there are children whose parents would gladly marry them off to us as we know only too well.' Said Erik.

'I am not at all proud of our behavior the past few days.' Said David as a cloud of depression started coming over him. 'Had I remained celibate until I met Beth, this would have been much better for me than passion and pain I had from my childhood sweethearts who both dumped me.' Said David.

'Please don't cry over spilled milk. I spent years doing this when my partner fell pregnant and ran off many years ago.'

Not wishing to put David off Beth he had nothing more to say. David simply didn't reply he needed time to think more about how his beloved had let him down. He believed that people should work harder on their marriages and that he wasn't perfect himself either.

After an hour of silence and as they were approaching Watendlath, David began, 'I have been a very weak man. I don't blame Beth, I blame myself. Her pregnancies to him were avoidable and all because of myself.

I let her down three times. Before she even knew him, and when she was still a virgin, she smiled at me, and later that same day said hello to me. She was mine for the taking and wanted to lose her cherry to me. The second time; was when I dumped her because she was carrying his child. Had I remembered that I ignored her advances a few months earlier, I might have acted differently. I mean I wouldn't have dumped her for Jennifer. I was upset that she was carrying his child, I was angry that she tried to deceive me. I can't blame myself for the second pregnancy she had with Roger. At that time my partner was pregnant, and I rightly stood by her. As for the third time, I do. I like my sleep and I can be a bit lazy. I didn't enjoy the sleepless nights with the baby and was too tired to make love to her. It was around this time that Roger impregnated her for a third time instead of me. Yes, Erik, just like in the novel Tess, I ignored her, and I only have myself to blame. Beth was a pure woman. She is simply an angel, but the evil of which I myself am a part in helped to sully this poor loving maid from heaven. A man should be stronger than his lady; instead, I have been duly weak and was unable to shield her from Roger. You see, Erik, life hasn't really changed. Men and women have always been the same, and if a novel were ever to be written about Beth, Roger and I, the reader would simply have a lot of Deja vu from not just reading a book by Thomas Hardy, but probably from Melvyn Bragg too!' He said as Erik had a pain in his heart from the monologue, which was too close to comfort for himself.

At Patterdale news about them spread fast and in turn to the neighbouring and larger settlement of Glenridding. In many ways, both villages were of one, and just an over mile apart. They had certainly walked a long way that day since the walk from Buttermere was over twenty miles. Erik and David were seen as superstars on tour. In the Ullswater valley with a population of around two thousand, life was running smoother than anywhere else in the country including the cities, which were mostly low lying and still more or less wiped out. Here, a renaissance of sorts was taking place. The shops were open longer hours, and coins were in use once more. Even so there was a shortage of men.

Some of the males had been sent to guard the shops in places such as Keswick, Grasmere and Ambleside. In turn all the single teenage girls were flirting and teasing these boys who were often closer in age to their parents than to themselves. Michelle, who would be David's second girl with the same Christian or in politically correct terminology first name on this trip, and one of the older ones, was a blond sixteen-year-old bombshell with a voluptuous body. She knew that the men were married. Even so she had dreamt of a beautiful night and was sitting with her friend, Debbie, aged fifteen in the local pub and waiting for the men to arrive after dark and sweep them off their fidgety feet. The days of getting a career after university were over. In England there was demand for only Cambridge and Oxford undergraduates, and they simply weren't of this calibre, Lancaster maybe, but this former grand institution like even Durham was now surplus to goods. In the whole of the UK, there were then just three universities, the third being Edinburgh and Scotland had more or less become a foreign identity, and there had been talk that one day, the Scots would retake Cumbria and add it to their own nation. While the Scots like the British had been seriously wiped out, were still a part of the UK the two countries were building more and more psychological barriers between each other. Luckily, no warlord had taken charge in either London or Edinburgh, and still recovering from the destruction in so many ways this post war period, without a Marshall Plan, was more demanding to say the least.

Back to more pleasant matters, with not enough manpower and fears for the future, sexual activity between men and women was worshipped. There was even a statue of a heavily pregnant young woman in the centre of Glenridding. In some ways she was something akin to a goddess; on top of that this former village was now looking like a prosperous Victorian market town. For some reason, Roger hadn't thought about visiting this valley, he had been too busy with his two families. At Buttermere when he was free to roam around, he didn't. He was torn between his love of Beth, his Christian values and all the other confusing areas of his life and was simply languishing at Buttermere with his insanity.

Had he come here; he could have found plenty of maidens to have got his very own baby factory up and running. 'My oh my! This is exactly what I was on about! Now it seems that procreation is a virtue here!' Said Erik as he was in awe of this thriving settlement with plenty of young mothers and pregnant women walking around, as thoughts of settling down there were on his mind.

'They might not be dressed to the nines, but their simplicity and appreciation of the simple things in life makes them so highly desirable.'

'As far as I can tell, they are dressed lovely. They look like the women from Pride and Prejudice.'

'And here we are wearing our Craghoppers!' Said David as they both started to chuckle.

Evening came, and sure enough the girls honed in on Erik and David as they saw them sat alone. The night was beautiful for David and Erik. Neither could resist these two young girls, who lived a few houses away from each other. They made love that night and again in the morning. During lunch, the two pairs of couples met up and had lunch at the local cafe, but just like the women, the men seemed more engrossed with their women than with their brothers-in-law friendship. The girls though, wanted to meet up the next day. In between the meet ups, there was plenty of passion despite their parents downstairs. Once again, they met up with each other the pairs for lunch and once again the couples went back to their love making dens. The next day and after being with them for three days, the men were completely worn out from making love so much.

This time they had a quiet word when the girls were in the cafe's toilet. 'Should we stay and not return home?' Asked Erik.

'I think we should. Beth and Sophie have really let both of us down. I am so in love with Michelle. I know I don't know her so well, but the energy from her that I receive, is so electric, like I cannot explain in words. I am so happy to be with her.' Said David.

'So, we are going to stay here, or what?'

'Erik, we can't. Apart from the fact we married two stupid women, the Illuminati will kill us if they have no more use for us.' He said as shivers went down both of their spines.

'Let's just spend another night with them and go!' Said David.

Around this time Beth was fretting since two weeks had gone, and her love of her life had not returned. Her fears that he wouldn't return seemed to be materialising. On top of that, the boys were having the time of their lives and spending a fourth night with the same girls from Glenridding. The longer that they stayed, the more in love that they were with them. As each hour went by, the mothers of the children of their nemesis, Roger, were increasingly teary eyed as their men seemed to be enjoying their lives without them. On top of that, it was high time for them to be menstruating too. At least, the virus was the least of her worries she was outside as much as she could and only washing her hands after going to the toilet and before she was preparing a meal or eating. In turn, Beth's hands were healing quickly and were becoming once again soft and gentle.

After putting their babies to bed, the sisters were sat in front of their lounge log fire. Both were sat their sullenly and pining over their men as the atmosphere was of one waiting to hear the latest update of death. Their miseries had been plunged back to the days just after the tsunami when despite the lack of media; they were still able to revise in their minds the death toll. At first, they had been hopefully that five percent of the population had survived, until eventually they realized it was far less than a percent point. Now it seemed; that both David and Erik had committed suicide since they were no longer able to cope with the shame from Roger's wicked acts against them. Both girls had pains running through their bodies and felt as though at times they were finding it as difficult to breathe as the corpses they saw almost everywhere during those early apocalyptic days.

Beth started to cry, and as she did, Sophie came over to her. Without her saying anything, she knew that they were in the same situation together. They had always been close, they were just fourteen months apart, but now their lives were more intertwined than ever. With the men gone, they would have to act as both mothers and fathers for the safety and love of their children. They already had five to look after, and soon and to their great terror, that number could very well double.

'I have nothing to say. I don't want to talk about our lot, but I implore you to survive. Every day we survive is another day of freedom for our children. They are so happy and content with their lives; and it is selfish if we as a miserable minority ruin it for them.' Said Sophie and with that Beth took a deep breath.

'Thank you, my dear sister. And what if they are still alive?'

'If they are, we will be the last ones to find out. What is to stop them from going to the new capital of the Lake District at Glenridding?'

'As evil as he was, Roger didn't do such a thing.' Said Beth hoping that their men had some morals.

'He was working more directly under the Illuminati than they were. Maybe, he was scared of men like himself taking over Fell End. Given the chance, I'm sure he would have put some maidens in the family way before he became the vicar.' Sophie said as fears over the unknown like some grim reaper went across their minds. Inside both the girls was the feeling that their men were having a good time in every sense of the word and with other young women.

'I am going to bed: early to bed, early to rise.' Said Beth poetically.

'Me too . . . Sleep is a healer, and during these early days we feel more tired as we both know only too well.' Sophie said, who like her sister was scared about her future but simply decided not to further fan the flames of fear any farther. If they were going to be raped, or to end up dead due to a plague, there simply was no hiding place for them. Once it was their turn for the grim reaper, just like they knew for everyone else back home and the corpses they had seen on their doorstep, there was nothing that they could do.

Alena was lying in Murat's loving arms when both of her daughters came in and disturbed them. 'Mummy we have caught something; we are both feeling ill.'

'What's wrong?'

'We both feel tired and have noticed that there is some smell here, like some poison making us feel worse.' Their periods were not due for a few more days, but it seemed that he really was the one all almighty.

'The Phallus Lives On!' Said the mother rejoicing. By then, Murat was fully aware of certain aspects surrounding the main characters in this weird and disturbing tale for him. What else could he do but stay quiet if he wanted to stay alive?

That night she felt as though her visions and dreams were coming more into focus, and that the message was clearer. As she closed her eyes, all she could see was her breasts enlarging, her bottom wobbling again, and her belly growing. There was no doubt about it, she was with child again and she wondered how she would survive without her husband.

After the fourth night at the Ullswater valley they continued on their tour and were in view of Grisedale Tarn, Erik looked at David. 'To be honest, I am starting to really enjoy life and fucking young teenage girls senseless!' Said Erik.

'To be honest I'm not. It is disgusting like some shallow drug taking. How can we expect a woman to love us when we have such thoughts of promiscuity?' David said piously.

'You have a point. Why don't we visit all the girls and decide which one we love the most?'

'No, I think that this is a terrible and disgusting idea. After a while, the excitement in any new romance fades. Not always, but it usually does. Hopping around from womb to womb will not solve our problems.'

'Well, I am turning back.'

'What about the Illuminati?'

'Fuck those dirty bastards!' Said Erik as he then started walking back towards the eastern valley.

'Don't be long; I will wait here for your return. I can't go back on my own; the girls will think I have killed you.'

David sat down and read some poetry from Wordsworth. He didn't know what else he could do. Once again and alone in his thoughts, David was thinking about how empty the hills were. The village down below was much more enticing than the path in front of him. As for Erik, he was furious. Not with David, but with life in general. If only he had been born fifty years earlier, he thought, when the living was easy.

Less than one hour later, Erik was back with David who was still immersed with his poetry. David was waiting for him to take him with him back to the girls in the prosperous village. Erik did take the lead, he looked at David. 'We had better go back to our fallen women, hadn't we?' David stood up, he wasn't entirely sure who he meant by his phrase, but as he saw Erik looking towards the west and he knew that it was about their wives. As for their latest conquests, they were schoolgirls, but school hours were mostly in the mornings only, and the men simply walked around the valley waiting for their Cumbrian women to return home. In Wasdale and Buttermere, due to the exceptionally rural conditions, bunking off school was easier and more common. In both of these places, survival took precedent to education and many families relied on manpower during harvest time.

Chapter

A NEW BEGINNING

The return was a most joyous occasion and heralded Beth's belief in her faith once more. Feeling humbled, she thanked the Lord Jesus and his maker in sending to her and Sophie back their men. Upon their sighting, both of the mothers wanted to pamper their men. They returned one fine autumn afternoon in the middle of October after eighteen days away, which in the hearts and minds of the men, which included of course David, should have been for much longer. As for the girls, they were so relieved to say the least as they entered their grounds. William stood there in awe as he saw David. He then ran up to him, 'Da da da!' With that David was flattered and like him, Erik was struck with emotion too.

'Da da da!' Said Jane who was copying her half sibling and half cousin as both women felt as though they were the cats who had got the cream. Neither of them men were the parents of the toddlers, but that seemed to be of nobody's concern.

Very quickly both girls left their husbands in the garden with their oldest children. Erik though was somewhat anxious. He needed to inspect their grounds. Instead, things were not what he had anticipated since the wives had been holding the forts up stoically. With that and just as a small white cloud weakened the autumnal solar rays, in one instant he felt duly brought back down to earth morally with a bang. He was a married man after all; he had taken his beautiful wife on as her husband along with her children in tow. Instead, he had recently behaved as some sort of prolific cad just like the man whom he was so glad to have parted from this earth. Then, he wondered if he was any better than The Beast himself.

The dinner was delightful. The men would do the washing up, and the women had some motivation to pamper themselves up. As such, they both went to the bathrooms and trusted the men to look after the children. Instead, they didn't do the washing up. David started reading fairy tales from his head, while Erik did some bungling and entertaining improvisations to everyone's delight. After a long while, the women came down and were delighted that their children had been taken on by their husbands as if they were of their own flesh and blood. Feeling so loved and so wanted, the girls crept into the kitchen and did the washing up themselves.

That evening as Sophie and Erik were making love and Beth had for the first time since David's departure some private time with him in the living room. 'David, sit down.' She said to him as she wanted them both to drink tea together in the dining-room.' He then sat down

'I am sat down.'

'I am with child.' She blurted out. 'And it is probably a multiple birth.' She said embarrassed to say the least.

'I don't know about that.' David said.

'Do you still love me David?' She said in fear that he would leave her and sensed that he had been sleeping around on his tour.

'Every night I wanted to make love to you the last two weeks when I was away.' He said as he tried so hard to block thoughts of Michelle out of his mind. It was indeed a funny old world. There he was the educated moralist, yet it was Erik who had helped shape his re found love of his wife. It wasn't what Erik said or did; it was merely his body language which seemed to chime in so well with his commitment into making the children happy while their spouses were beautifying themselves up earlier that evening.

'And now?'

'My feelings have not changed, but from now on, you will obey me rather than the beast who gave you the Stockholm Syndrome.'

'I am not the drama queen you think I am.' She said a little annoyed but equally she was pleased to see him taking the lead.

'I see things in black and white, but with you, the most beautiful girl in the world, I place the needs of my heart above my normally devout values based on piety. From now on, I expect you to devote yourself to me and to look after your children, who I will in turn take on as my own. In turn I will look after you. You are still very young, and once your youngest child with Roger is old enough to swim, dress and draw, I expect you to enter a second round of motherhood and we will have some mutual children together.' With that she wanted to burst out crying with relief. His words were full of magic for her, he wanted to be more of a hands-on dad than Roger. On top of that the long wait for him had sent her passion for him into overdrive and the lovemaking was simply of one of heaven.

David seemed somewhat more adventurous in the bed with her. With that she had more suspicions about his recent trip. She was sure that out of guilt because of his cheating, that in order to cover his tracks, he was giving her the love making of the lifetime. Even so, as amorous, and passionate as he was then, his prowess was still only a shadow of that of The Beast's.

In fact, she was partly correct. While David felt guilty for his cheating on her, having sex with other women was bringing out a more adventurous and passionate side to him. Whenever he was making love to her, at the back of his mind were the memories of his romantic nights with the girls he hoped were simply a part of his never to be repeated wonderful holiday. In turn he was more virile than ever.

One hurdle she still had to get over was the paintings in Roger's former bedroom, which she brought over from Buttermere. She believed that with the pictures as part of a mark of respect for him, Roger's evil eyes over her would be more benign since she would be showing some respect towards him as if it were some perpetual eulogy. As for Roger's sperm, she had to forget about this and never mention this again to David. He was a man and expected to have some semblance of honor. She then hung the paintings on the bedroom walls she shared with David and placed them along with her apparent foolhardy fortitude. In turn although in no particular order all five paintings were hung on the four walls. Who in the right mind would be able to endure what she had? David was already thinking that the paintings were somewhat improper for the children but didn't want to upset her.

At a timely moment he looked at her. 'Darling let's forget about the past, not worry about the future and live for the present and things will turn out beautifully.' Said David whose words were then chiming in so well with those of her own. Of course, as a mother with three children to someone else and perhaps a multiple pregnancy on the way, she felt that David was the best bet for her and that she would have to work harder as from then on with their marriage, if she were to keep him. Shivers then went through her spine as she was worried that she wasn't married. Roger had told her so, hadn't he? Roger still had a lot of power over her, and why not? She was carrying his children as well as himself literally.

When it came to the theory of power, this was an obscene and unwelcoming concept for her. He had had so much abusive power over her. As such, how could she have questioned herself over her slaying of him? Surely that was the best thing that she had done, to the man who apart from all the evil things he had done to her, to all the members of her close circle as well as to humanity, she should have been content that he was gone. His evil gave her the strength and the power to kill him, and this was the problem. Could she ever forgive herself for carrying out such a wicked deed? Of lesser significance for her was that he had confused her. This was a woman whose femininity was unshakeable, yet he was a man who with seductive persuasion had convinced her that she was born into the wrong body. She was the good Catholic girl who was pro-life and procreation yet he, had shaken her world to the extent that made her question her own thoughts on this matter subconsciously and hating her less than pure self, she was angry with him. How then, could this woman not relish in his demise of her own making, and, due to his monstrous provocation? From then on, she never wanted to see a sword again.

For Beth, the most powerful weapon against hate was love. She was a pacifist, and this made her feel so powerful. Knowing that he had deliberately used all of his wicked strength to force her to kill him; meant that he had won. For him who believed in the most twisted forms of power, she knew that in killing him she was in his eyes completely weak. She would have to live with this for the rest of her life. She was going to give birth to him and wondered how much extra power he might as her daughter, a born-again Roger, be exerting over her. Was it her remorse in her slaying of him that was hurting her, or was it her pride that had been wounded that was her problem?

One group of people who had been following the footsteps of the gentlemen's tour were the masked men from Cockermouth. They knew who would meet up with the young men. They had simply arranged everything and given descriptions to the women they believed were of the right calibre. In fact, they were a part of a group that had been planning everything decades in advance. They were the ones who would carry the sacred descendants of their hero. All they could was to wait for the telegrams to arrive between two and three weeks after the departure of the men at Wasdale, Buttermere and Glenridding.

November arrived in and Sophie was experiencing much worse morning sickness than Beth. Apart from her missed period, Beth didn't feel pregnant. David was acting so lovey dovey towards her and she could tell by the look in his eyes that he found her looking lovely in the first flush of this pregnancy. Sometimes, though, he would quickly think of Michelle from Glenridding, but would easily dismiss her from his passionate thoughts of the wonderful nights they spent together. Beth was doing a similar thing too, only for her it was somewhat more difficult, and at times she couldn't get Roger out of her head. They, David, and she, were both equals when it came to infidelity, but wise enough not to spark any serious mutual distrust between them both. As if that wasn't bad enough, the thought that he had impregnated her and was now inside her womb made her feel more sick than she expected from her pregnancy sickness. Other times when she had fond memories of him, she was delighted that he as a she would re-enter her life once again.

Around this time, Erik and Sophie had moved into the smaller house in the grounds of Fell End. Beth had at least one more child than Sophie, and although the junior sibling, as a couple and married to David, she was a partner in the leading Illuminati couple at Fell End. Mr Bell's credentials were far superior to those of Mr Alexander. He had studied, English literature and history at Lancaster University, but didn't gloat about this in front of Beth, he knew only too well how much she had wanted to have gained a degree. His former work at Grasmere chimed in so well with his studies too. As for Erik, the name Alexander had connections with courageous well to do Polish Jews who fought for the British after fleeing their homeland, as such, Roger had inadvertently done him a favour.

'Why do you think all this horror happened?' Sophie asked as the two couples were sat drinking tea one evening in the living room.

'The elite did this of course to wipe us all out!' said Erik.

'I am keeping an open mind.' Said David as Beth was proud of his thoughtfulness.

'Go on enlighten us.' Said Beth.

'When I was ten, there was this foot and mouth disease, all over Cumbria and everything came literally to a standstill here. There are three explanations for this. One it is part of Bible prophecy, Revelations, a warning that we were all doomed and the floods were an act of God. Another theory is that; when the population is too high then disease through cattle and humans is more prolific and that what we went through is nature's way of controlling us. Then there is the theory that the elite did all this so that they could have more space for themselves only.'

'Which one do you believe then David?' asked Erik.

'It is possible that what happened is a combination of all the three theories.' Said David.

'So, you are just sitting on the fence.' Said Erik.

'I am a Christian, am I supposed to believe in a loving God or a God who is angry? Erik spoke about nuclear explosions. These would have been with men on the trigger. Or maybe God chose these evil sinners to do such things. To be quite honest all of this is simply beyond me.' Beth said.

'So, regarding Hitler, do we sit on the fence on that one, or was he an evil mass murdering genocidal bastard?' Said Erik.

'He was evil for sure.' Said Sophie.

"So was Roger then.' Said Erik. All eyes were on the girls and more so on Beth. All she could imagine was that the tides were rising and either she could run through them with her answers or simply sit and wait for them to subside. On top of that, she was worried that the deafening silence might make her react in a way that was uncomfortable for her. Voices were ringing her head telling her to blurt out that Roger was the love of her life. Instead, and to her great delight, he, David came up to her and simply kissed her. In showing her more love, than a deceased Roger, she was happy with her husband once more.

Michelle and Debbie had beautiful memories of their night with David and Erik and three weeks since he left, Michelle realized that she was with child. As for Debbie, she wondered why she wasn't experiencing sore breasts, a missed period and nausea. On top of that, she feared that she might have been infertile. In turn she slept with as many men as possible, married ones included. At the end of another monthly cycle and ten male conquests, she was depressed. Yet again she wasn't pregnant.

December arrived, and this was still a sensitive time for Beth who was still in the early days of her third pregnancy. It was also the time when she received an official letter from Lancaster. On top of that, her sister had received one too.

Dear Bethany Bell,

As I am sure you are only too well aware, we are now living once again in feminist times. In turn as the lady of the house, it is with great pleasure that I am sending you this letter, which will make you proud of your husband, David Bell. Normally, as soon as we heard the wonderful news that your husband had managed to change a third parties' circumstances forever, we should have contacted you immediately. Instead, we decided to wait for news regarding any further third-party members involved with him, thanks to our close surveillance of him. In turn, please read on.

David Bell has successfully impregnated the following young women:

1. Melissa Bakewell. Born on the fourth of October 2007 of Wasdale head, Cumberland.

2.Michelle George. Born on the fourteenth of December 2005 of Cockermouth, Cumberland.

3. Michelle Mc Guinness. Born on the thirteenth of May 2004 of Glenridding, Westmorland.

While the first one is just a commoner, the second one has the blue blood of a kinship of yours who is also a lapsed Jew. The third is a descendent of the Irish brewery giant and once again of noble blood.

We will of course not be asking for any child support, but we do plan to re-house the former young teenage maidens to cottages around Loughrigg Tarn. In turn we expect David, to do his rounds there and to help keep the area as one happy family run baby factory.

While we have sent a letter to your sister, Sophie Alexander, regarding his impregnation of Julie Bakewell Born June 4th, 2005 from Wasdale, Cumberland, we have reason to suspect, that he may not be the father. Our suspicions arose when two other minors impregnated by him are not with child. We have reason to believe that on the night David cheated on Melissa that Julie conceived as a result of their act of love.

As an older and much more mature women; than these minors we expect the highest and exemplary behavior from you. As children they expect to be treated with preferential treatment and we do not expect any malicious comments or signs of envy from you or your sister whenever David and Erik will be going round to the baby making factory and making sure that these children are happy.

As the father and son of Roger, we have chosen David to continue with the legacy of your deceased and loving father of your children and anymore that you will conceive with David.

With the highest regards for you and your family Emma Noble.

Higher Executive Officer: The Department of Population Control.

With that Beth was shaken. Her sister had also received a similar letter regarding her husband's impregnation of the older Bakewell girl. As for the letter, she merely left it on the top of David's bedside cupboard. She also knew that; Emma Noble was acting on behalf of the villains she met at Buttermere. There was nothing to discuss. She certainly didn't want her origins in being dissected. The only way out of this; was death. David read the letter while Beth was watching him, felt resigned to his fate and like Beth simply didn't wish to discuss something of which neither of them had any control over. He wondered what to do, should he leave her for one of the other women or should he stay? Instead, Beth sensing that she was fighting against four other pregnant women of his, for his love she decided to simply excite him instead.

The only pleasant surprise for the readers was that the old county names of Westmorland and Cumberland, which had been romantically depicted in the novels along with Furness, had returned. Furness was the part of Lancashire that was a part of the Lake District, before all the above places had been swallowed into the new county of Cumbria.

Both of Alena's daughters had fallen pregnant to David. Instead, she had pleaded with her grandfather that only one of them would be officially recognized as the mother of Roger's children. As long as she was an item with Murat, she needed to have something she could hold against him. Simply put, if he crossed her, she could along with her father accuse Murat of raping a minor. As such the older child was to carry a baby without the name of the father, David Bell, being put onto the birth certificate.

After several days of passion, they were closer to each other than ever before and enjoyed their walks around the fell with the toddlers more than ever. Now feeling safe with David once more she didn't need to have sex all the time with him in order to keep him. A few more days passed by as a veil of sadness started clouding her thoughts once more. Her libido sank.

As the first trimester drew to a close, Beth noticed that she was noticeably bigger than Sophie. Despite that, she still had more energy than her sister. This was the time when her libido would return. Instead by chance, David found a letter underneath the wardrobe. Beth quickly grabbed it from him.

Some of my dreams have been compromised in my manifesto. I need David and Erik to act as my allies. In the short term, they will be allowed to procreate, but only as a last resort. So long as I have use for them, they will be looked after by me. In the longer term, their children will be destroyed and they too, if they don't agree to becoming eunuchs without balls. One way to reduce the pain would be for one of my sons to impregnate the girls who have none of my DNA and for my daughters to be impregnated by men who have none of my DNA. This is going to be a complicated process and will need plenty of strategic planning. These problems can be solved. A lot will depend upon my health. It is very important that I know who my daughters are, so that I don't impregnate them. I would like to visit the continent, so that my descendants can conquer the world with my own precious and Satanic DNA. In turn, non-descendants of my zoophillic mother and transgender father must be wiped out. It is a great honor to have been born in the bowels of Satan, my own mother; as such I will teach my children French. I will hypnotise them. Neither Beth nor Sophie will understand a thing. So long as the children are under my wings, they will become leaders ready to take on every continent. This means each child of theirs, every country within the continent. This with the generation after will go down to county level.

Lower levels such as, borough and parish are unnecessary due to the wipe out which turned out much better than even I predicted. In turn taking over the human race with me dead or alive is going the way, which would make my old hero Joe Epstein proud of me.

As much as my dream is my legacy for my perfect parents, I want to live forever. As a last resort, may I live forever and be reincarnated as both David's and Beth's daughter? During my final impregnation of Beth may she murder me immediately? In turn my soul will enter an egg, my mind enter a spermatozoa. We will then; be reunited in the mother's body and together become a fertilized egg. I say last resort, because Beth is unlike myself, and I fear that although I will live on, I will, as her child, be nothing like the zoophilic, transgender, paedophile, necrophiliac being I am as the child of my satanic mother, Sarah. As someone as pure, sweet and innocent as the Beth I first met before I excited her, I fear that as girl I will lead to instability. Simply put, as a good girl, people will walk all over me. This manifesto remains incomplete but will be revised yearly on every September as I gain more vision and I hope that in time; Beth will be as manipulative as I.

My love for Beth and David was sincere and true. I am devastated that in order to keep them, that a new act of parliament had to be passed preventing people from moving into unoccupied housing. As kind as it was from the lawmakers, as much as I will forever be indebted to their service towards me, the hurtful truth is that; neither Beth nor David would have voluntarily stayed with me.

Finally, I wish I had been born in another era. Even as I write this; my thoughts keep swinging due to my gender fluidity. At times it is so acute that the torment from not knowing who I am moved onto me seeing myself in my dreams, as a black woman, as a Jewish transgender singer or as a Muslim queen. The worst was when I made love to ewes and dogs; it was then that I fully accepted that I needed help.

If I could be born again as a tribal warrior, looking after my own kind I would be so lucky. The liberal agenda was a great experiment so that everything is now grey, but I must confess, and I am saying this as a former queen myself; that things have gone beyond the pale. As I myself am beyond repair.

After reading this Beth wanted to scream and shout. Instead, she found another letter.

Dear Greta,

Here I am in the Lake District; I have just got two teenagers pregnant. I am in wholehearted agreement with you in eating babies. I admire the purity of your actions. Of course, once the useless eaters have been wiped out it will be such an honor for me to make you pregnant as many times as you desire. Until then, keep up the image. If the tsunamis would be delayed, I am sure you would make a great first female president of the United States of America.

After reading the letter, which had supplanted her previous horror with something no better, she started screaming. 'Darling he is dead and buried.' David said.

'I feel sick thinking about making love until I have given birth.'

'Beth, we enjoyed the togetherness we had last night.'

'Please don't David, making love makes me think about him raping me.'

'You need to get over this.'

'How?' She said terrified.

'We simply need to have a New Beginning.' He said to her in sincerity. She didn't want to lose him, but what New Beginning could they have? All of their dreams had been broken. The New Beginning was that she was going to give birth to triplets and even worse was that the man she loved had died, metamorphosed into an unborn child inside of her womb as she felt as though she was constantly being abused by him.

'Make love.' He simply replied.

His words came exactly at the wrong moment in time for her. She then as she looked at him shone her eyes demonically at him as David was scared that she wanted to kill him. 'Roger, I don't want to be pregnant again, and again and again!' She screamed at him, as she thought about Roger's sperm mutating and making itself at home in David's testicles.

For her, he was in many ways whether he liked it or not Roger. Sexually, David was dead; in fact, she had forgotten when he was really potent at least in the sense of the beast. When she was pregnant the first time, he was passionate, but since then he seemed to lack much of his earlier sparkle in the bed, until The Beast raped him. Roger the parasite was simply using David's phallus as a means of living on forever. Erik then ran into their room. Beth burst out crying but managed to hand Erik the latest revelations beyond the grave, as he then realized that David wasn't harming her in any way.

Erik was feeling as sick as a dog while reading the letter. At least for him, it was Beth and not Sophie who was bearing the brunt of this perverted tale. He then left the room with both letters. As far as he was concerned, he had all of the necessary evidence to prove that Roger was a part of the depopulation agenda.

Sophie was reading the letters word for word. She looked as though she had aged a good decade. 'I must speak to Beth.' She then left the room. Erik followed her.

Sophie was then sat with her arms around her younger sister, and she began. 'Beth, that bastard is dead and buried! If only we ate him, maybe he is poisoning our hearts with his filth. Please Beth, our men deserve better than this.' Said Sophie. Poor Beth, she had eaten him, Sophie had eaten him as well as had David and Erik too. Of course, this was so disgusting and so terrible, that Erik had conveniently forgotten about this. Or perhaps he was going insane? Maybe he was losing his own mind. How could anyone forget that recently and for the first time in his life he had eaten human? Suddenly Erik started to turn white.

'What's wrong Erik?' David asked as he came in on the scene and noticed the morbidity after he had been outside in the pleasant outdoors for more than several minutes while the others were fully absorbed in the letters from beyond the grave. Suddenly Erik wanted David to kill him. He was scared that he would want to eat more human. It wasn't that he enjoyed it; it was merely that he had done it once and had to do it again.

Fortunately, during the next few days, things calmed down. Christmas came, and was a beautiful time for both families at Fell End. Although Ambleside had nothing like the population of the Ullswater valley, some of the survivors from high up, moved into the valley to dwellings they could previously have only dreamed of. Perhaps as many as one hundred people were living in the former market town. In turn some business activity was taking place. The presents that the oldest children received brightened up the hearts of William and Jane, were then aged twenty months. They were old enough to show their parents how much the Yuletide affair meant to them. In turn the families were happy and peaceful. With Beth being so sweet and nice to David, his passion for her was like that of an everlasting volcanic reaction. What could possibly go wrong? As for Timmy and Dexter, they both sensed that the atmosphere was much lighter than that of the previous season of goodwill when everyone at Fell End was in mourning over Jennifer and the fact that Roger was in their lives. Now all members of Fell End, simply felt that; love was all around.

January came, as did 2021. David and Beth had been through so much. Both of them had been traumatically humiliated and abused in every sense of the word by events. Even so, it appeared that nothing could go wrong. With the cold nights, they made sure that they were close to each other in the bed. It couldn't have been that cold, since they were always naked in bed together. Their quilts were warm after all. All they wanted was to be snug happily together.

Even so, her hormones were up and down, and she wanted David to be kept in check, psychologically. To David's horror she demanded to go away with him in their recently acquired two horsed carriage to the places he went on his travels with Erik. She took the twins with her, but left William with Sophie. She wanted the locals of Glenridding to see that both David and she were happily devoted to each other. She also vowed to somehow despite the cold weather show off her baby bump with pride. As far as she was concerned, this would show the world how much David and she were devoted to each other. They stayed for three nights at the

Patterdale Inn. The establishment where they stayed was around at the time of Wordsworth and was commercially more viable than the defunct hotels which were built for the electric age and mass tourism in Glenridding. David felt at times very uncomfortable. At least the locals were kind to them both. Even so, people spoke, they recognized David, and Michelle who was three and a half months pregnant on hearing about his arrival was curious. Shyly, she sat in the shadows observing Beth, and to her utter horror, noticed that her rival was even more beautiful than herself. After an hour or so she went home tired to bed and couldn't get him out of her head. Beth with her natural beauty didn't need much in the way of make-up but was so scared of being upstaged from David's flings; she made sure that she had everything at the ready. Apart from David's scarlet, silk maternity dress she had some creams from France.

Sat on a Gondola, that afternoon, the only boat in operation they went on a cruise around the lake. 'It is so much happier and civilised here. When our children are older, wouldn't it be good for them to have a decent school on their doorstep? I mean we could move in here if we ask them.'

'I am not so sure about that.' Said David.

'Well, if you hadn't gone around fucking all over the Lakes, I bet you would have jumped at the chance.' She said feisty.

'Look Beth, I am sorry for what I did, but let me tell you this: It doesn't matter to me as to what you wear, or the creams that you use. In the bear flash, I have never seen a woman so beautiful as you.' With that the two of them had nothing more to say. All she had to do was trust him. To show him that she was in control of her emotions so that he would never need to stray away from her again.

The Bell's ate their dinner in the guest's dining room. Beth was then delighted that after taking good care of the twins that she was able to visit the bar. Michelle came again too on the second evening of their visit. As soon as Beth went to visit the bathroom, she honed in on him as he was sat waiting for his wife. 'Hello David.'

'Hello Michelle.'

469

'You remember my name!' How could he forget her, in his eyes she was nearly so seductive as Beth. A Cumbrian like Jennifer with the sex appeal to match, but not quite like that of Beth's.

'I know you are married, and that's why I being not of a cruel persuasion, won't be asking you to come around to my home.'

'That's very kind of you.'

'One simple request of thee, is that you kiss my belly.' She then lifted up her dress as David bent his head down and kissed her small baby bump, the one that he himself had made. The feeling made him feel all male. A part of him felt as though he couldn't move his head away from her as he wanted to kiss her all over. As for Michelle, who had her hands gently on his head, it felt as though he hadn't left her three months earlier.

As soon as he lifted his head, Michelle walked off and he saw his wife who looked as though she had been crying. Beth then walked up to him and buried her face into his lap. She was so thankful that the babies were asleep upstairs since she felt more like a baby than those of her own. From then on, there was no more talk of moving to this valley. Like David, she was glad to be getting away from Patterdale.

Instead, as they were travelling the following morning, a police officer acting on the orders of the elite stopped them. 'Where are you going to?' He asked.

'We haven't decided yet.' Said Beth.

'Well to be honest where you are going is no concern of mine, but I received a telegram stating that David Bell is wanted in connection with Deborah Eccles and her failed pregnancy.'

With that he was forced to spend the night with Deborah Eccles, and to make love to her at least three times, while a civil servant was sat outside the room of the baby makers and taking notes. After each time they made love, they had to report to the male executive officer from the Department of Population Control. Beth simply couldn't sleep, but at least she realized that David was less unfaithful towards her than she had at first believed.

The next day, and one day later than they originally intended, they visited Keswick for lunch and called in at a restaurant. 'This town is named after cheese.' Said David.

'Why is it not called Cheesewick?' Asked Beth.

'In old English, the language was different and one of my great grandfathers came from Holland. He grew up on a farm, and I know that they call it Kaas over there.'

'And in German they call it kase.' Said Beth wanting to show him her intelligence.

After eating it was time for Buttermere. As they looked at the lake David was reminded of some of the Dutch words he had learnt from his grandma, who came over to England from Rotterdam to live with his maternal grandfather. 'Mere as in Buttermere, might be a strange name for an English word, but in Dutch, you can call this lake, Botermeer!

'What are you talking about?

'What do you think Botermer means in English?'

'Butter's Lake.' She said, and with that he kissed her on her lips.

Once again David was invited to Murat's as they walked around his farm at Gatesgarth, and the George's were living there with him. David felt very uncomfortable to say the least. Alena wanted to show Beth up obliquely and felt that the best way was to slap David across the face because of what he had done to her Michelle. The next day they left after staying just one night. From there they went the long way round via Loweswater, Ennerdale Bridge and Gosforth down into Wastwater. They stayed at the Wasdale Head Inn and David felt uncomfortable when a drunkard police officer came over to say hello. It was of course Wayne and fortunately he left.

Unfortunately for him, five minutes later he was back with Julie and Melissa who were both wearing maternity wear sat in the darkest part of the inn and keeping an eye on David. Both girls were also in their fifth month. As soon as her beau went to the bar to order hot chocolate drinks and chocolate brownies the former police officer went up to Beth. 'You and your husband seem to have a dirty habit of having kids all over the place. But I must say you are one hell of a looker.' He then placed his hands on her bump as she froze in horror and was completely taken aback when he started to kiss her on her lips and tried to fondle her breasts. As far as he was concerned, he was taking out revenge on David and making a fool out of Beth who in his eyes she was little more than a lady of the night. She then started to cry; Wayne didn't want any trouble and let her leave his presence at ease. She then walked to the bar and saw the two pregnant sisters with their hands all over her David. She was just about to go to their room and lock him out and went to collect her book lying on the table when the old man came back to her drunk as she approached her table. 'What do you say if we leave this beautiful threesome alone, keep my daughters happy while the two of us have some fun together?' Instead, she walked to David caught his attention and Wayne laughed at the Bells. 'Come on my sweet and innocent daughters; let's leave these makers of bastards alone in peace!' His daughters didn't know what to think, they were carrying bastards after all. Beth had gone to show who was the boss and if in the process David had been humiliated, then so what! Instead, she spent the night crying as he held her in his arms. The next day she wanted to leave but felt too weak to travel. It wasn't the most respectable of dilemmas as far as she was concerned. Too ashamed to venture downstairs she spent the whole day in the bedroom and David brought their food up to their room. By evening she felt somewhat more defiant and together she made love with David.

The next day they headed straight back over Burnmoor Tarn, Eskdale and the three passes, Hardknott, Wrynose and Langdale back to their haven above Ambleside, where a delighted William appeared to have been waiting for her ever since her depart.

During the second month of the year, Beth thought about how the last time she was five months gone that Roger was making out how she was looking almost full term. This time, she really did look full term even though she was only in the middle trimester. It was increasingly obvious to her, that she was experiencing more than just a single pregnancy, which from her past experience she knew only too well. One day as she went down to the lake at Waterhead she was somewhat filled with disgust. As she saw the mating amphibians, she wondered what choice the females had in all of this. In her mind she simply saw scenes of rape. She had to blank out these disturbed thoughts. If babies were made via coercion, then as far as she was concerned, we were all born victims of violence. Instead, it was better to think about her parents and how she and her sister came into the world through the love and devotion their parents had for each other. As luck would have it, David appeared, her face brightened, and they started kissing and she was happy once more. All he could do was stare at her body, touch her, kiss her, make love to her and that was all that; she wanted him to do.

Erik and Sophie were happy too. As for Greta, they could dress it as either a boy or a girl. For one thing at least, this special child was going to be easy to dress up at least. Sophie would go on short strolls with and without Erik. Even so, while she would still leave Jane with her sister, she still felt as though she had, as a then protective mother, to be in charge of Greta in every sense of the word.

Just as Beth was starting to believe that her life was entering another blissful phase, while out on her walk, she noticed David's two pregnant Michelle's' speaking to one another around Tarn Foot. As far as she was concerned, this wasn't heralding good tidings for her. What were these two sluts doing on her patch, she wondered? Luckily for her they were so busy talking to one another that they hadn't noticed her eavesdropping. Even so she felt sick as they were both comparing the night when they thought that they fell pregnant with her beau of all people. With David's mother's to be, encroaching closer and closer onto her territory, she felt as though some fatal virus was on its way and that the shame, like some mask, would engulf and suffocate her to death. Of course, once back with David, she felt fully at ease with the world once more.

Daffodil season arrived, and it was around this time that Beth had received once again a very official letter. She had been in fear of the authorities and their expectations of David having to go round and to excite the former maidens of his who were carrying his unborn children.

In short, he had been informed of the maidens' pregnancies just a few weeks after his return from his eighteen-night tour. Back in November, a man wearing a mask appeared in front of him while he was in the garden alone. He had been instructed not to mention anything to Beth. He was expected to spend a few nights with the girls from Wasdale. Instead, he arranged with the man that he would simply visit the girls during daylight hours at one of the cottages around Loughrigg Tarn. After two more weeks, both of the great granddaughters of George had been offered a second home next to The Howe as well as Michelle from Glenridding. Luckily for him, the girls stayed at home and tried to block him out of their minds. All that changed since he went on a tour with his wife and reminded them about him.

By this time with both girls now living close to them, Beth then knew that he was breaking the law by not sleeping with the girls, and she begged him not to risk his life. What she didn't realise was that he was discreetly visiting the women and didn't wish to rub this in her face. By this time, she then fully realized, that David had been set up by the seedy men she met at Buttermere into carry out their dirty agenda. It was then that Buttermere no longer had any appeal left for her. As her mind went back to the present, she was nervous to say the least as she was opening the letter from the Department of Population Control. She was so overwhelmed with anxiety that she had great difficulty in being able to open up the inside of the envelope.

Dear Mrs. Bethany Bell,

I hope that this letter sees you in good health. Normally under the circumstances of the minors, whom your husband impregnated it would be his duty to share his time with both you and the other three or four mothers to be.

As you are well aware, breaking the law is now once again a capital offence. After close analysis, my boss has said that a compromise may be reached. He has agreed that David Bell doesn't under the special circumstances have to go round regularly to the former maidens' cottages. With you being mother to several children, pregnant and an important Illuminati member our proposal for you which you agreed has been granted.

From the date of this letter, March the first, 2021, new guidelines have come into effect for David Bell. A similar letter is being sent to Sophie Alexander on behalf of Erik Alexander. Any minors residing close to Loughrigg Tarn will be given special permission to visit David Bell at his home of Fell End for their sexual and procreation desires. Given that the house is very spacious, we suggest that the former bedroom of; Roger De Cadenet, to be converted into the maidens' room. With the paintings above the heads of the girls while they are with David Bell, they will learn to respect you as the leading queen bee mother of the Illuminati.

Finally, as for the case regarding the case of Deborah Eccles and her failed pregnancy it is closed. We are proud to announce that; Deborah Eccles, born on the twenty-fourth of November 2005, of Glenridding Westmorland, has been successfully impregnated by David Bell.

ours Sincerely,

Emma Noble.

Higher Executive Officer of the Department of Population Control.

For Beth having to share her husband with his teenage fans made her feel very old to say the least. It seemed as if every night there was a either a pregnant teen or one trying to carry his child who was waiting for him. It was such an utter mess. At least David stuck to his guns and made sure that between the hours of 9PM after Beth had recovered from the breastfeeding until 7AM when she had to look after her family duties, he would be with her. With Roger's room almost as some kind of mausoleum and being the largest and with a King-size bed, more than one girl could sleep in it. Fortunately, since most of the girls like Beth, were pretty pregnant and pretty big, by this time the girls rarely stayed there overnight. Even so, both Andrea George and Claire Wood were showing less than the others, because they only fell in the family way once they arrived at the cottages close to Loughrigg Tarn in December and had more energy than Beth wished them to have. Simply put; she, Beth, wanted David, her husband, just for herself, especially as she was now heading towards her final trimester. Fortunately, Andrea and Claire had herd mentality, and given that the other mother's to be preferred not to spend the night at Fell End, they too decided to sleep in their own homes.

It was a usual evening for David he had just finished with his duties for the Department of Population Control, with a new maiden. Karen Carter; was the daughter of a single mother commoner. Her children would in turn end up being slaves for the elite. She had arrived along with three other maidens who were lucky enough to have been walking up the old man of Coniston on the day their native Barrow-In-Furness perished. Their parents, being working class scum were housed into former shepherds' bothys. Kind-hearted locals came with items of clothing and sleeping bags to prevent the children from freezing to death. When the girls were offered housing normally reserved for the elite, they simply couldn't refuse. On top of that and aged just thirteen, they were each expected to produce a crop of children running into double figures by the time they would have reached thirty.

She looked at him so hot and sultrily. 'Darling where do you get so much energy from?'

'It is simple my love. My job is to impregnate the girls and to excite them. When I make love to those who are already in the family way, I save my sperm for you!'

'Oh, David that is so romantic of you!' She said. They then kissed each other as they became increasingly passionate before making love. After it her mind had a pregnant pause. She then thought about his poignantly beautiful words. Why did he have to be with these other women or girls anyway? Why was it Roger's rather than his own semen he was carrying? If only the pain resulting from the father of her children's deeds would simply and finally come to pass. Then she could get on with her life? Then again how could she when all the evil around her seemed to go right back to Roger. The death of her parents, the corpses she saw all around her. Fortunately, David's love and devotion was so strong, that she trusted that nothing would come between them both.

Spring arrived. She was now entering the third trimester. Beth was huge. Her delicate frame looked as though it was being pushed to the limit. Even so, she still had plenty of energy and was amorous with a passionate David. A part of her was insecure as she felt that she had to fight for him. They weren't his baby's, and it was looking increasingly obvious for her that she was experiencing a multiple birth. How on earth could she cope without him?

As Beth and David were walking around the tarn one fine sunny afternoon in late March all she could think about were the three previous birthdays of Sophie. During the first one, all she heard about was the excitement taking place at Buttermere from her sister via the then defunct social media. On the second one, she had been badly bruised psychologically, was heavily pregnant but still didn't know what it was like to be a mother and had hundreds and thousands of followers on social media following her being fucked senseless by Roger and ripe pregnant. On the third one, she was a completely different person, a mother, heavily pregnant again and living with someone other than the father of her children and a very different person as well a very private one too. She had gone through enough changes, and one year on, on this fourth year, things had not changed so dramatically since Sophie's previous birthday.

Still holding his hand, she looked at the daffodils and found everything so beautiful. The flowers were a little bit past their best, but still beautiful. As she saw walked down to the tarn and saw the frogspawn at the water's edge, her mind went back to her maiden pregnancy and when his touch on her tummy was so warm and tender for her.

Back at Fell End, Sophie had prepared a lovely dinner for everyone. As she arrived back from her walk, she could smell something delicious. Instead of rushing inside, she simply looked around the outside of her home and was enjoying the sight of the primroses. As far as she was concerned; man couldn't produce anything more aesthetic. Life was the most beautiful thing on earth, and she believed that her children were of a wonderful testament to this.

With her carrying his babies for the third time, she couldn't get Roger out of her mind for long. She never wanted to have so many children at such a tender age. At best she wanted to have four children during her entire life, instead, aged just twenty she already had three, and in all probability was expecting triplets. On top of that, she would be expected to have at least two children to David. For Beth it made no sense to have depopulated the masses and for she herself to have several children. In fact: very little made sense apart from the immediate concerns of her family, her very own survival. In short, she was making sure that she was doing everything in pleasing David. He was a good man after all. Like Erik he lost his own child, and like her brother-in-law he was standing by his wife.

Under other conditions she could abuse him emotionally, but she was fully aware of the fact that he could easily live without her. Maybe once they had children of their own together, she would have some hold over him. Instead, for the time being at least, he loved her in a sweet and simple way, and she gave him the same kind of love in return. Had Roger not abused her and had she only made love to David, then as a faithful Christian woman, she would have been as devoted to her man as she was then feeling traumatised in her own mind. On top of that, other opportunities for him, in the form of other younger beauties than herself were staring her in the face as they came round to be fucked senseless by David as a regular event. It was incredible for her to see, how the powers at be had simply brainwashed the people into believing that this was acceptable behavior. Did any of the sheep following the elite's agenda have any morals? She wondered. All she could do; was put a brave face on and, simply be nice to David and together they would be able to get through with every challenge that came their way. Often, she would still remember her parents' views on fashion. As far as they were concerned, teenage girls simply dressed like prostitutes, and naturally, that were her own views on David's mothers to be.

In bed together with David one evening, Beth was in thinking mode. 'Fifty shades of Grey was selling more books than the Bible.'

'Yes, to think that if you asked someone to read the Bible meant that you were some religious far right lunatics, while if a woman forced her husband to read that stupid book it was considered normal.' He answered.

'Do you think this was God's revenge?' She asked him.

'It is difficult for me to say. It can be argued that all of the Bible's prophecies have come true. On the other hand, look at us. We are far from perfect ourselves, but I would like to believe that we are not evil.'

'I would like to believe that we are not evil too.'

'I will also have to live with the fact until the day that I die, that much of our mess is because I was too shy to make a move on you.'

'Please David, I am sure that God sees and feels our pain. Yes, we made such mistakes, but we did not deliberately cause pain to others. Our stupidity caused us both so much grief and enough guilt already.'

'How many fairy tales are there in life anyway? I am sure that with all the evil around even if we had the perfect marriage one of us, would have been cruelly taken away.' He said.

'Please don't be so morose, I would like for us to believe that given our love is so strong, and so true, that I would have found the job at Fell End instead of Jennifer and on the day of the holocaust it would have been your day off from work and we were walking around Loughrigg tarn together.' She said sadly.

'And carrying my child.' He said as tears then ran down his face. Both feeling sad, but without any more reproach for the other simply made love together and fell asleep. While for The Beast, sex was equated with death, for these two; love sex and life went hand in hand.

During the fourth month of the year, all was calm and peaceful with the loving Bells. David was more stable now that he was in a loving relationship and wanted in some ways to be the dominant one of the couple. In this sense Beth saw him as more of a man. Although sick and tired of having to make love to young girls, he decided not to dwell on it; it was nothing more than work for him, although he also felt as though he was merely a male prostitute of the New World Order. 'As I have already said to you, your children I will be taking on as my own. I will look after you. You are still very young, and once your youngest child with Roger is old enough to swim, dress his or herself and to draw, just when you are least expecting it, your second generation of motherhood will begin as we will have some children of our own together.' He said to her romantically.

'I count my blessings, no matter how hard life has turned out. I have you, the man I fell in love with instantly like no other! We have had some rocky times to get here. You are not so innocent either.' She said as she was in fear of him being offended from her remark and in fear of him running off with one of the younger girls, who was carrying his child.

They both smiled at each other lovingly. 'I know love.' he said.

'It is great that we can swim together and leave the children with Sophie.'

'We might have to change the routine a bit.'

'I know it is better to when the days are warmer, but my sister wants to go with Erik in the afternoons and we are hardier than they and can have our morning swims instead.'

'Sounds perfect with me darling . . .. Beth dear, I don't believe that you have a multiple birth.'

'Why is that?'

'If you were expecting a few, you wouldn't be able in your eight months to swim so easily.' She then kissed him. She knew that Roger was watching over her and looking after her as she was simultaneously carrying him. She hoped as a lady of faith that he was in heaven. She also knew that she couldn't say such a thing to David. She had to treat him as an equal and to understand his feelings. She had to show him that she had her eyes only for him and to understand that he too; and just like her, had suffered so much.

May came and Beth had never felt so happy since she had left her parents' home. She thought about how three years earlier she was getting ready for England. During the early days in the Lakes before William was born, her life was full of excitement with Roger. Equally she knew that he was disturbing her psychologically. Then she thought about how close she had been to taking her life and against her will and during her darkest days she fell again in the family way. Things though terrible, got somewhat better, albeit slowly and at the speed of a snail on its last legs. Fortunately, her hope never truly died.

Without modern life, she was enjoying being a mother. Life had really gone back to the days of Wordsworth. Without worrying about the shops, career or what was on TV her life was devoted to her family and nothing else. True, she enjoyed The Lake District and her outdoor activities there, but one day she would be able to have sporting activities not just with her beau, but with her precious children too. Of course, she needed him more than ever and knowing how lucky she was, she felt that her life was simply complete.

This was the penultimate month of her third pregnancy, and she was enjoying every moment of it as she felt all woman. Often, she would waddle to the tarn or to the lake with David, who wouldn't allow her out of his sight, in case she would go into an early labor. It was a strange feeling knowing that Roger was looking down at her from above, was inside of her womb and that his DNA was inside her husband's scrotum. It was almost as if he had split into three. Television had previously had a similar effect. For the masses the flat screens were real, and the celebrities were able to appear in more than in just two places, especially with all the memorabilia.

Late May arrived. 'Here we are in the waters of a tarn swimming together.' He said to her as they were drying off in the hot sunshine.

'Look, it seems your fans are watching us!' She said as she noticed a few of his mothers to be in the distance.

'They can't be real fans. If they were, they would be swimmers like you Beth.'

'What is that supposed to mean?' She said hoping that he would show her something less obliquely romantic.

'Beth, I would do anything to live on an island, just the two of us. Far away from the Maddening Crowd.'

'Oh, how I do love it and you so much whenever you quote Hardy.' She said.

'Oh, Beth if I told you that you have a beautiful body would you hold it tightly against me!' In turn she held her body into his loving arms. This turned into a kiss and led to them making love and nodding off together in the sunshine. As they woke up, they noticed some stupid and childish girls might be into voyeurism with their binoculars. Unlike many other women who were working hard on the farms, these women who were carrying the sacred descendants of Roger inside their rooms, were given priority treatment. With nothing else to do in their lives, and not into sport like Beth, watching David making love was as exciting for them as Pornhub had been for them along with some of their other so called more mature schoolmates. Beth and David simply went to the tarn together, and after their swim and drying off together, the spies also felt cheap. It was obvious to them that; David was genuinely in love with Beth, and that he only had sex with them out of his duty towards the New World Order. It was also a painful reminder that; they were just baby machines, who were expected to be impregnated by David only. As for Beth, she learnt to think more of her own luck, and simply felt blessed to be with him.

Just as in the painting, she was sat sweating in the uncomfortable heat with her legs open wide. She was in the garden, her son, her half child, half baby was proudly looking at her. He was sat between her legs, while she was breastfeeding her twins. Heavily pregnant, and, in a trance, her mind thought about the painting. At first, she found it vulgar. As a teenager it wasn't the sexiest of sights. Now though, yet still not much older, the painting had a deep and movingly beautiful meaning for her. Equally, all she could see in her mind outside was the picture indoors, which was so terrifyingly accurate. If only Roger could enjoy the sight of her now. This was all his work. The fact that his imagination had been so powerful, and a reality meant so much to her, he must have really loved her. His dream, which she herself was enjoying, was posthumously fulfilled, and now she was sure that she was carrying him. As for the scarlet stretch mark on her left breast, this was the least of her worries. David still hadn't made any comments, but at least he loved every inch of her body. All she could hope for was that Roger was living on inside of her and looking at her from above simultaneously. Having children at too young and tender an age was better than in being barren. She was finally at ease with the world. She was back into being her usual placid self.

Midsummer's night was dawning. She was so in love. He was so in love. The world around them was one big happy Garden of Eden. They had several adorable children. He loved her body; he made her feel like a lady who was simply a Goddess. 'Oh, when two hearts beat as one, nothing else matters!' She said lovingly to him.

'I love it when you recite my verses that I prepared specially for you!' He said to her with a smile on his face.

'You plagiarist! I might only be a young lady, but even I know you got those words from U2 and Metallica!' They then started to kiss and as the setting blood red sun was setting in the sky, they were turning as hot for each other as the sky was turning into every shade of red that one could simply only dream of. By this time, David had got over the fact that he could have had children with her, but due to his timidity hadn't. He loved children, and because it was her offspring, being a devoted stepfather came naturally to him.

Erik still had human flesh at the back of his mind. He was scared to say the least. Luckily for him he saw a child fall dead on the streets of Ambleside when he was there and quickly ran up to the deceased school infant and with all his strength, he ran up to Fell End. His eyes were bulging as he looked terrified, but still he seemed to know where he wanted to go.

Secretly he went to the kitchen while the others were outside in the garden. He then realized that he wouldn't be able to fit the boy, aged around five, into the pots at Fell End. In turn he fell asleep lying next to the dead little boy. In his light sleep, he had a dream about the son of his, whom he had never seen. In a fright he soon woke up. With no one around he put on his shoes and ran out stark naked carrying the dead young body in his arms.

The others detected strange body language from Erik when he ran in earlier and later on out of the house just then, but luckily for Erik, they hadn't realized that in his arms he was holding a juvenile corpse.

He knew of course about Roger's werewolf days and was terrified during his brief moments of calm that he himself could end up in being like Roger, a leader of a pack. Other moments he felt as though he wanted to put everyone around him out of their miseries. Once back in the valley, he simply dropped the boy off in the park and a pack of wild and hungry dogs ran over to the boy. By then the others had noticed Erik's mental health going downhill. During this time, the other adults prayed for his sanity daily. At times, they hoped that he would die peacefully, since they often wondered if his days were numbered.

Like Beth, Sophie was of course also heavily pregnant, but her baby bump looked much more compact since she was carrying only one child. 'My God Beth, you make me look so slim next to you.' Sophie said as they bumped into each other's path in the garden as they were wearing little in the way of clothing in the hot and sultry air.

'Please don't rub it into my face so much.' Beth said.

Thanks to her sister's personal attack, she needed David more than ever. At least she was never too big for him, since no matter what, he would always love her and would always give her his countenance.

Since Erik had now become the most disturbed member on the estate, Sophie had finally got her act together. Beth's love for David and his love for her, made Sophie think. She then thought to herself as usually around this time; that love conquers all. The same evening after he returned without the corpse Sophie had been waiting for him outside in the garden. He then entered the house as if he was a terrified little boy. 'Erik, love conquers all!' She said to him as she found him lying on their bed prostrate with his shoes on. Gently she took off his dirty outdoor footwear as if he were her sweet and little child. He then burst out crying. He cried and cried and cried. Her babies were already in bed. 'Just cry, you have every reason to cry. I am waiting for the man inside of you to let himself out of his sorrows.'

In short, there was nothing she could do. Although only in his mid-thirties, his body was worn out. His mind had metamorphosed into that of a child-man and was some kind of safety valve for him. Prior to his new self, the toils of his life had aged him decades mentally. He was simply too young to be suffering from insanity. Without any other available men, she would spend the rest of his life nursing him. David would have to give up his life of a gentleman and get his hands dirtier from working harder. In short, Fell End had one extra child than had been foretold. He was helpless alone, she would have to wash, feed and dress him. He was always with her, he needed her, and Beth had to spend more time looking after her babies and offer more help to her sister. Equally, he wasn't there at all. Their honeymoon had clearly ended as their long process of mourning over a living being had begun. And there she was sat on his bed one evening and after putting him to bed and staying with him until he fell asleep, she would wait until she would hear the unwelcome noise from the crows which waited for him to fall into his death of sleep before they would wake an exhausted heavily pregnant mother to be out of her pre sleep. He wasn't dead, but the Erik she knew had been taken out of her life while she would remain his devoted wife, in sickness and in health. Since the shrill of the crows heralded his silence, it was better to wait for them to screech their very prophesies of his demise than to fall asleep and be woken up to their terrific screams of a macabre kind. As such and sleepy eyes, she would wait for what she saw as modern dinosaurs to gloat over her husband and then when all was quiet, she would fall into her freedom from that of the real world.

Both girls were ripe pregnant and had gone on a gentle stroll together. Quickly the weather was deteriorating, with the wind picking up, mist setting in and rain falling down. Sophie who was constantly analysing Erik, was in fear that he had caught some virus and with a change in the weather whatever he had could spread everywhere. Both girls started to hold each other's hands. All of a sudden, Beth started screaming. A few giant-sized black crows were around them like swarms of locusts. The girls started flailing their arms as they were then apart from each other, the crows moved away from Beth but were circling around Sophie's middle. All she could see; was the crows flying around Jennifer just before she died in childbirth. If her beloved sister died too, then Beth would end up out of her mind she feared as she had a terrible mistrust for the future. Like Sophie she too had Erik on her mind. She then feared that insanity could be transmitted on to other family members, since according to the medical books, Erik was actually suffering from distemper or rabies. Maybe he had caught this from Roger. Back in his werewolf days, it was anyone's guess if the dwellers at Fell End were carrying some big surprise that one by one would devour their senses.

Epilogue

What a day to be giving birth, July the fourth 2021. It was exactly three years to the day since they had met Roger and a good two weeks past their due dates. It was in the early hours when Beth woke her sister up with her labor pains. Sophie waddled into Roger's room where she found her sibling. Beth seemed terrified. 'I hope that everything is going to be alright.' Said Beth trembling inside.

'Of course, it will.' Sophie said and inside she too was trembling.

The twins woke up crying and William walked in. 'Mummy, thirsty.' Said William in his broken English. It had been a warm night. Sophie left the room in order to breast feed the children. While breastfeeding, she was desperate to hold on. Her own labor contractions were starting, but now was not the time to disturb her sister who was lying in the same bed and in agony.

Given that they had the keys for each other's homes they were able to look after each other easily. Suddenly, Sophie could take no more, within what seemed like in no time at all she gave birth. David came in immediately after the arrival. He had been organising the room as a makeshift ward since Beth went into labor and hadn't thought about both women being in labor simultaneously. The umbilical cord was cut. The baby was dead. A flash went over his mind to the time of Jennifer's labor now was not the time for him to dwell on it. It was though, too late to protect Beth from this terrible sight and she was about to give birth too. 'Sister, don't worry about me.' A frozen looking Sophie said. All she had inside was her survival mode. She was handled hardships differently to Beth. It wasn't that she didn't care; she just found her cool manner best for her very own survival.

Since it was her third pregnancy it should be easier than this Beth thought. Instead, the sight of the dead baby seemed to have slowed down her own contractions. All she could see was dead babies everywhere as thoughts about the day of William's birth came back to haunt her. Erik was lying like a baby while Sophie was recovering from her labor. Luckily, there was little bleeding, and the three hungry babies would have to fight over her breasts. David decided that Beth would have to help out too with nursing until she went back into full labor. This was a time of emergency: this time he was terrified. Sophie's baby was a stillborn, and Beth reminded him of Jennifer. He then thought about the Crows and prayed that God would take his life instead of Beth's. Even David was in danger of suffering mentally but sought solace in God instead. He moved away from Beth who appeared to be in a deep sleep. 'Oh, merciful God, I thank thee for guiding me to this important day for my wife. If one of us must go, I beg thee to take my life instead of my wife's. She is the purest being who has ever entered this earth, and I ask thee to look after her, Amen.' He then walked back towards his beloved; she looked as though she was elsewhere. In fact, she had heard every word of his talk with the Lord and didn't want to embarrass him. All she wanted was to get through the labor and to enjoy every second with him.

While breastfeeding Sarah, Beth felt the time was up. Although it had seemed endless: Beth delivered safely, a beautiful baby boy. Only David was helping. Sophie was still weak from her delivery and found herself already having to nurse child-man, Erik. As for Beth, her child was alive, and Beth cried with happiness. As long as it seemed, it was only two hours long in duration that her labor had taken place.

Another two hours later and after giving birth to the second twin, Beth was relieved. Hopefully, there weren't any triplets after all. She then placed her hand on her belly, as she was so weak from everything and felt another baby move. At least she wouldn't be giving birth again that day, she hoped. This was the third child; the one Roger said would stay longer in her womb. She then fell asleep with her babies on both of her breasts and was lying close to Sophie who had since returned to her after David cleaned her up. She felt a little compromised having a former lover seeing her naked after giving birth and wished that she had never aborted Jan's baby especially since she was terrified of losing Erik. Like David, she too was scared of a terrible fate that might befall her sibling. It had been an easier labor than they had expected as they all waited morbidly during a seemingly ominous calm before the storm, of another corpse rebirth. Roger had bestowed unto Sophie a genderless baby, a stillborn baby what plans did he inside the womb have for Birth?

A few hours later she was woken up, she was giving birth again. It had been a most exhausting labor, she had six children. At least not everything Roger had said had come true. She wondered how she was strong enough with her petite frame to have survived everything. All she could poignantly think was that from the heavens above, Roger was her guardian angel and that she was the super mum of his genes.

As for Sophie, her baby was still born on the day when Jan had been murdered. She was sure that Roger was looking down happily knowing that she was just a test dummy for his preferred belle, Beth, who had three new-borns along with her twins who needed the help from their aunt's nipples too. In fact, Roger wanted Sophie to give birth to a stillborn. She had tried to kill him, and he had never forgiven her. She wondered what else he had planned for her, posthumously. She never wanted to have fallen pregnant with him in the first place. At least her first child with him was healthy. The second was a freak of nature without any sexual organs and was genderless, but a human being all the same of sorts and still in so many ways in good condition. The third was tragically stillborn. Sophie was well aware that Beth was more vulnerable than she was and was happy at least that it wasn't her younger sibling who had given birth to a freak of nature as well as to a corpse. Even so, she was still terrified of Roger. She was also terrified of herself. Had she simply cursed herself when once again she thought about when she implied that she didn't give a damn whether her baby was headless or not? At least her baby was only stillborn, without a head on it; she would never be able to recover.

Breastfeeding eight children was simply too much. With just four breasts between them, they decided that the new-borns were priority, and that the babies from the second pregnancy needed to be weaned off as soon as possible. At least the oldest children were no longer breast fed more than twice a day. In short, not only the latest additions were heavily reliant on their mother's milk. As far as she was concerned, under the circumstances, the weaning process was dragging on for far too long. All she could was to think about the present, and then the future would sort itself out.

For Beth something wasn't quite right since she had just given birth to the triplets. Of course, she was exhausted, but she seemed just as huge as ever. On top of that, all she wanted to do was to lie in the bed nursing her children while David was cooking and cleaning around the clock for her as well as looking after the garden and DIY. It was during this time that she felt that Roger was inside her body, and from her head down to her toes.

A month had passed, the new-born babies were being breastfed and the oldest ones were then being fed breast milk just once a day. As for those from the second pregnancies, they were still being breastfed three times daily. Sophie and Beth were certainly producing plenty of milk, but miraculously didn't look too exhausted.

Erik due to his insanity was torpidly confined to his bed. The horrors of the past nearly two years had to be blocked out of his tormented mind. Sophie as his dutiful wife; was acting sweeter than ever towards him. With her tender loving care, she hoped to arouse him out of his psychosis. As each day passed, it seemed that her tender loving care was simply to no avail. His response to her was like that of any of the old electrical appliances that were lying around obsolete since the National Grid packed up. As far as she was concerned, there was no hope for him. He was in a conscious state of sorts, but his mind was no sharper than that of the corpses she had seen on the day of the holocaust. Beth too was touched by the fate of her sister and felt as though the corpse rebirth of the man she once loved had been burned in embers of corruption. At least each day gave her hope. Three days had passed when he seemed to be choking and about to be dying from one of his uncontrollable fits of insanity. So long as the horror of him knocking on death's door wouldn't be replayed, and his condition remained in being stabilised, it gave her hope that their marriage might see some shafts of daylight between them both.

August was a calm month. Sophie had got back very nicely into shape, while Beth still looked as though she was about to drop. Even so, she was back to her routine of swimming, walking and being passionate with David. Still only twenty-one years of age, her body was much suppler than that of the older mothers she believed. Her belly was still hard so even though she felt much lighter after giving birth to triplets recently she was sure that this was a crop of quads. At times she had the odd fears about what she was carrying inside of her, but her solid rock was able to guide her through each day in harmony.

Miraculously, Erik started to feed himself. Miraculously, he started to wash and dress himself too. Sadly, he was in no frame of mind to speak. If Erik wasn't strong enough to build up their love together, she would be the catalyst. It didn't take her long as one evening was turning from one of misery for him to one as bright as a meadow at the bottom of a waterfall where the sun was shining radiantly on the waters which were flowing downstream and close to many flowers shining brightly in all of their regal splendour. Sadly, that was in her dreams, only. As she woke up, she was terrified, there he was. What was David doing in their room snooping in on them in the dark? As it transpired, it was Erik, and he had just been to the bathroom.

Another month had gone by. Erik's second corpse rebirth had taken place. Day by day he was getting stronger and wanting to help out with the work in the garden. The oldest children were now twenty-eight months; Beth's twins were sixteen months old and her triplets two months. She wanted to be free from being pregnant after eleven solid months. The triplets were healthy and strapping, if she was still pregnant, surely it was time for the Illuminati baby to rear its head.

In one sense, she was relieved that her days of waiting in fear for him to put her directly into the family way again were simply over. She could only blame herself. The first time it was because of her stupidity. The second time she got caught out was because of doing the right thing concerning Jennifer and not ruining her relationship. As for the third time, that was so unfortunate, she was a proud belle of her beau and safe as far as she was aware in their matrimony. Even so, she had seven children of his. In just three years, he had as far as she knew; three babies with her sister and one to the waitress. All she had to do was to think about David and for her Roger was in more ways than one; simply a virus who had been using David as a transmitter on his impregnation tour with all the young girls from the other corners of the park. Viruses spread easily; he was in his sixtieth year at the time of his death. He had confessed to having children in other countries. Over his forty year or possibly in his case nearly fifty-year epoch of producing children she had no idea as to how many he had. How many grandchildren did he have? Like a virus he had probably spread along with his posterity to all corners of the globe. And she, yes Beth, had helped him to achieve his dream in being a modern-day Genghis Khan, which as far as she believed was a fait accompli.

One evening, David and Erik were sat together in the living room. 'What was most interesting for the Illuminati was that they realized that they were not so strong as they thought they were. Simply put; they were parasites: luxurious ones in fact. Depopulation had given them the space that they wanted, but they were unable to cope with living without all the creature comforts of the modern age. One thing they believed in was the survival of the fittest; and things were not what they had envisaged. With the industrial clock put back to the Victorian days since there was no more electricity, it was peasant girls such as Beth and Sophie who found it easier to cope. In short, the elite were humbled. Of course, the biggest shock was when flood waters rose higher than expected and killed off most of the elite who wanted to take photographs of the dying plebeians!' Said David as Erik smiled. 'I would like to add that I consider myself a peasant too. If they were really true to their cause and wished to go down in history as noble people, then the elite should have considered the following. Firstly, it was a big mistake of theirs to have fuelled mass consumption which led to many environmental problems. Secondly, they themselves were no examples when their earth's footprint was incredibly much higher than that of everyone else's. Finally, instead of encouraging self-loathing and widespread depression and mental illness as a means of encouraging mass suicides, given that one Illuminati member had no concept of sustainability in their own private life, the best thing that they could have done for their cause was to have killed themselves. Instead, had history not been massaged, they would not have been looked upon kindly.' Said Erik.

David looked at Erik and was impressed with his speech. 'How can you speak of history in such a context?' David asked.

'We are writing history as we speak, and I am imaging that we are now fifty years down the road from now. I am sure those lunatics from Buttermere will be considered the saviors of the human race!" Said Erik as they both started to chuckle.

"With hindsight, the deceased Illuminati members would never have embarked on their mass genocide program. Had they left things naturally; the people would have voluntarily had less children. Instead, their forced programs of mass gender transitions, abortions and euthanasia programs destabilised the minds of many of their own family members as well angering the masses. Roger had been a testament as to how they had turned on each other too, when during the battle for supremacy, he killed off a rival of his, Helene Berger, who like him, was behind the genocidal program. Being much more consumerist than the rest of society, they themselves were responsible more than the humble servants. It is they, the elite, who were fuelling economic growth which created more environmental problems. Had these psychopaths been more of a stable persuasion they would never have embarked on a mass immigration program. Had they not done so, then most of the European populations would have fallen naturally. Had they not changed family courts into satanic courts, more parents would have stayed together and not necessarily had more children. In all too many cases, alienated dads were having in all too many cases, several extra children to make up for the ones that they no longer saw. In short, all they could achieve as they were sat in their ivory towers were white elephants." Said David as Erik nodded his head.

"Yes, they are failures of the evil empires which they themselves produced. And we will teach the children to spit on their graves." Said Erik.

In the final week of summer, Michelle McGuinness came round with her baby boy. Beth was distressed, "Can I speak to you privately?" What did she want? Beth wondered. "The girls and I have decided that with you having to look after six children that it isn't right us coming round and disturbing your privacy. As such we have concluded that it is better for those of us who are not pregnant and with a baby no less than three months to visit David just once a month."

"Thank you. This is so very kind and considerate of you."

"Please, use Roger's room for your family. In winter we will be discreet, we can do it on the sofa downstairs or wherever is best for you and in summer we can always be inseminated outside." Said Michelle. With that Beth was delighted. Life was turning out so well for her. "I also came round regarding other matters." Said Michelle as Beth was in fear and dread of them. "Don't worry. The Illuminati bosses have instructed me to spy on you and the children. I have no intention in doing so. Basically,

I have to report on you about the final baby, the sacred descendent of Roger. Instead, I will meet up with you for a coffee here, and together we can write the reports so that the lunatics running the asylum will be happy. I will also ask that they send you whatever supplies you might desire." Said Michelle.

"I don't know what to say." Beth said smiling.

"Don't mention it." Michelle said who knew Beth's story since her arrival in Cumbria and was ashamed that this terrible plight of hers had happened in her own county.

On September the twenty-fifth 2021 unexpectedly and the exact date of her marriage, Beth gave birth to a bouncing baby girl with blond hair. The timing was for Roger and his sacred bosses perfect. Yes, she could think about her marriage and think that the next day was the day he impregnated her for the third time and the day after was of his death. She now had seven children. She was simply too busy to analyze. She needed David more than ever. The autumn was warm, and he tended to their crops as well as restoring the house. He would collect firewood too. In short, her mind was focused on her man, her children and nothing else. Sophie was helping out with the breastfeeding. Deep down she was pleased that she had two instead of three of Roger's babies and felt compelled to help her younger sister.

Another winter had passed by, and during a drought and hot spell during the final days of spring, a sighting was to transform their lives. By chance, there was a strange being that wished to be unrecognisable and was walking somewhat nervously past Fell End. "David, follow me." David was a little scared but didn't wish to make him angry. Suddenly Erik jumped onto the man and his pistol fell to the ground. It was the rat masked man. David wanted to run off but was astute enough to realise that in doing so, he would end up on a wanted list. Instead, he took the pistol handed it to Erik. Then, David took off the mask and like Erik he was stunned. The face of Simon George had been revealed. "Take off your clothes!" David ordered as Erik was pointing the pistol at his head.

"I am going to shoot you with my second gun." Simon said.

"Do you want me to fire it now, or are you going to take off your clothes?" Demanded Erik.

"OK, I will get undressed." Simon then took off his clothes and was much more compliant than the two young men could have dreamt of. Like the others from the Cockermouth Illuminati, they often wore different masks in order to help them disguise themselves further. In turn, Simon felt very unlucky.

Shortly afterwards, Simon was tied to a chair with rope which had been lying around in the cellar for times of war. With so much money Simon believed that he could find a way out of his new prison. "What were you doing around here?" Asked Sophie terrified of him walking around their area.

"I was doing some surveying, before we move our headquarters from Cockermouth to Ambleside." Said Simon.

"Where are you meant to be staying?" Sophie asked.

"I was staying at the Queen's Hotel in Ambleside."

"How long are you staying there for?" Asked David.

"One week, could I go back there quietly?"

"No, you are our guest." Said Beth smiling at him

"The police will be looking for you." Simon said as he was hiding his fear.

"Are you going to telephone them!" Laughed Erik at his face.

Dinner was served. Simon enjoyed it and wondered what plans they had for him. He had survived the Nazis, surely, he could survive these laughable peasants. No longer tied up, Erik was watching and pointing the gun at him and Simon knew he was unable to spring any nasty surprises onto Erik. "We know why you were behind the LGBT agenda; we know why you wanted women to hate men. We are no longer interested in this." Said Beth. In turn he was relieved; he didn't wish to be interrogated about these issues. "Roger told me that you only wanted ninety-five percent of the population to have perished." She said. Erik was still pointing the gun at his head.

"Yes, sadly there are just four million people left on the planet."

"What were you going to do if there were a few hundred million?"

"Things would have carried in as before. Only, the housing crisis would have ceased. Also, Roger would have left you and Sophie in peace. Sadly, there were no other maidens as far as he was concerned other than you. We were thinking of sending him to Glenriddidng, but we were divided."

"Who is we?" Beth asked defiantly, as she felt even more like a whore of the elite.

"The members you saw from Cockermouth."

"Why would Roger have left the women alone with us after just their first pregnancy?"

"Had things not gone wrong, we planned to organise a big international event. The elite's beauties from all over the world were going to be impregnated by Roger." He said gloating over the fact that the men had no children of their own.

"And I guess those who didn't have his DNA would have been discarded of." Added Sophie.

"We should not be thinking like this. The wipe-out went wrong." Said Simon, as the others were shocked listening to him speaking without any emotion as if he was simply a cold-blooded lizard.

"As we are only too well aware." Said Erik.

"We want to burn the remaining Illuminati members from Cockermouth. Each day that you do not comply with us, we will cut of one of your toes or fingers." Said David.

"And I will put a bandage on and look after you." Said Beth surreally.

The following day, and hoping to save his life, Simon George agreed to pinpoint the homes of his henchmen. Along with petrol and matches in horse drawn vehicles a tied-up Simon was chauffeur driven with Erik pointing the pistol on his head, while David drove them to Cockermouth. A two-metre-high perimeter fence surrounded the properties of his allies. The petrol was doused onto the wood. Miraculously the whole border was ablaze. The residents had half expected this and didn't flinch. At least their gardens were safe. Once the wood from the fence had turned to char, their garden was saved. In the meantime, they had to stay indoors. Instead, the old oak tree in Busby's garden was set alight while the others, in their homes prayed. Instead, a branch that was ablaze set the grass on fire as it hit the ground and with the increased heat it spread onto the orchard. Busby was scared. At least his home wasn't alight. As for his neighbours, they were not scared, their gardens were safe. On top of that: the flames around the fence were calming down. For some reason, the parched grass which was ablaze had spread into the neighbouring gardens. The trees were in turn set alight. At least their homes were not alight. Even so, they had memories of forest fires in California which they had paid people to ignite. All they could do was to wait for their deaths. Throughout this time, a tied-up Simon was detained on David's and Erik's orders. When Simon realized his men had died, while he was still alive, he simply burst out laughing. Somehow and able to read his mind; Erik simply shot him in his face.

Beth had indeed never felt so happy with her life. She had seven children to look after, and David was her perfect de facto father of her children and loving husband. All of their energies went into bringing up her beautiful offspring. As for Roger the deceased father of her posterity, he was her best lover, and her children had the best genes any mother could desire for her litter. This loving concept of hers was surely the best way in not being succumbed by his power of hate.

It wasn't that she personally wanted her life to have ended up the way it was it was simply that she believed in making the most out of her situation. As much as there were times when she wanted to blame David for her less than morally blessed life, she also knew how cruel fate was. Instead of giving him hell, she would walk outside of the home and stand underneath the beech tree calm down and kiss him when she went back inside. She would always love David, and simply wanted the same from him too, towards herself. Roger had made one big mess of her after all. On top that, he was an old and ugly manipulator. Instead, of being consumed by him, she wanted to look on the bright side of life. As evil as he was, Roger had saved her life. As unfortunate it was that David wasn't the father of her children, at least he was with her until death do them both part.

As much as she knew deep down that she could have survived the floods along with David and had a traditional nuclear family with him, she tried not to dwell on it. If she did, she knew that her pain, sorrow, sadness, and regret would simply devour her instead.

A few days later and on the fourth of July and while David and Beth were admiring their orchard, a trespasser appeared in front of them. Equally, his positive energy didn't make the dwellers think of him as some dangerous person and he was basically some Jesus like figure. He was very tall with jet black long wavy hair. His stature around two metres or six feet seven was really something. "My name is Alexander and I have walked from Eyam in order to find you both. I wanted to come earlier, but with my enemies still around at Cockermouth I didn't dare look for you."

"It is an honor to meet you. My name is Beth, and I am sure you are the son of God."

"For me too, I spent some time at Cambridge, and your accent is more akin to that; than of Derbyshire." Said David.

"Well spotted, I spent my formative years near Saffron Walden, which is close to Cambridge." Said Alexander.

"With all the turmoil my mother moved to Eyam with me as a safe haven." Said Alexander.

"I just want to thank you for killing those Satanists at Cockermouth. I had a dream that you would and set off on foot before you had even carried out this act. You are right, Beth, I am the Messiah. As a thank you and anyway I believe that our lives have already been mapped out, I bring thee good tidings."

After a few more initial pleasantries Erik and Sophie appeared on scene. "Hello Mr and Mrs Alexander." Said Alexander to a shell-shocked Erik and Sophie. Suddenly a large vertical, oblong, white light appeared just above their heads. "Oh, merciful father, these four souls have suffered so much at the hands of Satan. I come here; four years to the day since the sisters came here for the first time. Back then, neither had been sullied by Roger De Cadenet. I humbly beseech thee that; these four beings will physically go back four years and in turn may their bodies be cleansed. Amen." With that, the others fell to the ground and kissed Alexander's feet.

"As for the children, can they be de Satanized?" Asked Beth.

"Oh, my wise lady, I am sorry, but I cannot change their souls. They wanted to wipe out my father, the Lord above and the day Simon George came here, he was planning to find out from you; my whereabouts."

"But this is crazy; we didn't even know you were in England let alone in Derbyshire." Said David.

"I know; I know their thinking. The world has been cleansed, go forth and multiply." Out of the seven billion souls who existed on earth recently David and Beth were each one in a billion. With that David and Beth looked terrified. "Erik and Sophie, you are both lucky and privileged to be connected with them. Even so, you are both good people and suffered too much at the hands of Satan. As for Beth and David: neither of you are perfect. Had you; four years ago, connected you would have been the perfect couple in every sense of the word. It was all a part of the plan, which even I myself as a very young man cannot fully explain. I am just eighteen years of age. Going back to your seven and two children: one day the earth will once again become overpopulated from mankind and Satan will cause havoc once more on the people when they return to their hedonism. Until then go forth and multiply with the love that you have as the two faithful couples you are." Said Alexander.

Amazingly, Sophie fell pregnant a few weeks after the demise of the Illuminati based at Cockermouth and Alexander's visit. It seemed that the spell had been broken. The fact that Erik was fecund after all, gave them all hope, that David too, could produce his own children. In the meantime, Beth was in no rush. She wanted a year of innocent romance with David before embarking into motherhood. As far as she was concerned, with her body being cleansed and rejuvenated, she was merely the guardian rather than biological mother of Satan and his siblings.

About the Author

STEVEN KAY

Steven Kay was born in Lancashire and he grew up in Hambleton close to Morecambe Bay and the Forest of Bowland. His father introduced him to the great outdoors and his mother showed him how to make the most out of his life. His education started in mathematics and at university transitioned to languages. Steven leads a simple life as a health-food enthusiast, he loves to go lake swimming, cycling, and camping. He maintains fluency in Dutch, and he intends to retire in Austria where the landscape reminds him of Cumbria but without the continual rains. In Austria he communicates fluently with the locals, and meets up with many flying Hollanders, who also appreciate the Low Countries rather than the Alps.

Finally, without a car and TV, Steven values love of a bygone era and the peacefulness it allows him to enjoy.

Visit the Author

STEVEN KAY

Facebook Fan Page:
https://www.facebook.com/authorstevenkay

Link to Title:
https://www.donnaink.com/product-page/in-wordsworth-s-shadow-by-steven-kay

Publisher Website:
https://www.donnaink.com

The Vicar of Buttermere

MERCHANDISE

Ironmantle Books

Ironmantle Books
An Imprint of DonnaInk Publications, L.L.C.
601 McReynolds Street
Carthage, NC 28327
Special Markets: contact@donnainkpublications.com
https://www.donnaink.com